MARIAH OF THE WIND

Nancy Flinchbaugh

Mariah of the Wind
Copyright © 2023 by Nancy Flinchbaugh

ISBN: 979-8-9871296-7-8
Library of Congress Control Number: 2023935840

Cover design by Nancy Flinchbaugh
Author photo by Madison Harmon; Photo editor Dean Elam

I dedicate this book to climate scientists, earth teachers, and all of you working to be a part of the solution to address our changing climate.

Acknowledgments

Writing a book is a long journey, with many twists and turns, and for me, a product of the communities in which I live and work. I thank all of you who are part of my many circles who inspire me and encourage me to write and speak up for the Earth.

Thank you to my writing coach, Kathie Giorgio, of AllWriters' Workplace and Workshop, for guiding and editing me through the process of writing this book.

Thank you to Deb Harris and All Things That Matter Press for believing in me and my story and for your painstaking work to edit this book and help bring it into the world.

I also thank the Sustainable Options for Springfield/Creation Justice Team Mission Group at First Baptist Church Springfield for being my community, Pastor Adam and Olivia Banks, Debbie and James Copeland, Marva and Tim Riley, Mary Anna Robinson and Steve Schlather. Thanks to Sherry Chen and others with Springfield Ohio Urban Plant Folk and Melrose Acres for leading the way and inviting me to work in the greenhouse and with this demonstration urban farm to plant and grow healthy food in southwest Springfield. Thanks to the Shalem Institute for Spiritual Formation and my Shalem Circle of Anita Davidson, Liz Kuhn, Steve Nelson, Esther Simonson and Karin Trail-Johnson for your love, encouragement and support.

I also want to thank all of you leading the way into climate solutions, the Creation Justice movement, Blessed Tomorrow, Citizens' Climate Lobby and so many more. You continue to inspire me.

Foreword

I wrote this book as a celebration of God's creation. I'm completely mesmerized by the gift of life, the changing seasons, the miracle of growing things. For this reason, I want to first acknowledge the Great Creator for the magnificence of Planet Earth. I hope that as you walk with Mariah through the pages of the book, you will catch glimpses of the beauty of the Earth. May this more fully awaken you to notice, appreciate and celebrate the serendipities of the natural world.

When we pay attention, we also become alarmed at the many ways we are destroying God's creation and creating difficulties for the future of life on our planet. I also wrote this book to encourage you to take action. I encourage you to ask: Why do so many insist that fossil fuels are the only way to supply our energy needs? This book suggests a simple answer to that question and offers one of the many solutions that need to be implemented now, before it's too late.

As my American Baptist pastor friend, Tom Carr, often says as we work together in creation justice efforts, "We save what we love." I pray that we will all work to save life on Planet Earth, the amazing gift entrusted in our care.

Listen to the wind, it talks.
Listen to the silence, it speaks.
Listen to your heart, it knows.
~Native American Proverb

PROLOGUE

"Tell me again, Daddy. I want to hear about the four winds," five-year-old Mariah coaxed her father while he tucked her into bed. "Please!"

Joseph Landtree, Jr. sighed. He pulled a chair over and sat. His face became dreamlike and his voice became soft as he began the familiar story which Mariah knew by heart, yet never tired of hearing.

"Once upon a time, in the great land of the Shawnee, a great wind from the west blew upon the land, sending away the warm days of the summer sun and bringing with it a new season of autumn. The leaves on the trees began their journey back to earth as they turned from green to brown and red and orange and yellow. And while the wind brought in the harvest and the end of the growing season, the wind also blew in new life in the gift of a little baby girl birthed to her proud parents, Rebecca and Joseph. Because she came in with the west wind, they called her Mariah.

"As the baby grew, drawing milk from her mother and strength from her father, the winds shifted and in blew the harsh winds of the north and winter. The snow fell, the animals went to sleep, and the trees turned black. The little baby continued to grow and learned to crawl and then to walk and soon she began to talk. She grew up to become a strong little girl who could solve problems and dance and sing.

"And the winds shifted once again, and the spring dew blew in from the east. The child continued to grow in imagination and creativity. She used crayons to paint the sky and she used her voice to sing of the woods and she used her heart to love the people around her.

"And one day, the Cyclone Lady came to the people and she blew in circles around the land, stirring the trees and swirling big clouds of dust, and the people were amazed at the power of the Creator and watched the strong lady with flying hair who would never harm the people of the Shawnee. Like the Shawnee people who once walked this land, Mariah learned to call her friend.

"As the great medicine wheel turned through the seasons, the south wind blew in summer and garden flowers blossomed. Green apples began developing on the trees. Strawberries and raspberries appeared in the fields. And every day, the little girl would harvest from her mother's garden. Her belly grew happy with the offerings of the good earth. And she loved the orange carrots, the green lettuce and spinach, the yellow and gold squash, the red tomatoes, and orange pumpkins. Mariah was a very happy little girl.

"And high above, she watched the thunderbird circle. When he blinked his eyes, lightning cracked across the skies. He, too, brought storms and guarded the gate to heaven."

Mariah's heavy eyes closed. Her father stopped the story short of full circle, with the thunderbird soaring in the south winds of summer. He pulled the bedspread up to her neck to keep her warm for the cold night ahead and gave her a kiss on the cheek before leaving the room.

1. BACK THEN

"Mariah! Come now!" her mother called.

Mariah lay back into the bed of leaves and closed her eyes. She could steal a few more minutes here if she tried. She knew her mother always called at least five or ten minutes before she really expected her to come. She didn't want to go inside yet.

Her once happy home seemed so dark these days. The wind brought change. During her birth year, she herself rode in on the wind. Now she didn't want to know what it might bring. This October, right after they celebrated her seventh birthday, her father's cough started to change. At first, she thought maybe a cold, but then the nightmare started.

The wind lifted the leaves beside her, and they swirled in a funnel. Could the Cyclone Lady be paying a visit? She learned to call the twirling woman friend in the stories her father told her at bedtime. But now it seemed the wind brought something bad.

She'd heard her parents whispering after they thought she was asleep. In between his coughs, he'd told her mother what they found on the X-ray. They were very quiet then, and she could hear her mother crying. She hated it when her mom cried.

She didn't quite understand what it all meant, but she could sense that it was going to be bad. A few nights later, she heard them whispering about what her mother would do when he was gone. Where would he go, she wondered. They didn't tell her a thing. She just figured it out that her daddy would be gone, and that her life would change. The leaves were falling. Change was coming. She didn't know what that meant for her, or her mom.

"Mariah! Come!" her mother yelled louder now.

Mariah stood, brushing the leaves off her jeans and jacket, and headed toward the house. She loved this time of year. She didn't want to go in. She turned back and watched the wind, picking up the leaves from the pile where she'd lain. They lifted into the late afternoon air and twirled, spiraling up. Magic! That wonderful Cyclone Lady.

Later, she told her mama about the magic of the Cyclone Lady. Her mother smiled and told her, "That's the mystery, dear. The wind brought you and the wind stirs up the leaves, and we just watch it all. Just keep watching, okay?"

2. NOW AUTUMN

The west winds of autumn stirred across the fields in the farmhouse where her mother lived the year Mariah was born. Her mother always told her that it felt like the wind had brought her. The labor lasted for three days. She didn't call the midwife until the third day. Even then, the wind whipped so hard, she said, some of the branches on the oak out front fell down into the yard. When the winds started, autumn was in full bloom. When they ended, there was nary a leaf on a tree all over the farm. Mariah's dad told her the Cyclone Lady brought her down that day. Her mother told her, "They call the wind Mariah, so that's what we named you."

Mariah slipped into her warm jacket to go out for a walk. She wanted to relish the beautiful fall season, during her break after the breakfast crowd and before going over to the diner to cook up lunch. Her days now fell into an easy rhythm of working at the diner in the morning and early afternoons, then enjoying evenings of freedom. In her job as short order cook, the people depended on her day in, day out, to be there, to make their meals, and to offer hospitality. Sometimes she felt like an old shoe, making her customers feel very comfortable. She liked serving them that way.

For some reason, this year the leaves seemed to be hanging on the trees longer. In October, Mariah liked thinking back to the year she was born. She liked believing the Cyclone Lady had dropped her down and taught her to fly. Today, she felt the wind picking up. She zipped up her jacket and pulled out a knitted cap from the pocket where she'd left it last winter. She snuggled it down over her head and smiled.

When she reached the edge of the woods, she entered the well-traveled foot path. A canopy of yellow and orange cast their colors over the late morning light. Here and there, water sparkled on leaves, still dripping with the dew. As the days cooled, the drops lingered longer.

Some of the leaves were falling now. She stopped to watch a yellow leaf twirl to the ground. She observed the tree from which it came. Strong, tall, generous, giving new life to the soil even as it shed its growth from last spring. She started to gather leaves, stuffing them into a pocket on her backpack. She took the long yellow elm leaf and imagined it as a feather in her cap. A brilliant red teardrop caught her eye. Were the trees sweating blood this year? She pondered over a three-pronged beaut of a maple, mottled with orange, yellow, and red. *What an artist*, she thought. She glanced around, looking for that talented one. There, across the way, a sturdy maple towered into the heavens.

Hundreds more leaves danced on its branches in the breeze, similar, yet each unique, holding on. Soon, though, they would let go, showering the forest floor with a carpet of color.

In the dense woods, the wind died down, but in the clearing ahead, she could see the leaves swirling. Perhaps the Cyclone Lady would visit. The seasons never ceased to amaze her. She needed to be outdoors, to walk, to watch, to observe. She breathed deeply, sucking in the brisk air, letting it fill her lungs and refresh her body and spirit. Always, when she greeted autumn, she came home to herself, born on the cusp of the wind in this season of change.

She once dreamed of becoming a scientist to study the wind. Becoming a cook instead didn't really bother her. But her natural curiosity still piqued now and then. Where did the wind originate? What caused it to blow? What caused it to make the leaves dance? How come the Cyclone Lady dropped her into this space and time?

In the clearing, she found her favorite stump and sat. She pulled a little notebook out of her pocket and then a pen. October 29, she began. Each day, she liked to chronicle her life and believed her secret journal kept her soul alive. All alone, she could try to figure it all out. She knew she was different, or at least that's what the people told her. She didn't think like them. They called her odd, queer, flowerchild, a dreamer.

"You just keep on being you," her mother always said. "You've got an ephemeral quality to you. Sometimes I don't think you're one of us. Maybe God put you here to show us something, and to give us a glimpse of heaven."

Mariah never knew if her mom said that because she wanted to believe she'd birthed a saint or something otherworldly, or if she really meant it. Before her mom left town right after Mariah graduated from high school, she hadn't ever thought to ask.

When you're young, she mused, you think a lot of things and you take it all in. But once you get a few years on you, you begin to ponder it all. Now she longed for her mother, to have some discussion about what it all meant.

As she'd blown in with the wind, it seemed like her dad blew out that autumn of her eighth year. Then her mom left just as she prepared to begin her adult life. They'd buried her dad in the cemetery down the road, but her mom had left for drug rehab. She held hope that her mom would wander in some day and explain everything. Mariah's stepfather had disappeared right about the same time.

Mariah had never liked the man. She kept her distance. He didn't treat her mama very well. Her mother cried a lot that year before she left. Ever since, Mariah preferred to keep men at a distance. She didn't want to trust them. She shut them out. She favored a quiet life, living with her old friend, Mrs. Applebee, and getting outdoors whenever she wasn't working in the diner.

Before her mama left, she'd arranged for Mariah to stay with Mrs. Applebee. The old lady needed someone to help her out and Mariah needed a place to live when she graduated high school. It seemed to work for them both, going on seven years now. Mrs. Applebee taught her all about cooking, and before long, she landed a job at Wind Song Diner at the edge of town. A perfect name of a place for Mariah to work and she felt it was her destiny.

Mrs. Applebee never ceased to amaze Mariah. Even though she'd just celebrated her eightieth birthday, she didn't show all those years on her body, just in the wisdom of her words. For a while now, Mrs. Bee, as Mariah liked to call her, had kept talking about love between a woman and man. She'd told Mariah all about Mr. Bee and she said she wanted something similar for her. She told Mariah to keep her eyes open and not to be surprised if the wind blew in a man for her one of these days. Mariah doubted that little bit of her words, but she tucked the thought away back in the recesses of the mind.

While Mariah slipped into daydreams, the leaves kept swirling about. She didn't get much written in her journal and already she needed to get back to the diner. On her way out of the forest, she continued to pick up leaves. She liked to give the customers something along with their bill. They would like the colorful leaves; she knew they would. They'd give her a smile and a faraway glance, probably remembering back to their own childhood, when they picked up the leaves themselves. Probably, they'd comment on the changing season and the fall colors. Probably they'd tell her, "Winter is a'comin'." Probably they'd look at her like they'd seen an angel or a forest sprite. She laughed. Was she fulfilling her destiny or just playing with them? Some days, she just didn't know.

3. MAX

Mariah rushed about, trying to keep all the customers happy with their midday meal. In her small workspace, she liked to keep everything tidy. She moved back and forth between the counter and the grill and microwave. Some of the customers liked sitting on the little stools at the counter. Those folks watched her every move. She wanted to appear as graceful as possible. She knew that in some fine restaurants, the chefs cooked out in front of the customers, stirring up oriental dishes or sizzling steaks to order. Her offerings were much less exotic, but she didn't mind being on display. She thought the people appreciated her show.

Some days, she flipped the eggs in the air; pancakes, too. She loved when little children came up and sat at the counter. She enjoyed making them laugh. And sometimes she could even tease a smile out of Farmer Sayers, who always came in after finishing up a morning of work. Of course, for years, Mrs. Sayers had served him lunch. But when she'd died of cancer the other year, he started coming into the diner. And like clockwork, he arrived every day, just before noon. He washed his hands and ordered some grub.

Mostly at lunch time, Mariah was busy making grilled cheese and hamburgers, French fries, an occasional salad or two. Here in Friendly, Ohio, most people didn't go for the vegetarian options on the menu, but she left them there, just in case. She kept some tofu on hand for stir-fry with veggies, seasoned with sesame orange dressing and soy. Every now and then, a visitor from another place would wander in and ask for it, or order one of her made-to-order veggie omelets with Bearnaise sauce. She could also make a mean Mexican taco, dripping with cheeses and full of three kinds of beans. Truth be told, Mariah served not just as a cook, but as a dishwasher, cleaner, manager, and bookkeeper. The only help she got was from Sally, an older woman who came in to help her over the lunch rush. The owner checked in with her from time to time, but Mariah essentially ran the place on her own.

On this particular day, she felt like she was waltzing on the top of the world. She served up a cheeseburger to Farmer Sayers with a smile, and darned if he didn't smile right back.

"Now, you enjoy that, Farmer Sayers," she told him. She winked. After a year, she finally could finally get a smile out of him. That was something. Perhaps if she worked a little harder, he would make conversation one of these days. That was the funny thing about people, she'd concluded. You can't push them, but sometimes if you just sort of let them be, they'd start to come out.

Turtles had always been her favorite. She loved their hard shell of a body. They could just go inside and hide when they wanted. She supposed she'd been doing that herself, despite her showy ways in the Wind Song Diner. Part of her still hid from people since her mother'd left. She didn't get too close to men—or women, for that matter. But she did take a liking to fellow turtles like Farmer Sayers.

The diner closed at 3:00 p.m. every afternoon, so Mariah usually had ample time to clean everything up and get ready for breakfast the next day. Her regular customers seemed downright respectful, the way they came in between 11:30 and 12:30 every day and were out of her hair by 1:30, 2:00 at the very latest.

So when at 2:15 the door opened, she found herself frowning. The wind caught the door, and it flew back on its hinges. Then she felt a cool breeze rushing into the diner. The gust lifted the leaves in her basket on the counter by the register and blew them all over the floor. As she rushed to pick them up, her last-minute customer fought with the flying door.

Once he wrestled it shut, he ambled over to the counter and sat by the register. "Sorry about that, Miss," he said, giving her a dimpled grin.

She didn't catch the humor and she really didn't want to serve this late guy. She knew he'd disrupt her cleaning routine with his order alone. And perhaps he'd do more damage with that silly grin of his. Probably thinking he's God's gift to women right about now, she imagined.

Mrs. Bee's voice echoed in her head. "Don't write them all off, Mar," she'd admonished just that morning.

Mariah checked him out as she wiped off the table behind him, recently vacated by the Earlys. A snug brown jacket covered broad shoulders, hiding his butt, but showing some tight blue jeans over firm thighs. His curly sandy hair fanned out from under the bright orange ball cap. He must spend some time in the woods. A hunter, perhaps? Sometimes the hunters dropped in for a midday break during their season.

"Be with you in a moment," she yelled to him. She knew people could get downright ornery if they thought they were being ignored. This little diner was teaching her so much about the human race. Some things, she tried to forget, but, for the most part, she loved the people of the little town and found their quirks and idiosyncrasies quite amusing.

The man tapped his fingers on the counter. An impatient one, she surmised. She finished up the table, restoring the catsup and salt and pepper, tucking the menu back by the napkin dispenser, and pulled her order tablet out of the pocket of her striped brown, gold, and orange apron. She floated around behind the counter, twirling with a little dance step she'd learned as a child when she'd learned to mimic the wind. She spun around one more time with a flourish, then stopped in front of the man with the firm thighs and sandy hair.

"How can I help you, sir?" she asked. She looked directly into his dark eyes that twinkled a smile into hers. She felt a surge of energy. *What was that? A spark? Is this guy some kind of magician? He might be serious trouble.* She tucked that thought away and slipped into her friendly waitress mode. "We close at three. I want to make you happy and get you out of here before too long. What's your pleasure today?"

He thumbed through the menu and then let out a sigh. "Thank you, ma'am. Call me Max. What's your name?"

"Mariah," she said. He was a flirt, just as she'd suspected, but she didn't have time for this sort of nonsense. "May I take your order?" She almost snapped at him, feeling a growing impatience as he appeared unlikely to make any snap decisions.

"They call the wind Mariah," he told her. "Did you just blow me in here? That was some kind of gust."

She laughed. "Right. I'll do anything for another customer right before I close up for the day."

"Ouch," he said as his eyes shifted dark and he clammed up.

Perhaps she'd gone too far. She didn't really mean to put him off — or maybe she did. Yes, she'd become quite adept at dodging the men in the town. Most of them gave up, but with new ones like this, she needed to build a fence.

"I'll take the Tofu Stir Fry with the Very Berry Orange smoothie," he said. "I'm not meanin' to tie you up. But tell me, how the hell does a little diner in a podunk farm town like Friendly have these vegetarian items on the menu?"

Mariah smiled. "You just never know what the wind might stir up, do you?"

She turned quickly back to her workplace to gather his lunch. What in the hell would a hunter be doing eating vegetarian?

She felt his eyes boring holes in her back. Or maybe he wasn't looking at her. She didn't dare pivot to find out. She moved smoothly, adeptly, starting up the fire under the wok and putting in the seasoning and oil to fry the tofu. When it turned brown, she placed it aside into a bowl and dumped in the veggies and steamed them just enough to soften, keeping the color bright. Later, she would add the spinach and the mushrooms.

Meanwhile, she kept an eye on her two other customers, passing out the leaves as they settled their bills. She handed the long yellow feather leaf to John Masters, the electrician working on the new station out by the edge of town. Sure enough if he didn't stick it in his cap and hand her an extra dollar with his money. "Keep the change, Mariah," he told her. "Winter's on its way; you might need a new cap."

She gave Farmer Sayers the multi-colored maple leaf, wanting to offer some cheer. "That's downright pretty there, Mariah," he said. "Thank you, dear." Again she noticed a few extra coins in the tip. She didn't aim to get money off the leaves. She couldn't take credit for God's creations. She didn't mean to be selling the beauty, just brightening their day. "I'm going to put this up on my mantel and think of you," he added. Well, she'd made an old man smile and admire the season. That was something.

Then, out of the corner of her eye, she caught Mr. Orange Hat watching her. A few moments later, she looked directly at him, and he winked, again. Trouble. She shivered. October, again. Always something. Sometimes a good wind, but sometimes the wind blew in something bad.

"That's a nice touch," he called as the door closed behind Farmer Sayers.

Now they were the only two left in the diner. She suspected this man could be a problem. She didn't want to acknowledge him acknowledging her. But she didn't know what else she could do.

She hurried back to assemble his meal, finishing up the smoothie, then placing his order in front of him on the counter.

"Now, you enjoy your lunch while I get this place cleaned up so I can go home," she told him. Perhaps that would shut him up.

She wiped off the tables vacated by the farmer and the electrician and filled the dishwasher. Then she grabbed the broom for a quick sweep of the floor, picking up some stray papers. She tallied the register receipts and entered them into the daily log.

Max began whistling something familiar. Her mother used to sing it when tucking her into bed at night. She knew it had something to do with the wind. Slowly, the words came back to her. "Seems like yesterday … We were young and strong, we were runnin' against the wind … I found myself alone, surrounded by strangers I thought were my friends … I guess I lost my way."

Eerie, this Max. Who was he? "Are you from around here?" she asked.

"Not really, maybe soon," he replied.

"Are you runnin' against the wind?" Maybe a little too nosey, but she wanted to know what had made him whistle that old song.

"I'm afraid so. How come you know that song?"

"My mama used to sing it. She loved Bob Seeger."

"My dad, too," he said. "So we got singing parents in common? Do you sing?"

"Now and then," she admitted. Not very often these days, but she still had her mama's voice.

"Hey, maybe you could back me up at Buck's Pub tonight? I could use some female vocals in my set."

"You're singing at Buck's? Don't expect him to take you on full time."

He laughed. "No, nothing like that. Just a little bit of music for an old friend."

"You know Buck?"

"You could say that. An old friend from way back. Buck didn't always live in these parts, you know."

Mariah knew that. And she also knew Buck like the back of her hand, which made her curious about Max. Buck didn't take up with very many people. No, he'd kept to himself ever since his wife died and he moved to Friendly. Mariah felt drawn to the old man for some reason, like a moth seeking light. She'd lost her mother; he, his wife. For the past several years, she'd often closed down the pub with him. A strange pair, the two of them, but they spoke the same language. Now a stranger'd come to town, claiming a stake on her friend? She knew Buck had a whole other life before Gloria died. He didn't like to talk about it much, but sometimes he opened up and she caught a glimpse of his past. So maybe Max was a part of all that.

"What are you running from?" she asked Max. There she went again, a little too nosey.

"Not running from, running against," he told her. "No easy times in which we live, darling. Don't worry your little head about what's going on out there, but it's not pretty."

Mariah cocked her head to listen. *What is he talking about?* "What are you talking about, Max? You don't need to hide the fact that we've got problems in this world. I know that all too well."

"No, ma'am," he shot back. "Not intending to offend. I just know a lot of women—and men, too—who prefer to hide their heads in the sand than worry about what's going on these days."

"Are you a worrier, Max?" Mariah asked, wondering why she kept quizzing him.

"Not generally," he replied. "Hey, my man's telling me to enjoy that pumpkin pie you've got over there. Could I have a serving with a scoop of vanilla ice cream? Then I promise I'll be gone soon."

"Your man?" Mariah asked as she turned to get the pie and ice cream. As an afterthought, she added, "Want the last of the coffee to go along with your pie?"

"Sure thing," he said. He tapped his book. "Henry David Thoreau, my man." He picked up the book and read out loud, "'Live in each season as it passes. Breathe the air, drink it up. Taste the fruit and resign yourself to the influence of the earth.'"

Max surprised her. First, he ate tofu, now this. Maybe she needed to get to know this guy. "Does the earth influence you?" she asked.

"Without a doubt," he said. "Look how it blew me in here today. And it's getting ready to blow me right back out." He took a bite of the pie, scooping up ice cream to go with it. "Thank you, Mr. Thoreau, for encouraging me to eat this pumpkin pie. Sure is good. You make it?"

"Mmm-hmm." Mariah allowed herself to smile. *What kind of a man quotes Thoreau, whistles my mama's song, and knows Buck?*

He inhaled the rest of his dessert like he hadn't eaten in days and sat, smacking his lips, while she scribbled out his debt. When she handed him a yellow/orange oak leaf with the bill, his hand closed over hers. She looked up, startled at the warmth of the hand, but also the intrusion. His eyes probed hers again, and that spark she'd felt at his first entrance ignited into fire. She pulled her hand away, and her eyes as well.

"Don't forget to come sing with me at Buck's tonight," he said. "I'll save the last set for you." He shrugged back into his jacket, picked up his leaf, and slapped a twenty on the counter before running out, almost quicker than he'd blown in.

Max lingered on her mind that afternoon as she cleaned up the diner. She didn't want to go sing with him, but Buck would think something was wrong if she didn't show up. She had more questions than answers with this one.

14

4. CONSIDERING WIND

Max started his hybrid pickup, silently coasting out of the lot toward Buck's place in the woods. As much as he loved good ole Buck, his heart was heavy. Looking back, he knew he'd left too damn much. But after the accident, he couldn't stay. He left his tenure-track position, his home, and a whole helluva lot more.

Pulling into the gravel road, he heard his setter, Gus, bark from inside the little cabin Buck had loaned him for the winter. In one room, he could tinker all he liked. The other would be a living space with a sink, a stove, a bathroom in the corner, and a wood-burning stove.

Gus and his project were about all he'd brought along from his former life. The university administrators had convinced him to take a leave of absence for research and he'd rented out his house instead of selling it. But deep inside, he knew he couldn't go back. The ghosts of Gabrielle and little Isabelle haunted every room of the house they'd once shared. He often wondered how could there be a God in heaven, one that would allow his love to be swept away by the rising river.

He hoped that pouring himself into research would be his liberation. Probably not, he realized, but the changes were coming too fast now. Rising oceans, burning forests, tornadoes and hurricanes leveling towns and coastal cities. He raced against time, tinkering, wondering if anything, let alone his little project, could make a difference. Perhaps, with Buck's help, they could pull it off.

He got some logs off the back porch and lit a fire in the stove. Grief had sucked so much out of him. Maybe bare survival would be all he could muster.

He picked up his guitar, strumming and humming. He needed a set list for the pub, but his heart wasn't in it. He suspected that Buck insisted that he sing because Buck knew all about the hellhole of grief and wanted to help Max forge a path forward. Problem was, Buck was still hiding away in the woods himself.

Funny how parallel lives ebb and flow, pulling apart at the seams, yet sometimes knitting back together in changing times, he reflected. Max fired up his laptop to check his emails and social media to see what new posts had popped up in his absence. When he'd agreed to move to Friendly, Buck promised to help him track down his assailants. Anybody trying to work for the climate these days got beat up by the big bucks of the PR firms hired by the fossil fuel companies. Sometimes, it felt to him like the whole world was going crazy; certainly things in the USA were off kilter.

It didn't take long to find words reaching their target. On Facebook, a troll had written: "You die." "Max Wahlberg worships the devil." "Dr. Wahlberg, you're full of lies. Quit deceiving the people." "We're watching you. Don't think you can slip out of town without notice. We're following you."

Boy, someone's been very busy.

He remembered hearing Greta Thunberg talking about Americans denying the science of climate change. "Where I come from, everyone knows we've got a problem. But here, you pretend it's not happening." *Yes, and it makes you crazy if you dwell on that too long.* What Max needed to know was how far the trolls would go. Would they stop with inflammatory words, or would they hire a headhunter to knock him off? Used to be if headhunters were after you, it was a good thing, trying to steal him away to a better job. Now the word had a completely different meaning.

He copied the most recent taunts into an email and sent it on to Buck and the private detective he'd hired while Gabrielle was still alive. He couldn't be sure they hadn't caused her accident. Sure, the river'd flooded, but Gabrielle hadn't been one to take chances. How her car swept off the road that day continued to be a question mark in his mind. The police couldn't find any evidence of foul play, but he didn't think they'd find much evidence in a flood anyway.

He pulled out a folder of set lists. They seemed too damn optimistic for these times. He didn't want to be a downer, but this needed to be real. "Send in the Clowns." "Papa was a rollin' stone". Just for Buck, he'd do "You've got a friend." He wasn't sure he could sing a set, let alone three. "Build it anyway." Gabrielle's favorite song. No, not that one tonight.

He searched his song files until he fingered the one he knew was back there. "They Call the Wind Mariah." He could do that for the sprite of a woman he'd just met. It was way too early for another woman, but there was something about her that lingered.

He reached for the oak leaf in the pocket of his jacket and showed it to Gus. "What do you think, old boy? A waitress who passes out fall leaves with the bill? She's something, ain't she? You'll have to meet her. Maybe I can bring her over sometime."

He listened to himself and then clammed up. *What am I thinking?*

Gus wagged his tail and put his leg up on Max's. Then he barked and jumped toward his leash hanging on the wall.

"Okay, old boy," Max said. "Let's go for a walk. That will do us both some good." Nothing like some fresh autumn air to clear out the mental cobwebs and set his feet on terra firma. Before winter settled in, he wanted to try to enjoy the season. God knew he needed the exercise.

"Sit," he told Gus, then buckled the leash onto his collar. "Okay, let's go." They left the cabin together, the man and his dog.

5. PRAYER

Mariah cleaned up in record time and then skipped down the street to Mrs. Bee's house on Main Street, right next to the big church that some folks called the God Box and others just ignored. "People don't believe in God much anymore," Mrs. Bee often told her. "They think they're too smart for a higher power. That's where they're so wrong."

Mariah understood that it's plumb hard to figure out God. But unlike those who looked the other way, she needed the Spirit in her life. Life wasn't an easy game. When her father died, the church became a rock for her and her mother. For several years, they went to that God Box and sat right up in front. She'd loved listening to the organ play the old hymns while the sunlight sparkled through stained glass, making the face of Jesus shine. The church people shared kindness, special presents at birthdays and holidays, and some extra food at the end of the month. The smiles and hugs had helped her get through those times. At least, until her mother's new friend, Bill, came into their lives. Then he forbade them going to church. Mariah snuck out some Sundays and tried sitting in the front all by herself. The people were still friendly, but it wasn't the same.

By the time her mother broke up with Bill and left town for rehab, Mariah'd quit going. With high school friends, she found other ways to get lit. First, they started drinking, then came the weed and cocaine. Even in a small town in Ohio, there was a steady pipeline of the stuff. Mariah could barely see straight the year her mother left.

That was when the rector's widow, Mrs. Bee, took her in. Didn't take much talking at all for her to turn around. Not only did she help her find her way back to God again, but suddenly, she had a big, beautiful, warm place to stay. By that time, her mother's dilapidated house wasn't fit for living and the mortgage company started foreclosure proceedings. The bills weren't being paid. Mariah lost her job at the grocery store and things got rough.

Mariah helped out and Mrs. Bee needed her. They bonded. Mariah'd never known her own grandparents, but she knew God had sent Mrs. Bee instead. No doubt in her mind about that.

Mrs. Bee was a funny sort, not the usual variety of old lady. But then Mariah believed each person to be a unique child of God. Come to think of it, Mrs. Bee had taught her that. It was Wednesday, so Mrs. Bee would be having her Tatting Society meeting. Mariah decided to visit the God Box before going home.

She rang the bell and Pastor Amy let her in.

"Well, hello, Mariah. How are you today? Come in out of the cold. Would you like some tea?"

Mariah loved Pastor Amy, almost as much as Reverend Bee. "Well, really," Mariah answered, "I just came to pray, the way you've been teaching us to meditate."

"Oh, okay," Pastor Amy said. "Could I join you? I could use a little inspiration myself. I'm trying to write my sermon for Sunday, and I know that I need to listen first."

"Sure," Mariah said.

"Do you want to meditate out here in the sanctuary or in our prayer room?"

"I like the sanctuary."

"Okay, let me get my singing bowl," Pastor Amy said.

Mariah found the silence to be comforting. And always it helped to settle and quiet her thoughts. She'd learned to listen for God in this new way. Sometimes she went on prayer walks now, where she mindfully took each step. Other times, she walked the labyrinth Pastor Amy had had them create out back of the church. And sometimes she did nothing but sit. Pastor Amy told her that God speaks in a still, calm voice and that you have to silence yourself to listen.

Amy came back in with a candle and the singing bowl. "Twenty minutes sound good?"

Mariah nodded.

Amy lit the candle on the table in the front of the first pew. She turned to Mariah and said, "May we be present to God, as God is always present to us." Then she hit the side of the singing bowl with a wood stick. The sound vibrated out into the sanctuary, resonating with Mariah's soul.

Mariah began to focus on her breath. As she breathed in, she imagined the wind of Spirit whooshing into her body, filling her lungs, lighting her heart, bringing her hope. As she breathed out, she let go of the disturbances of the day. She let go of the negative feelings she had about that newcomer. She breathed in the good and out the bad. The afternoon sun sparkled on Jesus' outstretched hand in the stained-glass window in the front of the sanctuary. She imagined putting her own in his and sat quietly with him, letting the afternoon be.

6. BUCK

Buck left home around 4:00 to get the bar open. He knew some folks liked to come in to eat. Thursday nights had become popular when he started offering music. On a work night, the locals didn't stay too late. So he scheduled the musicians for 7:00, two sets, and then off by 9:00. Weeknights, he closed up at 11:00. On the weekends, he stayed open until 1:00.

"Hello, Daisy, dear," he yelled as he unlocked the big wooden door. He loved the old bar that looked like something plopped into Friendly from medieval Europe. He'd wondered about the man who'd built the monstrosity more than once. But for the most part, he was content to enjoy it now. The old-fashioned lights perched along the side, and dark, thick oak beams stretched up along the walls and meeting in the center where a rotunda capped off the room. Outside, it looked like a castle. Inside, it looked ready for Sir Arthur. Heavy tables and captain chairs filled the room.

When he'd hung out his shingle five years ago, he couldn't resist starting a club called The Knights of the Round Table. Now those men were some of his best friends; they closed the bar down with him every Friday night.

But tonight he looked forward to Max, which reminded him. He pulled his cell phone off his belt and called his old friend. The call went to voice mail, so Buck left a message. "Hey, Max. I forgot to tell you. Dinner's free for our musicians. Come over now and we can catch up before your set."

Then Buck went to check out back. Sometimes there could be a mess out there from the night before. Every now and then, he'd find a broken bottle or trash from food to go. Coast looked clear this night, until he walked back toward the pub. He stopped in his tracks when he came to the dumpster. Scribbled on it in ugly bright red was a message of warning. WAHLBERG GET OUT OF HERE OR YOU DIE.

Buck called Sheriff Peabody, then went next door to Ace Hardware to buy some brown paint. He did not like the look of this. Not one bit.

Back at the pub, he waited for the sheriff, who took some pictures of the damage. Then he went out and covered up the message with the brown paint to match the dumpster. No use spooking Max before he got settled. He suspected this was just one more example of deniers trying to scare the climate scientists. He hadn't heard of anyone really getting hurt, except there were some question marks in how his family had died, and now Max's, too. He thought maybe he should tell Max, like the sheriff had recommended.

Buck didn't want anything bad to happen to Max, but he also wanted him to stick around. They had work to do. Which reminded him that he needed to check on a few things in his own research before he and Max put their heads together. With a little more work, their project might be ready. Maybe they could start with Friendly and light up the town with their newfangled contraption. Folks sure would like a break on their energy bills. With the university funding their prototype, it could be virtually free. But the electric company would be ticked off. He decided he'd worry about that bridge when he got to it.

"Great chili," he yelled to Daisy. "They're going to like this. Love this cornbread, too."

Daisy appeared in the doorway from the kitchen. "Thanks, Buck. These cool nights call for something warm for the belly." She came out further and stood by Buck's table. "I forgot to give you some crackers, cheese, onions, and sour cream to go on your chili. Do you want them now?"

"No, no," Buck said. "This chili doesn't need any doctoring up. Save it for the customers. They'll appreciate that touch."

"How you doin', Buck?" Daisy asked. She looked after him like she was his long-lost mother. And he appreciated it. He got really lonely some nights and she seemed to pick up on that. In fact, she often invited him over to have dinner with her big family on the holidays when they closed the pub for the night.

"Not bad," Buck said. "You know, my friend Max just moved into my cabin. In fact, he'll be showing up for some grub here in a minute. He's singing tonight."

"Who's Max?"

"Ah, Max," Buck replied. "He's out of the pages of my former life over at the university town. A graduate student of mine, and then a colleague. A good man, going through a hard time."

"Like you," Daisy said.

"Yes, like me."

Buck didn't elaborate, and Daisy didn't need to know all the details anyway. The parallels between what had happened to Max and what had happened to Buck himself back before he moved to Friendly were downright eerie. He didn't want to scare Daisy with it. He also didn't fill her in on the graffiti on the dumpster. She was focused on the kitchen and hadn't heard his conversation with the sheriff. Before she could ask any more questions, the door opened with a whoosh.

"Sure is windy in these parts," Max said as he sauntered into the pub. He eyed the room, checking out the beams, the lights on the wall, scanning the place. "Nice place, Buck. Where are the knights?"

Buck laughed and slapped Max on the back. "They come in Friday nights. Want to join us? The Knights of the Round Table will be gathering here for a healthy game of poker. We reserved the name Sir Maximillian for you."

Max laughed, too. "Really now? What happened to you, Buck? Moved to Friendly and took up poker with the knights? Will Sir Arthur be there?"

"Yes, I claimed that name right off. Pull up a chair and let's get you some chili so you have a full belly when you start singing."

Daisy stood quietly watching, until Buck talked about food. "Do you want a menu?" she asked.

Buck apologized then. "So sorry, Daisy. Max, meet our head cook and bottlewasher, who runs this place, Daisy Hildebrand, who likes me to call her Mom. Daisy, meet my old buddy, Max."

"Much obliged," Daisy said shyly and went over to Max. Max extended a hand, but Daisy wouldn't have it. "We do hugs in this town," she said. "Don't call us Friendly for nothing."

Daisy enfolded him in her big bosom hug. He sneaked a peek beyond him at Buck who gave him a thumbs up.

"Pleased to meet you, Daisy," Max said.

"Could I take your order?" Daisy asked again.

"Well, Buck recommends your chili. I'll take a bowl and whatever you serve with that, and could I have a beer?"

Daisy went back to the kitchen, and Buck to the bar. "What's your pleasure, Max?" He gestured toward the taps extending along the expanse of the bar.

"Wow, you're loaded. How'd you get a spread like that in a little place like this? Do they all really deliver kegs here?"

"Microbreweries are popping up all over the Buckeye state these days, each trying to make a name for themselves. And you know the brewers have been signing on to our bill to address the climate. Changing weather will affect growing hops. That might be the salvation of us yet."

"Don't I know it," Max replied. "I like a good dark beer. Do I see an Oktoberfest over there?"

"Ah, yes. That's a specialty of Buckeye Brew in Heidelberg, once a little German town next door. You'll like that." Buck pulled out a glass mug and leaned it to the side, filling it up for Max. He waited for the head to settle and brought it back and slapped it on the table. "So good to have you here, Max. A sight for sore eyes, you are," Buck told him, while hating that the haters seemed to be following Max here. For a night, he wanted to shelter his friend and welcome him to Friendly in a good way, even if someone else had other ideas.

7. MRS. BEE

Mariah finished up her prayers with Pastor Amy and went home to her favorite part of each day: dinner. Mrs. Bee said that a lot of what was wrong about America was that the family didn't sit together at an evening meal much anymore. They kept children so busy with sports and lessons and whatnot, that the poor parents could barely get them around from here to there. And, she commented, it was even worse for single parents trying to make ends meet on their own. There wasn't much time to sit and connect. But in Mrs. Bee's home, dinner together was not only part of the daily routine, it was an expectation, and, for Mariah, an anticipation.

Mrs. Bee's dining room included a picture window looking out onto the backyard. So dinner time included not just conversation with each other, but a deep connection with the Earth. Mariah knew Mrs. Bee would be asking about her day, and she had to decide how much or what she would tell about Max. Even if she decided not to share, Mrs. Bee had a way of drawing things out of her. Sometimes it was better to get things off her chest up front, even if she did want to hold them back.

"Mariah, dear, how are you doing, honey?" Mrs. Bee asked.

Mariah came to wash off her hands and gave Mrs. Bee a hug. "Good day. Beautiful out there, isn't it?"

Mrs. Bee smiled. "Yes, ma'am. We got all the lessons we need in the world in this season, or right out that window. I like learning from the trees. They teach it."

Mariah knew what Mrs. Bee was talking about, but she loved to hear Mrs. Bee's elaboration. She wished Mrs. Bee would write it all down. It seemed too much, too rich, to waste the words on Mariah. So recently, without her knowledge, Mariah had started recording Mrs. Bee's soliloquies on her phone. Someday, she could transcribe them all. She already had a title and cover for the book figured out.

"Such amazing living creatures, these trees. First off, they start from a little seed. Persistence. They teach persistence. That little seed waits until the time's right to unlock the potential within. And then that tiny little seed's got everything needed to grow into a huge structure. How do they do it? Even when we know a little bit of the science, the miracle is still so much to comprehend."

"How did you get interested in trees, Mrs. Bee?" Mariah asked.

"I guess it started with marveling at God's creation, Mariah, and God never stops creating, you know. Look at that maple tree over there. Those little whirly seedpods scattered all over our yard last spring, started sprouting up everywhere … in my planters, in your garden, in the yard. Amazing how that maple wants to keep giving life."

"Some people call them a mess in their yard," Mariah interjected. "Those little things are a pain to clean up."

"Yes, but just think what they can teach us. Now, what I want you think about, honey, is about all those little seeds inside of you. And what is God wanting to be creating in your life. Right now, we're heading into winter, so it's time to watch the trees and learn to let go. But in a couple seasons, it will be time to plant again.

"Let go, dear. See those leaves fluttering down. You need to let go of the past. I know you got hurts and I know life's not been all that easy for you, losing your pa and then your ma up and leaving town."

"Okay, so the trees even teach us how to do grief?"

"Yes, ma'am, they do. See those colors out there? See how the trees let go with such flourish? Such a show? They're going to get us all out there taking pictures of their autumn splendor. Now, we humans tend to put on black clothes and tear up when we're dealing with the loss and saying goodbye. But why do you think the trees' leaves are turning a hundred different brilliant shades? Why do you think that tree needs to shed all the leaves? Do you know the biology of that? Did you know they need to do that so they can weather the winter?

"Sometimes, you pass through dark times. Imagine these trees standing out there in the cold of winter. They got to preserve their strength in their trunks for another season. Ah, such a mystery, these trees."

"I never thought of it that way," Mariah said. Sometimes Mrs. Bee got deep, and that's what Mariah loved.

"Now, let's get some food on the table and pray," Mrs. Bee said, stopping her little lecture as quick as she started it.

The food out and the prayers done, they sat together and watched the trees without speaking for a few minutes. The wind was really strong. Mariah loved the way the sunset spread across the fields behind the house, casting beams of light through the yard and illuminating leaves breaking loose and falling back to earth, as if to illustrate Mrs. Bee's little sermon.

And the wind seemed to be picking up now and then, lifting the leaves and tossing them about, blowing some against the fence, even some up over the fence into the neighbor's yard. Mariah thought about Max. He'd blown in with the wind that afternoon and now she couldn't get him off her mind. She frowned.

"What's wrong, honey?" Mrs. Bee asked.

Mariah knew it. She couldn't keep anything from Mrs. Bee. Sometimes she wished she didn't wear her heart on her sleeve.

"Oh, I don't know," Mariah said. "A guy came into the diner this afternoon. An odd person. He quoted Thoreau, ordered vegetarian, and started whistling Against the Wind. I have no idea where he came from, but he's singing at Buck's tonight."

Mrs. Bee didn't say anything for what seemed like the longest time. Mrs. Bee's smile seemingly bent on coaxing a little smile out of Mariah's heart.

"Well, now," she said, after Mariah turned her smile into a frown, "I want to meet this man." And then she got as quiet as Mariah.

Mariah could hear her heart beating. She dared not say more. They sat watching the wind and contemplating together the change tossing the falling leaves about in the backyard. The unspoken words were sometimes louder than spoken ones, and Mariah knew full well Mrs. Bee understood her completely. Trouble was, she couldn't understand herself half as well.

8. SHUT DOWN

At Buck's pub, the regulars were starting to file in. The Poindexter twins were first, with their blond hair and easy smiles. They always claimed the corner round booth and soon others would join them. Next were Jared and Kyla, newly engaged. They sat side-by-side in a booth facing the little stage in front. They were kissing before they ordered. The music night brought a younger crowd. Buck watched Max as the place filled up. He detected some light in Max's eyes he didn't think had been there for a while. And he noticed that Max watched the door each time it opened.

"Do all these people live in Friendly?" Max asked.

"Many do, but we also draw them from neighboring towns. Down in these parts of Ohio, folks are looking for something to do at night. No big city next door. That's why I keep trying to create some fun for them. Make it not just a restaurant, but a destination."

"You're a regular businessman, Buck," Max said. "I didn't think you had it in you."

Buck laughed. "Me either. I opened a pub so I wouldn't have to drink alone. I found out quickly I'd either have to shut it down or make it work. It's given me something to take my mind off of other things, you know?"

"Man, I know," Max replied. "How do you do it?"

"One day at a time," Buck said. "One day at a time, and sometimes it's just thirty minutes at a time. Just trying to get through this hour and then on to the next."

The door opened again and Mariah sauntered in. Buck called to her, "Hey, Mariah, come have a seat. I want you to meet someone."

Mariah laughed, looking directly at Max. Buck looked at Max. *Ah,* he thought. *He's found who he was looking for.*

"I believe we've already met," Max said. He stood and extended a hand to Mariah, while explaining to Buck, "At the diner today. Glad you came out, Mariah. You gonna sing?"

Buck looked at Max, then at Mariah, and back at Max again. How had Max found Mariah after only twenty-four hours in town? Buck knew Mariah was one beautiful woman, with some wounds as deep as Max's. He also knew that she seemed to be a pariah when it came to the opposite sex. He wanted to shield Max from more pain, so he needed to get Mariah alone to tell her to go easy on his friend.

"Maybe," Mariah said to Max. "Maybe, one or two. I'd like to do 'Running Against the Wind.' You do that or just whistle it?"

"It's on my first set list."

Max's eyes sat easy on Mariah's. Buck continued to sense the energy between them.

"Okay, then," Mariah said. "I'll sing that with you."

"Maybe we should go practice in the back room."

Buck stifled a grin and kept quiet. Max didn't seem to be wasting any time.

"Let's just go with the flow and see how it happens, okay?" Mariah said. "And if there's time, I'd like to sing a song for Buck. Let that be a surprise."

Buck smiled. "Ah, you're so sweet, honey."

Mariah laughed. "I wouldn't go that far, Buck."

Buck knew she was actually sweeter than honey, apart from that side of her that held most men at bay. He looked at Max again and then watched Mariah's eyes lingering on the younger man as Max wolfed down his chili. Maybe no warnings were needed at all, he decided.

Daisy came out to get Mariah's order as the phone rang. Buck waltzed over to pick it up and, for the second time that day, stopped in his tracks.

"Buck Crawford? If you know what's good for you and your patrons, you'll get that place cleared out now. I planted a bomb that will go off in five minutes. And send Max Wahlberg out of town before someone gets hurt."

The phone went dead. Buck shuddered and froze for a moment. Then he went in the back room and pulled the fire alarm. Coming back out, he made an announcement.

"I'm sorry, our smoke alarm went off. There's a fire in the back room. I've called the fire department. I'm going to have to close for tonight. I apologize to all of you, but if you've already gotten some food or drink, this is your lucky day. No time to ring you up. We'll have a rain check on this music night until next week. Please leave quickly. I want you all to be safe."

Daisy came out from the kitchen in time to hear about the fire. She started to tell him all was well, but Buck used his finger to zip his lips, giving her a message to be quiet. Then he went over and stood next to her. He whispered, "Daisy, this is just something I have to do. I'll explain later. You go on home. I'll try to get the kitchen cleaned up before tomorrow."

The pub vacated quicker than it had filled up, and Buck left, too. In his car, he dialed the sheriff again. Feeling fear didn't do much for his ulcer or his peace of mind. Obviously, the fossil fuel troll was at it again.

9. POSSIBILITIES

Sometimes, Max decided, you seize the moment and don't look back. Max felt inspired by the spark and the fire. He grabbed his guitar case and followed Mariah out of the pub. "You need a ride?" he asked when she veered toward the sidewalk instead of the parking lot.

She looked at him warily. "My mama told me not to take rides with strange men."

Her voice held an edge and a smile at the same time. Max didn't quite know how to read that. But never one to mince words, he decided he'd jump off the cliff. "How about we go practice some songs for next week now? You can come back to my cabin, or we can go to your place."

Mariah looked conflicted. She hesitated.

Buck held his breath. He had just met the lady and maybe he was moving too fast. He was pretty sure they would have bonded over the music at Buck's. It would have been a perfect introduction. But now they'd done not much more than share a few moments, and a friend. He hoped that she might trust him based on Buck alone.

But Max also questioned himself. He was surprised that he was going after her. Sure, she was one helluva beautiful woman. Sure, she mystified him with her gentle ways. Sure, he loved that little touch of serving up an oak leaf with his bill. But he'd sworn off any relationships after what had happened to him. Partially because the grief was just too intense. It never went away. Most days, he could barely get out of bed. And there was the unresolved issue that tugged at the back of his mind. Had the accident been his fault? His internet stalker had threatened to kill not only him, but his wife and daughter. He'd closed his Twitter account after that, but it was too late. The guy knew too much about him.

Just as Max began to reconsider his invitation, not wanting to put another woman at risk, Mariah interrupted his thoughts. "Okay, but let's go to the church."

"The church?" Last time he'd ventured into a church was for the funeral. He'd told his best friend that day he didn't care if he never went back. His wife wouldn't like the fact that he gave up church in his grief, but she wasn't the one left all alone.

"Yeah," Mariah said. "I've got a key. We can sing in the sanctuary. It's really cool in there when you light some candles at night."

"I'm in." Going into a sanctuary with a beautiful woman at night wouldn't be the same as really going back. "My truck's over here." He put his hand gently on her shoulder and moved her in the right direction. "How come you've got a key to the church?"

"Oh, I go over sometimes and get things decorated for the pastor. I live next door," she explained.

Max went to the passenger door, unlocked it, and held it open while Mariah stepped up into the cab. She seemed confident and the high step didn't faze her. Max hurried around to the other side of the pickup to get in himself and get it turned on and warmed up.

The nights already were getting colder, and the first frost might come this weekend. Next would be Thanksgiving and then Christmas. Max didn't want to think about that right now. The holidays without his wife and daughter would be rough. He knew his mother wanted him to come home, but right now, all he wanted to do was hide with a bottle of whiskey and weather out the red-letter days.

"Why did you come to Friendly?" Mariah asked, jolting Max out of his pity party.

He looked at her, frustrated with her bluntness, preferring to be a stranger for a little while. He really didn't want to spill his guts before he knew her a bit. He decided to give her half an answer. Maybe later, he'd tell all.

"Oh, time to move on," he said. "I'm doing some research. Need some time to focus." There, he could tell her about his project. That would be easy. Telling her about his wife, that was something he simply could not do.

"What kind of research?"

"I'm working on a wind project," he said. "Actually, Buck and I are working on it together. Alternative energy, you know?"

"What are you trying to do?"

"Harness the wind, make it work for us," he said. "You know wind farms are popping up all over the countryside with those big wind turbines, right? We've got some here in Ohio. Indiana's got a lot now. But we're working on smaller turbines that will fuel a house and not interfere with the wildlife. Ones you can put on your roof, just like a chimney."

"Oh, that's cool," Mariah said. "We don't have much time to change our energy use, do we?"

Max looked at Mariah; her eyes were open wide. He could see a little darkness in the corner, a sadness. That she recognized the plight of humanity surprised him. He hated being a downer. Even with his students at the university, he never wanted them to give up hope.

"Are you concerned about the climate?" he asked. Maybe he'd misread the mournful look in her eyes.

"Well, yeah," she said, with indignation in her voice. "The birds are dying, the waters are rising, the ice caps are melting, and the storms are picking up. Thank you for working on the problem, Max. I've been trying to figure out what I can do. Will you show me your project?"

Max nodded. "Sure thing. But right now, lead me to this church of yours." He pulled out of the lot. "Left or right?"

"Left," she said. "Just down the street a way. It's not far."

Max laughed. "No, nothing's too far in Friendly, for sure."

They cruised down Main Street. There wasn't much traffic at that time of night.

"One more block," Mariah said. "Down here on the left." Max slowed as they passed a big house on the corner.

"That's where I live," Mariah said.

"You live all alone in that big house?" Max asked. "Do you have a family?"

Mariah laughed. "It is quite large. No, I live with Mrs. Bee. Her husband used to be the minister at the church. She took me in after my mother left town. I've been there ever since. And that's the church." She pointed to a large Gothic structure across the alley from the house. "Just park on the street," she told him. She jumped out of the truck before he could go open her door.

Together, they walked up the steps of the church toward the big, heavy doors. Max had goosebumps. It felt like an adventure, like he was about to step into a whole new world. He didn't know if he was ready to step into a church again, but telling Mariah that would require sharing the rest of the story that he'd rather keep under wraps for now.

Mariah pulled a key out of her purse and unlocked the door. The heavy door swung open easily. Max admired the carpentry on the thick portal. "After you," he told her.

She snickered. "That's archaic."

"I'm a gentleman," he said. "My mama taught me well."

"Whatever." She obliged, walking in ahead of him. She flipped the switch that lit the lights along the walls, mimicking the candles that might have lit a Gothic cathedral in days gone by, but now with look-a-like electric bulbs.

Max watched, mesmerized, as the soft light illuminated the cathedral. He looked up and noticed thick wooden beams, reminding him of Buck's Pub. Maybe the same architect had built both. He laughed, remembering when his old friend had suggested the pubs were really the sacred spaces in town where the Spirit brought out all kinds of people and truth.

Mariah flipped another switch, and the large stained-glass window in the front lit up.

Max stopped. "The man," was all he said. He liked that man and realized he really hadn't given him much of a thought since Gabrielle and Isabella died.

"Yes, Jesus," Mariah said.

They walked up the center aisle, side by side, their footsteps echoing into the large room.

"Did you know that sanctuaries are like upside down boats?" she asked him.

"What do you mean?" The idea was news to him.

"Look at this place. See the way the ceiling arches up to the center beam? Imagine turning that all upside down. Then it would look like a big boat, right? Jesus said he would make his followers fishers of men, right? So you come here to church, and they caught you! We're all in the same boat now." She laughed.

Max didn't quite know what to make of that. She was right. It was like an upside-down boat. But was that a true story, or just something someone made up trying to keep awake in church one Sunday? "For real?" he asked.

Mariah laughed again. "I don't know. That's what Reverend Bee told me. I do find the church helps me navigate the waters of life."

Okay. He'd just come in here to sing. No religious chatter, he wanted to say, but kept his preferences to himself.

They reached the front and Mariah sat on the steps going up to the altar. "We can sing here," she said.

Max got his guitar out and tuned it. His fingers were itching to play. He knew what his opening number would be.

She watched silently. He looked over at her and saw that she had a faraway look in her eyes. He did want to know more about her. He played a few chords, humming along to catch the melody, and then he jumped right into the tune. "Way out west ...."

Mariah looked puzzled. Then a smile spread across her face. Max was beginning to love that smile. He sang on, arriving at her name. "They call the wind Mariah." He probed her eyes, as he filled the upside-down boat of a sanctuary with the fullness of his tenor voice. "Mariah, Mariah." He sang slowly and deliberately, connecting with her eyes every time he sang her name. "They call the wind Mariah."

She kept smiling, but would look off into the distance, always returning to meet his gaze when he sang her name. When he finished, she applauded.

He got to his feet and took a bow.

"That's my song, you know," she said.

"No," Max replied sarcastically, then corrected himself. "Yes, your song. I played it for you, Mariah." He drew out her name slowly, surprising himself with the emotion he expressed. He wondered if it was just his old flirtatious nature kicking back in or if he was falling for this woman.

She changed the subject. "Funny, you're working on a wind project. You just blew into Friendly, and here we are. That's something, you know. Me, named after the wind," Mariah observed.

He started strumming his guitar, finding the chords for the next song he planned on singing. "Join me, Mariah," he said. "Seems like yesterday ...."

Mariah's face held wonder, then acknowledgement. Her eyes lit like a campfire, dancing into the dark. She smiled but didn't sing.

Max carried on without her. The words echoed his heart in this mess of his life. "Wish I didn't know now what I didn't know then."

When he led into the chorus, she joined him. It was a moment that would stay with him for a very long time. They sang together, "Against the wind." She matched his tenor with her soprano, carrying a harmony in a descant, almost ethereal in nature. In fact, Max looked up to see if the voice came from beyond. He hooked his eyes to hers, entwining his voice as well. Max launched into the second verse and Mariah dropped out.

Mariah got a faraway look in her eyes again. Max knew that look. He felt it so many times himself. He sang on. Once again, she joined him for chorus, matching him note for note as he closed it out. Their voices died away and Max finished off with a few chords.

Stillness settled into the dimly lit cavernous sanctuary. Here they were, safe, together, absorbing the words and the moment. For Max, the song held the angst of his present life. He was definitely running against the wind. Perhaps Mariah was as well.

"Can I sing one?" she asked. "I need to practice for church on Sunday."

"Okey dokey," Max replied. "What key?"

"Here, I'll do it," she said, reaching out to take the guitar.

"You play?"

"My daddy started teaching me when I was three."

She began to sing, and Max closed his eyes as her pristine voice filled the boat all the way up to the central ceiling beam, and to the bow. He knew it was Mariah, but it sounded like an angel.

"I pray you'll be our eyes ... Guide us with your grace ...."

The song rushed back to Max. He remembered singing it in choir in college. When she paused, he picked up the Italian words of the duet, popularized by Andrei Bocelli and Celine Dion. Mariah looked surprised but didn't skip a beat. She sang on, as if she had been singing with him all of their lives.

For a few moments, Max let his voice carry him into hope with hers as they sang back and forth. His Italian, her English, their unity. They sang together, "Let this be our prayer." He sang it, she sang it. They closed together. Then together, in Italian, they repeated the lyrics

Once again, silence descended upon them. Max could feel his heart beating. That song took him way back. And then, he remembered something else: that song at the funeral. He remembered Gabrielle's face looking down at him. He remembered Isabella calling, "Daddy!" He remembered his tears, the darkness, the confusion. He remembered running out of that church and never looking back.

"Mariah," he said, "this has been so nice, but I need to go." He couldn't tell her what he was feeling. He didn't want her to know.

"What's wrong?" she said.

He could tell she sensed his pain. That scared him, too. But he couldn't talk about it, he just wanted to go. His mind scrambled to make up a story she might believe.

"No, I'm okay," he lied. "I just need to check on Buck. I shouldn't have rushed out on him like that."

Well, that was something. Why did he leave his friend when there was a fire going on?

"Oh, yes," Mariah said. "We should go check on Buck."

"No," he said. How could he get rid of Mariah? She wanted to come along. He needed to be alone right now. "Um, no. That's okay, Mariah. I'll go. Let me drop you off."

Mariah looked hurt, and Max felt bad. She didn't understand. They'd just connected. He felt it every bit as strongly as probably she did. But it was too damn soon.

That song had transported him to their funeral, a memory he'd managed to hold at bay for three long months. He remembered the ghosts of Gabrielle and Isabella gazing down on him at their own funeral. At the time, he'd thought his mind played a trick on him or maybe he'd gone plumb crazy. Now he wanted to relive that moment. He longed to see them again and try to connect.

"I can walk," Mariah said. "I live next door."

Max packed up his guitar and, together, they walked back down the center aisle to the big doors. Mariah flipped off the lights; this time, she let him open the door.

"Are you sure you don't need somebody to talk with, Max?"

He shook his head. "No. I'm fine," he lied again. He hated lying to her. But that was all he could muster at the moment.

She walked away, into the night, crossing the alley. He watched her walk up the front porch steps and open the door. He watched her safely into the house before he walked over to his truck to drive out to the cabin and try to reconnect with his wife and daughter. He didn't care if he was crazy if it meant he could be with them again.

10. NOW WHAT?

Max never made contact with Gabrielle and Isabella that night, but he did have a heart-to-heart with Buck the next day. He started working with new fervor on their energy project and kept toying with the possibility of asking Mariah out on a real date. Part of him wanted to see where the connection between them would lead, but another part of him believed it was just too damn soon. October quickly passed into November as the days ticked by. He remained immobilized in his cabin, doing the work, mourning the dead, and trying to get excited about his next chapter. Some days, he still didn't want to get out of bed.

Gradually, though, he started to feel at home. Then Buck invited him over a few days before Thanksgiving. They talked about their project over lunch and shot the breeze until Buck dropped the bomb.

"The troll made it to Friendly," Buck blurted out. "I didn't want to upset you, but now I think you need to leave for a while."

"What?" Max asked. "What do you mean?"

"The night I scheduled you to play at the pub, he left a message for you on the dumpster out back. '"Max Wahlberg Go Home'. I didn't want to freak you out. I covered it up with paint. But remember when I evacuated the place because the fire alarm went off?"

Max nodded. He remembered well that night and the connections with Mariah, even though he never risked asking her out.

"Well, there was no fire. There was a bomb threat," Buck said.

"A bomb threat in Friendly?"

"The troll, I believe," Buck said. "But that's not all. I've also been receiving some emails saying that I need to get my friend, Max Wahlberg, to leave town or he might wind up dead."

"What?" Max asked. "What?"

"I know, I know. It's crazy. And I think they're only trying to spook us and keep us from doing our work, but I just don't want to take any chances. I think you need to leave for a while, Max."

So, a day later, Max called his parents to invite himself home for Thanksgiving, packed his bags, and hightailed out of Friendly. He ignored the weather forecast that said something about snow. He wanted to leave. Gus seemed happy to go for a ride. The snow started falling heavy as he cruised north.

An hour out of town, his old truck died. Out of gas. He pulled it over to the side of the road and got out, telling Gus to stay. He kicked the door. Stranded, in the middle of a storm. *Why didn't I check the tank before I left Friendly?* With gas always nearby in a small town, he hadn't given it a thought.

He climbed back into the truck and took stock of his situation. His cell phone didn't have much of a charge. He needed to call for help or they could freeze to death. That would be one way to end his pain, he supposed, and then he could join Gabrielle and Isabella, if there really was a heaven. But there was Gus. If he didn't have the dog, he could be like an old Eskimo, wandering into the snow to pass.

Before Gabrielle and Isabella died, stories of Indian women throwing themselves on their husbands' funeral pyres had baffled him. But over the last three months, he'd come to understand. Being left behind, alone, struck him as being much worse than quickly going up in flames. A sinister laugh bubbled up and out, echoing into the cooling car. Going out in a blaze together sounded like a good dream to him.

As he watched the swirling storm, he felt the anger and anguish within. His questions were endless. How could God have let it happen? Why did his wife and daughter have to die? Why was he being targeted for trying to save life on the planet? Were they really trying to kill him?

His mind flashed back to the day before when Buck had told him to leave. His friend had 'fessed up that, at first, he'd wanted to shelter Max from the nonsense, but when it kept intensifying, he decided he'd better come clean.

Gus licked his hand and he rubbed the dog's head. At least he had Gus. But this situation was not fair. He wasn't doing anything wrong, and he shouldn't have to run. Part of him didn't want to let the haters win. Backing down would help them accomplish exactly what they'd set out to do. He wondered if he'd been followed when he left town. If so, that could easily put the nails in his casket—unless, of course, he did it himself.

He fingered his cell phone. He needed to call someone quickly, if not for himself, for his dog.

Years of habit kicked in. Whenever he'd been in a bind, he'd always called his wife. "Gabrielle," he screamed, "why did you leave me?" He knew the accident hadn't been her fault, but he wanted to blame someone.

His outburst served to bring him to his senses. He knew that being an hour out of Friendly made it too far for Buck to reach him in the storm. He pulled up Google Maps, surprised that it worked with the satellites obscured with this heavy cloud mass of a storm, and searched for a nearby gas station, restaurant, or hotel.

And then he heard her. "Max-a-million Wahlberg, you are so not going to give up now." Her right hand petted Gus.

She'd always told him he was "one in a million" and liked to alter his name to illustrate the point. In the middle of love-making or just in an ordinary moment, she'd made him laugh and feel important. But this time, he knew she was wrong. He was just one more scientist fighting the rising tide of greed taking over the country. This time, the fire would take humanity down.

Gabrielle spoke firmly, insistently. "You cannot let them win. Do you hear me? Your work is too important for you to stop. No, Max. Stop that stinking thinking right now."

Negative thinking was another thing Gabrielle had always called him on. "The quality of your thoughts determines the quality of your life. Always dream, be positive, and concentrate on the good," she'd tell him.

"That's easy for you to say," he shot back. "How am I supposed to carry on alone?"

He collapsed into tears. His body heaved. His parka provided some warmth, but inside, he felt so cold. Gabrielle closed the distance between them. She reached out and enfolded him in her arms and then she held him, firmly, lovingly, passionately, the way only she could do. His tears streamed down his face and he licked at the salt.

Max didn't know how long she embraced him, but it was long enough for him to start to feel some hope, long enough to give him the love he needed to carry on. It was long enough to give him something to savor and hang on to for the days ahead. It might be snowing outside, but inside the car, he felt like he was on a sunny beach in the middle of a heat wave. The warmth of the love between them melted his heart back into gold.

After a while, she pulled away. "Max, there's a two-gallon gas can in the storage bin of your truck. It's behind the spare tire. I put it there just for you, my absent-minded professor. I knew you'd call me one of these days from some deserted highway when you forgot to fill up."

"Are you sure?"

"Yes, dear. You know I watch out for you. Now go get it and put it in your truck. I'll wait right here with Gus until you come back."

"Gabrielle?"

"Go now, Max, while you're still warm," she ordered.

As much as he didn't want to leave the warmth of her arms, he did as he was told.

Max leaned forward into the blowing night, fighting the storm to unlock the storage bin behind the cab on his truck. He reached behind the spare tire, where, sure enough, his hands landed on a gas can. He started crying again. His tears froze on his face, but he didn't care. He poured the gas into the tank, relishing the sound of the gushing liquid, one last gift from Gabrielle.

And then he remembered she'd said she would wait. He rushed

back into the cab, started the engine, and reached over to enfold her in his arms one more time. As the truck warmed, he felt life flooding back into his veins. Her love had always done that for him.

Gabrielle pulled away to look at her watch. "I can stay a few more minutes, Max, but you gotta get on down the road. Two gallons won't get you far and this storm is only getting worse."

"Do you have an inside line to the weather report now, honey?" Max asked giving her a wink.

Gabrielle smiled. "Maybe. They sent me down to save you."

"Who sent you down?"

"Isabella and my mom," she said. "They've been keeping an eye on you for me. You had them worried. Me, I sort of wanted you to just come join us. But the Big Boss said you still have some work to do. They all sent me."

Max looked at her incredulously. "What?"

"You heard me," she said. "Now, get this show on the road, Max. It's time to go."

He put the truck into drive and pulled out onto the snowy highway. "Just how far do you want me to go in this mess?" he asked her. Might as well get his marching orders before she slipped away. "Could you hang out with me 'til I reach Mom and Dad's?"

"You've got two gallons, Max. Remember? No, Max, not tonight. There's a hotel up the road about a mile; we should see its light soon. This is a blizzard. You might be there a few days before they can clear the road. But they've got good food, a warm bed, gas, and you've got your dog." As if on cue, Gus barked.

"Can you stay?" he asked. "Do you really need to get back? How 'bout you join me for a few nights."

"No, I can't, dear. You gotta get on with your life," she said.

"What does that mean? The hater is after me. I quit my job. Now I've gotten run out of town, so I'm going home to my parents. What am I supposed to do?"

"You'll figure it out, dear. You always do. By the way, I like Mariah," she said. "Look, there's the motel now. Pull in."

Max turned toward the parking lot of the motel and the wheels on the truck swerved out before he could control the wheel. They spun in a circle, almost in slow motion.

Gabrielle laughed and then she was gone. Max pulled up to a spot close to the door and walked in, hoping they'd take his dog.

He knew that for a long time to come, maybe even forever, he'd remember this night. He still wasn't quite sure if he'd dreamed her up or if he was just going crazy, but he was sure of two things. One, the folks up in heaven had his back, and, two, he had a job to do, so they weren't ready for him to come Home just yet.

11. WINTER DREAMS

Autumn passed quickly for Mariah. The winds cleared the leaves off the tree and then blew Max away, too. Buck said he went to visit his family, but that didn't sit right with her. The way he'd run out of the church that night seemed strange. Had he been running from her? She tried to ask Buck, but he was tight-lipped.

This December afternoon, Mariah looked at the clock in the diner, knowing she was cutting it close. "Sally, I'm taking my break," she called. She always tried to get out of the diner in between breakfast and lunch. The first day of winter beckoned. She'd planned a Winter Solstice celebration at Buck's Pub for later that night. She'd asked Buck to invite Max, but he hadn't made any promises. Mariah would be doing the music.

She pulled on her winter gear and hurried into the winter wonderland outdoors.

She loved the magic of this season almost as much as she loved her birth season of autumn. She could hardly believe the longest night had arrived already. It seemed before she'd had a chance to notice how short the days had gotten, they started lengthening back out into spring. She loved the rhythm of life changing through the cycle of each year.

She cherished the warmth of the fire and sparkling light of candles. She'd helped Mrs. Bee decorate last week and their house looked festive, all ready for their annual Christmas Eve party. But as much as Mariah loved the indoor ambiance of winter, she felt much more at home outside. As she traipsed toward the woods, she breathed in frosty air, enjoying the sensation as it cooled her lungs. She imagined delicate ice crystals dancing into her body, enlivening her entire being.

The snow streamed down, thick and heavy, covering the ground quickly. She wondered if folks would even make it to the pub that night. She twirled around, waltzing in a fantasyland of white. She didn't care. The winter slowed them all. Her feet would soon be plodding deliberately through inches of snow. But for now, they would only slip and slide. And then, sure enough, she fell right in the middle of a twirl, landing on her behind. Injuring nothing but her pride, she jumped up and glanced around, hoping no one had seen her.

She slowed her pace and walked meditatively, savoring the snow. The wind picked up a bit. The flakes flew sideways and some swirled in little cyclones, making her think of her Shawnee background. Sometimes, when she was younger, she'd heard an old woman talking to her. Even now, she could hear her words. Later, she'd learned the

Shawnees believed in a female God and she wondered if maybe she'd heard the voice of God.

Although she loved cooking up food at the diner to sustain the people of her little town, she needed something more. After talking it over with Mrs. Bee, she'd decided to go back to school and fulfill her childhood dream of studying the wind. She wanted to understand the created world and all she found so fascinating about it. She didn't yet know how she'd use her knowledge. Maybe as a teacher, maybe as a horticulturalist, or maybe, like Max, she would harness the wind. She loved the story of the boy in Africa who'd saved his village by taking apart his family's bicycle and making it into a windmill.

If a poor boy in Africa could do that, she reasoned, couldn't she do something to save the people of the earth? She might just be a poor girl in Friendly, but she had aspirations. Maybe she could help Max. He was already living her dreams.

Now enrolled in an online undergraduate program in earth science, she struggled to unpack the mystery of the wind in her online classes. She knew that when a high-pressure system met a low-pressure one, the dense molecules in the high-pressure system pushed downward into the less dense low-pressure and that created the wind. When a storm rolled in, the systems were meeting in the air. She'd learned that the low-pressure systems hovered around the earth most of the time, keeping the winds down. Now the heavens were swirling down and all around her, and, in this case, bringing the snow along. She felt happy to understand a little bit of the science of wind. She had the recurring thought that if she could really understand the wind, she'd also understand herself.

Last night, she'd finally spilled the story about her short-lived rendezvous with Max. Mrs. Bee always knew how to coax out her secrets, gently, in a painless sort of way. She admitted that, for once, she really didn't want to shut out a man, but then Max had closed her out instead.

She didn't understand why he'd run just when they were starting to stoke a flame. Mrs. Bee helped her get it all out and suggested there might be something about Max and his story that she didn't know yet. Mrs. Bee told her to give it time, that you couldn't rush things. "Sometimes, you have to let the heart wait until it's ready. If it's meant to be, it will happen," she'd said.

Mariah shivered. Even in her parka, the winter wind chilled her as she strained to walk through it. Originally, she'd planned to go to her path in the woods. Now she revised that to just staying on the sidewalk.

Already the town looked beautiful. She loved the way snow could paint the town white, covering up all its imperfections. After the glorious colors of autumn disappeared and the last green of the summer growth faded and the earth got put to bed with a drab, dreary blanket of grey and brown, the first snowfall of the year covered up the mess, refreshing the view and making things pure; a glistening white fluffy comforter laying on top of everything.

Outside, in the elements, she felt caught up in the midst of the change, whipped by the wind and living the storm. She liked this, too; it seemed an appropriate moment for the Solstice. She enjoyed winter roaring in like a lion. It felt substantial. A season changing had a right to stir things up.

She looked at her watch, realizing it was time to start back to the diner. She'd only come a few blocks, fighting the wind. The exercise had invigorated her. She spent the return trek composing her set list for Buck's, still hopeful that the snow wouldn't shut them down.

12. CELEBRATIONS

The snow had picked up something fierce by the time Mariah left the diner. She'd no more than gotten home when Buck called.

"I'm closing the pub tonight, Mariah," he said. "Can you sing next week instead? It's not safe out there tonight. Stay home, okay?"

"What else can I do?" Mariah asked. "I wanted to sing tonight. I'm in the mood." She'd felt something growing inside her since she'd sung with Max in the church. "Did you reschedule Max?" Even though she tried to make it to the pub most nights, she knew she didn't want to miss hearing Max sing. She hoped he'd invite her up to sing with him.

"Oh, babe, I'm sorry. Max left town before Thanksgiving. He'll be gone for a while," Buck reported.

"Where did he go?" Mariah asked, embarrassed that she didn't even know that he was gone.

"Home for the holidays."

"Could I have his phone number?"

Buck sighed. "I'll text it to you, okay?"

"Thanks, Buck," Mariah said. "Have a good night."

Mariah frowned. Christmas always was her favorite time of year, but having Max in the equation changed everything. Before, Mrs. Bee and the town people had been enough. But those sweet moments with Max made her long for something more. She'd finally let herself get attracted to a man and then what? He disappeared. First Dad, then Mom, now Max. She felt a familiar, dull ache in the center of her chest.

Mariah kept her feelings bottled up inside, but the next day, Mrs. Bee sensed her angst. She spilled out her frustration. Mrs. Bee always seemed to have an answer for her.

"Be patient, Mariah," she instructed. "He'll come back if it's meant to be."

But what if it's not meant to be, Mariah wondered. She knew sometimes God answered no to her prayers. Later in her room, she thought about calling Max, but chickened out. She considered the storm and hoped he made it wherever he was going before it got bad. Then and there, she decided to wait until Christmas to call him. It could be a present for them both.

***

The diner closed down the week of Christmas, which she'd loved in the past. This year, it gave her too darned much time on her hands, even with all the preparations. That morning, they baked the cookies and pies and stirred up the eggnog. They dressed the turkey and put it in to bake. She mixed up a green bean casserole, Mrs. Bee's favorite, and put it in the fridge. Then she peeled the potatoes, setting them aside to boil and mash later. Mariah even made the cranberry-orange relish, a recipe of her mom's. After the late afternoon church service, they'd get everything heated up and take the turkey out of the oven just in time for their guests. Mrs. Bee's family always came home for the meal, along with some of their town friends. Mariah felt happy to have Mrs. Bee's family coming, since she barely had any of her own.

With everything ready, Mariah decided to take a walk. As she stepped out into cold, she marveled at sunlight streaming onto snow-covered lawns. A fresh blanket of white had arrived overnight, covering up the dirty old snow. Mrs. Bee said that God was getting the world all dressed up for Christmas. Mariah had laughed, but enjoyed that way of thinking about it.

Tiny little flakes dotted the air, bouncing around on gentle gusts of wind. Some landed on her cheek, arctic kisses making her smile. They floated onto her jacket and melted into the fabric.

As she walked through the winter wonderland, she considered the miracles of the freeze. She loved that the season killed off harmful bugs and viruses. The cycle of life needed these dormant times. In her online classes, she'd learned not only about the wind, but the ways the plants survived through the winter. She thought she could learn from these aspects of nature.

She remembered learning about trees. When they shed their leaves, they could focus on hunkering down through deep roots, conserving energy to survive the cold. She looked at the towering black giants lining the street, standing as citadels of Friendly. Most outnumbered her by twenty-five years. She liked to think of them as her friends.

As a child, she'd named them when she learned their formal titles in school. Mr. Miles Maple. Mrs. Wanda Willow. Miss Elsie Elm. Sir Oliver Oak. As she passed them now, she reached out to touch each one, feeling their strength and absorbing some of it into herself.

These trees could bend with the wind. Sometimes the fierce drafts broke off a branch or two, but usually they stood flexible and strong. In the summer, their leaves danced in the breeze. Now, only the smaller branches waved with the gusts of winter.

Sometimes she worried about her old arbor friends. Could a tornado come through and take them all out? A nearby town had lost not only their trees, but most of their houses in a recent storm. She'd heard estimates of a hundred and forty-seven million dead trees in California, casualties of forest fires, drought, and the changing climate. She worried about whether the redwoods would still be there by the time she got to visit them. That was just one of the dreams on her long bucket list.

Time was running out for the people of the Earth to make changes, though, she reflected. Her father used to tell her that the Native American way considered seven generations when making plans and changes that affected the earth. But now, he'd said, businesses and governments barely considered what would happen in the current generation. Money trumps all. "Maybe you can change this, Mariah. I know I have failed," he'd tell her, lamenting that he couldn't even get his own father to make changes in his agricultural business.

She thought again of Max's project with the wind. Perhaps it was her destiny to help him. Was that what her father had meant? But the question of why Max had left remained.

A familiar tune her mama'd liked to sing came back to her now. "Dust in the wind. All we are is dust in the wind." The snowflakes continued swirling, sparkling as sunlight caught them midair. She figured you could call the snow dust in the wind, yet those delicate, symmetrical ice crystals, each unique, were formed in the clouds and showered earth with the mystery of life. She preferred to consider them miracles of life, so much more than dust in the wind. And she remembered Pastor Amy saying humans are made of stardust, formed from the supernova event that created our galaxy. We are born of a star. Maybe she'd write a new song about stars in the wind.

Maybe Max would come back. Maybe Mama, too. Just maybe, together they could make everything right. She must hope. Meanwhile, she searched for a rainbow as the sun peeked out for a moment, despite the falling snow.

13. HOWARD: MOVIN' ON

Got my marching orders this morning. They're sending me on to another town. Looks like I fulfilled my assignment in Friendly. Now I gotta go over to California where they are aiming to pass legislation about the climate and mess up our business plan.

Tree huggers want to stop our economy. Who the hell do they think they are? Don't they know the good Lord gave us all these resources to use in service to the almighty dollar and the future? We built America with these resources and we fuel the whole place with the fossil fuels. They are as necessary to American well-being as apple pie and baseball.

My job ain't all that bad, if you look at it properly. It's like I get paid to pull pranks. I'm harmless, really. Just rough them up a little bit. It doesn't take much to spook folks, I've learned. If they think you're watching them, they go under. All of the sudden, they are afraid to do what they're supposed to be doing, and that's what I like to see.

Take this Max Wahlberg guy. I've been messing with him for over a year now, because he's one of those scientists trying to let the cat out of the bag about the climate. Not only that, if his research pans out, that might put some of my fossil fuel employers out of business and we just can't have that, now can we? What would that do to my paycheck if the Maxes of the world win? No, sir. It's a free country and capitalism rules. It's survival of the fittest. Life is a competition, you see, and we're winning.

My job can be fun most days. Kinda like being the bad boy in the class, but getting paid to do it. Back in school, mess up and you got detention. Now I get paid for nasty deeds. A death threat brings in the big bucks. Toying with someone's reputation pays pretty damn well, too.

Pat me on the back or don't. Cuss me out, if you want. Won't bother me. All in a day's work. I might be leaving Friendly, but that don't mean Buck and Max are off my radar. They're still part of my assignment, but I usually just harass on the internet. Oh, boy, do I have their number. Every now and then, I have to totally destroy some of these folks to keep the paychecks coming. Destroy their reputations, I mean. That's what they deserve, trying to shut down American business. Totally fair stuff, you know. Some of us have to come out ahead in the game of the economy.

.

14. REBECCA

She checked her GPS one more time. Thirty miles, forty minutes to Friendly. Stopping at a light, she fingered her cell phone, paging through the Spotify Christmas playlist. She found "I'll be home for Christmas," and pushed it just as the light turned green. She hummed along as her old Toyota picked up speed. Off the major highways, she enjoyed traveling down the two-lane roads. The picturesque farms blanketed with the snow from recent storms felt somehow reassuring. She'd waited for a sunny day to make the final trek to her hometown.

She'd wanted to come home for years, but the longer she waited, the harder it got. She felt bad about Mariah, but her daughter was eighteen years old when Rebecca'd left and she figured Mariah could make it on her own. If she was being honest, she wasn't really thinking straight at the time. Her ex had almost killed her the night before she left. It took her a while to regain her bearings. The night she finally admitted she was an alcoholic, Mrs. Bee offered to take in Mariah. Rather than losing her job, she agreed to go into rehab. Rehabbing in South Carolina by the beach seemed the way to go, to get away from him and all her triggers in Friendly.

Her new life in Myrtle Beach gave her space to find herself again. Now that she'd received word her ex remarried and moved west, she needed to make a decision: go back to Friendly or stay on the coast? It depended on Mariah.

Rebecca'd decided to surprise her. She knew that Mariah would be at church on Christmas Eve. She planned to head directly to the church and get there for the service, which the website said started at five p.m. She hummed along with the Christmas music, hoping for a holy night.

15. CHRISTMAS EVE FOR MARIAH

At 4:45 p.m., Mariah and Mrs. Bee left their house and headed across the alley to the church. As Mariah walked into the candlelit sanctuary, she felt God's presence. As sad as she felt about Max, it didn't completely dim the joy of Christmas and that was something to be grateful for. She helped Mrs. Bee to her favorite pew and then took her place with the choir.

She'd promised Pastor Amy she'd sing "O Holy Night," her mother's favorite Christmas song. She'd sung it every Christmas since she was a little girl, but after her mother left town, she hadn't been able to get through it. She'd tried really hard, but her tears stopped her every single time. But then a few weeks ago, she'd been playing some songs on her guitar and decided to try again, just in case. She'd made it all the way through. She would sing it for her mama. She would sing it for herself. She would sing it for the Baby Jesus and the hope that came down at Christmas.

She still had conflicting feelings about her mother, but it was Christmas. She understood her mother'd needed rehab, but not why she'd stayed away so long, or why she didn't act like a mother anymore. There'd been nothing but silence since she'd left town.

Mariah watched the familiar folks filing into the pews, people she'd known all her life, and some who only came home for Christmas. They were bundled for the weather but unwrapped to reveal holiday garments of reds and greens. On a regular Sunday, the pews held more space than bodies, but on this night, the people squeezed in to be together. Mariah loved the crowd. She wished it could happen more often.

She scanned the room until her eyes rested on Mrs. Bee, who smiled. Mariah blew her a kiss. Then she saw Mrs. Bee mouthing the words, "Merry Christmas. I love you."

Mariah's smile widened as she blew a kiss in return and parroted the message back to her favorite old friend. She owed her life to that special old lady. Lately, Mrs. Bee seemed to be preparing Mariah for when she'd be leaving this world. Mariah didn't want to talk about it. She had enough stored grief for a lifetime in her heart already.

Mariah bowed in prayer, giving thanks for the blessings in her life. She said a special prayer for Max. When she looked up, she was surprised to see Buck ambling down the center aisle. She couldn't remember seeing Buck in the church before. He caught her eye and winked. He walked about halfway up and found an empty space by the aisle, just in back of Mrs. Bee. She noticed a single woman sitting in the pew not too far from him. It would be nice for Buck to have a woman. She wondered who she was, not remembering seeing her before, but she was hard to make out in the candlelight and seemed to be hiding under a bright scarf.

As the service started, Pastor Amy's voice soothed Mariah's heart as she led in prayer and read the familiar scripture telling of that night long ago in Bethlehem. As they sang the Christmas hymns, Mariah reflected that they sounded incredibly sacred on Christmas Eve. The candles flickered and, even in the dark sanctuary, she could see joy on the faces of the people gathered.

When the choir sang the "Carol of the Bells," Mariah enjoyed letting her voice merge with the others. Such a splendid evening, such heavenly sounds. Her heart felt full. Yes, it was a very Holy Night. And even if Mama weren't here in the flesh, she could imagine her.

Then Pastor Amy gave Mariah the cue. Mariah picked up the microphone and walked down the chancel steps to face the congregation, seeking to connect to the people, face to face. She aimed to make this song as special for them as it always had been for her and her mama.

She waited until Mrs. Frost, the organist, crossed to the piano and gave her a nod. As she began playing, Mariah smiled and started singing very quietly, "O holy night! The stars are brightly shining. It is the night of our dear Savior's birth."

Her voice lifted, opening into the space. "Long lay the world in sin and error pining, 'til He appeared and the soul felt its worth."

She gradually increased her volume. "A thrill of hope, the weary world rejoices, for yonder breaks a new and glorious morn." She continued, "Fall on your knees; O hear the angel voices! O night divine, O night when Christ was born. O night, O holy night, O night divine!"

When the next verse began, she sang directly to Mrs. Bee, who smiled warmly, maintaining eye contact with Mariah. "Led by the light of faith serenely beaming, with glowing hearts by His cradle we stand ... He knows our need, to our weakness is no stranger."

She bowed to Mrs. Bee as the verse ended, pulling her hand to her mouth and giving it a kiss. Her voice was strong. She found no tears streaming, only a radiating joy filling her whole body as she sang. She felt like a candle, shining as brightly as she thought possible.

She focused on her mama, remembering the years they'd used to sit right here together. She breezed through the second verse and went on to the final verse: "Truly He taught us to love one another; His law is love and His gospel is peace."

She still loved her mother, in spite of everything. She sang on, now making eye contact with Buck behind Mrs. Bee. "Chains shall He break for the slave is our brother; And in His name all oppression shall cease."

Then she looked past Buck to that unfamiliar woman in the pew next to him, no longer covered by the red scarf. She looked more closely. She kept singing, "Sweet hymns of joy in grateful chorus raise we." And then her eyes started to tear as she realized that woman was no stranger. That was her mother, home for Christmas! Trying to compose herself, she finished the song. "Let all within us, praise His holy name. Christ is the Lord! Then ever, ever praise we. Noel! Noel! Oh night, Oh night Divine! Noel! Noel! Oh night, Oh night Divine! Noel! Noel! Oh night, O Holy Night."

Her voice faded into the night. She replaced the microphone and stopped for a moment to smile at the radiant faces shining from the congregation below. She heard a cheer and someone started to clap. She bowed as the whole church broke out into applause. She heard a male voice yelling "Bravo". She felt their joy but couldn't believe it was all for her. She pointed up to the Christ window and bowed again. As the applause dissipated, she walked down the center aisle to Buck's pew. She gave Buck a smile, then said, "Excuse me," with an eye on her mother. She climbed over Buck and took a seat between him and her mother. A stillness descended over the sanctuary as she enfolded her mother in her arms and whispered, "Merry Christmas."

"Mariah, dear," her mother whispered back, confirming their bond as she held Mariah tighter than she'd been held in seven years. Later, there would be time for questions and anger, but right now, Mariah wanted to be a daughter again.

Pastor Amy stood and gave her Christmas homily, while Mariah and her mother sat and cried together, reunited on this very holy night, one that Mariah would never forget.

16. CHRISTMAS FOR MAX

Max had enjoyed being in his parents' home over Thanksgiving. His mom always served up a good spread and the family gathering felt comforting, despite his raw pain of grief. He helped with Christmas decorating and even baked cookies with his mom. And although he'd left Friendly, Buck stayed in touch and they continued their mutual wind project through emails and occasional phone conversations. Adhering to the time schedule set earlier, they refused to let the troll affect their important work.

As Christmas preparations continued, the nieces and nephews kept him busy. When he quit working each day, they wouldn't let him sit around and mope. He played Candyland and video games, tried out their new soccer balls. He taught the older ones to put some good old-fashioned English spin on the ping pong ball. The thirteen-year old Riley became his competitor by the end of the week. He played cards into the night with the older ones. He missed Gabrielle and Isabella. His sorrow circled him in the midst of the fun, but being with the family did him good. He laughed and cried. They watched "Miracle on 34th Street", went Christmas caroling at the nursing home, and even went ice skating downtown at the outdoor rink. He felt grateful for the gift of family.

His brother Marshall flew in from L.A. and they'd gone out to their favorite pub a couple nights. It had been nice to feel a sense of normalcy, remembering the good times they shared in the past. The bachelor life seemed to suit Marshall well and gave Max hope that perhaps he would eventually grow into enjoying singlehood again.

After the visitation from Gabrielle in the midst of the blizzard, he felt different. For years, he'd heard and read those "life after life" stories about those who died and came back, but he didn't quite believe it. But with Gabrielle showing up to tell him about the gas can? There was no way he could deny the reality of that.

As a scientist, he would always be a skeptic. But even the scientists these days were beginning to admit they couldn't know it all. Recently, his scientific journals talked about dark matter and dark space. This dark stuff filled up over ninety percent of everything and the scientists still didn't really understand it. The more he learned, the less he knew. One thing he did know for sure was that the mystery at the heart of life would defy understanding, at least in his lifetime.

The season pulled on his heart. When his mom asked if he'd join them at the church on Christmas Eve, he couldn't say no. If someone had asked him a few weeks ago, if he'd be caught inside a church again in his lifetime, he would have answered a definitive no. Now there he was, taking a shower and getting all decked out in his good suit, which had been still hanging in the closet from days gone by.

"Max, it's time to go," his mother yelled up the stairs.

"Coming, Mom," he replied. Once he made it downstairs, he was delighted by the aroma of freshly baked Christmas cookies filling the room. His little nieces and nephews were decked out in their holiday best. His dad wore a red bow tie and his mom matched him with her sparkling red Christmas dress.

"Photo op," his sister Janie hollered.

"We don't have much time," his mother warned.

"All the better," Janie's husband Mike quipped.

"In front of the fireplace," Janie directed. "Little ones, sit. Tall ones in the center. That's you, Max, Mike, Dad, Charlie. Ladies in front of the men."

"I can take the picture," Mom said. "We need to get the show on the road."

"No," Janie said. "You are the most important part of the picture. I'll take it, and then we'll do one without Mike."

Max smiled, but part of him could only remember the same time last year when Gabrielle and Isabella had been part of the family picture. He remembered holding Isabella in his arms. He remembered standing behind Gabrielle. A tear escaped and rolled down his cheek.

And then he heard her, as clear as day, a little voice calling to him, "Daddy, don't cry. Mommy and me are okay. We're just fine." "Did you hear that?" he asked Charlie, who was standing next to him.

"Hear what?"

"Nothing, nothing," he said, doubting his sanity yet again.

"You're not going to start talking about those reindeer on the roof again, are you?"

He laughed as the young children looked up at them.

"Is Santa here?" five-year old Darcy asked.

"Not yet, not yet," her father Charlie answered. "He waits until all the good girls and boys are sound asleep to come down the chimney."

"Okay," their mom said, "we are out of here."

The family pulled on gloves and parkas and walked out into the clear night.

"We can follow the star," his ever-quirky mom said. On Good Friday, she'd say it was always cloudy; and always sunny on Easter. He was pretty sure she was wrong, but she probably kept mum those years the weather didn't cooperate with her view of the world. To her, a clear night on Christmas Eve was a time to watch the stars and think about the wise men. Of course, a snowy night would be white Christmas dreams coming true. She had a way to spin everything.

The church was only a block away, so they didn't bother driving. The crisp evening air stimulated Max. He felt like his family was carrying him through this time. He drew comfort just being together. He walked with Charlie, until Charlie had to pick up one of his little ones. Then he walked with his mom, who put her arm around him. He felt her love and concern. He always did.

"I just heard Isabella," he told his mom, thinking she would believe him.

"She talks to you?"

"Just this once," he said. "She told me not to cry back there when they were taking our picture. She told me that she and her mommy are all right."

"How sweet," she said. "Bella showing up to let you know she's okay, that's a very special Christmas memory. They're watching over you, Max."

"Either that, or I'm going crazy," he whispered.

"No, no. Don't you think that. Remember what Gabrielle did. You couldn't make that up. You didn't make up Isabella, either. You're going to get through this. It's hard. It's hard for all of us, but love helps."

"I know, Mom. I just miss them so much."

His mom stopped and enfolded him completely in her arms. "I know, son. I know. So do I."

In minutes, they arrived at the church and filed in, taking seats about halfway up on the left where the Wahlberg family'd always liked to sit through the years. On the end of the pews were candles. Up in front, red and white poinsettias lined the chancel area. It was a beautiful sight; suddenly Max was glad he came.

The soft glow of candlelight brought to mind early mornings with Gabrielle when they would meditate and pray together, then journal to start their day. His life had changed so quickly the moment Gabrielle and Isabella were snatched away from him. Last year, they'd sat with him, right in this very pew.

The choir led with "O Come All Ye Faithful" and Max stood and sang along. The familiar tunes comforted him in his grief. After a time of greeting, the pastor invited the children up to the front to gather around the live nativity scene. They always brought in a goat and lamb for the service. The children liked to pet them. They let the kids sit in front through the rest of the service, with a parent. He volunteered to supervise Darcy so that Charlie could stay with his wife. Max remembered that Isabella had been mesmerized with the goat. And she'd also been restless. As a two-year old, she'd spent the service walking around the nativity scene, petting the goat and the lamb.

Eventually, Max had had to grab her and take her back with the family.

The service was mostly music, but he knew from experience the pastor would deliver a short reflection, followed by each person lighting a candle. Once again a memory flashed of last year, with Gabrielle and Isabella and all three of them holding the candles together.

A soloist began to sing his favorite song, "O Holy Night." He closed his eyes, feeling the warmth of Darcy, who leaned back on him where they both sat on the floor by the lamb. The voice echoed out into the sanctuary and into the cavern of Max's empty heart, filling it up just a little. And his heart brought a sudden flashback to the night in the church with Mariah. He started to wonder if she, too, might be in church on this night, if she was singing, if she was thinking about him? He'd cut her off. He knew he had some explaining to do. Gabrielle had said she liked Mariah. That made him feel better. To be perfectly honest, he knew that he liked her, too.

17. REUNION

At Pastor Amy's church, the ushers walked down the aisles, passing out little candles. They stopped at the pew where Mariah sat with Buck and her mom. Buck took three candles out of the basket.

The choir began to sing "Silent Night" and the congregation joined in. Pastor Amy lit the ushers' candles from the Christ Candle in the center of the altar, sending them back out to the congregation. The ushers again walked down the center aisle, lighting the candles of those at the end of each pew, who passed the flame on down their rows, gradually brightening the entire sanctuary.

Buck received the light and passed it on to Mariah. Mariah accepted the light and shared it with her mom. Their faces glowed in candlelight. Mariah's tears continued rolling down her face even as she smiled into her flickering candle. Her mother's arm encircled her, firmly planted around her shoulder. It felt good. She felt loved and happy.

All of a sudden, Mariah remembered that she was supposed to be playing the guitar with "Silent Night", the way it was originally sung when the church organ quit working the year it was written. She caught Pastor Amy's eye, worried that she might be upset. Instead, Pastor Amy offered a radiant smile that Mariah could read across the considerable distance between them. Pastor Amy'd never met her mother, but she must understand. Mariah smiled back.

Mariah had a lot of questions for her mother. Why she'd stayed away for so long didn't make sense to Mariah. Rehab doesn't take seven years. It was nice she'd come home for Christmas, but that didn't erase all the hurt Mariah felt from the years of absence.

As the song ended, the organist played a transitional interlude. Pastor Amy held her candle up, and the others followed suit. The choir led out, "Joy to the world, the Lord has come! Let earth receive her king." Again, Mariah and her mother made their own duet. This time, her mother found the alto to Mariah's soprano, as their voices cascaded down together the "And every heart, prepare him room!"

The rest of the evening passed in a blur. Mariah, her mom, and Buck fetched Mrs. Bee and the foursome hurried next door to ready the house for the Christmas Eve feast. They warmed up savory dishes, popped the pecan and mincemeat pies in the oven, tossed salads, pulled cold offerings out of the fridge, and completed last minute preparations before the guests started to arrive. Mariah wanted to ask her mom so many questions, but helping Mrs. Bee kept her too busy to even stop.

Finally, at almost ten, after all goodbyes were said and the clean-up was finished, they sat in the living room and at last Mariah found time to talk with her mother. "Mama, why didn't you tell me you were coming for Christmas?"

Mrs. Bee, who'd been sitting in her easy chair, got to her feet. "I'm going to leave you two to talk this out. It's past my bedtime and I'm worn out. Goodnight."

Mariah rose to give Mrs. Bee a hug. "Merry Christmas! Thank you for everything. See you in the morning. I have some surprises for you."

"Oh, my," Mrs. Bee replied. "I'll look forward to that."

Mariah sat again. "So tell me, Mama, why didn't you call and tell me you were coming?"

Her mother laughed nervously, but then smiled. "I wanted to surprise you. A Christmas present!"

Mariah hesitated. Her mother had lived in distant Myrtle Beach for the past seven years. Although they'd talked briefly on the phone from time to time, Mariah no longer felt the bond with her mother that she had growing up.

"Okay," Mariah answered, trying to summon her common courtesy. "That's nice. Thanks, Mom." She knew she should be grateful, but she didn't feel it.

"Thank you for singing 'O Holy Night'," her mother said. "My favorite song and breathtakingly beautiful. That was the best Christmas present I could ever get. Your dad would have been so proud of you."

Mariah didn't say that she'd thought about her mom when she'd decided to sing the song and had been thinking about her as she sang it in church. Sometimes she felt a disconnect between her love for her mother and the reality of who her mother'd become. Instead, she said, "But Dad didn't go to church."

"Oh, but he loved to sing, and teaching you to play that guitar and sing was one of his greatest joys. Of course he would have been proud, honey," her mother said.

Mariah shrugged. Sometimes people made the dead into something they never were during their lifetime. She knew her dad had liked to hear her sing, but "O Holy Night"?

"Mom," Mariah said, "I'm really tired. It's great to have you here. Let's get you situated in the guest bedroom and call it a night. We can talk in the morning. And I'm sorry, I don't have a present for you. I didn't know you were coming."

"Mariah, I told you hearing you sing tonight was the best Christmas present I could ever want." Her mother stood and came and kissed Mariah's cheek. "I want to spend more time with you, honey. I'm sorry I've stayed away so long."

Mariah didn't know what had prompted her mother's sudden

change, but she guessed it might be a good thing. Right now, however, she just wanted to go to sleep. Mariah grabbed her mother's suitcase and pulled it up the stairs. "What did you bring?" she asked her mother. "Do you have rocks in here?"

Her mother laughed. "Just presents, dear. I have some surprises, too."

Mariah turned open the covers on the guest bed, partially to be hospitable and partially to make sure the sheets were clean. Then she hugged her mom and said goodnight. "Sleep tight," she added as she left the room.

18. OLD YEAR COMING TO A CLOSE

Buck called Max on Christmas Day. "Merry Christmas, old buddy. Let's get together. A new year's about to begin. We need to finish our project. When you comin' back?"

"Merry Christmas to you, too. Is the coast clear?" Max asked. "Do you really think it's safe?"

"Ain't heard nothing since you left town. I think the guy's moved on. They're just trying to spook us up a little, you know. Mission accomplished," Buck answered. "You left town. He's gone, focusing on some other climate scientist now. Come on back, Max."

Max didn't respond. As much as he wanted to return, he didn't agree. He wasn't sure it safe with that crazy troll on the loose.

"You still there?"

"I'm here," Max said. "I just don't want to put anybody in danger. I don't think I could live with myself if someone else dies because of me."

"Max, don't talk like that. It's not your fault that Gabrielle and Isabella died. Don't put that on yourself. That was a bad storm, an accident. The fossil fuel PR guy may sound scary, but he's just roughing us up. He wouldn't kill anyone."

"I'm not so sure about that, Buck," Max confessed. "A bomb threat at your pub? That's a little too much. Too big of a risk. We don't know for sure what happened to Gabrielle and Isabella—or your wife, for that matter."

"Stop it, Max. Accidents happen. You gotta let go. I know it's a weird coincidence, but you can't let this troll stop you. That's their goal, to shut you down. I've installed new security cameras at the pub, at my home, and at the cabin. If he comes back, we'll get him on video and press charges. We can't let him control us. That's exactly what he's trying to do. We can't let him win, Max. The stakes are too high. If he did kill Gabrielle and Isabella, that's all the more reason to not give up. We need to nail him. Hell, I'll hire a private investigator if you want."

Max laughed. "A private eye? That's what we need. But I don't know, man. I just don't know."

"Come sing a set for my New Year's Eve party at the pub, Max. You still owe me. Remember, that was part of our original agreement. You stay in the cabin, you provide music at the pub."

Max laughed. He could only resist his good friend for so long. "You got me. I'll show up around six to eat and I'll sing a set or two. And if the offer is still on the table, I'll move back into the cabin. Then we can put together our goals for the new year. I do want to finish our wind project. It's never been more important."

"Great. And, Max," he said, "Mariah's singing a set, too. We'll see you New Year's Eve."

"See you soon." As Max hung up the phone, he wondered why Buck had mentioned Mariah. Maybe she'd said something to their mutual friend about him. He'd assumed that by now he was off her list, keeping company with the rest of the men she'd spurned over the years.

But as he prepared for bed, he remembered the candles at church on Christmas Eve and he remembered Gabrielle. And Isabella's little voice reaching out. He felt a flicker of faith and with that faith came hope and the faint possibility that he could love again.

19. AFTERNOON WALK

Mariah cleaned up the diner for the day. Her mother really did seem to be turning over a new leaf. Gratitude swelled in her heart. Taking off her apron, she remembered Max coming into the diner, ordering vegetarian and quoting Thoreau. She replayed his voice singing her name in the sanctuary: "Mariah, Mariah, they call the wind Mariah." Then their voices blending together with "The Prayer" and his haunting solo, "Running against the Wind."

Once more, she wondered why he'd run. And she wished he would come back. Buck was tight-lipped, but had said, "He'll be back." She could only hope.

She grabbed her coat and walked out, turning the sign to "Closed" and pulling her hood up over the long curls she'd forced her hair into that morning. She'd be singing a New Year's Eve set, as well as a few songs with her mama. After the weekend, her mom would go back to Myrtle Beach.

Shadows fell early on Friendly at this time of year. She wished now she had her camera to catch the light playing on the landscape. She reminded herself that she could instead be present in the "eternal now" as Pastor Amy called it. "Be here now," she'd said. "We only ever live in this very moment."

The earth slept, dormant after the first frost. Mammals hibernated. Mariah couldn't remember when she'd last had a vacation. The diner would close for New Year's Day. Her mother and Mrs. Bee had planned a feast and invited Buck over.

The white sky offered a stark blank canvas for the trees. The black, leafless branches stretched up toward the heavens, air roots to the sky. She imagined their roots, just as big, stretching deep underground. She aimed to be grounded like the trees.

A crow winged up into the sky. A squirrel scurried nearby, then dashed behind a bush. The wind blew gently. She breathed deeply, taking in the refreshing cool air. The leaves were matted together now after rain and snow, beginning to decompose. The circle of life spun on.

Yet she worried. The threat of climate change cast shadows over the beauty. Changes were coming fast. Polar caps were melting. Warming seas changed weather patterns. The nightly news seemed to constantly report on weather disasters. Venice, eighty-five percent under water. Wildfires threatening the California coast. Islands sinking. She didn't understand how people could deny the obvious truth.

And she wondered what she could do. She kicked a rock. She would take more classes on the environment. Maybe Buck and Max would let her help them with their wind research. She turned toward home. Tomorrow, she decided, she'd set some goals for the new year. Just cooking at the diner would not save the planet. She needed to do more. Like her Native American ancestors, she yearned to do her part in keeping the Earth healthy for the next seven generations.

20. SINGING IT OUT

Max shuffled into the bar around seven thirty to the sounds of a familiar voice singing "Welcome, Back," the theme song for Mr. Kotter. How fitting. Singer Luke gave Max a nod and Max waved back. They'd shared the stage a while back. The holiday crowd filled the place, as did the aroma of Daisy's fine chili. His stomach grumbled. He scanned the room, looking for her, Mariah, sitting at the bar. His whole body reacted. Feeling a little foolish, he took a minute to get himself under control. An unsettling thought crossed his mind: *was she the real reason I ran?*

Mariah, engrossed in conversation with Buck, hadn't seen him enter. He wondered if maybe he should leave well enough alone. He'd just passed the seven-month mark since he lost Gabrielle and Isabella, but it still seemed like yesterday. He put down his guitar and waited for Buck to come around. He had time.

In younger days, he'd always hurried. Not anymore. That was another of the many things grief had taught him. He leaned back, stretching his feet out to the opposite bench, and sang along with a Jim Croce song. "If I could save time in a bottle ... I'd save every day like a treasure and then again, I would spend them with you." Then he whispered, "Come back and haunt me tonight, Gabbie. Let me take you home."

Buck caught his eye, pointed at the stage, and then flashed ten fingers twice. Okay, twenty minutes to down a beer, wallow in self-pity and then sing his heart out. As his stomach growled again, he ordered a bowl of Daisy's famous chili and he reviewed his first set list, which he'd worked up on a very dark night after he left Friendly in November. On his second set, he'd ramp things up a bit, trying to manufacture some hope for the new year. Maybe, he mused, he'd even convince himself.

Buck slid into the booth next to him, slapping down a mug of Devil's Dark, his favorite, along with a basket of their jumbo fries.

"Ah, you remembered," Max said, immediately downing a hefty swig of the beer.

"Not much 'bout you I forget," Buck tossed back. "Missed you, bud. Glad you're back. We've got work to do." Buck patted him on his back, then looked into his eyes. "How's it going, Max?"

"I don't know," Max said. "Honestly? Some days, I think I'm getting a handle on it. Had some good times over the holidays. Being with my family helped. But just sitting here, a song comes on and it takes me back and I'm wallowing again." Max picked up the mug and took another long drink. "I just don't know."

Daisy brought out his chili and welcomed Max with a smile. "Good to see you back, Max. Don't be a stranger."

When she left, Buck picked up the conversation. "I know it's hard. Every day, I start over. Some days, I don't want to get out of bed. This bar keeps me going."

"Do you ever think about going back?"

"Back where?" Buck said. "There's no going back."

"I mean back to the university. Back to teaching, back to the students, the academic life."

Buck got a faraway look and his eyes darted around the pub. Then someone called Buck up to the bar. Max sat pondering the question for himself. Personally, he wanted to go back. Not this semester, it was too late for that now, but maybe this summer or next fall. He'd needed to get away, but some days, he regretted leaving. He drained his beer and motioned for another.

He glanced back at Mariah. Their eyes locked for an instant before she looked away, then back. He beckoned to her to come over. She smiled but didn't move. A moment later, she jumped down from her perch and sauntered over, holding a glass of red wine. She wore a bright red, soft sweater dress that showed off her curves and sparkled with little specks of gold. Her lips were covered in a shade of red, and around her neck were gold hearts. He sighed.

"Wow, Mariah. You look stunning," he said. "You really dressed up for the party." So much for holding back. So much for taking it slow. He might have all the right intentions, but beautiful women had a tendency of tossing them out the window for him. And he knew she was something more, deep within. That was something he'd liked to explore. He imagined taking her home to learn more about her. Who was he trying to fool? He wanted her.

"How are you, Max?" she asked as she slid onto the bench beside him, giving him a caring smile and sipping her wine.

"Oh, I've been okay," he lied.

"Where did you go? One day, you were here, and the next day, gone."

Ouch. Here it comes. Before she could light into him, he said, "I went home to spend some time with my family, over the holidays, you know." Changing the subject, because he didn't really want to let her in, he asked, "You singing tonight?"

She smiled shyly. "Yes, Buck put me on to do a set after you. Do you want to sing that song together we sang in the church. Do you remember?"

Max chuckled. Oh, he remembered all right. He wasn't likely to forget her angelic voice. "Okay." Man, he was going down fast.

Buck shouted, "Hey, Max, you're up."

He looked at Mariah. "Can we finish this conversation later?"

She flashed him a smile, showing off her dimples and clear delight. "Sure thing, Max," she said.

Max sprang into action, carrying his guitar to the little stage where he tuned it briefly and then sat on the bar stool to sing. He addressed the crowd, talking into the mic. "It's good to be back," he told them. "I'm Max Wahlberg, and I'm going to sing a few songs. Life can be hard, you know. Downright depressing at times. Seeing as I've gone through a hard patch this year, I want to sing a few sad songs. Sometimes we gotta just be with the pain."

He started out with "You can Cry if You Want To," singing the Paul Brandt song he'd learned a while back. He saw Mariah scoot back over to her seat at the bar, but she seemed to be focused his way. He paused at the end of the verse and gave her a smile.

After that, he sang "Lonely" by Noah Cydrus. Knowing that was a little over the top, even in his state of mind, he then launched into "You've Got a Friend," singing directly to Mariah. Man, he needed to get a grip on himself. Before he jumped over the cliff, he probably ought to learn to fly again.

21. AULD LANG SYNE

Mariah returned to the bar and ordered another glass of wine. Her mother seemed engrossed in a conversation with Buck, which left Mariah to listen to Max. Her heart felt warm toward him. He'd come back and he seemed to still be interested in her. The music, the wine, and the festive atmosphere soothed her.

Max finished some sad songs. Then he started singing "You've Got a Friend", looking directly at her. She gave him a wide smile. She enjoyed his ability to sing the song; he almost sounded like James Taylor on the CD her mom had played back in the day. Her heart swelled. Perhaps Mrs. Bee was right. Maybe something would happen between them after all.

After Max's set, it was Mariah's turn. She called her mom up for the first song and they did "Auld Lang Syne," Karaoke style. Buck usually reserved one night a week for Karaoke, so Mariah liked to take advantage of that equipment when she sang, engaging the crowd in some sing-alongs. It took the pressure off her to perform and the crowd liked it, following the words projected on the screen behind the stage.

Tonight, the pub patrons seemed to really enjoy singing. As her mother returned to her seat at the bar, Mariah engaged the crowd. "How you all doin' tonight? Ready to party? Let's have some fun." She replaced "Auld Lang Syne" on the screen with "Roll out the Barrel."

Some guys in the back started holding up their mugs, swinging in time with the music.

At the end of the song, Mariah talked to them again. "Let's have a barrel of fun. One last chance to celebrate this year. I hope you and yours are enjoying the evening. I am Mariah Landtree and I'm here to help you close out the year. My mama and papa tell me I blew in with the October wind the year I was born. You know, they call the wind Mariah?" Then she launched into her signature song.

During the first verse, she noticed Max singing along. Feeling bold with a couple glasses of wine in her stomach, she stopped before the chorus. "Max Wahlberg, would you like to come up here and help me sing this song?"

"Sure thing," he answered. He harmonized to her melody as she began the chorus, "Mariah, Mariah, they call the wind Mariah."

Then she whispered, "Why don't you sing the next verse," so he did. When they got back to the chorus, they sang together again. She led on the third verse and, together, they took the song home. The crowd cheered and clapped.

"As long as you're here, Max, let's fortify them with some religion for the new year. You might know this song from Andrei Bocelli and Sarah Brightman, but here at Buck's Pub, we serve you up 'The Prayer' with Mariah Landtree and Max Wahlberg." She wanted to feel those good vibes of singing this song with Max again.

Mariah started. "I pray you'll be our eyes and watch us where we go." The chattering in the pub died down. She had their attention as she sang on, but when Max started singing Italian, the folks began clapping and everybody was focused on the stage. Mariah sang the English lines, Max the Italian. They batted the lyrics back and forth, captivating the crowd. Her heart swelled with joy as she felt the warm vibrations of Max's tenor connecting with hers.

On the last verse, Mariah sang, "Guide us with your grace."

Max answered with. *"Hai Acceso in noi."*

"Give us faith so we'll be safe."

"Sent ooche ci salverai."

Max took Mariah's hand and together, they bowed as the crowd clapped, rising to their feet to give them a standing ovation.

"More! More!" the patrons took up the chant.

"I'm glad you liked that," Mariah said, smiling. She felt almost giddy with the cheers from the crowd and her heart rumbled something fierce, standing so close to Max. "Thank you, Max," she said, then needed to do something to keep her from saying something more to him. So instead, she said, "And now I'd like to ask my mama to come up."

Max gave her a kiss on the cheek. She blushed and pulled out a familiar song to focus on. Her mom arrived at her side and she whispered, "How about 'Those Were The Days'?"

"Sounds good."

Then Mariah had a thought. She raised her voice to call to the first singer, who was engrossed in a conversation with a woman at the front booth. "Hey, Luke, do you have your fiddle with you tonight?"

"Sure thing, doll," he replied.

"Could you come up here and help my mama and me with 'Those Were The Days'?"

"Be right there."

Mariah and Luke had worked the song up a while back and she loved to hear him playing the tune on the violin. She thought it would be the perfect song for the end of another year. And it was a song her mother had taught her after her father died. A big song for a little girl, but now she could appreciate it.

Mariah said into the microphone, "My mama came home for Christmas this year and I'm so happy to have her here." She gave her mom a kiss. "Now, I think this next song is a fitting one for a New Year's Eve night. I want each of you to think back over the past year and remember those days. Those were the days."

Luke stood in place by the extra mic and Mariah gave him the nod. His violin's minor key pierced the night, pushing out the haunting melody. A hush fell over the room. Soon, Mariah and Luke sang, "Once upon a time, there was a tavern ...." She laughed as she saw some of the people raising their mugs and glasses of wine when they sang about them raising a glass or two.

She stood back from the mic and gestured to her mom to pick up the next lines. Then they shared the mic, singing on as Luke's fiddle sizzled along and kept the haunt going in between the verses. She felt drawn back in time to those days before her mother'd left town and the fun they'd had singing, before her mother's second husband moved in and her mother started drinking too much. The lyrics made sense in the context of their lives.

Mariah dropped out on the next verse and her mama sang, "Then the busy years went rushing by us."

A tear ran down Mariah's cheek as she thought about the years that had rushed by without her mama, but she stifled a full-out cry and joined in with her mom, on the chorus. As they continued the song, she looked out at the pub and noticed there were very few conversations. Everyone seemed intent on the performance.

When they came to the la-la-la's, Mariah hooked arms with her mother and began twirling around as they sang. Luke's strings added to the festivities as he also began to dance.

She and her mother harmonized on the rest of the song, drawing out the last line very solemnly, "Those were the days, oh, yes, those were the days."

Mariah felt dizzy with joy when the crowd again cheered her performance and called for more. She took her mother's hand and they bowed together, laughing. And then she told them, "I think that's the end of my set. I need to catch my breath! But Max has a few more for you."

Mariah gave Max a hug and went back to her seat at the bar, and Max ushered in the New Year with a more upbeat set. Finally, he called Mariah and her mother up at ten 'til midnight to repeat "Auld Lang Syne."

Buck joined them to lead the count down. "We've got thirty seconds left on the clock of the old year and I've got Daisy here with our version of the Time Square Ball." She curtsied as she showed off the pole with a lighted ball attached. "Pick up those noise makers we put on your tables and get ready to make some noise! Ten, nine, eight—" Daisy helped the ball drop manually. "Six, five, four, three, two, one ... happy New Year!"

Max turned to Mariah, closing the distance quickly. "Happy New Year." Not waiting for a reply, he gave her a kiss that she could feel all the way down to her toes. Mariah enjoyed the bliss for a moment, before turning away to find her mother and Buck doing the same thing.

She laughed and gave Max a knowing look. She broke away to hug Buck and her mom and wish them both a happy new year, too.

After that, Luke took over music duty, and Mariah went to sit with Max. They had a couple more drinks before Max asked Mariah if she wanted to come back to his place for a nightcap. She'd had enough to drink that any reservations she might have had had disappeared . As soon as she agreed, they said their good-byes to her mom and Buck and were out the door.

22. EARLY HOURS

Later, Max couldn't be quite sure what he was thinking when he'd brought Mariah home that night. Neither of them could have been thinking straight. He'd had a few beers and he knew she had at least three glasses of wine. She seemed very happy, but not out of control or drunk.

They sat on his living room couch for a while and he put on some soft music. He lost little time in returning to her, hoping for another kiss like the one they'd shared to usher in the new year. It had felt good to kiss her, and he wanted to do it again and again.

They didn't talk much; a word here or there. At one point, he announced, "I really like you. I missed you."

"Why did you leave?"

"Good question. You know, I think I was scared. Not ready. It was hard losing my wife and daughter. It's only been seven months. I just didn't think I could get involved again so soon."

"But now you think you can?"

"I'd like to try," he said. "If you're willing?"

She nodded. "I like you, too."

After some more kissing, he asked if she'd like to stretch out on his bed. He didn't intend to go any further than some heavy petting with their clothes on, but once there, his instincts seemed to take over and she seemed almost as aggressive. She started taking off his clothes and then he helped her with hers. He suddenly realized that he didn't have any condoms. He promised himself they'd stop before going all the way.

However, he found it hard to deny her what she clearly wanted. Much later, he realized the wine probably affected her more than the beer did him. But in the moment, he was solely focused on making her happy. Before long, they soared together into the rafters of the little cabin, ushering in the new year with pure joy.

23. NEW YEAR

Mariah knew she'd drunk too much wine that night. There were things she couldn't remember about New Year's Eve. She knew she'd sung with Max and with her mama. She remembered the countdown and a nice kiss to celebrate the new year with Max. And she knew they'd left shortly thereafter, going to his little cabin in the woods. The rest blurred.

She made it home the next day in time for the New Year's dinner that her mom and Mrs. Bee prepared without her help. She tried to slip in the front door, unnoticed, thinking they'd be busy in the kitchen, but that didn't work.

"Mariah," Mrs. Bee called, before Mariah could run up the stairs. "Why didn't you call us? We were worried about you. Where've you been?"

Oops. Why didn't I call them? Good question and she knew exactly the answer, but she didn't really want to tell Mrs. Bee, and she didn't think her mother-in-recovery would be too impressed, either. She'd had more wine than she could hold and went to Max's. She opted for some white lies.

"I'm so sorry. Max invited me over to his place. I meant to call, but it was way past my bedtime. I fell asleep." Well, that was sort of the truth. "But, Mom, didn't I tell you where I was going when I left the pub?"

"Uh, no," her mother replied. "You said good-bye, but you didn't say you were going home with Max."

Mrs. Bee raised her eyebrows. "Mariah, I know you like Max, but I think you know better than that. Slow down. Give it time." Then she clamped her mouth shut and went back to her dinner prep, but Mariah could see her shaking her head and muttering under her breath.

"Mariah, do we need to have a talk? And you should know that you need to be very careful about drinking. Alcoholism can be genetic. I don't want you to follow in my footsteps," her mother said.

Geez. Talk about the third degree. What right does my mother have to talk to me like that after all she'd done?

"I said I'm sorry," she groused. "What more do you want? I need to take a shower." She scooted upstairs before they could grill her more and find out what had actually happened. The whole episode was embarrassing enough without having to admit to them that she couldn't remember.

When Mariah came back downstairs later, she realized their earlier conversation had put a damper on the New Year's luncheon. Mariah was exhausted. Mrs. Bee and her mom seemed a little perturbed with her but didn't directly address the situation again. Then shortly after lunch, her mom left for Myrtle Beach, and the holidays were officially over.

***

After the weekend, she had to work again. Morning greeted her front and center and her head hurt. But she couldn't delay anymore. Already she'd pushed the snooze button twice. Once more and she'd be late. She rolled out of bed into her daily routine.

She went to wash off the night and relished the warm water streaming over her head and body. She switched the shower head to massage and let it do its magic on her back. Memories of Max's hands on her shoulders flooded back. Memories of Max and his cologne. Memories of laughter.

She scrubbed her body clean and let the water roll over her longer than usual. She felt a new longing within her. For so long, she'd avoided men. But now, even though she couldn't remember, she knew something awakened in her that night. Her whole body felt different.

She shifted into automatic, drying her hair, getting dressed, and going out the door. There was much to do in a short amount of time to be ready for the first customers right at seven a.m.

Although the longest night was past, she still had to walk to work in the dark. She could do without that, but she tried to make it friendly and bright in the diner in the morning. She hurried the short distance to the diner and heated up the grill, put on the first pot of coffee, and popped some muffins into the oven. When Farmer Sayers arrived at five after seven, she was ready.

"Happy New Year," she greeted him. "How ya doing, Farmer Sayers? What can I get for you this morning?" He always ordered the same thing, but she went through the motions to be polite. And, in all honesty, some days she needed to hear the familiar answers that felt like a comfortable old blanket in a world that keep changing.

"Just give me the usual, but could I have an apple with that?" he asked.

"Ah, an apple." Mariah winked. "Changing it up a little bit here in the new year?"

"I promised my daughter," he told her solemnly.

"An apple a day keeps the doctor away," Mariah said.

A moment later, the bell on the door jingled and in walked Max. Her heart lurched and her body tingled all over. Another memory surfaced.

She blushed. "Look what the cat drug in," she said, trying to hide that she was flustered. "Good morning, Max." She turned on her waitress voice, hiding deep within. "What can I get you?"

"Your veggie omelet with your Very Berry Smoothie and a black coffee," he said. Then he looked her up and down. "You're a sight for sore eyes."

Mariah turned back to the counter and dumped a bowl of mixed veggies on the grill then stirred up the eggs and milk for Max's omelet. Once again, she immersed herself in busyness, trying to keep all the emotions brewing under her skin from getting her mind all messed up. Max did something to her that she didn't understand. She felt more than a little embarrassed that she didn't even know what happened that night. She knew he was watching her every move.

"Did you read the paper?" she asked, trying to deflect his attention away from her for a spell.

"No. Should I?" he asked, locking his eyes on hers.

Something in the way he looked at her gave her a tingle that surged all the way down to her toes. Another memory came back. She blushed again. For years, she'd watched the natural world outside. Now she wanted to explore more the miracle of her own body which awakened in a new away when Max was around.

She handed him the paper, still wrapped in plastic. "You tell us," she said, hoping he didn't notice her red face.

Max did as he was told, and she turned back to finish his omelet, putting it in front of him before handing the farmer his bill with a little sheet of paper.

"Resolutions for the New Year," he read aloud. "I done made my New Year's resolutions, Mariah. Can't you tell? But I'll fill this out for you and bring it back tomorrow."

Mariah laughed. "Where did Farmer Sayers go? Who is this new man that had breakfast in my diner this morning?"

Farmer Sayers laughed with her. "You don't know me, Mariah. You thought you did, but you don't. The best is yet to come! See you tomorrow, dear."

The bell hanging on the door jingled and she could hear him chuckling to himself as he walked out into the brisk morning. She turned back to her only customer and her heart took a leap as Max closed the distance between them. "Gotta jump while the skillet is hot," he said and then his mouth found her lips. His body enfolded hers as his tongue probed the recesses of her mouth, sending shock waves into her core.

He came up for air. "Ahh," he said. "I've been wanting to do that all morning. Ah, Mariah." He paused, looking deep into her eyes. "I'm falling for you hard." Then before she could respond, he locked his lips on hers again, just as the bell jingled and her old high school friend, Corky, walked in.

"Caught ya in the act," Corky declared in a loud voice. "I knew there was something going on here."

Mariah pulled away from Max. "Good morning, Corky. What can I get you?"

Mariah went back to her job and Max went back to eating his omelet. Corky placed her order, while Mariah worried about who her friend would tell about the kiss she'd seen.

24. MAKING ENERGY

Winter rushed into Friendly in full fury shortly after the new year. An unusual storm system from the north dumped three feet of snow. Then polar temperatures made digging out extremely difficult. Folks bundled up and created small paths through the snow; it was the best they could do. Most of the cars ended up staying buried.

Max kept busy with their wind project. Mariah buckled down on her studies. They often met at the pub at night, where they worked on their laptops. Max helped her with her homework, as well as staying focused on the project. January came and went, and they continued an easy friendship with no repeats of New Year's Eve.

Max wasn't sure how to proceed. Mariah seemed a bit remote. Valentine's Day was coming up. His mind spun, seeking the next step. Maybe he could invite her to his place and explain himself. Maybe he was the one who needed to open up. He couldn't get New Year's Eve out of his thoughts. And yet neither of them talked about it. He stayed silent in his uncertainty. He couldn't figure her out. And, if he was being honest, he couldn't figure himself out. Maybe it too early for him to be jumping into a relationship, no matter how much he found himself drawn to her. The grief counselor had recommended waiting at least a year, to avoid making potentially painful mistakes.

Then there were his thoughts about Fall. More and more, he wanted to go back to teaching.

He checked his email. He was waiting to hear from the patent lawyer, and, finally, there it was. They could launch their baby now. He forwarded it on to Buck and then jumped to his feet and took a spin, twirling about like he'd done swing dancing with Gabrielle.

Mariah looked up at him. "What's up?"

"We got our patent! Full speed ahead." He called the bartender over and ordered the newest IPA, Dancing Dragon. "Time to celebrate. What do you want, Mariah?"

Mariah ordered organic ginger ale.

"No wine tonight?"

"No wine," Mariah said, then looked away. "I'm off alcohol for a while."

"Why?"

"Just taking a break."

He took out his guitar and strummed a few notes. "Okay," he said. "How's the weather?"

"Spring is coming," Mariah exclaimed.

Max let out a breath he didn't realize he'd been holding. "I don't think the groundhog saw his shadow."

"Do you believe that?" Mariah asked. "I thought you were a scientist."

"Scientists don't know half as much as they think they did do."

"What do you mean?"

"Dark space, dark matter. Ninety percent of everything and we don't understand it at all," he said. "Have you taken any classes on space? Have you studied the stars, Mariah?"

"Not yet," she said with a dreamy look in her eyes. "Should I?"

"I would recommend it. There's an amazing astronomer at Ohio State. He lectures to sold out classes every semester," Max said. "He's a good friend of mine. He'd help you see things with a whole new perspective."

"How could I do that? I can only take classes online," Mariah said. "Right now, I just don't see how I could afford to quit working and go to school."

"Have you ever looked into scholarships? I can help you. We're trying to encourage women in science these days. You sell yourself short. Mariah. There's a whole world waiting outside of Friendly."

Mariah frowned. "I can't think about that right now," she declared.

"Why not?"

She opened her mouth to reply, but snapped it shut without saying a word, leaving Max convinced that he'd never figure her out.

The door opened and in walked a man Max didn't know. Strangers stood out in a small town where everyone knew everyone else. This one looked like he had money. His black loafers shined, even in the low light of the pub. His hair was greased into place in an old Presley look. He wore a Mister Rogers-style sweater over a button-down white oxford, but somehow, he didn't have the Mister Roger's Neighborhood vibe. In fact, something about him made Max nervous.

"What can I get you, sir?" Daisy said.

"Gotta a menu?" the man asked with a sneer in his voice as if Daisy were trying to hide something.

"They're on the tables, sir."

"Do you know him?" Max asked Mariah.

"Never seen him," Mariah said. "He's got a gun," she whispered.

Looking again, Max noticed a holster hanging off the man's belt, with a handgun tucked inside. Max shuddered. Ohio's conceal and carry law made it legal, but he didn't like it one bit.

The man sat and thumbed through the menu.

"Can I get you something to drink?" Buck asked from the bar.

"Just give me a minute, won't you? Don't get yourself in a tizzy, now," the stranger barked back.

The man seemed determined to be upset. He'd walked in with a chip on his shoulder. Max watched the guy rise to his feet, take his gun out of his holster, and fire two shots into the air.

Max sprang into action. He'd been trained well for active shooters at Ohio State. Universities all over the country were trying to be prepared in light of more and more incidents of gun violence at schools. He whispered to Mariah, "Get Daisy and Buck back in the kitchen and call 911." Then he dove for the man. By the look of the stranger's face, Max surprised the hell of him. Act quick or get out of the way was what they'd taught him. The obsession he'd had with martial arts during younger years had finally paid off: he knew how to take a man down.

The gun flew out of the stranger's hand and Max wrestled him to the ground. The sheriff arrived minutes later, put cuffs on the man, took Max's statement, and led the gunman away.

Max started to go into the kitchen to tell them the coast was clear and passed by the booth where the shooter had sat moments earlier. A leather briefcase leaned against the wall, at the end of the bench. On closer examination, he read the letters AST engraved in gold. America's Solutions for Tomorrow. The troll was back. He needed to tell Buck—and the sheriff.

Fortunately, it was early enough in the evening that there were no other patrons in the pub. Max went into the kitchen to tell Daisy, Mariah, and Buck it was safe to come out.

"What happened?" Daisy asked.

"People are plumb crazy these days," Max said. And then he turned to his friend. "Buck, it might be a good idea to close down for the rest of the night."

"The sheriff took the guy, right?" Buck said. "Why shut down?"

"The sheriff will be back to investigate," Max said.

"Yeah, but that's not a big deal," Buck said.

"Maybe not, but can I talk to you a minute?" Max pulled Buck back into the kitchen to explain about the briefcase.

"Oh," Buck said. "Yes, I'll shut down. We need to fill the sheriff in on this." Buck walked back out into the bar. "Daisy, put up the Closed sign. Then you and Mariah can go on home. You deserve a break. Max and I will stay here to clean up and wait for the sheriff to come back. Mariah, do you mind?"

"No, not at all. That was spooky," Mariah said. "I was just about to leave anyway." She picked up her books. "Catch you all later."

As soon as Daisy and Mariah were safely out of the pub, Max called Buck over to the booth. "Look at this," he told Buck, holding up the briefcase.

"Please tell me that America's Solutions for Tomorrow is not back to haunt us again."

Max looked down. "I told you I shouldn't come back."

"We're in this together, Max," Buck said. "I'm glad you're with me."

America's Solutions for Tomorrow sounded like the name of a savior, but they knew that man was serious trouble. "We need to call the sheriff back," Max announced. "He needs to call the FBI."

Two hours later, the police reports were complete and the FBI had been contacted. They would be investigating in the morning. Max and Buck left together, but not before Max took a good look around the parking lot for unknown cars or men in trench coats. There was no reason to believe the thwarted shooter had acted alone. Max gave a nod to the cop in the unmarked police car before unlocking his truck and driving away.

***

Max watched Mariah take a long drink of her ginger ale. He wished she was drinking wine instead of ginger ale. He knew he could lure her home if she had a few glasses of wine. But she hadn't had beer or wine since New Year's Eve. He poured a glass of red wine and placed it in front of her.

She pushed it away. "Not tonight, Max," she said.

"I thought you liked red wine," he protested.

"I told you, I'm not drinking wine right now."

"Okay, okay," Max said. Better quit pushing the wine. She obviously didn't want it. So Max downed it himself. He went back to work, running the bar for Buck for a few hours. He asked the boys in the back if they wanted refills, carried their dirty mugs to the sink, and filled new ones with their requested brews.

Everyone seemed happy. He picked up his guitar. And that was when all hell broke loose.

The college students over in the corner opened fire first. They sprayed paint, dodging around the bar like little kids, shooting it out in a free-for-all. He watched them destroying the place and yelled, 'Stop right now or I'm calling the police."

As if in response, yellow paint splashed on the mirror above the bar. Red paint covered the beer labels on the keg spigots. The students themselves looked like rainbow-spattered children after a few rounds.

Mariah just laughed. And laughed and laughed and laughed.

Daisy came out from the kitchen and wrestled a gun from a student and started shooting at Max, then Mariah. The students joined in and sprayed Daisy.

Max couldn't imagine how he'd ever explain this mess to Buck. Then, just when he thought it couldn't get any worse, a quiet man in the corner stood. Max squinted at him, trying to place where he recognized the man from. And then his eyes dropped to the shirt, which bore the initials AST. Max thought the sheriff had locked him up. So how did he get back to the bar?

Again the man pulled a gun out of a holster on his hip. "Now," he ordered, "I want you kids to stop your silliness and get out of here. If you leave quietly and calmly, you'll have no problems. Ladies, you're free to go, too." He motioned to Daisy and Mariah. "But Max Wahlberg, you stay right where you are."

Max considered his options, not wanting to put anyone in jeopardy. If the man let everyone else leave, Max could stay put and let them go. Once the pub cleared, he'd press his luck. If it was his time, so be it. He could join Gabrielle and Isabella. Hopefully, though, his training would pull him through one more time.

"Leave," he told the patrons. "Do what he says. Just walk on out."

Mariah seemed reluctant, but Daisy took her by the arm and led her out the door, whispering something that Max couldn't make out.

Max found his mind asking the same old tired questions. Why was he the target for trying to slow climate change? Why were the greedy ones so determined to shut down alternative energy projects that just might save life on the planet? How could they be so successful in confusing the people? Had they killed his wife? Did they murder his little girl? Would God really let such evil triumph and destroy the human race?

As the bar cleared, Max shook himself back into focus and once again considered his options. As much as he missed his wife and child, he realized that he didn't want to die. Not yet. He wanted to fight for his life and for the life of the human race. He'd sacrificed too much to give up now. His enemy stood across the room and a showdown was inevitable. The stranger had a gun; Max had only the truth.

He found himself praying for the first time in a very long time. He bargained and promised about his future. "God, please!" he pleaded silently.

The man took aim. Max heard the shots ring out. Was this his end? He didn't feel the bullets. He stood, frozen, unable to move his feet on the wooden planks of the bar's floor. More shots. He heard a voice. The shots became pounding.

His feet were free. *Where am I?* he wondered. He felt bed clothing and grabbed the blanket. He sat up with a crazy grin on his face. Someone was knocking on his door. He felt his chest. *I'm still alive! No bullet holes. Someone's knocking on the door.* "Thank you, Jesus," he said with deep emotion.

Max slipped into his bathrobe and hurried to the front door. He opened it to a welcome sight. "Buck! What are you doing here at this hour?"

They embraced each other on the porch.

"Can I come in? It's a little cold out here. My heat went out."

"Oh. Yes, yes. Come in. I'm sorry. You startled me. I was in the middle of a nightmare," Max explained.

"Tell me about it—in the morning. If you don't mind, I'm going to stretch out on your couch and get some shuteye." Buck pulled the knitted throws off the couch, put his head on a pillow and lay down, pulling the blankets over him.

Max rubbed his head, then got another blanket to throw over Buck before he went back to bed. The nightmare could wait. Once more, he thanked God that it had only been a dream.

25. GREENHOUSE

Mariah turned on the music. Mrs. Bee, Pastor Amy, Gloria, Lisa, Sherry, and Karol would arrive soon for the planting party. One of her favorite times of year came every February when she began to plan and plant for spring.

She danced to the classical music as she looked around one of the joys of living with Mrs. Bee. One of her favorite places in the whole world was this large greenhouse behind the house, a stone's throw to the God Box next door. Reverend Bee had cultivated award-winning tomatoes here during his lifetime and many other flowers and vegetables as well. He'd always told the congregation that he learned a lot about life in his greenhouse. He'd liked to share his gardening lessons in his sermons. Mariah remembered all of his stories. She'd started writing them down for Mrs. Bee, who couldn't remember so well anymore.

"If you listen to Jesus," he once said, "you're transported into the natural world of God's creation. Our Lord lived closer to the plants and trees and bees than we do these days. He often found examples among the growing things to teach us how to live. In the greenhouse in late winter, I understand the power of a seed. It's a metaphor Jesus used for faith."

Mariah pulled her phone out of her purse and searched for Matthew 17:20. She read it silently to herself. "Truly I tell you, if you have faith as small as a mustard seed, you can say to this mountain, 'Move from here to there,' and it will move. Nothing will be impossible for you."

Today they would plant the seeds. She'd chosen them carefully. Some, she ordered from the Heirloom catalogue, some from Organic Roots, and others she'd saved from last year's garden. Now she placed them all out on the little table.

Pastor Amy came in first. "Would you bless the seeds?" Mariah asked. "I'd like to have a little ceremony before we start to plant."

"Certainly. I'd be most honored. Thank you for inviting me. I found some of Reverend Bee's old sermons in the church archives where he refers to this greenhouse. I'm so glad to get to experience it firsthand."

"You found his sermons? Oh, my gosh, aren't they wonderful?"

Amy nodded. "It's amazing to me that you remember them. We pastors put hours into sermon preparation, but research shows that most of you don't remember what we say a few hours later, let alone years later. How is it, Mariah, that you remember still?"

Mariah didn't really understand how memory worked. Some

experiences had launched into her consciousness at some time in the past and embedded there. Others she tossed out as soon as they arrived, like when her stepfather and mom would fight. Reverend Bee's sermons had provided an oasis in her troubled young life, words she replayed and treasured in her heart.

"He spoke for God," Mariah said simply. "How could I forget?"

"That's just so cool to me, Mariah."

The door opened to let in Sherry, Lisa, and Gloria. They managed gardens for the elementary school in town, so Mariah provided them a corner of the greenhouse to plant for the children. They brought their own seeds.

Following closely behind, her retired friend, Karol, shuffled in. "How ya doin'?" she asked.

"Happy," Mariah replied and then sang, "It's a beautiful day in the neighborhood."

"Would you be mine? Could you be mine? Would you be my neighbor?" Karol sang back slightly off key.

They both laughed. Mariah had offered some space to Karol when she moved into the retirement community at the edge of town. When Karol had her own house, she'd cultivated vegetable starts under lamps in the winter and often gave Mariah tomato plants for her garden. Now Karol helped Mariah with her gardening and Mariah shared the harvest with her. Karol liked the raised beds that Reverend Bee had installed in his later years; they made it easier on older folks who didn't want to give up gardening.

Mariah heard whistling just before Mrs. Bee arrived, a smile spreading across her face. "Good morning, loves," she said cheerfully. "Thank you all for coming to the planting party. I've brought lunch in my crock pot for all of us. So please stay when we're done and make an old lady happy, okay?" Then Mrs. Bee looked at Mariah. "Do you have somewhere to plug this in, dear?"

"Oh, sure. Thank you, Mrs. Bee. Let me take it." Mariah then took the crockpot over to a table by the wall and plugged it in. Then, not wanting to waste time, she said, "Okay, ladies. Let's gather around. Pastor Amy will bless all our seeds and soil and then we can begin."

Pastor Amy instructed, "Hold your hands out, over the seed packets, palms down." She did it herself and the others followed suit. "I will pray, and, as I do, I ask that you send prayer energy to the seeds. Imagine love pouring out of your hands onto them." She began to pray. "We thank you, most Holy One, for the gift of life you give to each of us. We thank you for the mystery of these tiny seeds that hold within them the potential for new life. We pray that you help each of them to fulfill their unique destiny and become the plants they were created to be. We pray for this soil that will hold them as they begin to unfold. And we pray for all of us who will care for them here, remembering to water them just the right amount. We give thanks for the sun which heats this place, as well as our solar panels. Bless the seeds, the soil, and all of us as we participate in the miracle of your unfolding creation this year." She paused, then added, "Please send your love and light to these seeds as we continue silently in prayer together."

Silence fell among the women as they stood side by side, making a semi-circle around the little table. Mariah cracked her eyes open to watch. They obviously took the directions very seriously, seeming to concentrate even with their eyes closed. She imagined the light of God enfolding the seeds with love. She sent love to the seed-starting mix as well.

After about five minutes, Pastor Amy said, "Amen."

Everyone opened their eyes. Ostensibly, nothing had changed, yet for Mariah, something had shifted. She felt they were standing on holy ground. "Thank you, Pastor Amy. Can you all feel that energy?" she asked.

"I know," Gloria said. "God is here."

Pastor Amy said, "Yes, God is always with us, but when we pray, we become more aware of God's presence with us."

Mariah turned off the music for the prayer and fingered her iPad, already plugged into speakers, to share her new Spotify planting playlist with the group, creating musical ambiance for their party. First up, the old Peter, Paul, and Mary song her mother had always played in the spring: "Inch by inch, row by row, going to make my garden grow." The words of the song were happy, uplifting. Mariah hoped the seeds would be happy, too.

"Okay, time to fill up your trays with our seed starter mix," she told Mrs. Bee, Pastor Amy, and Karol, who were working with her. She turned to Gloria, Lisa, and Sherry. "Looks like you've brought everything you need."

They started with the tomatoes. Mrs. Bee followed Mariah's direction, talking nonstop. "Now we're putting you in, little tomatoes. You just go ahead and do your thing. We'll be watching you now. We promise to give you the water you need, then you and God do the rest."

They worked through the morning. They sowed seeds of peppers, lettuce, spinach, zucchini, cucumber, squash, and many herbs. In one section, they began flowers for the church garden and the pots on Main Street.

Halfway through, Mariah started to share. "I remember one sermon Reverend Bee gave called 'Not Yet'. He talked about how nature takes its time. These seeds, which came from plants last year or maybe several years ago, are waiting. Sometimes, we want things to happen right now. But with nature, you have to wait. All winter long, we wait for spring in the 'not yet' time of frozen earth. But waiting time holds importance, too. We know that old people are often closer to God because they've learned to slow down and wait better than eager young people. When you slow down, you see things you never saw before. Reverend Bee said he visited the greenhouse every day and liked to just sit there. Somedays, change is slow, and others, he said, he could almost see the plants growing. But, he cautioned, if you're in a hurry, you won't notice. You'll just judge everything in your own terms."

Mrs. Bee agreed. "Oh, lawdy, yes. I see so much more even with these feeble eyes of mine just sitting around than when I was young. I sit in my chair by the window and I watch the world go to bed in the winter and wake up in the spring. It's a miracle right in front of us, going on all the time, but, so often, we are too distracted to watch and listen."

"My papa always told me about the Shawnee who lived here before the white man came. They rose each morning and greeted the four directions, giving thanks. They honored the seasons. The Native American traditions teach us to reverence the earth and to nurture it. Somehow, when I participate in spring planting, I feel like I connect with my ancestors of the Shawnee," Mariah said.

"Are you an injun?" Karol asked.

"Yes, and could you please say Native American?" Mariah said.

"Oh, I'm sorry," Karol said. "No harm intended."

"Well, okay," Mariah said, "but we consider that a putdown. I'm proud of my Shawnee heritage. I've been learning more about them as I grow older. They were pushed off the land when the Europeans came in, but they were quite wise. A lot of their practices were trashed when rapid development moved in. Now, our Earth is hurting and we need to listen to what they taught."

"That's deep," Karol said. "Maybe Pastor Amy should have you preach it one of these Sundays."

"That's a great idea, Karol," Pastor Amy said. "Earth Day is coming up." She looked at Mariah.

"I'll work on it," Mariah said, accepting the challenge.

The women continued planting, filling flats until the last seed was planted. Then they gathered at the long table in the front which had earlier held the seeds. Together, they cleaned it off and covered it with a bright flowered tablecloth.

Mariah distributed plates, silverware, and glasses from Mrs. Bee's house, brought over in a large tub. "No need to use paper products and plastics to throw away," she said. "We need to preserve the Earth."

Gloria said, "Paper plates are much easier. Why bother?"

"We must preserve the Earth," Mariah said again. Disposables were the status quo these days and it made it sick to her stomach when she thought about all the landfills and the trash generated all over the beautiful country. But she knew better than to argue and thanked them all for coming. "Sometimes, you just need to lead by example," her mama'd said.

26. COFFEE AND THE CORONAVIRUS

The morning after his crazy dream, Max was surprised to find Buck on his couch when he woke, but then he remembered that Buck's furnace had gone out. Rather than unload on Buck, Max set the coffee maker up for a fresh brew and left a note: *Push the red button for caffeine, went for a run, be back in an hour.* He signed off, *Max 6:30 a.m.*

Max walked out into the early morning with his dog Gus, appreciating the fresh air. The winter days trapped life inside and he yearned for spring, even though his grieving heart wasn't quite ready for daffodils. To damn much pain, remembering Gabrielle and her gardens, and then his daughter and her joy with the first signs of spring. Just when she'd begun to explore and ask questions, it all got cut off. He kicked a rock, his anger at the injustice simmering close to the surface. Sometimes he felt like a volcano about ready to blow. Just when he thought he'd gotten over that phase, it all came back to him. He broke into a slow jog and then a run. Gus matched his pace. He turned off his negative thoughts and relaxed into the rhythm of his feet falling down onto the country road with soft thuds. His dog's paws made almost no sound at all, other than sometimes the click of nails on the asphalt. His breath evened out to match his stride. The gray skies didn't do much for his spirits, but soon, the endorphins lifted his heart just a little bit. He headed toward the diner, then thought better of it and circled around back toward home. Better touch base with Buck and get cleaned up before going to see Mariah.

Buck greeted him when he walked in. "Have some coffee? I just made pancakes. Plenty to share. There's some of Mrs. Bee's strawberry jam. I'll cook you up some eggs if you want. We need to talk."

Max smiled. He guessed he'd have to forego morning breakfast with Mariah and wait until lunch time. "Did I remember to tell you to make yourself at home?" he joked.

"I went home to get some supplies for breakfast. And Rover. My furnace man should be over by eleven," Buck explained.

Buck's German shepherd's ears perked up at his name.

"Stay," Buck told him. Gus stretched out on the rug in front of the fireplace, while Rover sat at Buck's side in the kitchen.

The cabin felt cozy on the cold winter morning. Max enjoyed having company and enjoyed even more the cup of coffee Buck poured, followed by a stack of pancakes with the strawberry preserves. He wasted no time digging into the grub and downing his coffee, holding up his plate and cup up for more.

"Oh," Buck said with a laugh, "I'm your waiter, now?"

"You've done worse," Max said.

"That, I have." Buck nodded, smiling.

Max remembered some of the stories Buck had told him about his youth. "Tell me again about that time you—"

"Not now, Max. We gotta talk. Have you been reading about China?"

"China? What about China? Are they ahead of us? Did they already do our wind project?"

"No, no, no. That's not what I'm talking about. Wuhan. Did you hear about Wuhan?"

Max thought for a moment. Wuhan. Where had he heard that name recently? Then he remembered. "The virus at the market?"

"Right," Buck answered. "I think this is the big one."

"Why?"

"Have you read the reports?"

"Hmm." Max hesitated. He remembered reading about it, but he'd skipped over the story. "Uh, I just read a little. What are you talking about, man?"

"It's spreading quickly. They have no immunity to it. People are dying, Max. They say it's just a matter of time until it gets to us." Buck rubbed his forehead. "Could be a big problem."

"A pandemic? Is it possible? Here?"

"Of course," Buck said. "The first cases are already in the U.S."

"Oh, man," Max said. Suddenly, he remembered Gabrielle's pandemic research from her master's degree. She'd lived the possibility night and day, worrying, talked about it. It was a matter of time, she'd say. He'd calm her down, tell her to stop thinking about it, give her a massage and then a romp in the sack, and she'd be distracted. For a while. He could still remember her fear, her insistence that it wasn't a matter of if, but of when.

"We gotta prepare," Buck said, "before it's too late."

"What do you suggest?".

"I don't know, Max. But we're scientists, right? We should be able to do something."

"Yeah, but we're *wind* scientists. Wind and biology are two different things."

"Give yourself some credit, Max. You know a lot more than you're letting on."

"Gabrielle worried about this. She wrote a paper on it," Max said.

"Did you read it?"

"Did I have a choice?" Max laughed. "Yes, I read that thing many times, many nights as she wrote and rewrote. Scary stuff."

"Do you still have it?"

I suppose it's up there in the Cloud where she left it. I could probably find it. Do you want to read it? But what can we do?"

"Wouldn't be a bad idea to read it over."

"Okay, I'll look it up. Now, how about some more pancakes and let me get my day in gear? We've got our wind project. That should be our focus."

"Right, but I'm just saying we can't ignore the possibility of a pandemic."

Max didn't want to think about it. Instead, he wolfed down another plate of pancakes, feeling only a little guilty when Buck got a call from the furnace guy who'd shown up early.

Once Buck left, Max pulled out his laptop to buckle down on the job at hand, working on the wind-let, as he liked to call it. Their little windmill would attach to a roof, a boat, or even a car, once they developed the technology. He liked the idea of the moving vehicle the most because wind would be in constant supply.

Then he remembered Gabrielle's paper. He hunted it down and emailed it to Buck. In her paper, she'd laid out, point by point, what they could do to be prepared. For Gabrielle, he'd make a point to have that discussion with Buck real soon.

27. SIGNS OF SPRING

Mariah repeated the pregnancy test before going to work. Yesterday, it had read positive, but the directions recommended a second test to confirm. She'd held on to hope, but deep inside, she knew. Her body felt different, so she'd quit drinking wine. Reality hit her dead center and she found herself wanting to forget. She went through the motions of getting ready for work and managed to keep the thoughts at bay through the morning.

Now, with her break at hand, reality surfaced. She finished cleaning off the tables from the breakfast crowd and headed out for a March morning walk to distract herself. She shivered, and stopped to zip up her jacket, put on her gloves and pull the hood over her head. Fortunately, the clouds cleared enough to let the sun shine onto her path. She took a deep breath, gazing up to the heavens, closed her eyes, and felt the warmth of the sun's rays on her face.

Nature would welcome her, regardless of her situation. She decided to visit the cemetery to search for signs of spring, just around the corner. She checked her cell phone calendar. Only sixteen days until the Spring Equinox. She loved spring, almost as much as autumn.

New life would be growing all around. Oh, and also within her. A different kind of spring. She needed to tell Max. *What would he think? What do I think?* They barely knew each other; too much alcohol on New Year's Eve was a sorry excuse for bringing a new life into the world. Although their friendship continued to grow, so far, neither of them had mentioned that night. She felt embarrassed more than anything. But now they needed to talk.

Walking through the residential area, she saw purple and yellow crocuses blooming brightly in Mrs. Weld's front yard. Next door, at the Turners' house, the daffodils were hanging brightly on their green stems. She snapped shots of both with her cell phone and waltzed on. She stopped to admire the dogwood at the Marvel's house. Tiny buds clung to the otherwise barren branches. She squatted down to capture pictures of them, with the blue sky as backdrop. Her heart warmed with the joy of them all.

Next, she crossed the street to enter under the old stone gates of the village cemetery. Founded 1842, the sign read. She tried to imagine life back then. The Village of Friendly was founded in 1840, and, soon after, they'd created this place to bury their dead. Through the 1800s, they'd started filling the empty hills with the remains of their dearly departed. She imagined Friendly was a small place back then. When she arrived at the 1918-19 section, all of a sudden, there were many graves. Babies, toddlers, young people in their prime, and those past it, too. A historical marker explained the Pandemic of 1918-19 which had caused Friendly to bury half of its citizens. She tried to imagine the horror. Then she smiled, secure in her knowledge that something like that could never happen again, not with all the medical resources available in the 21st century.

Near the marker, she noticed a forsythia bush covered with yellow buds. Spring seemed to pop up like that, almost overnight, offering a flurry of color after the dreary browns and greys of the winter landscape. She took special care to photograph the bush, with close-ups of the yellow buds, letting the background remain fuzzy. Last time she'd come, these branches were just brown. *So much potential within a branch.*

Placing her hand on her stomach, she thought about the potential of the new life inside of her. Her emotions were mixed. She welcomed new life every spring. Having a child would be a miracle, an amazing responsibility. But this was unplanned, unexpected, and in such a new relationship. She hated thinking about being a single mother. *Where would we live? What would Mrs. Bee say? How could I support myself and the baby if Mrs. Bee kicked me out and if Max didn't want anything to do with the child?*

Walking on, she went downhill toward the creek. On the banks, wildflowers sparkled. Smooth and tender white snowdrops hung down like little streetlights off curving stems. She walked through the grasses, trying to avoid stepping on the delicate purple flowers with white centers, the buttercups, and the dainty white flowers with pink stamens. Such a canvas of delight all around. She didn't know all their names. Every year, she intended to look them up, but always managed to forget. For now, she contented herself with capturing each of them with her cell phone's camera. Later, she could share them with the patrons in the diner and maybe get some prints made.

That the little flowers sprung from barely warmed ground amazed her. Just when it seemed winter would last forever, wildflowers emerged victorious. Sometimes late snows covered them, but they opened again on days of warming sun. To her—and Mrs. Bee agreed— wildflowers signified hope.

She thought about how her people, the Shawnee, must've felt when the wildflowers started popping up, signaling the spring. Surely they'd been excited. She loved reading the book about them her father had given her years ago. She wished she could go back in time and talk to them now about spring.

She touched her stomach again. She remembered that quote from

Carl Sandburg. "A baby is God's opinion that life should go on." Babies were something like the wildflowers, springing up just when you least expected it. Still, she knew better than to have unprotected sex. *Why was I so careless?*

She needed to talk with Max, figure out how to tell him. Maybe she should invite him to dinner or ask him to go for a walk. Maybe she should ask him to go to the church and sing. She was already entering the third month. She'd missed a period now and then, but after the second one never came, she'd known. By the time she told him, it would be beyond the point of no return, not that she considered that as an option anyway. Regardless of what he might want, her baby would live.

On impulse, she sent him a text: Max, could we talk when I get off work today? Around three? Meet me at the diner.

There. She'd done it. She'd get it off her chest and find out what she was afraid to know. Unless she changed her mind again.

Her eyes focused on the geese. Two by two, they roamed the creek banks. Some floated on the cold water. She remembered her dad once telling her that geese mated for life. That was what she wanted. But she worried that she'd have a baby without a partner. Even the geese did better, she chided herself. She stopped to sit on a bench and prayed that God would look after her baby, that Max would welcome the child, that all would be well. The geese stayed in her thoughts as she walked back to work.

28. THE ASSIGNMENT

Looking out the window, Max shook himself. He could do better than this. He shrugged out of his clothes and made his way to the shower. There was nothing like a hot shower to provide a fresh perspective on life. The gentle streams of water cleansed the sweat off his back. He soaped up, then rinsed off. He squeezed out some shampoo and massaged his head, soothing his scalp and cleaning his hair, which was getting a little long. Perhaps he needed to visit the barber, but part of him liked the wild man look. Now he could grow his hair down to his waist, without Gabrielle around to complain. He could become a regular mountain man. Well, maybe a man of the Ohio hills.

Gabrielle. He remembered the showers they shared together. He quickly turned the faucet to cold, letting frigid water douse his fantasy. He refused to spend another day wallowing in the past.

Once dressed, he felt much better. He planned a morning of work on the wind project, then would head over to the Wind Song Café for lunch. Goodbye, Gabrielle, he mouthed. And then he looked up and saw her sitting there.

He did a double take, shook his head, and went into the kitchen for some coffee. Gabrielle was *not* there. He knew better. He would not let his grief drive him crazy. "Stop it," he muttered underneath his breath. As much as he might believe she visited him in the snowstorm, he had no interest in talking to her ghost on a regular basis. If he wasn't careful, he'd step off the deep end into God knows where.

He warmed his hands around the cup of coffee as he sat down at his computer, focused himself, and opened his project workbook. But a hand reached over and closed the workbook, right after he opened it.

"What the ...?"

"No, Max," a familiar voice demanded from behind him. "Not today. Today, you need to start getting your town and your people ready for the pandemic. You've got other work to do."

That word, twice in one day. Pandemic. He hadn't considered it for years. "Pandemic?"

Gabrielle stood in front of him and took his hand. "Come with me and I'll explain."

She led him over to the couch and pulled him down beside her. She grabbed both of his hands, then dropped them and gave him a hug. Hallucination or not, being in her arms again felt damn good to Max. He squeezed her hard, feeling the familiar soft curves of her body easing into his. He didn't want to let go. Her love seeped into all his cold spots, taking away the aches of mourning, lifting his soul into a wild space of joy. For a moment, he could pretend she'd never left.

Gabrielle pulled away. "I came to put you to work, Max."

"What? They sent you down to give me a job? What kind of joke are they playing on me? Why did they take you away in the first place? That was wrong. Dead wrong. Did you tell them? Gabrielle, what happened? How did your car go off the road? Who did that to you?"

Max quickly worked himself into a frenzy, yelling at his wife. He stopped mid-sentence. "I'm sorry, Brie." He began to sob. "I just miss you so damn much."

"I know, honey," she said. Then, with her long slender fingers, she dried the tears running down his face. "I know it's hard. I'm sorry. It was an accident. These things just happen. Nobody wanted that. It's not fair. It's nobody's fault. It just is, and you must go on now. You still have your whole life ahead of you. And you have work to do."

"Oh, really? Why can't I just join you and Isabella? Why do I have to stay here all alone? Whose idea was that?"

"Nobody's idea, Max. It's not that way. But you've got to move on, and you *do* have work to do. That's why I am visiting today."

Max hung his head. Gabrielle began to massage his neck.

"Honey, a pandemic is coming. I want you to implement my plan," she said.

"Me? Implement a public health plan? How would I begin? Who would listen to me? I'm just married to the dead expert. Does that qualify me?"

"Max, you know the drill. My thesis lays it all out. You need to get this to the authorities before it's too late. At least talk with the Friendly Village Council. Will you promise me that?"

"Are you sure a pandemic is coming? Buck was just talking about it. But really? Is it going to happen here?"

"Yes, it's already happening. It's just a matter of time before it hits Friendly. You need to get them ready. Get the tests. Have a plan to test people and quarantine the ones who are positive. You can do this, Max. You can save a lot of lives. That's why they sent me down."

Max shook his head. "Brie, really? Why now? Why me?"

"Promise me, Max. Promise me you'll try," Gabrielle said and gave him a kiss.

Max pulled her into his arms and lengthened the kiss.

Gabrielle pulled away. "That was good, but I've gotta go. Tell me you'll try. Promise me, please?"

"Your wish is my command, dear," he said, repeating a phrase he'd whispered to her almost every single day of their marriage.

She chuckled. "Good, that's good. Thank you, honey."

Max kissed her again, wrapping his arms around her and holding on. Maybe if he didn't let her go, she would stay

This time, Gabrielle didn't pull away. Maybe they would let her stay to help. The least he could do was to ask.

"Hey, if they sent you down on assignment, why don't you ask permission to stay until it's all done? I might need your supernatural power to accomplish all you want me to do." Max presented his case. A perfectly logical suggestion, except for the fact that he was talking to a ghost—or a figment of his imagination. Teetering on the edge of sanity, he jumped off the cliff, leaning into another kiss.

A few minutes later, Gabrielle laughed. "I could always ask. Who knows, maybe they'll say yes."

"You check on that and get back to me," Max told her. So much for getting into his wind project this morning. "Can you stay put while you ask? I don't want you to go back up there, or wherever you came from, if they won't let you come back."

"It doesn't work that way, honey," Gabrielle said. "Now, you do your work, then go talk this all over with Buck. He'll know what to do. And in the meantime, don't neglect Mariah. She's good for you. She has a surprise."

Max sat upright. Mariah? He looked over to ask more, but she was gone. His cell phone buzzed. He picked it up and saw a message from … Mariah. That was very eerie. Maybe the Addam's Family would move in next.

Mariah's text invited him to meet her after lunch. But now he wanted to go as soon as he could. He could work on his laptop in the café. Yes, he could sit there and let Mariah keep filling up his coffee cup, and then order a delicious lunch. He wasn't all that hungry after Buck's pancakes. Honestly, he didn't need any food, he just wanted her company.

Wait a minute. He'd just asked Gabrielle to stay around. He couldn't be with Gabrielle and Mariah at the same time. But Gabrielle would not come back. No, he realized, he'd need to masquerade as a public health authority without her.

Rather than think about the insanity that his life had become, he packed up his laptop and left.

29. THE ANNOUNCEMENT

Mariah arrived at the diner just in time to turn on the coffee, put on the hot water and turn around the sign to Open. She was happy from the many signs of spring she'd witnessed on that short walk, but then she felt a wave of nausea and grabbed a package of saltines from the big jar on the counter. Whew. Had she really sent that text to Max? Had he even responded? *What was I thinking?*

She grabbed her cell phone and searched for the text. He'd replied: *I'll be over for lunch and hang out, doing some work.*

She typed back: *Let's go to the lake when I'm done.*

He responded immediately: *Okay, see you soon,* just as the doorbell rang, announcing her first lunch customer.

Farmer Sayers whistled as he came in.

"It's a wonderful day in the neighborhood?" she asked.

"Can't complain. Can't complain at all," he said. "I think I turned myself over a new leaf, that I did."

Mariah smiled. "So your New Year's resolution is holding on?" She admired those who could pick a goal and stick with it.

"Not only that," he said with a twinkle in his eye. "Can you keep a secret?"

Mariah looked at the impish grin on the old man's face and couldn't wait to hear what he had to say. "What? What have you done now, Farmer Sayers? Tell me. My lips are sealed."

"I got myself a date with Mrs. Adams for tomorrow night. Yep, I got myself a date. I figured it's about time."

"Mrs. Adams, the retired schoolteacher?"

"That's the one. She lost her husband a few years back. I met her at a grief group. I think she likes me, if you know what I mean."

"Oh, yeah," Mariah said. "Yeah, I know what you're talking about." She closed her eyes for a minute and thought about Max. "Spring's just around the corner. A great time for romance."

The door opened again and the farmer clammed up as the village gossip waltzed in. "Why, Farmer Sayers, fancy meeting you here." The newcomer, Mrs. Maple, known to pass all the news and more around the small town, took a seat across from the farmer.

"Oh, no," he said. "Looks like I got company."

"Looks like you do," she replied. Then she turned to Mariah. "Could you turn the TV on for the noon news and serve me up my usual?"

Mariah went over to turn on the TV, a new addition to the diner. The owner thought they needed to keep up with the other establishments that sometimes mounted TVs on multiple walls and occasionally at each booth. She understood the rationale, but didn't like it. She associated TVs with her stepfather. He'd kept it blaring in the living room all the time he was home. To her, it had interrupted her peace of mind and kept a constant state of tension in the room. Now at the diner, it interrupted the flow of conversation. People paid less attention to each other when they had a TV. Fortunately, some days, she didn't turn it on and no one seemed to notice.

"Channel 7 News at noon for March 5, 2020," the announcer began. Mariah tuned it out and started Mrs. Maple's order.

Then she remembered her other customer. "Oh, I forgot. Farmer Sayers, what did you want?"

"The usual," he said. "I'll take your grilled chicken sandwich with tomato, lettuce and mayo with a side salad, some fries, and coffee. Then let me know what kind of desserts you've got back there."

The door opened again to admit Max, and Mariah's heart skipped a beat. His hair was growing out. He was a handsome man before, but that longer hair did something for him. His eyes sizzled into hers and she turned away. She didn't mean to play hard to get, but for some reason, she didn't want him to know how he melted her heart. If she laid all her cards out on the table and then he rejected her and the baby, she didn't know what she'd do.

"Good afternoon, Mariah," he said, then tipped his hat to the other residents. "Just fix me up that stir fry of yours with some rice and a Pepsi."

"Sure thing," she said. He kept smiling from where he sat in the back corner. She watched him pull a laptop and notebook out of his satchel, then settled in behind the counter, finishing up the other lunches and starting on his. She could get used to this, having Max coming in to do his work. They could work together.

The news blared on, disturbing the tranquility of the little diner.

"Could you turn that up?" Mrs. Maple asked.

Mariah frowned. Why did she have to come in here to watch TV? Didn't she have a TV at home?

"COVID-19 claimed its first victim in the United States on February 29," the newsman reported. "The governor of Washington State has declared a state of emergency."

Mariah looked at the TV. "What's that?" she asked.

"A hoax," Mrs. Maple said. "Just a hoax. Don't worry your pretty little head about it. It's nothing, dear."

To Mariah's surprise, Farmer Sayers agreed with Mrs. Maple. "The Democrats are up to their old tricks," he explained. "Don't worry, it's nothing."

"I wouldn't say that," a voice piped up from the back of the room.

Max. Mariah looked at him, then the others, bracing for a confrontation. People argued so much in her little town these days. She steered away from political conversation in the diner. Such talk never seemed to resolve.

The announcer continued, "The President has banned travel from China and may be closing other travel down soon."

"This sounds serious," Mariah said.

"Don't worry, be happy, dear," Mrs. Maple said with a wink. "The President himself said it's a hoax."

Mariah saw Max roll his eyes. She went back to work, bringing out Mrs. Maple's chef salad, hoping to keep her quiet for a few minutes. Meanwhile, she poured the farmer a coffee and took a can of Pepsi with some ice over to Max. Then she went back to the grill, finished off the grilled chicken and pulled the fries out of the deep fryer and let them drain while she fixed up the chicken sandwich.

"Here you go," she told the farmer, placing his meal down in front of him.

"Those fries aren't good for you," Mrs. Maples admonished him.

Farmer Sayers snapped, "For your information, I ain't your child. I'm not about to let any old woman tell me what to do."

Taken aback, Mrs. Maple mumbled, "And you're not my old man."

"Peace! Peace!" Mariah urged. "Do I need to separate you two?"

"And are you their parent now?" Max laughed.

"I thought you came here to work," Mariah reminded him.

"Did I get your dander up, Mariah? So sorry," Max laughed again.

"Stop it," Mariah said. She blushed and turned away to work on his stir fry.

Meanwhile, Max continued the conversation with the farmer and Mrs. Maple. "It's not a hoax. It's a serious concern."

"What are you talking about?" the older man asked.

"I know, I know," Mrs. Maple said. "The liberal media are saying this could spread like the flu epidemic of 1918-1919. Half the people of our village died back then. You see it in the cemetery."

"Fortunately, that won't happen again," Mariah said. "We have much better medicine now."

"Sure do," Farmer Sayers said. "Why, look at the Ebola scare we had a few years ago. Started in Africa and we nipped that in the bud real fast. We'll do it again."

Mrs. Maples chewed her salad. The farmer took a bite of his sandwich. Max looked like he wanted to say something, but kept silent.

When Mariah finished his lunch, she took it over to Max and sat across from him. "Can I join you? Just for a minute."

"Of course, Mariah. We need to talk about your text," Max said.

"Yeah, but not right now."

The door opened again and a family came in with twin three-year-old boys.

"Not right now," Mariah said again as she stood and went over to take another order. "When I get off," she called back over her shoulder.

The afternoon passed quickly. Max worked and Mariah served the customers and cleaned up after them.

After the last of the lunch crowd left Mariah flipped off the TV and went back again to sit by Max. She felt shy. One look in his eyes and she felt that energy surge that happened every time she looked at him. She didn't know what it meant. She'd never felt anything like it before. Instead of sharing her very big news, worried about his reaction, she stuck to what she decided was a much safer subject: the news.

"What do you think of this new flu? Will it be bad in the US like it's been in China? What's going on?"

"Well," Max said, "it's hard to know. It could be a major problem. My late wife did some research on this stuff. Most experts believe it's just a matter of time before we have a major pandemic. With all the international travel, a virus can be transmitted very quickly."

"What can we do? We can't stop it?"

"Well, once it starts spreading through the community, it's very hard to stop. Mostly, people get well, but some die. Actually, Gabrielle wrote her thesis on this sort of thing. She has a lot of ideas on how to minimize the problem.

"Do you know the mayor?" He switched gears, remembering his orders from Gabrielle.

"Of course. You haven't met him yet? He often comes in. I'll introduce you the next time you're both here."

"Good. Yes, this COVID-19 could be a problem. We'll see." Then he changed the subject again. "So, you want to go to the lake?"

"Yes," Mariah said. "I thought we could go out to the lake. It's so beautiful outside today. Spring is coming." She really wanted to get him out there to tell him about the baby. Just thinking about it made her nervous, so she changed the subject herself. "Tell me, what are you working on there? Is that your wind project?"

"Yes. I said I'd tell you about this, didn't I? We're very close, Mariah. We just got our patent approved. We've got a manufacturer lined up. We'll begin production next month, as soon as they get all the parts and get the production line together. Our little mini-wind turbines should be available for sale soon. Buck and I are planning a party to celebrate as soon as we can make it official. Then you and Mrs. Bee can get one for your house."

"They fit on houses?"

"Yes, that's the whole idea. Take the house off the grid and let it manufacture its own energy. No more fossil fuels needed. Got it?"

"Cool. Very cool. You are living my dreams, boy. I always dreamed of harnessing the wind. You're actually doing it."

Mariah started thinking about the wind, her destiny. And here, the father of her unborn child sat right in front of her, ready to pull in the breeze and make it useful. Classic. Perfect. But then she froze. Words stuck in her throat. She could feel fear pulsating in her heart. What would Max think about the baby? To escape, she jumped up and took off toward the kitchenette, telling Max, "I need to finish cleaning up."

"Hey, when do we leave for the lake?" Max called after her.

"Um," Mariah answered, "give me twenty-five minutes, okay?"

"Sure. I'll just sit here and get some more work done."

She busied herself as her heart kept beating faster and faster. Earlier, she'd known she had to tell him. Now she felt lost and afraid. Would he be upset? What if he didn't want to be a father? She scrubbed the counters with vigor, trying to erase all the bad things that could happen when he found out about the baby. No way she could tell him. No way.

Max busied himself at his laptop, but the food he'd eaten lurched in his stomach. *What was I thinking?* If Gabrielle came back to help coordinate a public health initiative to deal with the pandemic, there wasn't any chance that he'd be starting up a more serious relationship with Mariah. He had no business leading her on.

On the other hand, Max knew he needed to move forward with his life. He needed to focus on what was right in front of him. He watched the beautiful young woman cleaning the counter. He watched her muscles as she was scrubbing and saw strength. He flashed back to the day they'd met right here in the café. From the first day, he'd felt drawn to her. She was beautiful with her long brown/blonde hair. Her voice was incredibly sweet. When she sang in the church, her voice had an ephemeral quality, almost angelic. And she seemed just so damn positive. He thought back to New Year's Eve when they'd both had just a little too much to drink and he'd taken her home. What a night. He closed his eyes and there she was in his bed again. And as soon as he felt that goodness, he wanted to kick himself. He knew better than to take advantage of her in that situation. He should have waited.

Max made a stop in the bathroom to relieve himself before the trip to the lake. When he opened the door to go back to his booth, he felt relaxed and happy to be alone with her. He smiled at Mariah and she smiled back.

"Almost done," she told him.

He started packing up, stuffing his book back into his bag, powering off and zipping his laptop into its case. Then he checked his cell phone one last time.

Mariah hurried to his booth to clean it off, turning back to smile at him as she leaned over, and giving him a view of her backside. Once again, he thought of New Year's Eve. She said she couldn't remember much about that night. Damn. There wasn't a single thing he could forget about it.

She took the cleaning cloth back to the sink, and Max looked at the empty booth he'd vacated, now sparkling like new.

"Come on, let's go to the lake," Mariah said.

He followed Mariah out of the café and waited as she turned the sign to Closed and locked the door. With the slam of the door, Max silently said, "Goodbye, Gabrielle. I will always love you, but I'm moving on."

Once outside, Mariah leaned back against the door and took a deep breath. On her exhale, she said, "Ah ... freedom. We get to go look for spring. I'm excited!"

Max grinned down at her as they walked toward his truck at the back of the lot. He liked her enthusiasm for life and her pure joy. It reminded him of his daughter, Isabella, just a little bit. Izzy had always helped him lighten up. And he hadn't had much frivolity in his life since Izzy and Gabrielle died. But now, his smile widened into a grin, almost hurting his cheeks as it seemed to want to extend beyond the contours of his face. He laughed out loud and felt the weight he'd been carrying lessening just a little bit.

He held open the door to his pickup and Mariah climbed up into the cab. He slammed her door and started whistling as he circled back around the truck and eased into his seat on the other side. He reached over and took her hand. "You don't have to sit way over there," he told her. "Come closer." He let go of her hand and patted the seat beside him.

Mariah scooted over until her body was cozied up next to him. I could get used to having a woman beside me again, he realized.

Mariah turned on the radio, found an oldies station, and hummed along to an old James Taylor song. "You've got a friend," she sang, looking at him.

"Sure do," he replied. "I sure do, honey." Yes, he decided, he liked the feel of having Mariah sitting next to him. He didn't want to go home alone. Maybe he could take her to dinner. He smiled at the thought of more time with her.

"What's so funny?"

"Nothing, dear," he said. "Just thinking about maybe how we could go over to the Cove for some food after our walk. Are you up for that?"

"Oh, yeah," Mariah said. "I love the food there. I haven't been there for a long time."

"So, you said you wanted to talk with me about something?"

Mariah went silent.

Max had learned in the school of marriage that sometimes the silences were the most delicate situations in a relationship. He knew better than to assume, complain, or ignore. The silence meant something was hard to express. From dealing with Gabrielle's silences over the years, he knew Mariah needed time and encouragement.

First, though, he let the silence sit between them for a minute. Then he tightened his arm around her, massaging her shoulder a little. He turned off the truck after he pulled into the lake parking lot and turned to look at her. Overcome with her beauty and the closeness of her body, he couldn't stop himself from moving in for a kiss. The kiss was a form of silent encouragement, an invitation to tell all, he told himself.

The kiss led to other things. Max flashed back to high school and spring days parking with his girlfriend, all alone on a deserted road by the lake. Now Mariah was straddling his lap and she pressed against his manhood. He reached down to unzip her jeans ... and suddenly she lurched away and cowered on her side of the seat, leaning into the window and door.

"What's wrong?"

"I'm pregnant."

Max's passion disappeared, his face dropped, and his heart skipped a beat. He looked at her with disbelief. "You're pregnant?" Then he remembered New Year's Eve, the passion—and the fact that he hadn't had a condom.

"Oh, no," he said "You got pregnant New Year's Eve?"

She nodded and started to cry. "I barely remember what happened. And now I'm pregnant."

He tried to slide over to her and pull her into a hug to stop the tears, but she leaned away. He wanted to hold her while she cried. He'd rather comfort her with his body because he sure as hell had no idea how to comfort her with words.

A baby? He did the math. Here they were, March. Eight weeks, nine, ten, heading quickly to the second trimester, the point of no return. A mental lightbulb lit up. That was why she'd stopped drinking wine. While he felt very attracted to Mariah, he was not ready to set up another home. He'd often told himself he would never do that again. Not after losing his wife and daughter. He couldn't risk it.

But this wasn't about him, although it was. Really, this was about Mariah. It was her decision. He should see first what she wanted to do. He blurted the question without thinking about how it would sound. "What do you want to do?"

Mariah placed her hand on her stomach gently and looked at him with serious determination that told him what was coming, even before she mouthed the words. "I'm going to have this baby, Max."

He put his head down and covered his face with his hands. It wasn't the response he knew she wanted, but it was all he could manage. He again kicked himself for having unprotected sex, not to mention taking advantage of her in the first place.

"I'm so sorry," he said. "This is all my fault. You didn't deserve this. I'm so sorry."

"I knew I shouldn't have told you. You don't want the baby, do you?" Tears streamed down her face as she turned away from Max, pressing herself into the door. Then she opened it, jumped out, and started running across the parking lot toward the lake.

Max knew better than to let her go alone. He considered himself a good runner, but she must be a sprinter. Her legs stretched out as she lengthened the distance between them.

She reached the lake path and kept running. He followed, close behind. Gradually, his longer legs helped him start to close the distance.

Finally, he caught up, but Mariah kept running, her breathing labored. As she wore out and slowed, suddenly she tripped and started to fall. He caught her in mid-air, but because he was running, too, he lost his balance and her weight pulled him down. They fell together, but he rolled to make sure she came on top, cushioning her fall, even as he felt his own body hit the ground hard.

He found himself lying on the cool spring earth with Mariah on top of him, crying. She looked confused and upset at the same time.

"You don't want the baby, do you?"

Max knew he needed to say something, but he just couldn't. Not yet.

"I'm not going to get rid of it," Mariah said, filling the silence. "I'll raise her alone. I'll be okay. She'll be okay. We'll be fine. You don't have to do a thing. If you think she's a mistake, I don't want you around."

He couldn't put his head around all of those words strung together so fast. He felt steamrolled. "Whoa," he managed to say, trying to stop the deluge. "Mariah, stop. I need a little time to think. Don't jump to conclusions here. You've had time to think about this for a while. I'm just finding out. You've blown me away. I need a little time to process this, Mariah. Please, give me some time."

Mariah pulled herself off him and stood, extending a hand to pull him up. He pretended to take her assistance. If he let her pull him, he'd just yank her back down. She might be strong, but not strong enough to pull a grown man up from the ground.

"Could we go to dinner now?" he asked. "Let's talk about this, Mariah." That was the least he could do, offer her some food. Maybe once he'd had some time to think this through, he'd know what he wanted to say, what he wanted to do, and how the hell he was going to handle this situation.

"No," she said. "Take me home. I want to go home."

Once again, Max covered his face with his hands and let go of a deep breath, puffing up his cheeks as his shoulders dropped. "Okay, let's go," he said. He wasn't up for a fight right now. "I'll take you home."

They walked silently back to the truck and didn't speak a word until he pulled up in front of her house. "I need a little time, Mariah. Just give me a little time, okay?"

"Do I have a choice?" Mariah asked. Then she opened her door and turned back to him with a flourish of finality as she said, "Goodbye, Max." She didn't look back as she walked up to the front door.

Earlier, he'd delighted in Mariah's joyful, childlike nature reminding him of Isabella's two-year-old bliss. Now, she was more like the other Isabella he remembered too well, the one who could be very unreasonable and throw a tantrum at the drop of the hat. Couldn't she understand he needed time? Max sat there, stunned, feeling numb. *I need a drink. A lot of drinks. I need ... something.*

31. PATENT LAWYER

The next morning, Max overslept, woke up groggy, slowly remembering he was due at Buck's for a trip into Columbus to meet with the patent attorney over their wind turbine. He jumped into the shower, trying to shake himself out of his hangover and usher in some sanity to the day. He thought back to the reason he doused himself the night with every sort of alcohol he could find in his pantry. Seriously, he deserved this. Absolutely nothing was going to make him feel better for a very long time.

Nevertheless, he blew his hair dry to bring out the natural wave and put on his best suit. He looked respectable enough, even though he knew behind his Sunday best lurked a despicable man. He poured a bowl of Lucky Charms out of the box and added some milk on top of that. *What am I thinking?* St. Patrick's Day and Gabrielle, that's what. March.

A dead wife comes back to guide her husband through a public health plan for a pandemic? Impossible. He laughed out loud. He took a spoonful of Lucky Charms, letting the sweetness remind him of better mornings, laughing with Gabrielle. But when the cereal moved on down his digestive track, his stomach rebelled. He hightailed it to the bathroom where it all came out, splattering the charming colors on his best suit jacket as he emptied the contents of his stomach into the toilet bowl. He cleaned his face, then tried to wipe off the suit with a washcloth without success. Plan B found him changing into his khakis and his white OSU-monogrammed button-down Oxford shirt for a special touch, topped off with his navy blazer.

His head was pounding. Although he knew he couldn't put anything in his stomach now, he grabbed an ibuprofen and washed it down with warm water. That would have to do. He picked up his briefcase to head over to Buck's.

When he glanced back at the kitchen, looking at the mess that would be waiting for him when he returned, she was there again. Gabrielle. He tried to ignore the hallucination, but she blew him a kiss. "I'll be waiting for you when you get back, Max. We need to talk."

"Right, Brie. I'll catch you later. I'll be back mid-afternoon for your talk," He said with a touch of sarcasm. When he closed the door, he shut out the ghost and the hallucination that threatened his sanity.

Buck was waiting in the front drive, looking at his watch, when Max pulled up. "Cutting this close, aren't you?"

"Sorry, man. I'm hung over. Could you drive?"

"Why didn't you call? I would have come and picked you up," Buck said. "Okay, okay. Come on then, let's go. We've got rush hour traffic to contend with, you know? I doubt we're going to make this appointment, but let's try."

Max laughed. He knew Buck's driving style. Buck would have them there early, but he got it. Buck wanted him to feel bad for being late. Like he didn't feel bad enough already.

Once on the road, Max tried to zone out for the ride to Columbus. He didn't feel like talking. He feared if he started, he would spill the beans about Mariah. He felt the pill taking a slight edge off his hangover, so he closed his eyes, trying to catch up on the sleep that wouldn't come the night before. This was supposed to be a good day. They'd worked hard for this one. He just hoped to God he didn't throw up again.

Despite his alcohol consumption the night before, the meeting with the patent attorney proceeded without a hitch. He let Buck take the lead, contributing only when needed. The patent process was complete and approved. Not that the whole process had been easy, but now that they were on this side of it, Max breathed a sigh of relief. They thanked the attorney for all of his good work, paid the bill, and left with the prize: a patent for their mini wind turbine. They were on schedule to open the factory as planned.

32. GROWING THINGS

Mariah watched the evening news with Mrs. Bee. Their mouths dropped open in unison, as they listened to the accounts of the coronavirus sweeping the globe. The announcer reported that it had started in an open market in Wuhan. It was a novel virus and people were dying. The President had stopped international travel from China.

"Is it going to come here?" Mariah asked.

"I don't know, dear. I certainly hope not."

Mariah didn't feel like worrying tonight. She turned off the TV. "Let's talk about something else. Or better yet, let's go visit the greenhouse," she suggested.

"These old bones just want to sit, dear. You go and come back and tell me about it," Mrs. Bee said.

"Okay. I'll take my camera. You're going to be surprised. I was just in there today. I'll be quick. Stay right there!"

"Oh, I'm not going anywhere, except to bed in a little while. Now you hurry along and enjoy yourself," Mrs. Bee said.

Mariah skipped along the little sidewalk toward the greenhouse, then slowed her pace. The late afternoon sun warmed the air and cast shadows across the yard. She took a deep breath in, inhaling the fresh joy of spring. The trees were budding. Tiny new leaf green starts covered the bushes in the side yard, luminescent in the sun. *Such a sacred time of year.*

She opened the greenhouse door expectantly. The fragrance of growing things flooded her nostrils as she started to explore the fruits of their planting. First stop, the tomatoes. She remembered Mrs. Bee praying over them and Pastor Amy blessing the seeds. With all of that attention, what could those little seeds do but spring forth? They were so tiny, they were already forming little tomato plants. In a few more weeks, they would be ready to plant outside. Mariah couldn't wait. She snapped a picture of the whole lot of them, then adjusted her camera to take some close-ups.

She waltzed around the greenhouse, humming her favorite garden song: Inch by inch, row by row, going to make my garden grow. She photographed the peppers, the unfurling lettuce, the little dark green spinach plants. Then she went on to the squash family. They all looked so similar when they sprouted. It was hard to believe they would be so different, forming green zucchini, yellow butternut squash, and spaghetti squash. She captured them all with her lens and couldn't wait to show them to Mrs. Bee. She hurried on to the herb garden plants, stopping to smell their fragrances. The oregano, basil, mint, and cilantro delighted her. She wished she could include the wonderful smells in the pictures. She finished up with the flowers, amazed at all the happy plants already in the process of becoming. She could almost see them as they would soon be in the gardens, delicate cosmos, hearty marigolds, butterfly-attracting zinnias, and incredible sunflowers towering toward the heavens.

Her heart was full as she finished up with some landscape views for Mrs. Bee. She took another deep breath, inhaling the cool, delightful air. The fresh oxygen given off by growing things enlivened every pore in her body. She bent over, exhaling onto the sunflower starts, showering her own carbon dioxide on the little leaves.

Suddenly, she stopped and rested her hand on her belly, thinking about the baby. Her smile faded. Caring for a garden took time and some expertise, but raising a child? How could she even think of doing such a thing? Could she raise a baby alone? She must. Abortion and adoption were out of her universe of possibilities.

She knew she needed to tell Mrs. Bee, who probably already suspected something was up. Maybe tonight. After a photography show of the growing things, she could segue into the new life growing with in her. She worried about what Mrs. Bee would think, what she would say.

Mariah walked slowly to the house. Dark shadows stretched across the yard. The sun had completed its journey to the horizon and light wisps of color faded into gray as night descended. Mariah dragged her feet, reluctant to go inside. Telling Mrs. Bee would be hard. But she summoned her courage and opened the back door. She held her shoulders resolutely and called as she entered, "I'm home!" She laughed. "Mrs. Bee?"

No answer. Mrs. Bee's chair was empty. Her bedroom door was closed. She'd obviously gone to bed.

Mariah transferred the pictures to her laptop, then edited and selected the best ones to show Mrs. Bee. At breakfast, she would do show and tell.

***

The next morning, Mariah's stomach didn't feel so hot. She couldn't sit at breakfast with Mrs. Bee when it took all her energy to deal with the nausea and get ready for work. *I'll tell her soon*, she promised herself, knowing that the longer she waited, the harder it would become.

33. PANDEMIC UNFOLDING

Max tuned in to the governor's press conference. Each day, a new announcement. Life as they knew it had changed, and not in good ways. First the governor had closed the schools for three weeks. Next came the restaurants. Carryout permitted, but not dine in. Now all but essential businesses were shut down. For how long, Max wondered.

"Social distancing" became the new norm, the recommended way to protect everyone from the spread of the virus. While in Washington State, California and New York, the virus spread like wildfire, in Ohio, the governor and his health director sought to flatten the curve. In Friendly, Max planned to keep the virus at bay.

He implemented Gabrielle's plan with fervor. Every morning, she provided direction. Fortunately, he was able to order tests from the World Health Organization for research purposes. Later, he heard the President had turned down the tests for the country as a whole. Max focused on the little town of Friendly to protect the people he had come to know and love: Buck, the Knights of the Round Table, Mrs. Bee, Pastor Amy, and, most of all, Mariah and the baby.

Mariah refused to talk to him. And now with a stay-at-home order in place, he couldn't even try to visit her. The baby still scared him. But he missed Mariah and kept reliving that night the baby was conceived. With everything turned upside down, he struggled to come to terms with it.

And he had another daily visitor: Gabrielle.

Every morning, she dropped in. She kept it short and to the point. She also repeatedly told him to move on with his life. He suspected she knew about the baby, but he didn't raise the subject.

Max slipped into a new routine. At night, he reminisced about Mariah. In the morning, he sipped his morning coffee with Gabrielle. In these days of social isolation, he felt anything but alone, although he feared his grip on reality was slipping away a little bit more each day.

He kept busy. Their factory had finished the first batch of wind turbines the week the governor ordered all non-essential factories to cease production. That shut them down, but Buck appealed to the governor. Now they awaited the verdict. Although energy was essential, the Ohio legislature favored coal and other fossil fuels. In the past, they'd enacted tax breaks and incentives to encourage alternative energy, but, more recently, they kept shutting down those earlier incentives, putting to rest anything related to renewables.

Max scratched his head. Here, in the midst of a viral nightmare, the government shut down business and enacted war powers overnight. The American economic system ground to a halt, creating a horrendous fallout. Meanwhile, the planet continued warming and the clock continued ticking on the time left to turn around the climate problem. The government refused to take action. People noticed cleaner air, a result of less driving and pollution from the shutdown. but that didn't mean they would start taking climate change seriously. The only thing anybody could talk about now was COVID-19.

The President continued to deny climate change and thumbed his nose at any policy or treaty that would try to save the future of human life on the planet. He protected the fossil fuel industry at all costs, even subsidizing the billion-dollar industry. The people elected by the right-to-life crowd seemed intent on hammering the nails in the coffin of humanity.

Max didn't get it. Not at all. For years, he'd worked to develop this alternative energy project and, by God, with Buck's help and some down time in Friendly, they'd pulled it off. Poised on the brink of launching their dream, they could now start taking back control of the energy production in the country. Energy would be placed back in the hands of common folk as in the days of old when people relied on wood fires to warm the house and cook. But Max knew change like this would not happen without a fight.

His thoughts revisited the thug who'd dogged him to Friendly. He knew the guy was paid to conduct a calculated campaign to terrorize climate scientists, but that knowledge didn't help him much when he himself was the target. The Koch Brothers knew what they were doing. They carried out a very effective campaign, starting with the Tea Party, and all of their little organizations to use niche issues to inflame the voters.

The average Joe-on-the-street voted for candidates who promised to preserve their gun rights and stop abortions, while the corporations took over the Supreme Court and attempted to leave democracy in the dust. He feared for the future and for Mariah's unborn child. Gabrielle and Isabella were now safe on the other side. It was the people still here that he worried about.

Cataloging his worries, Max realized he hadn't checked in on his brother in L.A. yet today. He texted: How are you, bro? Anything you need? Marshall had taken a job out there a couple years ago and moved across the country to chase the sun and California girls. But he'd come down with COVID-19, and was suffering all alone, sequestered in his Echo Park condo.

Max aimed to encourage him at least once a day, believing connection was important. Most days, Marshall was too tired to talk.

Max did not want to lose his brother. Every night, he said a prayer for Marshall, something Max had quit doing after Gabrielle and Isabella died. He didn't know what else to do.

Max hated the virus. People died in isolation, in the hospital. Those who got sick, but weren't dying, stayed home, also alone. So many around the country were in similar situations. Marshall reminded him that the statistics were on his side. Most of the young recovered.

Their mother rallied the troops to support Marshall. Even though he'd proclaimed he didn't believe in God years ago, that didn't stop his mother from getting his name on every prayer list in town. She posted it on Facebook, too. Max himself didn't like Facebook much, but every now and then he checked in to see the latest pictures of his niece and nephews. His mom had gotten well over two hundred of her friends praying for Marshall with one simple post. Facebook algorithms seemed to favor the prayer requests and health updates over almost anything else. Max didn't see that as a bad thing, although those same algorithms had swung the past election, too.

Max flipped off the press conference and focused on the task at hand. He needed to touch base with the mayor. Even though Mariah wouldn't talk to him, she'd made sure that he got to know the mayor. Now he worked hand in hand with Friendly's boss to implement Gabrielle's plan. Their goal was to keep Friendly free of COVID-19 for many months to come.

Each day, the local radio provided an update on the situation and recommendations. The people of Friendly learned early on what the symptoms of the dreaded virus were. Sore throat, dry cough, fever, and, later, difficulty breathing. The health clinic conducted tests daily of anyone with these symptoms. So far, they'd had no positives.

They initiated twenty-four hour check points at the roads leading into and out of the town. Anyone coming back into Friendly from places with active cases had to self-quarantine for fourteen days. Those coming to make deliveries were asked to unload and leave as soon as possible. Free masks were distributed to anyone interacting with town residents. Quarantines were planned for anyone diagnosed with the virus. Contract tracing would work back two weeks for those infected and require quarantine also for all those who had been in contact with the infected person.

Gabrielle seemed pleased with Max's efforts, but Max was getting worn out.

Meanwhile, Max kept thinking about the baby. Mariah still refused to talk with him and he wondered what to do. If he offered marriage, he wondered if she'd accept, or if, like many women, she'd be perfectly willing to raise babies without a man around.

At four in the afternoon, Max had had enough of working. He put on his jogging clothes and headed out the door. Maybe a good run would bring him some clarity.

34. MAUNDY THURSDAY

Friendly shut down was a different place. Mariah tended to Mrs. Bee, did the grocery shopping, watered the plants in the greenhouse, and tuned in to daily prayer with Pastor Amy on Facebook Live. She missed the contact with people in the cafe. She prepared meals, but only to-go orders. The people wore masks when they came to pick up the food, and seemed nervous and uneasy. They'd been told that the coronavirus could lurk almost anywhere: in the air, tiny respiratory droplets, on a piece of paper touched by an infected person, lingering longer on metal. Mariah could feel their fear. She worried she could have the virus and unknowingly transmit it to them on paper products. Some people who had it were asymptomatic. She wondered if she could be one of those.

The mayor's daily messages on Facebook Live, however, claimed that not one case of the coronavirus lived in Friendly. "We are friendly people here," he started each broadcast, "but we have banned the coronavirus from our town." Items being shipped into the town were quarantined until the virus would die. Healthcare workers and first responders were given COVID-19 tests every week. Anyone with similar symptoms was also tested. Across Ohio, the number of cases continued to rise. Mariah felt comforted to hear that Friendly was virus-free, but worried when the Health Commissioner reported they suspected a hundred thousand undetected cases in the state.

In the past, the Episcopal Church had always hosted a Seder meal on Maundy Thursday. Mariah lamented that the pandemic necessitated shutting down one of her favorite traditions. Pastor Amy sent out an email encouraging people to prepare the foods of the Seder to eat, promising a Facebook Live service to remember both the Seder and the Last Supper. The food of the Seder helped the Jewish people remember their Exodus from Egypt. As they told the story each year, they remembered the way God redeemed their people. Some of the special things they prepared were *maror*, horseradish, to remember the bitter times, *matza*, unleavened crackers, because they didn't have time to let their dough rise when they fled, and *haroset*, a dish made with apples, nuts, spices and wine, as a symbol of the mortar and the work they did for the Pharoah in Egypt.

Mariah and Mrs. Bee decided not to fix the Seder foods, which would require another grocery run, but planned to tune into the Maundy Thursday service live, after their meal.

Mrs. Bee cooked lentil soup and homemade oatmeal bread and,

together, they cut up apples and oranges. At the table, Mrs. Bee told her, "I miss the way my husband conducted the Maundy Thursday service. We would have a meal together, then do foot washing. After that, we would leave silently, in the dark."

"Foot washing? Why? I've never done that."

"Well, you know in the Bible that it says that Jesus washed the disciples' feet. It was the role of a servant. That was his way, you know, to serve."

"Did the people like that?"

"Yes, I think so. The women washed the women's feet and the men would do the other men. I always thought it was an exercise in humility and helped you understand the mind of Christ."

"He was really something, that man Jesus," Mariah said.

Mrs. Bee leaned back in her chair and put her hands on her belly. "He was trying to help the people. A healer, a lover, telling them to love each other. And they killed him. Why did they do that?"

"I don't know," Mariah said. "It's hard to understand. Wasn't it God's plan to forgive us?"

"Maybe," Mrs. Bee said. "Or maybe God just made something good of a bad situation."

"What does God think about the coronavirus?"

"Good question, Mariah. One that I'm not quite sure how to answer. Let's ask Pastor Amy." Mrs. Bee chuckled.

Mariah didn't know if that was a nice thing to do, to put her on the spot like that. But during the Q and A at the end of the service, Mariah could write in the question.

"I love your soup, Mrs. Bee. And this oatmeal bread ... out of the world! Thank you for making this simple meal for us. I feel sorry for all of those people living alone during this social isolation," Mariah said, changing the subject.

"Yes, what about that friend of yours, Max? Have you checked in on him?"

Mariah blushed, then didn't know what to say. She felt bad that she still hadn't told Mrs. Bee about the baby. She shook her head and hoped Mrs. Bee wouldn't pry.

"I understand he's helping the mayor with this coronavirus. Somebody told me the other day, the reason we have no cases in Friendly is largely because of Max. Did you know that?" Mrs. Bee asked.

"So I heard," Mariah said. "I wonder how he knew what to do?"

"Isn't he a scientist from Ohio State, like Buck?"

"Yes," Mariah said. "A wind scientist, not a biologist, though." Mariah didn't like the direction of the conversation. Mrs. Bee always knew more than she let on and now she seemed to be able to read right into Mariah's soul. She felt trapped with nowhere to hide.

"Hmm," Mrs. Bee said. "I thought you took a liking to him?"

Mariah looked down. Yes, of course she liked Max. But what if he didn't want her baby? That scared her more than anything. All he'd said was he needed time. She was the one who'd jumped to conclusions and cut him off. She found herself getting more emotional than usual these days, perhaps pregnancy hormones.

"You know he's still grieving," Mariah said. "He just lost his wife and daughter last year. He's not ready for a relationship." Mariah hated herself as soon as the words left her mouth. She was digging a hole she'd have a hard time crawling out of later. She should just tell the truth, but fear stilled her tongue.

"You could at least call him," Mrs. Bee said. "We can't eat that big Easter feast all by ourselves. Why don't you plan to take him a plate? You could drop one off for Buck, too, while you're out there."

Mariah smiled. She supposed she could do that. "Maybe," she said.

Then it was time for Pastor Amy's service. Together, they watched Pastor Amy talking about how the disciples met for the Passover meal. She explained how the Seder meal helps the Jewish people remember their story as a people. She talked about Jesus and his disciples at the Last Supper. Then she told them to get something to eat and drink at home to participate in the communion ritual. Mariah cut off two pieces of oatmeal bread and found some red wine. *The best communion feast ever*, she thought.

At the end of the service, Pastor Amy turned off the lights and extinguished the final candle. The screen turned black as she said, "Now we accompany Jesus to the cross. I encourage you to spend the next two days considering how you can follow Jesus. What is the suffering that you experience? Remember, we are his followers."

When Pastor Amy wrapped up the service without the usual opportunity for questions, Mariah sighed with relief. Mrs. Bee had probably forgotten anyway. Mariah wasn't sure why she didn't want to ask Pastor Amy to explain how God views the pandemic. but she was thankful for the reprieve.

The two of them observed the silence after that, and didn't speak much the following day, either. Good Friday passed quietly. Usually the schools closed, but they already were. The eerie silence of quarantining in place spooked Mariah. And the coronavirus was killing. Over five hundred thousand cases in the US and twenty thousand deaths already. That was a lot of people.

Just how *did* Max know how to keep it out of Friendly? Mariah wanted to know. What did Friendly do that other cities didn't? Maybe she'd go over and find out with a plateful of food on Easter.

35. GOOD FRIDAY BEGINS FOR MAX

After a fitful night, Max decided on an early morning run to greet the sun before coffee with Gabrielle. He shrugged into his jogging clothes and entered the world of spring just as the rising sun cast a diffuse glow on the fields around his house. He breathed deeply, inhaling crisp, fresh air as he kicked up his heels and fell into an easy cadence. He focused on his breath, counting as he ran. Breathing deeply, in and out. Meditation in motion, Gabrielle had dubbed it when they'd run together every morning before Isabella. Even now, nothing calmed him like a nice run.

Today, he especially needed to clear his head. Between COVID-19 and the turbine factory appeal, nothing felt easy on this bleak day. But the sun was shining, and that was something. "Wrong," he whispered to his mother who said the sun never shone on Good Friday.

Back when he'd spent a lot of time in church, Good Friday was an important day. Being the day Christians remember the death of Jesus, it always gave him pause. When he thought about Jesus, he thought about a good man who tried to walk the straight and narrow. He thought about someone so connected to the Higher Power that he must've almost dazzled the crowds with light, just like the dew sparkled on the leaves on the trees just now.

He knew the story well, and he knew that many Christians thought it was God's plan that he be put to death. But Max didn't really buy that. If he'd been sent as a messenger, Max didn't believe having him killed off was the original plan.

He didn't understand why people were downright evil sometimes. Jesus preached love. He said that's all God wanted us to do: love. What was so threatening about that?

How could civilization reach its current pinnacle and yet be hellbent on destroying itself in the same breath? The fossil fuel industry baffled his mind.

The filthy-rich couldn't be happy with enough billions for many lifetimes. No, they wanted more. And so far, they seemed to be successful in preventing decisive action on the climate. Couldn't more money be made by stockpiling fossil fuels and developing alternatives? Why must they expand the use and subsidies of fossil fuels in every way?

The truth of a warming planet wasn't a controversy. They turned it into such by hiring public relation gurus to put doubt about climate change in the American psyche. Certainly, those who watched certain "news" channels still believed climate change was a joke. The hype about fake news twisted truth into lies and lies into truth, creating enough confusion to allow the businesses to do absolutely anything to make money.

Max tried to wrap his head around the current president. How could he rise to be the leader of the best country in the world and be so confused and narcissistic? Max didn't have a TV, so he didn't watch the daily briefings during this COVID-19 pandemic, but he read enough in various news sources to know that man continued to make an absolute fool of himself. And yet he was still the one in charge.

The Roman Empire and almost every civilization's downfall had resulted from greed. The USA was tumbling a lot quicker than anyone imagined. The federal government had been spending beyond its means for decades. Now it was catapulting the national debt into the stratosphere.

Max stopped himself. Somewhere between the country road and the main drag of town, he'd quit counting and his thoughts had taken on a poison of their own. He looked up as he jogged down the tree-lined streets of Friendly. He liked this little town. But it was eerie. People were staying home, indoors. He missed the social network he'd come to love, taking lunch with the locals at the diner, catching up with the Knights of the Round Table on Friday nights, and then there was Mariah.

He passed the church and remembered Mariah's angelic voice. He ran by her house next door and felt his whole body warming up. Then he remembered the baby and he cooled off. A child. Another child. How could he have another child when he hadn't been able to protect the first one? And what sort of crazy person would bring a child into this day and time?

Would it be a son or a daughter? Should he marry Mariah, just do the right thing? He'd said he needed time, and that was the truth. This was a lot to wrap his mind around.

He looked at his watch. Time to start for home. He'd do coffee with Gabrielle and lunch with Buck. Since the social isolation had begun, he and Buck decided they were a household, so they gathered daily for a meal. It helped keep Max on terra firma. But this was the day they'd get the verdict of their appeal and Max was afraid it would put an end to everything they'd worked for in the past five years. He picked up his pace and started back to Buck's country estate and his hideaway, seeking strength for whatever might come.

36. FRIDAY WITH MARIAH

Mariah woke early on Good Friday, before sunrise, but feeling tired, she moved slowly. By the time she showered and dressed, she could see the beginning of day outside. Her mother always told her the sun never shines on Good Friday. Today smashed that idea to pieces. She considered the colors of the sunrise, God's handiwork layered through the sky, out Mrs. Bee's picture window. Light pinks and oranges heralded new day and reminded her that mothers were fallible. Hers was no exception. Ever since her mother had gone back to Myrtle Beach, Mariah kept her in the doghouse. But soon, she would be a mother, too and maybe she could do better. She admitted she wasn't off to the greatest start so far.

On Christmas Eve, when her mother had first come back to Friendly after all those years in hiding, Mariah had been excited. After pleading with God for so long to bring her back, she'd been filled with joy. Her amazing Christmas seemed too good to be true. She'd never desert her child like that in the first place. She put her hand on her stomach. She *could* do better. She would not treat her child like that.

Her stomach churned. She needed to eat something, but wasn't sure she could keep it down. Her mother'd always recommended bananas, rice, applesauce, and toast, the BRAT diet. It had certainly helped after the flu and during her first trimester. Maybe her mom was right about some things.

She popped a piece of whole wheat bread in the toaster. If she could keep that down, she'd have a banana. Meanwhile, as she made some chamomile ginger tea, to calm her stomach and aid digestion, she thought about Good Friday. She liked attending church with the somber music and focus on Jesus' last words. Since starting her job at the diner, she'd missed out. But because the service would be broadcast on Facebook Live because of the pandemic, she could listen in at the diner while she worked. She decided to do the Stations of the Cross in the church garden to commemorate the day.

Years ago, the Episcopal Church had commissioned a local artist to make statues in the area behind the church. When Mariah had needed an escape as a child, like after the loss of her father and then from the trauma in her house with her abusive stepfather, she'd liked to visit the flowers in this garden. She'd volunteered in the place all summer as a way to escape her troubled home life. She knew the statues well. They'd comforted her over the years, especially when her mother had left.

There was no activity in Mrs. Bee's room yet, so Mariah decided to walk the stations of the cross as her Good Friday ritual, before going in to work. She left a note on the table and slipped outside.

She loved the quiet at dawn. The ball of the sun hung over the greenhouse, catching the dew on the new leaves of the trees, making them sparkle. The glistening drops seemed to dance. It hardly seemed like a day of mourning at all.

Mariah had discovered over the years that nature would just go on being its pristine self in the midst of whatever calamity life might dump on it. When her daddy'd died, the sun still came up. How could it shine, she remembered wondering, when her whole world had just fallen apart? And yet, the steadiness of the natural world often calmed and soothed her in the midst of struggle.

She opened the wrought iron gate, the entry to her favorite space. Some wildflowers were popping with color across the lawn, but most of the flowers were still sleeping in the ground. A few daffodils greeted her at the first station of the cross where Pontius Pilate sentenced Jesus to death. The man looked disturbed. His hands were suspended in time, folded over each other, washing his hands of the blame. He'd said he didn't want to send Jesus to his death. The people made him do it. Right. Just what her stepfather always said when he was beating her mother. According to him, it was all her mother's fault. She didn't believe either of them.

Mariah took a deep breath. A deep sadness filled her heart as she considered her own time of suffering. She knew about shifting the blame. She also knew that Pontius Pilate's hands would never be clean again. That kind of blame can't be washed away. Well, she supposed Jesus forgave him on the cross, but … she remembered crying all day long by this statue when her mother first left. Once again, she wondered how her mother could do that to her own child.

Not wanting to dwell on her mother today, she moved on to the next station, where Jesus takes up his cross. Pastor Amy always told her that God will give you the strength you need to get through the day. Looking at Jesus bowing under the weight of the cross, she knew that even though she could make it, some the burdens were almost too heavy.

She walked on. Jesus falls at Station Three. It was hard to comprehend what it might feel like to have to carry the cross on which they were going to kill you. She could relate. Losing her father, then dealing with the mean stepfather who'd made their lives hell, then losing her mother had been hard to carry. She could remember those days she'd wanted to stay in bed all day long.

Mariah moved on and plopped down on the bench beside Station Four, where He places his hand on the shoulder of his mother. He comforts her. She couldn't imagine what it would be like for a mother to lose her child. Even though hers was only weeks old, she loved the unborn baby with all of her heart. She so much wanted to meet this little person growing inside of her. She tried to imagine that, someday, her child would be big enough to comfort her.

Mariah checked the time on her cellphone. She needed to get to the café soon, so she hurried through the rest of the stations. Pausing for a moment at Station Five, she looked at the pain in Simon's face as he carried the cross for Jesus. Taking on someone else's burden could be painful, she knew. How she'd mourned for Farmer Sayers when he wouldn't speak, as she tried to break his shell. That the old turtle was finally poking his head out and opening up made her so happy.

At the sixth station, she admired the statue of the woman wiping the face of Jesus. It always reminded her of the gentleness of her own mother, wiping her face with a cool cloth when she had a fever as a child. Her mom did love her, she knew that. Mariah felt her loss like a stab in her heart.

At Station Seven, where Jesus falls again, she wished she could stop and have a good cry, but she moved on to Station Eight where he meets the women of Jerusalem, saying goodbyes. There had been too many goodbyes in her life, including her abrupt goodbye to Max. She needed to give him a chance. Then Jesus falls again at Station Nine, and Mariah hurried on because she needed to get to work, but she also didn't want to absorb any more pain. They take his clothes at Station Ten, an act of cruelty. And at Station Eleven, they nail him to the cross. She couldn't comprehend how one human being could do that to another, let alone how Jesus kept loving through it all. She knew that was the requirement of all the followers. She paused at Station Twelve, Jesus, dead on the cross. This was what she'd come for. Good Friday, not good at all. This was what she needed to remember today. And then, at Station Thirteen, where they put his body in Mary's arms, she looked away from the pain. And finally, at Station Fourteen, they put him in the tomb. The end of the story for now. She looked at the good man, the man she followed, dead, and tried to imagine his love and the confusion of all of those who loved him at that time.

She thought about people suffering around the world in the present day as they lost their loved ones to COVID-19. She felt tears running down her cheek. She was very emotional these days. She'd read that pregnancy caused that, hormones gone wild. She allowed herself to cry. It seemed appropriate.

Then, as she made her way to the gate, she saw a flash of a person running by. Looking more closely, she recognized Max. She cried harder and waited until he was long gone before exiting the garden and walking to the café.

Max opened the door to his little cabin. Sunlight struck the kitchen table and danced on the face of his wife.

"Hi, Max," she said. "Have a nice run?"

In the moment, Max forgot he was talking to a ghost and just appreciated her presence. "Yes," he said. "I needed that. Crazy times in which I live here. You got out just in time."

"Don't say that, honey. You've got a good life here and much more to do. Take a shower. I'll wait for you."

Max liked having her wait for him while he cleaned up and prepared for a new day. He kissed her on the cheek, ran his hand along her shoulder, feeling the connection they always shared, then went to change. He slowed his pace to a crawl with a long shower, trying to stretch out Gabrielle's presence. He knew she'd want to get down to business and would evaporate as soon as she gave directions.

When Max returned to the kitchen, he started coffee and then pulled out a skillet to make some eggs. He popped a couple pieces of bread in the toaster before turning to Gabrielle. "Can I interest you in breakfast, dear?" He laughed. "I wouldn't want the friendly ghost to go hungry on my watch."

Gabrielle smiled. "I don't need any food, but you go ahead. I've got all the time in the world."

"Really?"

"Max, they didn't send me back down here to be your wife. I'm here to stop the pandemic, that's all. Maybe it seems unfair, but you need to get on with your life. Focusing on what we used to have isn't going to help you in the long run. You've got other fish to fry."

Max gave her a long look. Did she know about Mariah's baby? He laughed to cover his confusion. "Oh, yeah, I need to fry me some fish. Right. Come on, Gabrielle. Listen to yourself. Put yourself in my shoes. What the hell would you do if I came back to haunt you?"

"Calm down, Max. Someday, you'll understand. Right now, we have a mission," she explained. "We're protecting Friendly for you and your unborn baby."

"How do you know that?"

"Mmm …," Gabrielle said. "We have an overview of life going on. It's hard to explain. We watch life unfolding. But usually we focus on our new life up there."

"Okay, okay, so you know." Max shook his head as pulled his toast out and started to butter it. "What should I do?" he asked as he sprinkled his toast with cinnamon and then sugar, plated his eggs, poured a glass of water, and grabbed another cup of coffee, before sitting across from her.. "We're just getting acquainted and now she's pregnant?"

"That's your fault. You've gotta step up and be a father again," Gabrielle said.

"No. I'm not doing it. I promised myself I would never do that again the day you and Isabella died. I can't take any more grief."

"Max, you have life. Don't blow it. You can't live your life on hold. Life happens. Death happens. But you have today. Make it count. You like Mariah. You're lonely. It's a good thing. Perhaps not what you thought you wanted, but she's everything you need."

Gabrielle quit talking and silence hung in the room, an unwelcome visitor. Max tried to wrap his mind around the scene unfolding in his kitchen. His ex-wife telling him to step up and be a father again with another woman and their baby. He couldn't quite comprehend this twilight reality. He got up from the table and started toward the door to escape.

"Max! Come back here. Running isn't going to get you anywhere. Get back here, right now."

Gabrielle still knew how to control him, that was for sure. Her wish was his command, but when it came to Mariah? He found it extremely bizarre that Gabrielle was not only aware of the situation, but was also trying to dictate his next move. He took a deep breath. "Let's get back to work," he said.

"Okay," Gabrielle said, "but remember what I told you. You'll be happier, Max. I know you will."

Max closed his eyes. Perhaps when he opened them, Gabrielle would be gone and he could return to the saner insanity of his life. No such luck.

"Yes, let's get to work," she said. "You've been doing a great job, Max. Friendly is well-protected, but we can't let up. When the virus comes to town, we've got to be ready. Remember, test, isolate, investigate, quarantine, and test some more."

"I think we've got the message out," Max said. "People are watching the mayor's daily Facebook videos. They are self-monitoring. The health clinic gets a lot of calls from people trying to sort out their symptoms. So far, anyone with anything close to the symptoms of COVID-19 has been tested."

"And no positives yet, right?"

"Correct."

"But don't jump to conclusions based on the negative test readings. In Seattle, they've found that they may get false negatives up to forty-five percent of the time, so it's possible some of those people actually have the virus."

"How can that be? Are the tests bogus?"

"Sometimes, the virus may not be well-established in the body. They do a nose swab, but the virus may be in the throat or hasn't spread to all the mucous yet, you know? Our tests from the World Health Organization are probably more reliable, but even then we can't be sure. So still tell people who have symptoms to self-isolate until two weeks after the symptoms are gone."

"That's hard," Max said. "That's really hard."

"Yes, but consider the alternative. In New York, the hospitals are overrun with dying patients and many of the staff are sick. You don't want that in Friendly, do you, Max?"

"Of course not," Max said. "But do you really think we can beat this thing?"

"Check the news. There was a little town in Italy that followed protocol like what I outlined in my paper. The science explains how to proceed. I imagine the USA would be doing the same thing except we lost ground and the wisdom gathered for these times because the President abolished the National Security Council unit created to deal with health crises before the pandemic. I didn't live long enough to try out my approach, but I thank you for picking up the ball. Friendly is small enough. We can make this work," she insisted.

"Okay. So right now, it's important to get those with symptoms to stay home, even if they tested negative?"

"Exactly."

"Okay, I'll ask the mayor to start including that in his briefings and make sure the health clinic tells the patients as well. But you know, it doesn't look good for America. The number of cases and deaths grow each day. Pretty soon, we might have more cases than any other country in the world."

"I know, Max. We have to be in it for the long haul. We must be vigilant. Seven months from now, when your baby is born, we want a healthy community for him, don't we?"

"Him? I'm going to have a son?"

Gabrielle just smiled. "See you tomorrow, Max." And then she was gone.

Max fired up his laptop, emailed the mayor and then the clinic's only doctor. He followed up with a press release to the Friendly Gazette. Mission accomplished, he gathered his things together to take over to Buck's for the conference call on the turbine factory.

He was grateful he had actual work, because the last thing he wanted to do right now was sit around and think about the baby and

Mariah and what the hell he was going to do. But, even as he tried to focus, Gabrielle's words kept playing in his mind. Was this really what he needed? What he wanted? Could he step up and be a father again? He knew the answer to that last question was that he really didn't have a choice.

38. COMING CLEAN WITH MRS. BEE

Mariah cruised on autopilot through the morning at the café, tucking the misery of the Stations of the Cross in the back of her mind as she processed orders, cooked and packed the food up for the customers. Being busy helped keep her worries at bay. She fried a lot of fish for the Catholics in town, the Good Friday special.

Everything had changed with the pandemic. The "new normal" felt like living on the edge of a dream in the sleepy time of early morning. Mental confusion surrounded the shape of ordinary. She'd seen enough on TV to learn that everyone felt the same way.

She missed interactions with people, especially in the cafe. It was hard to communicate through the masks. She hated asking people to repeat themselves, so often she just nodded and pretended to understand. Then there was all the packaging, wasteful, from her point of view. She hated Styrofoam containers. She'd ordered recyclable paper products, but they wouldn't come in for another week. It bothered her that every single item needed to be packaged with something that would end up in the landfill.

She missed the community of people in the diner as she cooked and cleaned. Necessary for safety, but not fun. She hated worrying with every customer that she'd infect them or they'd infect her. It was such an awful thing, this virus. The mayor said they'd keep it out of Friendly, but she wasn't stupid. She watched the nightly news. The virus was spreading like wildfire across the country and almost everywhere in Ohio, too. Could Max really keep it out?

She worried about Mrs. Bee and the baby. Thinking about the two of them at the same time once again reminded her that she needed to come clean and confide in Mrs. Bee. Then she needed to call her mom. It was Good Friday. Might as well get all the difficult stuff out today. Then Easter would bring a brand new perspective for them all.

She cleaned up the counters, following the Health Department's protocols. It took twice as long to do everything. The virus mainly passed airborne, they said, yet they told her to clean all the surfaces. She wondered about inside the air ducts. Some people thought it was moving through the heating and air conditioning systems. She'd heard singers could project the virus out twenty-seven feet, a fact both eerie and disturbing. And sad. Fortunately, the owner of the diner planned to have a drive-thru window installed soon. That would minimize her concerns.

Her thoughts turned to how she could explain her pregnancy to

Mrs. Bee. "You wanted me to get involved ... well, I went a little too far." Maybe it was as simple as that. "We got carried away."

She hurried so she could get home before she changed her mind. She worried about what Mrs. Bee might say. In the end, she realized there was no easy path, she just needed to do it.

Mrs. Bee sat in her chair, dozing, when Mariah walked in at a quarter after two. She closed the door gently, trying not to disturb the older woman, but she opened her eyes nevertheless.

"Hello, dear," she said. "Or should I say Happy Good Friday? No, I guess not." Mrs. Bee laughed a little. "We should be properly sad today." She patted the chair beside her easy chair. "Come sit with me and let's grieve together."

Mariah planted a kiss on Mrs. Bee's cheek before sitting down. "I went to the stations of the cross before work this morning. A good thing to do on Good Friday, right?"

"Oh, yes. It used to be so crowded in the garden on Good Friday back in the day. I'm not sure anybody but you pays attention to those old statues anymore." Mrs. Bee looked out the window toward the garden by the church. "You spent hours there, didn't you? Reverend Bee would tell me to pray for you whenever he saw you there."

"Thanks. I needed all the prayers I could get. Still do. Especially now. I need to tell you something."

"What is it, dear? You know you can talk to me. Tell me, what's going on?"

Mariah let out a deep breath. She realized she'd been holding in her fear. She relaxed a little at Mrs. Bee's words. "Well, I know you've been telling me to give a relationship with a man a chance for quite a while."

Mrs. Bee smiled. "It's Max, isn't it? I knew there was something going on there."

Mariah blushed, surprised. Sometimes, she thought Mrs. Bee was just like God. She seemed to know things happening in Mariah's life before she understood them herself.

"You've been trying to fool me, but I knew," Mrs. Bee said with a kind smile.

Mariah grinned, too. "Well, yes. I like Max. I like him a lot. But then he left Friendly and he's struggling with grief, like I told you last night. But there's more."

Mrs. Bee got very quiet. She smoothed her hands over her legs, looking at Mariah with a caring gaze that made her feel warm and loved.

It was time. Mariah couldn't hold it in anymore.

"On New Year's Eve, I went over to Max's. I had too much to drink. We got carried away. You know I don't usually drink much." Mariah

122

took a deep breath in and then let it all out. "I'm pregnant," she said. Then she hung her head in shame.

Mrs. Bee continued to look at her with that loving gaze. Then her eyes lit up. "You're having a baby with Max?"

"Yes. I'm pregnant with Max's baby." Mariah was relieved that she'd finally told the truth. It felt good to tell someone.

"Oh, honey," Mrs. Bee said. "The first time you were together? Are you sure?"

'Yes, I'm sure. October. The baby's due in October."

Mariah was surprised that Mrs. Bee didn't condemn her or scold her or even tell her she'd made a mistake. She asked, "How are you feeling now?"

"Well, I get sick a little in the mornings, but mostly, I feel good. A little tired sometimes."

"I mean how do you feel about the baby?" Mrs. Bee clarified.

Mariah hadn't expected this question. She paused. How did she feel about the baby? "Well, of course I feel stupid for letting this happen. I feel embarrassed. I've been afraid to tell anybody, even you and Mom," she stammered.

"I understand," Mrs. Bee said. "It's a hard situation for you. But how do you feel about the baby?"

"Oh," Mariah said with a gentle smile, warmth radiating from her heart. "I love this baby." She put her hand on her belly. "There's a new life growing inside of me and I'm going to do everything I can do to be the best mother you ever saw."

"That's my girl," Mrs. Bee said. "That's my girl. You'll do just fine." And then Mrs. Bee said nothing, giving Mariah permission to speak or be quiet, too.

Mariah let the comfortable silence fill the space between them. She felt like someone had lifted a heavy backpack of books off her shoulders. Her heart felt light. If Mrs. Bee thought she'd do just fine, she knew she would.

After a while, Mrs. Bee asked, "Did you tell Max? He needs to know."

Mariah burst into tears. "I told him and I haven't spoken to him since."

"What did he say?"

"I don't think he wants this baby, Mrs. Bee." Mariah sobbed.

"Did he say that?"

"No, he just said he needed time."

"Give him time then," Mrs. Bee said. "He'll come around."

"What if he doesn't want the baby?"

"Honey, you told me Max is grieving. Maybe he's afraid to be a father again. Can you imagine how it would feel to lose your three-year old child?"

Mariah nodded.

"Go wash your face, honey. It's going to be okay. Just give him time."

"I brought fish dinners home for us," she told Mrs. Bee when she came back to the living room after washing up. She was exhausted. She wanted to take a nap, but she also needed to eat. "Do you want one?"

"In a little while, Mariah. Why don't you go lie down and rest. I'll wake you up in a couple hours. Then we can have a nice fish dinner and afterwards, you can call your mama. You need to get this off your chest. Oh, and I wondered, did you see the doctor yet?"

"No. Should I do that? I didn't think about that."

"Yes, yes. Monday, make an appointment. I'll go with you if you want. You're already in your second trimester."

Mariah nodded again. "I'll do that. It would be wonderful to have you come with me." Mrs. Bee always knew just what she needed. She hated to think that Mrs. Bee would be gone someday. "Thank you," she said. "I do need a nap." She kissed Mrs. Bee again on the cheek. Mrs. Bee enfolded her in a big hug, holding her firmly long enough for Mariah to feel very loved and relaxed. In Mrs. Bee's arms, she could only believe that everything would be just fine.

"Now go on, you," Mrs. Bee told her.

And Mariah did. She went up to bed and fell soundly asleep until Mrs. Bee woke her two hours later. They shared an early dinner of fried fish and coleslaw and green beans with some hush puppies on the side. The warm food soothed Mariah and she decided it tasted delicious, even if she had made it herself.

They didn't talk much during the meal. Mariah appreciated that silence was perfectly okay between her and Mrs. Bee. When you felt close to someone, words often weren't necessary. Mariah had learned that during the years they lived together. Mrs. Bee often even told her, "You don't have to talk, dear."

After the meal, they cleaned up together. When the dishes were dried and put away, Mrs. Bee told Mariah, "Now you go on upstairs and call your mama. Then come back down and we can watch a show together before I go to bed. You'll feel better, honey. You know you will."

Mariah frowned. She knew she was dragging her feet on this one, but Mrs. Bee was right. She'd planned to tell her mother today, but if Mrs. Bee wasn't there to prod her, she knew she'd procrastinate again. She felt too much distance from her mom. Mariah's anger, always simmering just below the surface, tended to come out in ugly comments when her mom called.

Part of Mariah didn't want to share her baby with her mother. She doubted her mom would be as supportive as Mrs. Bee. Did she even want to expose her child to a grandmother who would come and go and not really be there for the long haul?

Mariah stood by the window, watching dusk settle on the Stations of the Cross garden. It wasn't surprising, she reflected, that the statue of Jesus talking with his mother would be the only one she could see clearly from the window.

Mrs. Bee interrupted her procrastination. "Honey, it will be okay. Go upstairs and make the call and get back down here, before I go to sleep."

Mariah smiled, knowing she needed the nudge. As much as she dreaded this call, she went upstairs to make it happen. She pushed her mother's numbers before flopping down on the bed. She closed her eyes, listening to the phone ring, worrying that her mother was going to answer, worrying that she might not.

Her mother picked it up on the second ring. "Mariah, is that you? Honey, I'm so glad you called. I've been thinking about you, it being Good Friday and all. Such a sad day. I miss you, honey. How are you doing?"

Mariah hadn't expected her mom getting all gushy on her. "I'm okay," Mariah said. "I'm okay."

"I'm so glad, dear," her mother said.

Mariah didn't feel like small talk, so she let it out. "Mom, I called to tell you I'm pregnant."

Her mother didn't respond for what seemed like the longest time. Mariah kept quiet, waiting for a bomb to drop—or had her mother hung up?

"You're pregnant? Oh my," her mother finally said. "How are you feeling?"

Mariah paused. The same response as Mrs. Bee? Unbelievable. Part of her didn't want to answer, but her manners kicked in. "Well, I'm tired a lot. But I'm excited about the baby. I'm excited about being a mother. I will never leave my child."

"Ouch," her mother said. Mariah thought she would start defending herself then, but instead she said, "I'm sure you'll be a great mother. You're such a loving person. I have no doubt that you will be a good mother. What about the father? Who's the father? Does he want to be involved?"

"It's Max and I don't know. He's still thinking about it. I haven't talked with him since I told him. Not that he hasn't tried to talk with me, but I'm mad because he said he had to think about it."

"Oh, yeah, that's hard. I see how you could feel that way. He seems like a good man. I think he'll come around. He'll be a good father. And I know you like him a lot. I could tell that when I was there. I'm not surprised."

Mariah didn't know what she'd expected, but her mother sounding kind, supportive and concerned about Mariah's feelings was not it. Then she reminded herself that Mother was always all of those things — when she was around. Mariah's anger obscured the mother she'd always known and loved. In her anger, her mother became a monster, an ogre at a distance that Mariah had decided to dislike and mistreat.

"Mom, I don't get it. Why did you stay away for so long?"

"I'm sorry, Mariah. I needed to heal. I went through rehab and got a job. I didn't want to come back and risk falling in with my old crowd who knew me as a happy drinker. I didn't want to run into your stepfather, either. I should have kept in touch with you better. I'm sorry.

"That was the hardest thing I've ever done, honey. I know you don't understand. I don't know if you will ever forgive me. But I couldn't take a chance of backsliding. I needed to stay sober."

"But you left me all alone, Mom. Why didn't you take me with you?"

"You needed to finish high school. I went into residential treatment. You couldn't stay there with me. Did you really want me to pull you out of your senior year?"

"Well, yes. I could have finished up somewhere else."

"Maybe I made a mistake. I'm sorry. I thought you'd be better off in Friendly. It seems to me you've turned out okay. You landed on your feet, Mariah. You're doing very well. And now you're going to be a mother. I'm so happy for you, dear."

"Okay. Thanks, Mom," Mariah said. "I gotta go. I told Mrs. Bee I'd do something with her before I go to bed. I just wanted you to know. Bye for now."

"Goodbye, Mariah. I love you so much. You're going to be a great mother."

"Okay, bye," Mariah said. She couldn't say the love word. Not yet. Part of her still wanted to punish her mother for leaving, but she wanted to see things from her mother's point of view.

39. TROUBLE RETURNS

With California on lockdown, the climate activists quieted down, too. Harold wanted out of the place. The mandatory mask order made him feel like a criminal. What happened to American freedom? He took pride in his appearance. He didn't like covering up his pearly whites. Perhaps he could go back and rough up Max in Ohio where the governor only recommended masks. He asked for permission to move on and received the green light much quicker than he imagined. They arranged a new identity to cover his tracks from his last romp in the Buckeye State. The boss arranged for a new Ohio license plate and new identity cards, which arrived within a week.

He bid adieu to his Airbnb the night before he left. He'd miss the sweet little guesthouse in Silver Lake, but he couldn't say as much for Los Angeles traffic. Now he cruised onto Highway 2 at four in the morning, glad to miss the morning rush. The City of Angels was navigable by car, but not for large chunks of the day, and not always at a reasonable speed.

Howard liked to plot his travel in advance. He'd mapped it all out last night and now he mentally rehearsed the trip in his mind. First turn, Exit 17A, head east on Interstate 210. He would pass just south of the Angeles Forest and almost to Mount San Antonio before turning north on 15 leading to Interstate 40. Then a straight shot clear to Oklahoma City in nineteen hours, if all went well, passing through Arizona and New Mexico. Arizona had been getting a couple hundred new cases of the COVID-19 a day. He might do drive-thru and gas stations, but he'd wash his hands, maybe even use a mask and keep using his hand sanitizer after each stop. Freedom means not wearing a mask, and also wearing a mask when it's in your best interest.

Thirteen hundred miles for one day was a helluva lot of driving, but Harold loved the open road. If he downed enough coffee, with a little luck, he could pull into Oklahoma City by midnight, catch some shuteye and take off again by seven. Worst case scenario, he could split the trip in half and sleep in a roadside park. Then he could cruise into Ohio the day before Easter Sunday, or on the holy day itself, the day the President planned to reopen the country.

The governors didn't agree, but he dreamed about spending a fine evening in a tavern with mugs of beer. Perhaps that tavern in Friendly would be open. With his wig and moustache disguise, he doubted anyone would recognize him.

40. APPEAL ON THE WIND TURBINE

After checking in with the mayor, Max tidied the cabin and prepared for his Zoom meeting with Buck and the attorneys. This was the day they'd learn the verdict on their appeal. Although many factories were shut down during the pandemic, the governor had made an exemption for essential businesses. As an energy factory, they should be exempt. But the Ohio legislators catered to the fossil fuel lobby, so their wind factory may be jinxed. He hoped not.

His phone rang, interrupting his thoughts. Buck's number scrolled on his cellphone. "Good morning, Buck," he said.

"Morning, Max. Why not come over for this call? We'll be strong together and console each other if needed."

"Okay. Be right over." Max shoved his papers into his briefcase and grabbed a jacket for the cool April weather. Five minutes later, he was knocking on Buck's front door.

"Come in, come in," Buck welcomed him. "Nice to have someone else in the house. Gets mighty lonely sometimes. Thanks for coming."

"Don't I know it. And now we're not the only ones. I heard yesterday that loneliness is as lethal as smoking fifteen cigarettes a day. This pandemic's not good for anyone."

"That's what's wrong with me," Buck said. "Okay. Now I understand."

"Yeah. But what's worse? To be alone or to love again and risk death? I don't know if I have it in me to go through all that loss again."

"Ah, Max, you're young and attractive, not a surly old man like me. You need to get out there and have some fun. What about Mariah? It seems like there are some sparks flying there."

Max covered his face with his hands. "Oh, man," he said. "Right. Mariah." He hesitated for a moment before spilling the beans. Max and Mariah were friends, but Max needed to get it off his chest. "Yeah, one night in the hay and now she's pregnant."

"What? Mariah is pregnant? Max, how did you let that happen? What were you thinking?"

Max cringed. "I wasn't thinking, that was the problem. New Year's Eve, alcohol, attraction off the charts. She's beautiful. We got carried away."

"I thought better of you, man," Buck said. "Of course, you're going to make it right. You've got to."

Deep down, Max agreed, and yet he continued to argue—with himself, more than with Buck. "A baby, Buck? It's too much. I promised myself I would not go there again. After losing Isabella, I can't do it."

"Max, you can't stop living just because Gabrielle and Isabella died. You know they wouldn't want that for you. Your time is not up, son. You've got a bright future ahead of you."

"Right. So bright, it hurts my eyes. A crazy president, climate change, and now the pandemic. What a wonderful life. Who would want to bring a baby into this mess? I know I don't."

"But, Max," Buck argued, "you're a good dad. I watched you. We need good dads to make good people who are equipped to deal with the mess we know is coming. And Mariah is one fine woman. You can't walk away, Max."

"Please, don't say anything to Mariah about this until we work things out, okay? I'm already in the doghouse," Max pleaded.

"You got it, but know I'm expecting you to make this right."

Max didn't want to hear it. The clock gave him the perfect out." Hey, man, it's time for our meeting."

"So it is," Buck replied.

Max was weary of online meetings, but he also realized they opened up possibilities. When he left his job at OSU, they'd asked him to teach online. At that time, Max could barely get out of bed in the morning, and teaching was the last thing he wanted to consider. As time passed and he became more comfortable with the online format, he thought he might be able to teach a few remote classes in the fall.

Their attorney greeted them as they joined the Zoom call. "Good morning, Buck and Max, good to see you."

"Same," Buck said. "Thanks for helping us out on a holy day."

"Well, I know it's Good Friday, but we don't take this day off. And right now, all days seem to blend into each other. Such is the strange reality of working from home. My wife reminded me this morning that Easter is Sunday. You know the President wants places to reopen on Easter."

"This is too damn early," Max said, remembering Gabrielle's thoughts on the matter.

"Yes, well," the attorney said. "Even the President can't make that happen."

"Now he says it's all up to the states," Buck said.

"If he'd taken some leadership in the first place, he would've issued national orders. Then the states wouldn't be left to fend for themselves. How can he expect to be in charge of opening when he refused to be in charge of shutting down?" Max asked.

"Okay, okay," the attorney replied. "But that's what we've got at this point. Tell me, who would want to be in charge of this mess?"

"Look," Buck said, "let's talk business. What do we do if they deny our appeal?"

"We can take it higher," the attorney said. "Is that what you'd want to do?"

"Yes," Buck and Max said in unison.

"I hope that won't be necessary," the attorney said. "I think there's someone in the waiting room, let me see."

The attorney from the State AG's office appeared on the screen. "Good morning, gentlemen. I'm Rob Hastings, an assistant attorney in the Office of the Ohio Attorney General. Our boss couldn't be with us this morning, but he asked me to extend his greetings on behalf of our office and the governor. You know the governor is a strong supporter of Ohio State and follows their academic accolades, as well as their sports. He asked me to commend you both for your pioneering research in the development of energy for the future."

Max and Buck raised their eyebrows and looked at each other.

"Well, that's mighty nice to hear," Buck replied.

"And you can pass back to the governor that the people of Friendly have been very impressed with his leadership during this crisis," Max added.

"Not everyone is so pleased," Rob said. "I'm sure he'll be glad to hear of your support. The legislature wants him to open things more quickly. They're also trying to silence our female health commissioner."

"Not the first time men have tried to shut down women," Max said.

The attorney gave Max a look. But then he laughed and said, "The governor got around that easily, telling them that he's the one that makes the calls."

"Yes. But his own party seems more concerned about the economy than people's lives," Max said.

"That's not entirely true," Rob said. "The governor has received widespread support from Republicans in Ohio and across the country, and also from the President.

"But let's get down to business. I know you're anxious to hear what I have to say. The governor instructed the Attorney General to approve your request to open your factory as planned, as an essential business. Our gas stations and other energy producers are essential and open for business. Therefore, your energy factory is deemed essential as well.

"He wants you to know he follows what you are doing. He applauds your efforts and believes it's instrumental to the future with our changing climate. Your plan to eventually employ twenty-five people in good paying jobs is something we're all for. Thanks for doing your part to grow our Ohio economy.

"We reviewed your social distancing plans. They comply with the governor's orders. Do you have any questions?"

"No, no," the attorney said. "Thank you so much, Rob. That's good to hear. Please extend our appreciation to the governor, who happens to be a neighbor of mine."

"He mentioned that," Rob said. "He said to tell you he missed the spring cookout this year that you usually provide for the neighborhood."

"Yes, so much has been cancelled this year," the attorney commiserated. "Tell him I hated having to cancel to keep us all safe."

"We can open our factory, then?" Max asked to clarify.

"You're good to go," Rob replied. "And, oh, the governor also would like to order two of your devices when they are available. He wants to try to hook them up to his guesthouse."

"Sure thing," Buck said, winking at Max. "We'll even give him a discount."

"Well, good day, then," Rob said. "Best wishes on your endeavor. We do like to see new businesses up and running. It's admirable that you're forging ahead in these difficult times."

Rob left the call. Buck and Max thanked the attorney and signed off, too.

"This calls for something good," Buck said. "How 'bout I fire up the grill? How does a celebratory lunch of sirloin and grilled veggies sound?"

"Okay," Max said. Although he avoided red meat for the most part and preferred a vegetarian diet, he still liked a good steak now and then. He would deviate to celebrate good news, even if it was Good Friday.

"Let's eat on the deck. I've got a warm jacket you can wear," Buck suggested. "You work on getting the veggies ready and I'll get started on the meat. Here are some skewers." He pulled a bowl of brussels sprouts, cherry tomatoes and carrots out of the refrigerator. "I already steamed them a bit. Just put them on the skewers, add some seasoning and bring them out to me. They should grill up real nice."

Max and Buck enjoyed the afternoon together, hanging out on the deck. The birds were chirping, the steak was delicious, and the veggies were grilled tender and juicy. In their country haven, all seemed right with the world. Fortunately, Buck didn't bring up the baby again and Max sure wasn't going to talk about it. They dined and reminisced and planned, talking about their new factory, hoping for better days ahead.

41. IN BETWEEN

On Saturday morning, shortly after breakfast, Mariah received a text from her mom.

Mariah, your dad wrote you a letter before he died. He told me to give it to you once you were grown. I think it's time for you to read it now. He put it in a metal box and asked me to bury it next to his grave. It's under the planter that we put there years ago. I buried it down about four inches. Take a shovel. Let me know when you get it. I don't know what it says.

A letter from Dad? Why did her mom text instead of calling? Without thinking, she called her mom.

"Mariah. You got my text."

"Mom, why? Why did you keep this from me for all of these years? Why now all of a sudden?"

"Oh, Mariah. Actually, I forgot about it, or I would have told you to get it at Christmas. When you told me you're pregnant, I remembered. Your dad said to give it to you when you were all grown, ready to have a child of your own. This is exactly when he wanted you to have it, honey."

"What does it say? Did he show you?"

"No. He asked me for the paper and supplies to get it ready. He did research on how to make sure the paper wouldn't disintegrate inside the box. He told me exactly what to buy, but then he wanted to do it all by himself. He made me pledge not to look in the box. He wanted you to read it first and then decide if you wanted to share the contents with me."

"I'm going to go get it, Mom," Mariah said. "This is so cool. I've only got a little time before work, but I'm going to go dig it up. I hope I can still read the letter."

"Call me later, Mariah. I'm eager to find out what he wrote. I'm so happy he did this for you. He loved you so much," her mother said.

"Bye, Mom. Thank you," Mariah said and looked at the clock. Yes, she could dig it up before work. A few minutes later, she hurriedly told Mrs. Bee all about it and then kissed her goodbye. She stopped to get a shovel out of the greenhouse.

On her way to the cemetery, she thought about the weirdness of this Holy Saturday. Ever since she was a little girl, she always felt sad on this day between Good Friday and Easter. After they killed Jesus, she tried to imagine what it was like for his disciples on that day, and then the next. Their wonderful leader, gone. Dead. Lying in the tomb.

She remembered when her daddy died. She didn't think her mother smiled for a whole year after that. She didn't laugh much herself. It was awful. Death is so final. She puzzled over the fact that someone could be so alive, with you one moment and then just gone. A lifeless body lying there.

At the funeral, she'd tried to wake her dad up. He looked so good, just like himself asleep. She knew he wanted to wake up and be with her. They had a ritual. She came into her parents' bed in the morning and woke him up. He always laughed and gave her a hug and a kiss. Then he would smooth her hair and look deeply into her eyes and say, "Good morning, sunshine."

But at the funeral, her dad didn't wake up. He didn't hug and kiss her. He didn't call her sunshine. Instead, her mother started crying right in front of everybody. That was when Mom's bestie Lois took Mariah by the hand and led her into the next room. Mariah never forgot her words. "Your daddy can't wake up because he went to be with Jesus."

The explanation raised more questions than it provided answers. How could her daddy go to be with Jesus if he never even knew the man? As far as she knew, her father never went to church.

Mariah hurried down the sidewalk until it ended at the edge of town, and then jogged on the grass beside the road, covering the short distance to the entrance of the cemetery. Here, the wildflowers were mostly gone, but now brilliant red tulips surrounded the sign which announced The Village of Friendly Cemetery.

Why did Dad write me a letter? And why did Mom wait so long to tell me about it? Okay, so Dad wanted her to wait, but she still could've told me.

She knew her dad's grave was tucked into a corner at the back of yard, just before the small stream that meandered near the edge of the cemetery. Mariah jogged up the hill and then back down. As she spotted the grave, her pulse quickened. Suddenly, she felt a movement in her tummy. The baby? She touched her abdomen and felt something pushing from within.

On her arms, goosebumps formed as she wondered if her dad was present as well. She wondered if it was an omen. Maybe her child would be a boy and she could name him Joseph, after her father. The name signified dignity, history, and a sense of promise.

What would he say if he were here now? That question really intrigued her. She would soon find out if the message had made it through the years.

Sometimes, she couldn't remember him very well. She remembered him being sick. He'd told her to do good in school and make the family proud. He'd always hugged her. She never doubted his love. But her memory of him was fuzzy around the edges. She could hear him calling her sunshine, but fog obscured that sun in the corridors of their shared past.

She stopped in front of the grave and bent down to push the big planter aside. She frowned at the empty pot where nothing grew anymore. Her mother had quit tending it years ago when she took up with her stepfather. He didn't want her to pay tribute to her dead husband. Mariah could understand that in a way, but it wasn't fair. Mariah had been too young to tend the planter, but she'd visited her daddy's grave all by herself in those years. She could've been doing that more recently. She decided to get some seedlings from the greenhouse to honor her dad with flowers through the summer. Better yet, she could go back after work and plant some pansies and Easter lilies until later. Spruce it all up for Easter and plant the seedlings later.

She remembered the year after her daddy died when her mother had planted so many pretty flowers here. She could see their beauty in her mind's eye even now. Her love of nature came directly from her mom. *What did I get from Dad?* She guessed she was about to find out.

Digging for a buried treasure excited her. She wished Max was there, or her mother. It seemed she was always alone for the important things.

She stuck her shovel in the earth, pushing hard. The ground under the pot felt like rock. She could barely penetrate it. Fortunately, recent rains had softened the earth around the pot. Mariah changed her strategy, digging outside the circumference of the pot, and then slowly down toward the center.

Would the message even be legible? How would the paper hold up after being underground for over eight years? Her mom had said her dad did research to keep it safe. She imagined the metal box would help. She hoped his plan worked.

Once she removed the dirt from the perimeter, she started wedging the shovel in toward the center, hoping to strike gold, or whatever kind of box it would be. The ground continued to feel as hard as rock. She again wished Max were here or that she had some water to loosen the dirt. She chipped away slowly at the hard earth. She checked the time. Still an hour until she had to be at work. She could do this.

She summoned all her energy for a hard swipe into the center and suddenly, she felt the shovel hit not just dirt, but something hard. Bingo! She used the shovel gently now to clear away the dirt by the metal box. She stuck the shovel under the box and tried to loosen it. She laid it sideways to try to dislodge it. And, finally, it broke free.

Mariah dropped the shovel, knelt down and tugged on the little metal box. She pulled it out of the ground, cradling it in her hands. She could hardly believe it. A treasure box from her father, waiting for her all these years. She started to cry.

She debated whether to open it or wait until tomorrow. She hoped to visit Max tomorrow with leftovers from Easter dinner. Maybe she could open it with him, or, better yet, tomorrow morning with Mrs. Bee. She could open it as part of their Easter morning ritual. They liked to do Easter baskets together, buying each other little treats. Mrs. Bee hadn't gone shopping this year, because of the pandemic, but she'd given Mariah directions on what to buy. Waiting to open the box would give Mariah an awesome Easter surprise, a gift from her father.

She cradled the little box in her right hand, carrying the shovel in her left, and started back toward town. The box had a latch. Curious, she tugged and lifted it up, tempted to open it. Why not? But the shovel started to fall, and she pushed the latch back down, rearranging the shovel in her other hand.

No, after all these years, she could wait one more day. She tucked the little box into the spacious pocket of her jacket and jogged toward the diner. She resisted all through her shift.

At the end of her workday, Mariah hurried home to collect some garden tools and borrow Mrs. Bee's car to buy some flowers.

The store seemed like a twilight zone now. Normally, she liked shopping at the grocery and chatting with the other customers. Now she could barely recognize people and, because of COVID-19, she needed to maintain a safe distance. She searched quickly for an Easter lily for Mrs. Bee and another for her dad's grave, along with some pansies. She just wanted to get out of there. She felt much better when she removed her mask in the parking lot.

She stopped by the cemetery on the way home and planted the Easter lily in the center of the planter by her dad's grave. She filled in around it with purple, yellow, and white pansies. She smiled at her handiwork, glad to once again be honoring her dad.

42. MAX AND GABRIELLE

Saturday morning, Max looked wistfully out the window as he ate breakfast, wishing he could share with Gabrielle. As if called by his thought, she appeared, materializing out of nowhere, startling him. Okay. Right. His wife, the ghost, dropping in for her morning visit.

"Did I frighten you?" she asked with a smile.

"Yes," he said, somewhat indignantly. "Just think if the tables were turned. How would you feel, having a ghost pop up at your kitchen table for breakfast?"

"I know," Gabrielle said. "It's very strange, but nice to spend time together, don't you think?"

Max didn't answer. The more these breakfast meetings continued, the more he worried about his sanity. No denying she delivered great instructions, stuff he could not possibly know himself. But how could she be possible?

"We've got work to do, Max-a-Million," she said. "Easter is tomorrow, and with that comes visitors. Families will gather and people will come in from out of town. This is a dangerous time. So far, we've done well keeping the virus out of Friendly, but tomorrow will be a workday. Technically, we should quarantine all the visitors for fourteen days, but I know that won't go over very well."

"What do you recommend, then?" Max said. "We already have checkpoints screening newcomers. But mostly we rely on honesty and the temperature check. What if they're asymptomatic or pre-symptomatic, or if they don't tell us the truth?"

"Yes, that's a problem," Gabrielle admitted. "Maybe the best we can do is to track the visitors. We need to know who they are visiting and for how long, then follow up with tracing our residents. Most of these people will be gone before the end of the day. If they brought the virus in, that's what we need to be concerned about, right? So, ask those they visit to monitor themselves for symptoms and to quarantine for ten days."

"Okay, dear," Max replied. "They won't like that, but I guess it's manageable. They've been working around the clock anyway. With the churches closed, it's not like they will be in church tomorrow."

"Max, when are you going back?"

"I already did."

"Right. Christmas Eve. But really, Max, when are you going back?"

"It's hard, Gabby. Try losing your child and your spouse in one fatal sweep. Then tell me what you think about the great Almighty."

"But I know you believe, Max. The facts that you're sitting here, talking to me, and helping Friendly deal with the pandemic show that you have a big heart."

"How do they explain up there when bad things happen down here? Do you really understand it all now? What's it like on the other side, Gabby?"

"Oh, Max." Gabrielle tucked her long hair behind her ear and looked gently into his eyes.

Max felt confused, spooked, and downright sad. He waited for an answer, hoping for enlightenment. He needed something to hold onto in the darkness of these days.

"It's all good. Believe me. It's all good. Someday, you'll see. Someday, you'll be with me again."

"It's all good? How can you say that? It doesn't look so good to me," Max complained. "Can't you give me a little glimpse of the hereafter? Something to hang on to?"

But instead of unlocking the secrets of life on the other side, Gabrielle evaporated into thin air. Max bowed his head, completely exasperated. But before he could wallow too deeply in the angst of his current reality, the phone rang.

"Max?" the mayor said. "Are we ready for tomorrow?"

"Uh, yes. No. Um, I think we need to make a few adjustments," Max stammered. He slipped back into his false guru mode where he pretended to know it all, but was really following the orders of his dead wife. "We will have visitors coming in for Easter from out of town. Really, we also should track the ones that have come in since last Saturday. Sometimes people take the week as a vacation. We need to track who they visit. We can call the people they visit on Monday to ask them to quarantine and to let us know if they get symptoms. Tracking and quarantining our people should do the trick, okay?"

"Righto, boss. I'm on it. Thanks so much, Professor Wahlberg. What would I do without you?"

"So far, so good," Max said. "We're liable to see a case soon, being so close to Columbus. The Franklin County case numbers have been going through the roof. It's just a matter of time before the virus arrives here. We will be ready, sir."

"Yes," the mayor agreed. "I believe we will. Have a good day, son. Get out there and have some fun."

"Goodbye, sir." He wondered how in the hell could he have fun in the midst of this mess?

43. TROUBLE CONTINUES

All the way from California, he gunned his rental to the max whenever his fuzz detector let him know the coast was clear. Still, he found it surprising no one pulled him over. He felt like Mario Andretti speeding along. Every now and then, he put the pedal to the metal and made it up to a hundred, but then hovered between seventy-five and eighty-five the rest of the time. What he really enjoyed was traveling in the states that had eighty as the legal limit. Most of the roads he traveled were well below that. He played games with the cops all the way across Arizona into New Mexico, where he decided to stop after a good eleven hours on the road. He treated himself to take-out and pulled off at a roadside park until early in the morning, when he hit the road again.

He pulled into Oklahoma City in the mid-afternoon. Road-weary, he checked into a motel for the rest of the day and night. In the morning, he fueled up on coffee and donuts at a Dunkin Donut drive-thru and pushed on for thirteen hours to Indianapolis. Now in Indiana, he hit the sack early after a nice steak dinner. With only a skip and a jump to go to Friendly, with a little luck, he could get there in time for Easter worship. If the churches had been reopened. He liked to make good impressions and nothing like a Bible-beating service to get him motivated.

On Easter Sunday, as he neared Friendly, Howard slowed down to think. First, he wanted to peek in on Max and Buck. Social isolation played havoc with his sleuthing, but he looked forward to the challenge.

44. HAPPY EASTER

On Easter, Mariah woke before dawn, feeling downright happy. She slipped downstairs to play Easter bunny. She laughed aloud as she filled two baskets with bright colored plastic grass and hid Hershey chocolate and Reese's peanut butter eggs around in the grass. She retrieved the cascarones made the week before, placing six in both baskets. She'd learned how to make the confetti-filled eggs from a friend in high school. Instead of dyeing hard-boiled eggs, Mexicans dyed empty eggshells and filled them with confetti, topping them off by gluing on a circle of tissue paper. They made a mess when cracked over someone's head, but it sure was a lot of fun. She already planned to crack one on Buck when she dropped off an Easter dinner plate. If she could summon the courage to also take Max dinner, maybe she could break the ice by cracking one over his head as well.

If she could find the nerve.

Now she fingered the treasure box she'd dug out from beside her father's grave the day before. She placed it into her Easter basket. Soon, she would read the words her dad wrote to her on his death bed. It touched her heart to have this box.

Next, she placed her new earrings in the basket. Mrs. Bee had told Mariah to pick out the ones she liked. Butterflies, sunflowers, and daisies. To Mrs. Bee's basket, she added gloves. One set for gardening, one for washing dishes, and one just to keep her hands warm. Even in the summer, sometimes she complained all her fingers were cold, from poor circulation, probably. Mariah had also purchased them both tomato plants to plant in the backyard pots. She placed these near the baskets and then set citronella candles next to them. As the days warmed, they loved eating and hanging out on the deck in the evening. The candles would keep the mosquitoes at bay.

Finished with the baskets, Mariah went to prepare their breakfast.

She expected Mrs. Bee in the kitchen at exactly eight; like clockwork, that lady. Mariah still had an hour to herself. She decided to start off her Easter with a time of reflection in the greenhouse. She grabbed her journal and a pen, along with her cell phone, and slipped out the back door.

The lengthening days brought the sun up earlier, already warming the greenhouse. Mariah stopped inside the door and sat down on the plastic chair, tucking up her feet in a lotus position. She set her phone timer for fifteen minutes and let her eyes slightly close. In that way, she could still see the growing things without really concentrating on them.

It gave her a sense of awareness in the present moment. She absorbed green hues bathed in diffuse light. Breathing deeply, she inhaled the oxygen of the growing plants and showered them with carbon dioxide on her outbreath. Settling into a rhythm, she slowly inhaled and exhaled for a while and then let her breath settle into its natural flow.

Time hung suspended in the sacred silent space of growing things. Surrounded by the new life of the plants, she felt fully alive. She smiled, contemplating the new life growing within. The baby moved. She placed her hand on her stomach, feeling the bump ripple, like a small wave. She beamed love and light to the child while absorbing the miracles all around.

Just as she completely lost herself in contemplative silence, her timer chimed. Mariah stopped the alarm, picked up her pen and began to write. She wrote about the baby and Mrs. Bee. She wrote about the treasure box from her father. She wrote about Max and the possible visit today. She enjoyed the luxury of uninterrupted time to listen to her heart.

She expressed excitement, but also her fear. What did her dad write? What would Max say?

Mariah often wondered if people could follow along on the happenings down here on Earth after they died. She'd heard stories about people coming back after dying. They called it life after life. She bet her dad would love to come back today, if he could, to watch her read the letter.

Mrs. Bee didn't talk about it much, but every now and then, she heard from Reverend Bee. She explained it so matter-of-fact like, as if he just stopped by for a visit.

"You look beautiful," she told the tomato plants. "Coming along nicely," she said to the cucumbers. "We're taking you outside next week," she told the rows of lettuce and spinach.

Some people also said that plants could sense humans and listen. Mrs. Bee said she always talked to her plants, and it seemed to help — or at least it never hurt them.

"Happy Easter, all you beautiful growing ones," she exclaimed as she turned to leave.

Once back in the house, Mariah finished up breakfast preparation just as Mrs. Bee came down to eat. She cheerfully welcomed her. "Happy Easter, Mrs. Bee. Your breakfast awaits you."

"You're so kind, Mariah," Mrs. Bee replied. "I don't know what I'd do without you. Some days, these old bones don't want to move, but you keep me going. I love you and Happy Easter."

"Christós Anésti!" Mariah said, remembering the Easter that her high school friend took her a Greek Church for a long service the night before Easter. "That's what we said at my friend's Greek church on Easter," Mariah said and then translated, "Christ is risen, in Greek."

They quietly munched on breakfast together. Mariah enjoyed the tacos made with corn tortillas, eggs, and various delectable items. Mrs. Bee let Mariah know she liked them with sounds of approval.

When they finished, Mariah cleared the dishes and loaded them into the dishwasher while Mrs. Bee moved into the other room, taking up residence in her easy chair.

When Mariah entered the living room. Mrs. Bee said, "It looks like the Easter bunny visited last night."

Mariah acted like a surprised child. "Oh, my. I wonder what he brought. Let's take a look," she said with a smile.

She kneeled on the floor, lifting a tomato plant and candle. "Ah, a tomato plant for each of us. The Easter Bunny knows us well. And a citronella candle to keep the mosquitoes away on the deck. Perfect. Way to go, Easter Bunny!"

"Way to go, Mariah." Mrs. Bee chuckled.

Mariah delivered Mrs. Bee's basket to her lap, with the joy of a child on Christmas morning. She oohed and aahed as Mrs. Bee discovered the candies and the gloves. "Thank you, Easter Bunny," she said. "Thank you, Mariah."

Mariah looked surprised. "Me? What did I do?"

Mrs. Bee laughed again. "Okay. Open yours then, Mariah."

Mariah pulled chocolates out of her basket, opened a peanut butter egg and popped it in her mouth. "What's breakfast without dessert?" She took the earrings out individually, showing them to Mrs. Bee. "Thank you," she said after each one.

Then she stopped. "Mrs. Bee, I have one more thing to open. The box I dug up yesterday at my dad's grave. One last present from my dad."

Mrs. Bee said, "What a treasure! You told me you were going to dig it up. I forgot to ask about it last night."

"I wanted you to share this with me, on Easter." Mariah showed Mrs. Bee the metal box, with a raised rose design on the top. "I don't know if he made this or not."

"Oh, yes, I think so," Mrs. Bee said. "Your father made some things like this for Reverend Bee for the church. On the altar, we have a rendition of the Last Supper made in pewter. Your dad repaired that for us."

Mariah smiled. Now was the time. She moved the latch and opened the box. "So far, so good," she reported.

Red velvet lined the little box. Mariah ran her finger around the top of the soft cloth which felt fresh and new. On the velvet lay a piece of folded paper, about two inches wide. Mariah looked at Mrs. Bee, then she picked it up and placed it on the table, inspecting the box a little more. She carefully felt the red velvet on the bottom of the box and noticed some bumps. She realized there was a fold in the cloth and unfolded it to reveal another piece of paper and an arrowhead. She pulled them out of the box, feeling the cool black stone and cradling the smaller piece of folded paper.

"Go ahead, dear," Mrs. Bee said. "Open it up. Read it aloud if you want."

Mariah put the arrowhead on the coffee table and opened the little paper. There, in her father's distinct handwriting, she found a simple message.

"You, my dear, are Shawnee. My mother's mother was a full-blooded Shawnee woman. I spent much time with her as a child. She taught me that, as a Native Americans, we inherit their teachings of the Earth. 'All things are connected. Whatever befalls the earth befalls the children of the Earth.' – Chief Seattle of the Suqwamish and Duwamish tribes. 'In every deliberation, we must consider the impact on the seventh generation.' The Great Law of the Iroquois. Treasure these teachings. Encourage your family to live by this wisdom. I tried and failed. Perhaps you will succeed."

"Your father was a very wise man," Mrs. Bee said. "I remember him speaking about Native American philosophy."

"Yes, I do, too. He told me the stories of the Shawnee before I went to sleep. Wow, this is a legacy. Can I do what he failed?" She looked at Mrs. Bee, feeling honored and concerned at the same time. "Wow," she said again.

Then Mariah picked up the larger paper. She placed it on the coffee table and unfolded it gently, trying not to tear it. It opened into a sheet of notebook paper. She leaned over and began to read.

"My little buttercup, you are the apple of my eye, the smile in my morning coffee, and the best thing that ever happened to me. I am so sorry that I had to leave you before you were grown."

She stopped. "Wait," she said. "I'm going to take a picture of this so I have a copy. I don't want to lose this." She used her cellphone to snap the photo, then returned to reading.

"Someday, I hope you'll get to experience love of a child of your own. There's nothing quite like this experience. Having you come jump on the bed and wake me up in the morning has been one of my greatest joys. Thank you so much for the love you shared with me. I am so blessed to be your father.

"I want you to embrace love, Mariah, should it come to you. Live each moment fully. You never know when life may be taken. I was too busy trying to get myself established in business some days and didn't treasure the moments with you and your mother enough until it was too late. Don't let life pass you by, Mariah.

"And now, I want you to know there is another box waiting for you near the farm where I grew up in Mansfield, Ohio. This box, however, is not buried in the ground. It is kept by the law offices of Marley and Masters in their safe. It's a box that was passed to me from my father.

"Mariah, my father and I didn't speak in his later years. He never forgave me for leaving him to move south to marry your mother. I was afraid to look in that box when he died. His attorney contacted me several times and indicated that there was something good in that box, but I just couldn't go get it.

"Maybe it was embarrassment, guilt, or anger that he wouldn't accept my choices. I'm not quite sure. But we were estranged in life, and now in death. But you, buttercup, perhaps you can mend the fence between us.

"Go visit the attorney and open the box. Perhaps there will be something there to help you.

"Know that I will love you always,

"Your devoted father."

Tears streamed down Mariah's face. Mrs. Bee handed her a tissue.

"So sad, isn't it?" Mariah said. "He had regrets, didn't he?"

Mrs. Bee shook her head. "Mm hm, yes. Yes, he did. But I think he wants you to do things differently. Don't you think?"

"Yes. He wants to give me advice so I don't make the same mistake. That's nice. And I think he was a little too hard on himself."

"Yes, he was. Your father was a very kind man. He did work hard, but he also loved your mother with all his heart, and you, too, his little buttercup."

More tears streamed down Mariah's face. "This is so special. What a gem. Oh, my gosh. The words of my father. He wants me to live each moment fully. Do I, Mrs. Bee? Do I live fully?"

"Yes, I think you do, Mariah. I think you try very hard to live your best life. You do very well for all the challenges you've had to face." Mrs. Bee handed Mariah another tissue. "Here, dry those tears. Be proud of yourself, Mariah. Your father would be glad you're such a wonderful young woman."

"Okay," Mariah said. "But these are happy tears, tears of love for Daddy. I still miss him so much. He says there's another box. What do you think is in it, Mrs. Bee? From his father?"

"I couldn't even guess Mariah. You'll have to call the law office tomorrow and go up and find out. Sounds like you might have an inheritance."

"Or maybe an apology. Maybe his father wanted to say he was sorry before he died?"

"Or that. Hard to tell."

"I'm going to call Mom," Mariah said. "I need to love her while I can. I think Daddy would want me to do that, don't you?"

Mrs. Bee nodded but didn't say anything. Mariah thought she probably didn't think too highly of how her mother deserted Mariah, either. But forgiveness was important and she knew in her heart she needed to forgive, and that her mother would be so happy to hear what her father had written.

"I'm going up to my room to call her, then we can watch church together in a little while."

Mariah's mother answered on the first ring. "You okay, baby girl?"

Mariah grinned at her mother's caring voice. Was it the baby? Or was she always like that? "I'm fine, Mom. Happy Easter."

"Happy Easter to you, too, honey. Is Pastor Amy doing a service? I'd like to watch," her mother said.

"Yes, at ten. I'm singing. You know she has someone do special music each Sunday, recorded in advance. She recorded me earlier this week." There were a few blessings of the pandemic. It was cool that her mother could watch from Myrtle Beach. Pastor Amy kept asking them to look for the silver linings. That was one.

"Awesome. I can't wait."

"Mom, I got Dad's letter."

"Oh, honey, that's wonderful. I'm so glad. What did he say?"

Mariah pulled the letter out of her pocket and began to read.

"Oh, my gosh," her mother said.

Mariah could hear her mother sniffling. She stopped reading. "Get a tissue, Mom. I'll wait. This is deep." As she waited, Mariah considered what it must be like for her mom to hear from a dead husband after all these years. Had he written a letter to her as well? For the first time, she considered her mother's grief.

When her mom came back to the phone, Mariah asked, "Did you get a letter, too, Mom?"

"Oh, yes," she said. "He wrote me twelve letters and instructed me to open one each month the year after he died. Those letters saved me in the early days."

"Mom, did you know Dad's grandmother was Shawnee?"

"Yes. Your father was very proud of his Native American heritage. He often fought with his father over that through the years. His dad seemed to want to keep it under wraps, whereas your dad wanted to follow the Native American ways."

"That's cool," Mariah said. "I know he used to tell me stories about

144

Cyclone Woman, the thunderbirds, and the four winds, but I didn't know about his grandmother. Did he tell you about a treasure box in a safety deposit box in his hometown?"

"No, I don't remember that."

"Listen to this," Mariah said. She continued to read the letter explaining about the box at the law offices of Marley and Masters in Mansfield Ohio that he neglected to open after his father died, but which he encouraged Mariah to receive. Over the phone, she heard her mother sobbing. "Are you okay, Mom?"

"This just brings back so many memories, you know. Some good, some bad. Your father's separation from his family was sad. They didn't like me. It created a giant rift. His father tried to get your dad to come visit quite a few times. I know he felt bad. He even talked to me and asked me to convince your dad to forgive him. I tried, but your dad would have none of it. When his father died, the lawyer called once a week for two months, trying to get your dad to come read the Will."

"Why didn't you go, after Dad died? Maybe they could have helped you."

"I didn't think your dad wanted me to go. I didn't know if they would welcome me. It was too late. I wasn't part of their family. They barely knew me."

"Mom, then what do you think? Should I go?"

"By all means. Do you want me to come with you? Call the attorney's office in the morning and see if they're open. Make an appointment and I'll aim to come home and take you there."

"Oh, Mom, this is so cool to have this letter from Dad. I love it. This is the best Easter present ever. It's almost like he came back from the dead, like Jesus."

Her mother laughed. "Well, I'm not sure I'd go that far, but it is a wonderful thing. A good thing for your dad to do for you. Can you send me a copy?"

Mariah found the photo in her phone she snapped earlier and texted it to her mom. "Done. On its way."

"What?"

"I just texted a photo of the letter to you."

"Technology. I forget. Some things are so easy these days."

"Mom," Mariah said, "I gotta go. Mrs. Bee and I are watching church. It starts soon."

"Right. Thank you so much for sharing your dad's letter. It's a great Easter present for me, too. But watching you sing will be my best present ever. Talk to you later. Love you, Mariah."

"Love you, too, Mom."

45. MORNING RUN AND BREAKFAST WITH GABRIELLE AND ISABELLA

Max woke up before dawn on Easter. He remembered Gabrielle had always insisted on going to an Easter sunrise service. Now that he could sleep in as long as he wished, sleep eluded him.

No sunrise service for him. He'd greet the sun with a morning run. Connecting with the Earth with pounding feet and settling into a stride summoned his heart into the present moment. The fresh morning air energized his spirit and awakened him deep within.

His mom always told him you only got one life to live and so you better do it good. Of course, his Hindu friends begged to differ. They believed you kept coming back until you got it right. He didn't know which he preferred. One chance to reach for the stars, or multiple tries until you found your moon. Whichever, he knew he still had a long way to go, either in future lives or in this one right in front of his face.

He placed one foot in front of the other as he entered the Village of Friendly cemetery. Monuments to former lives cluttered the grass and a few daffodils bloomed, heralding spring.

He experienced freedom as the scenery flashed by, even as he knew that things would change soon. He sprinted down the road, leaving Friendly far behind. Eventually, he slowed to an easy jog. When his watch chimed, indicating his halfway mark, he pivoted and headed back home. Gabrielle would be waiting, and that was something.

A half hour later, Max stopped in front of his cabin and pulled open the door, looking inside to find Gabrielle sprawled out on the couch, Isabella right on top of her. Max did a second take. "Pumpkin?" he called. The little girl jumped up and ran all the way to the door.

"Daddy," she yelled, jumping into his arms. He enfolded her in a big hug, lifting her high and circling around as she giggled.

Then he stopped and looked past Isabella to her mother. "An Easter surprise?"

"He is risen," Gabrielle said. "So are we."

Max's heart stopped. They were risen? He felt Isabella's warmth and it felt so good to hold his little girl again. He looked down at her, kissing her curly locks. "I miss you, baby," he murmured into her ear. His heart flip-flopped between joy and confusion.

"Oh, Daddy," Isabella said, "it's so good to see you. Don't worry about us. We're okay. Mama says it's you we need to worry about."

Isabella looked at her mother, who held up her index finger in front of her lips and made a "Shhh" sound.

"Happy Easter, Daddy," Isabella said. Then she climbed down from his arms. "Mommy said we came to work," she said with all the authority of a stern task master.

Again, Max looked at Gabrielle, who shrugged her shoulders and agreed. "She's right."

Max needed a shower, but he didn't want to risk Bella leaving, so he turned on the coffee maker, grabbed a bagel, pulled some cream cheese and an orange out of the refrigerator. Then he sat down at the table. "Do either of you want to share my breakfast?" he asked, even though he knew Gabrielle had always turned him down in the past.

"We're not like that anymore, Daddy. We don't need food, right, Mommy?" Isabella explained.

Okay, risen in a spiritual sense, but not alive in the here and now. Right. Sure. What? As Max's thoughts turned somersaults in his head, Gabrielle and Isabella continued without a pause.

"Right, dear," Gabrielle agreed. "You go ahead, Max. I know you're hungry after that run."

Max took a bite, then announced, "Okay, Isabella, I'm reporting for work. Are you going to join me?"

"You bet," she said, and ran over, climb up into a chair next to him. Her mother sauntered over more slowly.

"What are my orders today?" he asked Gabrielle.

"No Happy Easter?"

Max smiled. He got to his feet and went around behind Gabrielle. "Happy Easter," he said dutifully, then touched her chin, turning it to the side to meet his face and closed in for a full mouth kiss.

After a long, welcoming kiss, she said, "Happy Easter, Max. I love you."

He paused, looking into her familiar blue eyes. "I love you, too, Brie."

"Hey, don't I get one?" Isabella interrupted.

Max laughed. "Sure, sugar. How could I ever forget my beautiful Bella Babe?"

Isabella pointed to her cheek. Max placed his lips firmly on the selected site and made a noise to make her giggle as he laid a smacker on her.

"Love you too, pumpkin," he whispered as a tear ran down his cheek.

"Love you, Daddy," Bella replied.

"If I'd known you were coming, I would have told the Easter Bunny and hidden some eggs for you to find," Max said.

"It's okay, Daddy. Mommy said we're here to work," Bella replied. "Let's get down to business."

This time, Max just looked at Gabrielle and laughed out loud. "Yes, ma'am. What's our business, Bella?"

Gabrielle's eyes clouded over. Max sensed trouble, recognizing that expression on her face. "What is it?" he asked.

"COVID-19 has arrived in Friendly. Time to take action."

"How do you know?"

She looked up, then explained gently, "I just do. Consider it an early news break. Remember Farm Fresh, that fruit and vegetable packing company in the next county? Several people who work there tested positive. Juan Ramirez lives in Friendly, but works at Farm Fresh. He's positive."

Max rubbed his face with this his hands. "Oh, man," he said. "How sick?"

"That's the good thing. Juan is coughing a little, not too bad."

"What do we do?"

"Contact tracing and testing," Gabrielle said. "That's where we start. You know the drill. We've been talking about this."

"Yes, we're good to go. The mayor hired a contact tester last week. They know what to do. And we could quarantine them at the state park cabin, if they agree to go."

"They might not trust a government official enough to leave their house," Gabrielle cautioned.

"Well, then, we'll just take care of them at their house. We can deliver food." He paused. "This is about to get real hard, isn't it?"

Gabrielle didn't say anything for a while. Then she talked very slowly. "Max, the point is to keep the virus out of Friendly. I know that we haven't completely succeeded, but if we stay ahead of it, we can minimize risk."

The phone rang. Max picked it up, noticing it was the mayor. He turned on the speaker phone so Gabrielle could hear.

"We've got a hot one," the mayor reported.

"What do you mean, hot?"

"We've got a guy at the checkpoint with an elevated temp."

"How high?"

"One-o-one."

"Yup. That's a problem. Does he have any other symptoms?"

"He won't talk, but none observable," the mayor said. "He has Ohio plates. Says he's been traveling."

"Did they offer him a cabin at the state park?"

"Yes, and he actually seems excited about the idea," the mayor said.

Max looked at Gabrielle. She gave a thumbs up and then said, "Yes."

"You got company, Max?" the mayor said. "Am I interrupting something?"

Max laughed. Oh, man. No way was he going to answer that question. "Oh, yeah. It's okay, though. Carry on."

That made Gabrielle start laughing. Max put his hand over the phone, pointing toward the door. She settled down, but her quiet grin spread from ear to ear as Max suppressed a laugh himself.

"Should we put him up at the state park, then?" the mayor asked.

"Yes, by all means. And, Mayor, did you hear about positive test results at the Fresh Fruit plant? I believe at least one employee lives in Friendly. Better check on it. If he's positive, you could offer a cabin to his family, as well."

"Who? Do you know something I don't know?"

"Check out the Juan Ramirez family on the edge of town. You know who I'm talking about?"

"I can find out," the mayor assured him. "Now get back to whatever you were doing." He chuckled. "I apologize for interrupting you."

Max turned red as he hung up the phone. Gabrielle let out the giggles she was suppressing since Max threatened to kick her out.

"What's so funny, Mommy?" Isabella asked.

"Your father."

"Glad I can still make you laugh," Max quipped.

"Always." She kissed Max's cheek and took Isabella's hand. "Tomorrow, then?"

"Yes, tomorrow."

"See you, Daddy," Isabella said.

"Love you, pumpkin." Max blew a kiss as his two favorite ladies disappeared into thin air.

46. TROUBLE AT THE STATE PARK

Well, I'll be darned. Free accommodations at the State Park. Howard followed willingly as the sheriff's cruiser led the way. *I should be sitting pretty for a couple weeks. Quarantined with free grub and a whole house to myself. Could it get much better?*

Howard rubbed his neck. His throat burned and he felt exhausted. Long days behind the wheel had worn him out. He coughed. He knew he didn't have COVID, though, no chance. The fever might be connected with his sore throat. Maybe strep? He realized he needed a break.

A little bit of nature always helped a guy rest and relax at the end of the day. With his computer and hotspot handy, he could have a field day harassing the people on his list. Tracking Max and Buck would be a little harder. He needed to get permission for surveillance, but his supervisor was working on it. With the green light, he could access all the data to track them from afar.

Just out of town, they passed by a large lake and dam. The cruiser slowed, barely creeping along. So much for gunning it. Howard followed dutifully behind the car, beginning to worry about the terms of his stay. How closely would he be monitored? Could he leave the cabin? Maybe he'd agreed too quickly to this little arrangement. Sweet could turn sour quicker than a jackrabbit.

He knew he didn't have COVID-19. Hell, he protected himself like a beekeeper, all dressed up in that white suit to collect the honey. No way he planned to let that virus get into his body. Well, maybe he did buck the mask policy from time to time, but he knew he wasn't at risk. So maybe it didn't really matter if he quarantined or not, as long as he played the game. He wouldn't be infecting anybody, being squeaky clean himself. He rubbed his neck again, coughed, and took a drink from his water bottle. His throat burned as the liquid went down.

The sheriff pulled up to a cabin and a woman in a white shirt with a little emblem on it got out of the passenger side. Quite a looker, Howard noticed. He parked close by and the woman walked over and stood by his car.

Howard unbuckled his seat belt and scrambled out. "Good morning, ma'am," he greeted her. "How can I help you?" If they included her in the deal, this wouldn't be all bad.

She backed up. He counted. Six feet of separation. Right.

"Hello, Howard," she said. "I would shake your hand, but under the circumstances, that is not allowed. Welcome to Friendly. My name is Debbie Shore. I'm a public health worker with the local health district. I'll be your contact for the next two weeks. Any issues, call me. Got it?"

Howard smiled, but, secretly, he plotted his next move to get her into the sack. He could enjoy her beautiful body on company time.

"Sir?" she asked.

Howard shook himself. Had she asked a question? Had he missed something while messing with her in his mind? "Okay, sure," he replied. "Whatever you say."

The lady put on a mask and closed the distance between them. She handed him a paper and a mask and then quickly stepped away. "Could you please put on the mask, sir?"

Howard complied, although he didn't like it one bit.

"Here are our guidelines for the quarantine," she said. "Our goal is to protect our town from people coming in from regions with COVID-19. Because of your elevated temp, out of precaution, we are putting you up here for two weeks. What you get is free lodging and free food. What you must give in return is your commitment to keep to yourself, stay within walking distance of this cabin, and submit to daily health checks. I know you already agreed to this at the checkpoint, but now I'd like to ask you to sign this agreement before we proceed."

She stepped close again and handed him a clipboard with a red X where he was to sign. Normally, he didn't sign anything without reading, but today, he was too busy looking at the beautiful woman in front of him to take time for that. He hoped she'd visit the cabin. Would he dare make a move?

He signed the paper with flourish and handed it back. "Now can you show me to my palace?" he asked, laughing. Always needed to add a little humor.

She took a pair of keys from her pocket. "Here you go," she said, handing them over while turning her head as if he smelled bad or something. She stepped further away as soon as he took the keys. "It's fairly self-explanatory. If you have any questions, call me." She tore off a duplicate copy of the agreement he'd just signed and handed it to him. "My phone number is on this sheet. A local restaurant will bring you meals. We will also deliver a package of food each week, for snacks and in between."

"Sounds like you're taking care of me very well," he said. "Will you be coming each day to do the health checks?" He certainly hoped so.

"Sometimes," she said.

He thought she might be smiling under the mask, at least her eyes seemed very bright. It was hard to tell. But then she got back into the cruiser and it took off.

He realized she hadn't told him when the food would arrive. He wasted no time giving her a call. He could get used to this. It wasn't bad to have a beautiful woman always on call.

47. THE SERMON

Mariah and Mrs. Bee settled into the living room to watch the Easter service. Mariah reclined on the couch, while Mrs. Bee stretched out on the recliner.

"There are some advantages to the pandemic," Mariah exclaimed as she searched for the service with the remote.

"Yes, going to church in the comfort of our living room isn't all bad. In fact, it's mighty nice for an old lady like me," Mrs. Bee said.

The screen drew them in as they watched their friend Carl Forbriger playing a prelude of familiar Easter hymns on the organ with great finesse.

As the service progressed, Mariah got to her feet. An unquenchable thirst had become her companion in pregnancy. "Want anything from the kitchen?" she asked Mrs. Bee.

"Oh, no, dear. Thank you."

When she returned, Pastor Amy was standing front and center with a smile spreading across her face. She made announcements, then introduced special music to lead into the time of prayer. Mariah wondered who would be doing the special music, and then laughed as the video she'd recorded earlier in the week began on the screen.

Listening to her performance, her mind skipped back in time to that night she'd sung this very song in the sanctuary with Max. She could still remember him, answering her, blending his voice into hers. She put her hand on her stomach. She'd felt their connection that night, and, suddenly, she could also remember New Year's Eve in a way that had been blacked out before. She remembered his words. She remembered her own. She felt the love, the electricity exchanged between them.

The baby moved.

Their child had been conceived in love. She was sure. She smiled as she listened to the verse, "Just like every child needs to find a place." She thought, *my child will have a wonderful place in this world.*

"That's beautiful, Mariah," Mrs. Bee praised.

"Thanks," Mariah said. "I love that song."

The service continued, with prayers and scripture, but Mariah slipped away in daydreams swirling around Max and their brief times together. She decided she would definitely visit him later, and, if her courage served her well, she might even discuss New Year's Eve. She wondered if he'd admit his feelings and their connection. She knew now their rendezvous had been much more than a one-off sexual encounter. In her gut, she'd always suspected it, but until she'd remembered the actual encounter, she'd worried.

Pastor Amy interrupted her inner reverie. "We come to Easter today, in the midst of a pandemic, listening again to the words of our holy scripture. We come looking for hope. We hear again the familiar story on the third day, when all hope was gone, Jesus appeared to Mary Magdalene and the women at the tomb.

"We live in dark days. Many businesses have closed. Some of you in Friendly have lost your jobs. The virus seems to be raging out of control in many places. Although we have been fortunate in Friendly, we must keep up our guard now. These are trying times. We feel despair as Jesus' followers must have felt that day at the tomb.

"But Jesus once again brought good news, appearing to the women. He called Mary by name. He appeared to let her know he was not dead.

"The miracle of Easter is that love cannot be destroyed. That even though we are walking through the valley of the shadow of death, God is with us. And even though thousands are dying of the pandemic, there will be hope on the other side. The miracle of Easter is that, like Mary, each of us have a story to tell. Each of us are important. We must all seize the glory and use our unique gifts in service to the Most High.

"So I want to tell you today, don't give up.

"Beloveds, it's spring. Go outside and observe the flowers. Right now, the daffodils and tulips are in full bloom. But a couple months ago, those flowers were hidden in bulbs buried in our gardens. Hope is like that. It waits. It's patient. It knows that something is coming and it doesn't give up.

"During this time, I encourage you to listen more carefully. Take this pandemic time to cultivate your spiritual practices, friends. What bulbs are residing inside of you? What new thing will God do with you in your life?"

Mariah placed her hand on her bump, feeling the child growing within. Her baby was her bulb. She felt its presence with joy, her love child.

"During this time, we offer Centering Prayer virtually on Wednesday evenings, and we will also be starting up new virtual small groups, Circles of Hope. Know that you are not alone. Sign up by emailing or calling me if you would like to participate.

"Get outside, watch the flowers. Visit our church garden where the perennials will be blooming again soon. Let God lead you into hope for the future, for this day, for this very special moment."

"That's nice," Mariah said to Mrs. Bee. "That's real nice."

Mrs. Bee nodded and said, "Mm, hm. Real nice. I like listening to Pastor Amy. She's very different than Reverend Bee, but that's okay. Each pastor's got their own way."

Mariah absorbed the words, feeling a glow and excitement about being pregnant. Now she looked forward to visiting Max. The future looked bright.

Mariah closed her eyes, transporting herself to another time and place with Max where she'd felt safe in his arms. She placed both hands on her belly. She wanted her baby to feel that safe love, too.

Max and Gus made it to Buck's at noon for Easter dinner. Gus nuzzled Buck's dog, Rover, who barked and bared his teeth in greeting. Buck opened the door to let the two canine friends out to romp, while their human counterparts prepared for a feast. Buck had gone all out with a glazed ham, sweet potatoes, and coleslaw, topping it all off with a peach pie from the Wind Song Diner for dessert. And he'd dressed up in a spiffy white shirt and black tie and dress pants.

"What's the occasion?" Max asked. "All this for me?"

"It's Easter. Can't wear fancy clothes much these days. Nowhere to go during the pandemic. So I figured on a holiday, I might as well put on some good threads, listen to church, and make my own kind of ritual."

Max looked hard at his friend, surprised. "What's got into you, man?"

"Just turning over a new leaf, I guess," Buck said. "I left my dreams behind when Marcia died. Now, after many seasons of grief, I'm ready to get on with things. Our factory is opening, we got our research going on, and who knows, I may even make it back to teaching one of these days."

Max slapped Buck on the back. "Good for you," he said. "I'm not there yet, but I'm happy for you, Buck."

"Grief takes time, Max. You can't rush it. Have you read anything about grief? That might help."

"Really, no," Max said. As he admitted that, he realized he should be. Ever since he'd been a little boy, he'd liked to read about anything and everything. Google searches helped, but nothing could quite replace the power of a book. "Any you recommend?"

"Well, there's a fairly new one out called *Finding Meaning*. You've probably heard of Kubler-Ross and the five stages of grief?"

Max nodded.

"But this guy, David Kessler, adds a sixth stage which he calls 'Finding Meaning'. I think that's where I'm at. I really want to throw myself into our wind turbines full gusto. I think I'm going to be open to love again. I don't want to give up. There's an opening in my life to do something new, to make a difference. Did you listen to Pastor Amy's sermon today? I would recommend that. Go home. Listen to the recording on YouTube. Maybe she'll inspire you."

Max shrugged. "Okay, I'll listen. I haven't been too keen on going to church since Gabrielle and Isabella died. But I did go at Christmas and I know I need to get back. Just not ready to go whole hog."

"I just suggested watching one sermon," Buck said. "Just one. Now let's get busy on this dinner."

Max really enjoyed the home-cooked meal. "Thanks for cooking," he told Buck. "You're getting pretty good in your old age."

"I'm not all that old."

Max laughed. "Okay, okay. You've just got a few years on me there." Then he changed the subject. "So the President wanted everything to start opening up again today? The governors didn't agree."

"Maybe not," Buck said. "But you notice some of them are very careful not to disagree with the President."

"Right," Max said. "This president demands absolute loyalty. Have you listened to our governor's press conferences? You get the idea that he disagrees with the President. Often, he says the exact opposite thing about how to respond to COVID-19– but when he mentions the President, he talks as if they are friends. He'll say, 'I talked with him the other day.'"

"Crazy," Buck agreed. "If everything starts to open up again, what will happen?"

"The number of cases will go through the roof. You know I'm advising the mayor on this?"

"Yes, I heard about that. What makes you an expert?"

Max looked down at the floor. He took another bite of ham. "Great ham," he said. Then he took a bite of sweet potato. "Mm, good."

"Cat got your tongue?"

Max covered for himself. "Gabrielle was into this stuff. She wrote a master's thesis on it, from a public health perspective. I thought you knew about that."

"I asked you a question," Buck said. "How did you become an expert on COVID-19?"

"I just reread her paper. She laid it all out. The Center for Disease Control has the protocols for an outbreak like this. It's not rocket science. But when you have a President bent on 'draining the swamp,' as he calls it, reason gets thrown out the window. He defunded the pandemic response department after he took office. Now the country is ill-prepared to deal with an outbreak of this magnitude. Controlling the spread in a small town like Friendly isn't difficult, if you know what you're doing and are willing to follow the science."

"Science has become a dirty word these days, hasn't it?" Buck asked. "We're the villains. How did that happen?"

"Money, Buck. It's all about money. When the history books are written about our times, the truth will show how greed destroyed our nation. It's the common cause of the downfall of most civilizations throughout history. We just didn't think it would happen to us, did we?"

"It's not over until it's over, Max. I'm not ready to give up. There's November. There's a new day coming. We can work our way out of this. Why are we doing a wind project if we have no hope? Come on, it's Easter. Lighten up, man."

Max wanted to hope again, but the light seemed to be burning very dimly in the corridors of his mind. The current state of reality compounded his bleak feeling. Since he'd lost his wife and daughter, a generalized feeling of depression had clouded most of his thoughts. Now with the pandemic, economic shutdown, and rising death toll, the scenery of his life seemed even darker.

Max felt good about helping the mayor with the Friendly response to the pandemic, but the daily visits of the ghost of his dead wife were taking a toll. And now that his daughter visited, too, well, maybe he needed to see a shrink. He doubted teledoc, the new normal, would cut it though. Would Gabrielle stop dropping by if he got a good counselor or read a few books on how to navigate his grief? His bottom line question was whether or not she was no more than a figment of his imagination in his deranged and damaged psyche.

After eating, Max helped Buck clean up and did the dishes that needed hand washing as Buck loaded the dishwasher. Then he excused himself. "Thank you, Buck. Delicious food, good company, what more could a man want?"

"I can think of plenty of things." Buck laughed.

"Yes, well," Max said with a smile. "And then there's that."

49. THE VISITOR

After arriving home and deciding a nap was in order, Max slept soundly on the couch until he heard his dog barking and then the doorbell rang, startling him from his slumbers. He woke, feeling disoriented. Where was he and what was that noise? Before he could get up, he heard knocking.

"Max," a female voice called.

Certainly not Gabrielle, but familiar. He looked down at his boxers and went back to his room to pull on some jeans and a T-shirt. Gus barked again. He didn't remember letting him out.

"Anybody home?"

"I'm coming," Max yelled. "Just a minute." He paused in front of the mirror to comb his hair. Not every day a female visited the boonies. In fact, the last time a live woman had graced his place was New Year's Eve. Oh. Suddenly, he recognized the voice. Mariah.

Max hurried to open the front door, and his dog rushed in, waiting for a pat. Max gave him a cursory touch and ordered, "Sit."

Gus scurried to his bed, stepped in, then sat erect, looking at Max with mournful eyes. Max commanded, "Gus, lay down." The canine dropped horizontal but continued to make eyes at Max who shrugged and said, "Dogs." Then he smiled. "Good afternoon, Mariah. Do you want to come in?"

Mariah nodded. "Of course."

"Well, I wasn't sure with this pandemic going on and the baby and all. Do you want me to wear a mask?"

"Have you been out? I think we're safe. We don't have any cases in Friendly," she said.

"Um, that's not exactly true. We do have a case as of today, in fact."

"Oh, no. Who?"

"A family man who works at the fruit and vegetable factory in the next county. Juan Martinez. Do you know him?"

"I don't think so. How did he get it?"

"Probably at work," Max said.

"Oh," she said. "But we're still safe, right? You're working with the mayor?"

"I hope so, but we need to be careful. Well, come on in. Do you have something for me?" he asked, looking at the bag she held on her arm.

"Yes. I almost forgot why I came." She laughed. "Mrs. Bee and I want to share a plate of our Easter dinner with you."

"Well, thank you, Mariah. That's very kind."

Mariah handed the dinner to him, saying, "I thought you'd be starving. You know, batching it? But I just dropped a meal at Buck's on the way over and learned you two had your own feast already."

"Yes, men can cook too, you know," he said. "Buck's a regular gourmet and I'm not so bad myself when I put my mind to it." Conversation came easy with Mariah. He took the bag out of her hands. "But don't worry. I will thoroughly enjoy this home-cooked meal. Thank you for thinking of me."

Mariah smiled and Max returned the smile. Then she looked at him seriously. "Max, could we talk?"

Max's smile disappeared, not knowing what to expect. Part of him wanted her to stay forever, but on another level, he felt terrified at the prospect. He could hide behind the governor's orders, recommending social distancing, or he could break the silence between them and get real. He opted for the latter, being really tired of being alone. "Sure," he agreed. "Have a seat there on the couch and put your feet up. What do you want to talk about?"

"Us."

He needed a few moments to compose himself, so he plopped down beside her on the couch and looked at his dog. "Gus, come," he said. The dog walked over and placed his head right by Max's hand. "He knows what he wants," he told Mariah, "and he gets it." He complied by scratching the dog's head behind the ears. "Dogs have a way," he added. Bracing himself, he asked, "You want to talk about us?" He suspected she wanted answers. Their situation was a loaded topic and he couldn't even begin to know what he wanted to say. But sitting there with her feet up on his couch, Mariah looked like she belonged. He realized he could get used to having a woman around again very quickly.

"I'm sorry about New Year's Eve," he began. "I should have just taken you home."

"Max," she cut him off, "do you remember that night?"

"Yes. I remember every single minute of that night. Actually, I can't get it out of my mind."

Mariah smiled. "I remember, too," she said. "Today, during church. Pastor Amy was preaching and all of a sudden, it all came back. I thought I blacked out about it because something bad happened. But it was all good. There was something so strong between us. Max, I know you felt it, too. This baby of ours was conceived in love."

Max's mouth dropped. He hadn't been expecting that. Love? That was a pretty strong word. Was that what happened between them? Was that why he ran the other way? Was he scared? Not ready? Still grieving?

160

"Mariah," he said, fumbling for words. "Mariah ... I love your name." He continued to stall, not knowing what to say. His attraction for her pulled at him. Ever since he'd met her, she occupied a part of his thoughts. Gabrielle and Isabella were there, too. But Mariah was front and center. When she'd gotten mad at him at the lake, he hadn't known what to do. Now here she was, perhaps extending an olive branch, and he didn't want to say the wrong thing again and upset her. Max took Mariah's hand and traced a heart slowly in her palm.

"Maybe God wanted this," Mariah said.

"God did this?" Max couldn't keep the horror out of his voice.

Mariah started crying. Max grabbed some tissues off the coffee table and handed them to her. Guess he'd put his foot in his mouth there. He didn't want to argue, but he also didn't believe that God went around, causing people to make babies. He held himself completely responsible for his bad decision, although it had seemed perfectly wonderful at the time. After she dried her tears, he said, "What's wrong?"

"I don't think you want the baby. I think you think it's a mistake. But I don't feel that way. I love this baby and I believe it was conceived in love."

"Mariah," Max said. If there was one thing Max had learned during his marriage, it was how to comfort a crying woman. "Come here." Mariah scooted over a few inches and leaned into him. "It's going to be all right. You're right. There's a connection between us. I feel it, too." He wrapped his arms around her and pulled her close. "We will make it through this. I promise I'm going to love this baby, too."

Then he decided to come clean. "To be perfectly honest, I can't get you out of my mind, but I'm scared. You're an incredible woman. You've touched me deeply. You get under my skin with all of your little quirks and caring ways. But this is all so new to me. Adding a child into the mix as we're just getting acquainted will be difficult." And then he surprised himself as his own tears started to flow. He was embarrassed, unable to remember the last time he cried. Once he started, he couldn't stop.

Mariah wrapped both her arms around him and held him tight. "It's okay, Max," she said. "Everything's going to be okay. I can feel it in my bones."

"You can feel it in your bones?" he asked as he held her close. He chuckled, remembering Buck had said almost the very same thing earlier. "Buck's been listening to his bones, too. Your bones talk?"

"Oh, yes," she laughed. "My bones talk."

For a time, they sat there together, holding each other. The baby bump between them felt real good. Maybe just what he needed to motivate him to get up in the morning. The factory and the wind project only went so far. Mariah and the baby were right beside him in true color. Of course he would always love Gabrielle. Her visits delighted him, even if she was a ghost. But a live human woman would help much more. They'd already made a baby. He even thought he might love her, although he wasn't ready to say the words. Maybe he just needed to look forward and get on with his life.

"Well, then," Max said. "Let's agree you've got yourself some wise bones. I see what you're saying."

"Hey, Max, did you go to church today?"

"All the churches in Friendly are closed," Max said.

"Yes, but you know Pastor Amy conducts virtual church? She puts the video up at ten, but you can watch anytime on YouTube. She even has an online meditation group and they are setting up small groups called Circles of Hope."

"Okay," Max said. "Come to think of it, yes, Buck mentioned it. He said Pastor Amy had a good sermon today. Seemed to motivate him to turn over a new leaf."

"Exactly," Mariah said. "Could we listen to it? I'd like to hear it again and I think it might do you some good."

"You think I need to get religion?" Max asked. For the second time in one day, someone wanted him to go to church. Gabrielle would say it was a message from God. Oh man, that hound of heaven must be coming after him hard.

"It might help," Mariah said cautiously. "You've been through a lot. I know that can cause you to lose your religion. Trauma can also motivate you to draw closer to God. If you let down your guard, you might let a whole lotta light in, Max."

Max sighed and took a deep breath. He could almost hear Gabrielle cheering Mariah on from the other side, but this time, Gabrielle was not in the room. Mariah touched a chord very deep inside of him. That pain of loss did wrap around his soul and keep him in a perpetual state of anger. He knew he needed to let go of that anger. A few times, the veil started to be yanked away. But most of the time, the blackness of his despair kept any thought of God at arm's length.

"Whew, Mariah," Max responded. "That's deep. You get me."

"I know," Mariah said. "When you first ran away from me and the baby, I felt hurt. I've been angry with you ever since. But as I prayed about it, I started to realize what you must feel. I could feel it in my bones."

"Your bones again?" Max laughed. "I gotta get me some of these wise bones. Why don't mine talk to me?"

Mariah laughed, too. "Maybe they are talking and you're just not listening."

"Teach me. How does one listen to their bones?"

"Well," Mariah said. "First, you gotta be quiet. Then, you listen deep inside yourself and sometimes you hear exactly what you need. I think it's called intuition."

"Oh, okay," Max said. "A woman's intuition, that's what you're talking about?"

"Yes, but men have it, too. I think it's a matter of being open to hear the truth within. It's a stereotype that only women have intuition. If men listen, they can hear that inner wisdom, too."

"You're probably right. That's probably what Buck was talking about earlier. I'll make a point of listening more. It's really about trusting yourself, isn't it? I know I've been so damn confused since I lost Gabrielle and Isabella. Nothing made sense after all that."

Mariah comforted him. "You're doing okay. You've got me and soon the baby. You'll be okay, Max. Try to listen the next time you need some guidance. I bet your bones will speak loud and clear. Now, can we watch Pastor Amy?"

"Just a minute," Max stopped her. "There's something I want to do first."

He placed his hand on Mariah's cheek and turned her face gently toward his. When she gave him a go ahead with her cute little smile, his lips found hers and he kissed her with all the passion he could summon on a Sunday afternoon, because he did really care about this woman. She was carrying his child and now he knew they would be sharing a life together. He could feel it in his bones. Ah-ha! There it was already. And as he kissed her, he let his hands rove over her back, feeling her strong spine. Then he caressed her shoulders, feeling her bones so close to his, rediscovering home.

Later, Max remembered their conversation and smiled. He'd enjoyed Pastor Amy, but he'd enjoyed Mariah even more. How she made it from his living room couch, back into his bedroom, he couldn't be sure. Conversation and dinner, sharing the food she brought over. More kisses, more connections. They found an easy rhythm that surprised him. The day cemented her into his heart.

50. TUESDAY MORNING

Mariah woke up singing on the Tuesday after Easter. Spring called to her from outside her window. She placed her forehead on the screen, taking deep breaths of the fresh morning air while she listened to the birds singing and enjoyed the bright new green leaves covering the trees. She smiled, feeling joy deep inside like a waterfall in her heart. Finally, things seemed to be going her way. Life hadn't been kind to her in some ways, like losing her dad to death, then her mom to Myrtle Beach. But good things happened, too. Mrs. Bee had become her oasis and her mother came back. Now Max had shown up and gave her a baby to love. Things seemed to be looking up.

Mariah did worry about COVID-19, now that the virus had arrived in Friendly. Just two cases that they knew about, but it could spread. Max had explained how he was working with the mayor on social distancing protocol and contact tracing to limit its spread. Last night, he'd called before she went to bed and told her to be careful. She hated worrying that every customer at the diner could potentially be a threat to the baby. Most people wore masks when they came to pick up food, but not all. She decided to put up a sign saying masks were required. Maybe that would help. The drive-thru window should be open in another day.

Now that Max was on board to be a father and her partner, it would be easier. But, she realized, come to think about it, he hadn't mentioned marriage, or even living together. Maybe she needed to ask him, but didn't want to rush him. He needed time and he'd admitted he was scared. He had been through a lot.

She worried how Mrs. Bee would get along if she moved out to be with Max. Maybe Max could move here instead? Time would tell. There were many months to go until those decisions needed to be made. Mrs. Bee had already told her she would be welcome to stay with the baby. She'd always thought Mrs. Bee needed her, but did she need a baby and a man, too?

On Sunday night, when Mariah'd realized that she would spend the night with Max, she called Mrs. Bee to explain so she wouldn't worry. She knew Mrs. Bee didn't approve of sex before marriage, but she didn't give Mariah a hard time when they finally did catch up on Monday night at dinner. She knew that Mrs. Bee liked Max and thought they should get together. Perhaps that was old-fashioned, but Mariah was happy about it.

She replayed their conversation in her mind.

Mrs. Bee had inquired, "How's Max?"

"Good. He said we should talk every day. He's coming around."

"I knew he would. I told you he's a good man. You can't go wrong with him, Mariah."

"Yes, a very good man. I'm in love, Mrs. Bee."

"And does he love you back, Mariah?"

"Yes, I think so."

"The answer to my prayers, then," Mrs. Bee explained. "I think you two can do well together, but it won't be easy."

"I know, I know," Mariah said, "But with Max, I think it will be much easier than alone."

"I certainly hope so," Mrs. Bee said. "I do hope so." Then she'd gotten a faraway look in her eyes and Mariah didn't pry. Instead, she sat quietly as they ate. *Sometimes it's okay to just let life happen*, Mariah thought. *Let Mrs. Bee dwell in her own thoughts. Sometimes old people worry too much.*

Now, as they finished breakfast on Tuesday morning, Mariah announced, "I'm going to call the attorney's office now. Want to listen in?"

"No, you go ahead. Let me clean up the dishes. You go call and report back what you find out."

A woman answered on the first ring. "Law offices of Marley and Masters. How may I help you?"

"My name is Mariah Landtree. My father, Joseph Landtree, Junior, once lived in Mansfield, and so did his father, Joseph Landtree, Senior. I understand that when Senior died, he left a box for my dad with your law firm. My father never claimed the box and I didn't know about it until recently. My dad passed away twenty years ago, but I just received a letter from him that he wrote shortly before he died, telling me to contact your office. Do you still have the box?"

The secretary remained silent. Mariah began to worry. It was barely thirty seconds, but it seemed like a lifetime. "Are you there?" Mariah asked.

"Oh, I'm sorry," the woman replied. "I was just checking to see if Mr. Marley could take your call. I remember your grandfather very well. It was shortly after I started working here that he came in and made these arrangements with Mr. Marley. That was a long time ago."

"Wow," Mariah said. "You knew my grandfather? What was he like?"

"He was a very proper man. Very tall and kind. When he brought us the box, he knew he didn't have long in this world. He wanted to reconcile with your dad, but knew it was too late. He wanted to make up for the breach. But I should let Mr. Marley explain. You're lucky to catch Mr. Marley here. He's rather old himself, mostly retired now."

"Mabel," Mariah heard a male voice say, "I'll take that call now."

"Yes, sir," the secretary said. "I'll transfer her in."

Mariah heard some clicks and then the attorney's voice boomed, "Marley here. How can I help you?"

"My name is Mariah Landtree. I understand you have a box left here for my father, Joseph Landtree, Junior, by his father, Joseph Landtree, Senior." She repeated the story she'd told his secretary.

"Mariah, you say? A daughter of Junior Landtree? Let me see here. Let me get that file. I don't believe there was a daughter at the time. What is your birthdate?"

"October 7, 1995."

"Hm," Mr. Marley replied while rustling some papers. "Your father died in 2001, so I guess you're possible." He chuckled. "What is your mother's name?"

Mariah rattled off her mom's name and birthdate. She hoped he didn't ask for her grandfather's birthdate, because that was a piece of information she'd never been told. She'd also never thought that she might have to prove her identity. "Do you want my birth certificate?" she asked.

Marley laughed. "Well, yes, just to be careful, when you come in, young lady. I do have something here for you. I only wish your grandfather could be here to give it to you, but I do have a film of his Last Will and Testament that you can watch. It's a dinosaur, though, you know. Back then, we didn't have cell phones and all these modern contraptions. When would you like to come?"

"As soon as possible. My mother offered to come with me. She lives in South Carolina. We could come Friday. Would that work?"

Mr. Marley laughed again. "Bring me in on my day off," he grumbled.

"Oh, I'm sorry. I didn't know. I can come another day."

"No, I'm just teasing," Marley said. "I stay home most days now. Friday is no exception. Sure, I can come meet you Friday. Ten a.m.? Will that work?"

Mariah thought. She'd have to get someone to cover at the diner. "Could we make it four in the afternoon?" she asked. "I work over the noon hour, so that would give me time to close up and get over there. But I can get someone to cover for me if you need to meet at ten instead."

Marley laughed. "Oh, my, my schedule is rather open these days, you know. They want me to conduct my business on Zoom, but I much prefer in person. I'd rather wear a mask and social distance than talk on the computer. I can be here at four. But speaking of that, please do wear a mask. And besides, I need to give you the box."

166

"Yes," Mariah said. "Thank you so much. And, Mr. Marley?"

"Yes?" the old man said.

"Do you know what's in the box?"

"Let's wait until you have a chance to hear your grandfather explain. Then you'll understand."

"Okay, right," Mariah responded. "I will see you on Friday at four then, hopefully with my mother."

Mariah hung up and went to give the good news to Mrs. Bee. Then she called her mom. Fortunately, her mother could get off a few days off, and promised to arrive Thursday night after dinner. Mariah sang to herself as she started to dress for work, looking forward to Friday and the treasure from her grandfather.

51. STATE PARK QUARANTINE BLUES

On Tuesday, Howard woke from a fitful sleep and started coughing again. He needed to get out of bed, but his lungs ached. He felt like he was living on the North Pole, even under two blankets. Sunday night, he'd managed to slip out undetected, and even made it all the way to Max's home in the dark.

Damn dog had started barking just as he pedaled up to the house. He remembered the treat he packed in his bike bag that would make that canine calm down, if the house was unlocked. The big bone he tucked away for such emergencies came in right handy. He got off the bike, pushed open the door, and gave the dog the bone just in the nick of time. Worked like a charm. The dog settled down like a baby, giving Howard time to explore. He went into the living room quietly and even made it to the bathroom to relieve himself. No disturbance from the bedroom gave him courage to explore more.

Now, looking back, he saw the foolishness of his ways. COVID-19 must've affected him. Normally, he didn't take chances like that. Knowing the lay of the house might come in handy in the future, though, when he wanted to rough up Max and scare him a bit. But he knew better than to walk into a house with people sleeping in a bed. It was a good way to get himself shot. What was he thinking?

He remembered using his cellphone flashlight to guide his path. He'd started to cough near the bedroom and tried hard to hold his breath, walking quickly by, but not before he noticed two bodies in the bed. Max must be getting lucky.

The dog continued to chew on the bone, and even wagged its tail at Howard when he slipped out the front door. Howard climbed up on his bike and pedaled away. After putting some distance between him and Max's house, he'd turned on his electric motor, taken some swigs from his water bottle, and began to relax. Damn cough had almost got him busted.

His phone rang, before he could force himself out of bed. He grabbed it off the nightstand. "Howard here."

"Good morning, Howard," a cheerful voice responded. "How are you today?"

"Not so good," he muttered into the phone. "Not good at all." He started coughing as if to illustrate his point. He wished he were just play-acting for the health department official. Feigning illness was a whole helluva lot more fun than actually being sick.

"What symptoms are you having?"

"Well, you hear me coughing. I feel a little chilled and my lungs feel heavy."

"Any difficulty breathing?"

"Well, I'm talking, aren't I?" Howard snapped back. "I can breathe."

"But you said your lungs are heavy? Is that making your breathing difficult?"

"No, I don't think so."

"If you get worse now, I want you to call me," she said. "We have some rooms reserved in the hospital for COVID-19 patients."

"Oh, no. I'm not that sick," Howard said. "I don't need to go to the hospital." He didn't tell the lady, but that would be like going to prison as far as he was concerned.

"Could you take your temperature for me, sir?"

She asked so nicely. Howard remembered the easy looks of the woman who checked him in the other day, but he couldn't be sure if this was the same one.

"Sir?"

"Okay, just a minute. I'll be back." He put the phone down and went into the bathroom to find the digital thermometer they'd given him with his welcome pack. He stuck it in his mouth and waited. He knew Sunday, his temperature had been over a hundred, and wondered what it would be now. Geez, he was on fire.

Max moseyed on back to the bedroom and picked up the phone. "One-o-two point three," he told her.

"Take care of yourself," she answered. "We will be dropping off some meals for you today. If you need anything, just call. And stay put. We don't want you spreading this around."

"I ain't going nowhere," he said. True enough at this time. He felt like hell warmed over. He certainly wouldn't be taking any night rides anytime soon. He didn't mind having someone taking care of him for a change. In fact, he found it mighty nice. Being a motherless child had gotten old quick. Perhaps his COVID symptoms would stay with him for a while. He could take some pampering.

52. CHECKING IN

When Mariah arrived at the diner, she shifted into autopilot, turning on the lights, heating up the grill, getting the staples out of the refrigerator. She checked phone and email messages for the orders and went to work.

About midway through, she felt the baby kick and that, for some reason, reminded her of Max. She'd planned to call him from the diner.

He answered on a single ring. "Hello, darling," he said and started to cough.

"Max!" she said. "Are you all right?"

"I think so," he replied. "Just some sinus stuff going on, you know. Spring."

"You weren't coughing the other night," she reminded him.

"I know. But, you know, something new is opening up every day. It's nothing." He coughed again. "Let me get some water. I'll be right back."

That gave Mariah time to worry. Could Max have COVID-19? She'd thought they were safe here in Friendly. Two people already infected and Max? If Max got it, would she? She'd slept with him Sunday, woke up with him Monday. That would definitely put her at risk.

Max came back. "Did you hear someone coughing Sunday night?" he asked.

"No," she said, "But I also slept like a log. I don't think a chainsaw would have woken me up."

"Okay," Max said. "Forget that. How are you doing, Mariah? I want to see you, but I'm going to get a COVID-19 test and I'll wait. I don't want you to get this."

"It may be too late for that, Max."

"I know," he confirmed. "I'm sure I heard coughing Sunday night. I heard Gus barking, too. I just quite can't piece it together."

"I slept like a baby with my baby," Mariah said. "No, I didn't even know you got up. I didn't hear the barking."

"Okay," Max said. "Maybe I dreamed it." But that didn't explain the new bone that had shown up by Gus' dog bed that morning. Max knew he hadn't given him that bone.

"I had a good dream last night," Mariah said. "Want to hear it?"

"Sure," Max replied with a smile in his voice. "Did it include me?"

"Yes" Mariah laughed. "As a matter of fact, it did." Just then, the diner's phone rang. "Max, I've gotta get this. Probably an order."

"Okay, then. Call me when you're through. I want to hear about me in your dream."

Mariah flipped into work mode, but in her thoughts, she focused on Max and their baby and her happy dream that she hoped would come true.

53. FRIDAY MORNING FOR MAX

Max answered the phone in a fog early Friday morning. Checking the time, he realized he'd overslept. "Hello?" he croaked.

"Malcolm Fox here," came the reply.

"Good morning, sir," Max answered, wondering why the health commissioner was calling at the crack of dawn.

"Good news, Max. Your test was negative."

"Son of a gun. I guess I do have spring allergies."

"Get some over the counter stuff for that, and be safe," Malcom ordered. "And, Max, be careful. We need you."

Max got out of bed, continuing to cough, but glad to have a negative diagnosis. He decided to hop in the shower. Hot steam would soothe his sinuses. He wanted to phone Mariah, but he didn't feel comfortable calling this early. He finished his shower, perked some coffee and set up shop at the kitchen table to check emails and figure out what needed to be done with the business. With the factory up and running, soon they would be turning out the mini wind machines in bulk. They needed to get the marketing in gear.

As he sat down to eat, Gabrielle materialized at the table in front of him.

"Good morning," she said with a warm smile. "Glad you don't have COVID, honey."

"Ain't that the truth?" he shot back. "I worried when you told me to get tested, thinking you knew I had it. But really, you didn't know?"

"I'm just a ghost, Max, not God."

"Oh. So just where do you fit in the hierarchy then?"

"It's not that way, Max. You wouldn't understand, but someday, you'll see."

"But, hey, can't you give me a little preview, honey?"

"That's not why I'm here, Max," Gabrielle said. "Let's get to work."

"Okay, boss. What do you want me to do now?"

"Teach them how to prevent the spread of the virus. Get the message out that masks and social distancing will do the trick."

"You want me to speak to them? I am so not the evening news guy."

"Max, I know, I know. But ask the mayor and health commissioner to spread the news. Currently, people are getting mixed messages about precautions."

"Tell me about it. The President refused to wear a mask."

"Well, yes," Gabrielle said. "But he gets tested continually."

"But people listen to him. When he doesn't wear a mask, when he makes fun of people who do wear masks—"

"Max, stop. We agree the President doesn't set a good example. That's why, here in Friendly, it's so important to get those in charge to counter his message. If they hear it three times a day on the President's news channels, they need to hear it more from local people. You've really got to talk this one up."

"It's a hard sell, you know," Max said. "Ohio voted him in."

"Max," Gabrielle said, "I believe in you. You can do this."

"Right," Max said sarcastically as he finished his eggs. When he looked up, she was gone.

Max sighed. Every morning, Gabrielle showed up. Every morning, his life seemed normal and bizarre at the same time. Having Gabrielle at the table plopped him back down into the comfortable reality of yesteryear. But he wondered what Mariah would think if she knew about his breakfast meetings with his dead wife.

Pushing the thought away, Max got busy. He called the commissioner back, talked to him, and then rang the mayor.

The mayor wanted to give him a hard time. "You can't argue with the President," he said. "He doesn't like that."

"This is not about the President, Mayor," Max said. "Don't make it about him. We must keep Friendly safe. We need every man, woman, and child to take this virus seriously."

"That's a hard sell. People think it's fake news."

"Mayor, the people respect you. Be a leader. Follow our governor. You got this."

"Okay, okay."

Max was fairly certain the mayor watched the channel he referred to as Faux News. As pandemic days continued to wreak havoc, Max also knew they—with the President's sound bites—would downplay the threat, minimize the problem, and deny the necessity of masks.

Politicians were complicated beings. How the mayor could laugh about the President one day, then say you can't go against him the next baffled Max. The mayor supported his work with Buck on the factory, too. Maybe it was only because they were becoming entrepreneurs and he saw potential economic benefit to the town. Either way, the man had agreed to get the word out, and that was the important thing.

Max poured another cup of coffee and walked outside, seeking solace with the light of day. But the wind stirred the remaining leaves of autumn, lifting them up and swirling them about. Dark clouds moved across the sun and a storm manifested. Raindrops began falling while Max stood, immobilized. A shadow loomed not only across the landscape, but his entire life.

He stepped back toward the house and noticed a piece of paper sticking out of the mailbox on the porch. He had a bad feeling as he pulled the paper out of the box to read. The words jumped out at him like a flaming fire.

Max didn't want to believe it. He pinched himself to make sure he wasn't dreaming. Then he started pacing around his little cottage. The wind continued to blow and thunder cracked outside. As he reread the message slowly, the venom spread its poison deep into his psyche, reopening a wound of his life as yet unhealed.

I TOLD YOU ONCE, TWICE AND THIS IS YOUR THIRD WARNING. BUT YOU DIDN'T LISTEN. NOW YOU'VE GONE AND OPENED A WIND TURBINE FACTORY. CEASE AND DESIST OR YOU'LL BE SORRY. I'M WATCHING YOU. I KNOW YOU HAVE A NEW WOMAN FRIEND. YOU WOULDN'T WANT ANYTHING TO HAPPEN TO HER, WOULD YOU? GET WITH THE PROGRAM, MAX. THERE'S NOTHING WRONG WITH FOSSIL FUELS. YOU'RE WRONG. WISE UP, OR YOU'LL BE SORRY.

Max knew he needed help. He couldn't face this alone, but he couldn't put Mariah in danger. Maybe Gabrielle would know what to do, but there was no knowing when she would materialize again, so he called Buck and invited himself over. Then he searched for the church number online and dialed Pastor Amy, figuring there was nothing like a little foxhole religion. Somehow, he would find a way, but for now, the lightning brought only momentary relief from the darkness.

54. HOWARDLY INSANITY

In the state park cabin, Howard's condition worsened by the hour, but before emailing his boss man to secure his next paycheck, he had to earn his keep. He actually enjoyed writing threats and posting them on social media. Perhaps it brought him pleasure because he could imagine the recipient squirming. And, always, the underlying mission was his patriotic chore. He'd patted himself on the back many a day as he worked to shore up the USA and the fossil fuel industry. He congratulated himself that he'd helped the whole country move full steam ahead. Roughing up the climate scientists and alternative energy leaders came with the territory.

Howard opened his climate scientist spreadsheet on his laptop and slowly made his way down the list. His posts from eight different Facebook accounts kept them guessing. And at the beginning of each month, he started new accounts. For the little lady down in Texas, he posted an article by their PR firm that proved the climate always changed itself up. Quack! Quack! Read the truth here. Climate Change is Fake News, he wrote. He used the same article a couple more times as he posted on the others' pages. Then he posted some weather forecasts, showing snow in April on some of his other assignments. "Global Warming? Seriously?" he commented along with the forecast. His goal was to create a modicum of doubt in the mind of the readers. He didn't have to do much to get that question mark well-placed. He repeated the posts on their Twitter accounts for good measure.

Thinking now about his little visit to Max's countryside retreat, he considered the note he'd dropped in the front porch mailbox. That foray had also yielded helpful knowledge about the layout of the cottage and the existence of the lady friend. A threat to a girlfriend would definitely be effective at messing with Max's mind after what had happened to his wife and daughter.

He knew Max suspected foul play in the car accident. There, Max was wrong, but it was great fodder for playing on his fears since he believed that Isabella and Gabrielle had been intentionally killed. Let Max think that Howard would come after his girlfriend. It could be just what it would take to scare him off.

Howard planted a few more flaming comments online, laying one on Buck and some folks he trolled in California, until he started to cough again. He popped a eucalyptus cough drop into his mouth, but that only worked for a minute before his cough erupted again. Coughing wore him out. He already felt tired and heavy. He pushed himself to finish his email to his boss, explaining how he was risking life and limb in service to the public relations firm. He included information about his fever and his cough and the fact that he believed he became infected on the job. Nothing wrong with making the boss squirm a little, as well. Despite what the President kept saying, Howard knew the science. The writing was on the wall.

His day's work done, Howard returned to bed. The moment his head hit the pillow, he started coughing again. Not only did he have a fever, a sore throat, and this damn cough, but his lungs felt heavy. Maybe he should call the nurse, but what could she do? COVID-19 had no cure. A vaccine might not come for another year. He'd better just hunker down and wait the crap out.

He dozed off, sleeping fitfully until his phone rang. He reached for it, fumbling to answer. "Howard here," he choked out, caught off guard.

"Did I interrupt something?" the nurse asked. "I'm sorry."

"No, no," Howard said. "What's up?"

"I'd like to bring our physician's assistant to check on you today," she said.

"Could that wait until tomorrow? I'm fine, just tired. I need to rest," Howard said.

"Okay," she agreed. "First thing, then. We will arrive at eight thirty sharp. Be ready. Good-bye, Howard."

Howard turned on the TV for company. The newsman prattled on about tornado warnings for southwestern Ohio. Howard wasn't able to focus on any of it. Instead, he found a bottle of sleeping pills, deciding to take a long nap and wake up with—if he was lucky—the virus and storm far behind.

55. FACING FUTURE

Mariah snuggled in her blanket, stealing a few more minutes in the warm, cozy bed, before launching out into her big day. The day would start per usual, breakfast, then working at the diner, but she planned to close up early. Her mother had promised to arrive at noon. Together, they would drive to Mansfield to visit her grandfather's attorney. She was excited, but also sad, thinking about the estrangement between father and son.

Life could be tough. Grief is hard. It can turn life upside down and inside out in the blink of an eye and cause people to go crazy. Those were the first lessons she'd learned with her father's death. But she'd also discovered the importance of appreciating the little things and finding joy in each moment.

Her mother taught her the first lesson that year her father died. Mariah wailed. Her mother cried softly, sometimes whimpering as she cooked. Some days, she just moaned in the upholstered rocker, going through a box of tissues in an afternoon.

Mariah had tried to comfort her mom. She'd repeated what her mother told her when she skinned a knee. "It will get better, Mommy. It hurts now, but you'll be brand new tomorrow."

But her mother didn't get better. Autumn passed. Leaves fell. The beauty faded into winter days of gray and her mom still cried. After a while, Mariah gave up trying to help her. Especially when she started going out at night. She left Mariah with the next-door neighbor, Mrs. Merkt.

Mariah liked being in a place where people still laughed. Mrs. Merkt talked to Mariah all the time and Mariah found it easy to talk back. She could tell Mrs. Merkt anything. She explained about her mother's endless sobbing and the kind older woman seemed to understand.

Mrs. Merkt also taught Mariah a most valuable lesson on a spring day that had never faded from her memory. Wildflowers had popped up overnight and bluebirds sang. In her yard, Mrs. Merkt pointed out signs of spring and told Mariah, "Just when it seems like all is dead, God sends little miracles, breaking through the ground. See that flower? Here and there. See those new leaves springing up? Mariah, look for little flowers in each day. That makes all the difference."

Mariah had watched carefully for all the spring flowers as they bloomed that year. Her appreciation for nature blossomed. But Mrs. Merkt meant something more about looking for the miracles, and Mariah learned to do that also.

Mrs. Merkt had taught her to look for miracles. A smile from a friend, a chocolate chip cookie, the warmth of the sun, reading something new in a book. She taught to always look for the rainbows in a storm. Mariah decided she wanted to grow up to be just like Mrs. Merkt.

And Mariah did. She made a habit of finding rainbows. She discovered them in nature most days. The simple act of taking a walk made her feel better. She found the goodness of people in her life. She thanked God for Mrs. Bee. Getting pregnant like she had could have been a major problem, but she could see blessings coming. And she really liked Max.

She'd often been accused of wearing rose-colored glasses. Maybe so. But ever since she'd watched her mom's life fall apart and ever since Mrs. Merkt taught her to look for the rainbows, Mariah had chosen happiness even in the midst of bad things happening around her.

Today, she prayed for some new rainbows in her life. She would unlock the mystery of her father's treasure, a gift from her grandfather. Perhaps she would even meet some cousins she'd never known she had. She might have a big family after all, and that would be wonderful.

Max hightailed it to Buck's. He knocked and called, "Buck?"

"Door's always open, Max. Coffee's on." Buck poured a cup of coffee for Max and placed it on the kitchen table. "What's up?"

Max pulled the wrinkled paper out of his pocket and shoved it on the table in front of Buck. "This." He frowned.

Buck picked up the piece of paper and read the message from the troll. "Oh, no, he's back?" Max could hear the fear in his voice.

"Appears so. What do I do now?" Max dumped the problem on his friend, hoping for answers.

"What do *we* do now?" Buck corrected. "He's after me, too."

Much to his discomfort, Buck insisted that before they discussed it further, they pray. Max protested, but his friend wouldn't be swayed, so he closed his eyes and pretended.

"Okay," he said, when Buck finally concluded his prayer, "What does God think? Should we run? How can I protect Mariah and the baby? What am I going to do?"

Buck responded thoughtfully. "I believe he's just trying to scare us, but we need to take it seriously, of course. We both have reason to think otherwise."

"Right," Max agreed. "I called Pastor Amy. I'm talking to her this afternoon."

"Good," Buck said. "Let me know what you two decide. That's good, Max. We can't face this alone. Do you want me to go with you to see her?"

"No, but I'm glad you're in my camp, Buck." Max paused. As much as it bothered him when Buck started to pray, he himself had already called Pastor Amy. "Maybe I'm about to get me some foxhole religion. What else can I do at this point?" Max took a few sips of his coffee and stared out the window.

"We'll get through this together. You talk to Pastor Amy and then come back and we'll figure out how we can handle this. Come back for dinner and we can hash it out?"

"Sure, Buck. Thank you. I better be going now. You be careful now. I'll be back at six?"

"Yep, six sounds good. I'll make you some of that Indian food you like so much. Cooking will give me something to do so I can think about this, too. See you soon."

Max returned home, grabbed a snack and opened his laptop in the easy chair. He appreciated that Pastor Amy offered him a Zoom counseling slot at one p.m. when he'd called. She'd explained she kept time open each day for pastoral counseling. People were scared, confused, and lonely, more so due to the pandemic. She believed listening was her call.

He pushed back on the recliner, propped his feet up, and cradled his computer in his lap. He clicked on the Zoom link a few minutes early. So many emotions swirled around inside his head that he couldn't think straight. One thing he knew for sure: he would not put Mariah and the baby at risk. If that meant leaving town, closing the factory, or moving to Timbuktu, so be it. He would not live through the nightmare of losing his wife and child again.

Pastor Amy appeared right at one. "Hello, Max," she began. "Could I start with a little prayer?"

"Sure," Max replied. First, Buck, now Pastor Amy. It was a bit much, except for the fact that Max admitted he wouldn't mind some divine intervention at this point. *Bring it on*, he thought.

"Dear God," she said, "bless this time together. Open our hearts to hear what's happening with Max today. Surround us with your love and clarity of vision to face this situation with wisdom and charity. We pray in the name of Jesus, Amen."

Max suddenly relaxed. The tension building in him since he'd opened the note started to subside.

Pastor Amy asked, "Where are you now? What brings you here today, Max?"

Max sucked in his breath. Good question. Somehow, he thought the pastor would help him resolve his dilemma, figure out a way to protect Mariah and the baby. He realized that might be too much to ask. "I don't know where to start," he said.

"Tell me what is important. You don't have to tell me your life story, just what you think I need to know to understand your situation this afternoon."

"Okay," Max said. "Okay. Let's see. I had a happy childhood, not too far down the road. I excelled in school, married my college sweetheart, and we had a little girl. I finished my Ph.D. the year Isabella was born. My wife, Gabrielle, worked as a public health administrator at the time. Me, I'm a wind scientist. Worked with Buck, actually, at Ohio State. We taught, did research together. Just recently, we opened a wind turbine factory."

"I didn't know all of this, Max," Amy said. "You've had quite a life."

"Past tense," Max noted. "Everything sparkled. Great job, great wife, adorable kid. I thought I had it all."

"And then?"

"And then Gabrielle ran the car off the road in a big storm, and high

180

water carried the car into a nearby river. By the time the car was recovered, Gabrielle and Isabella were dead. They tried to revive them, but it was too late."

"Oh, Max, that's terrible."

Max started to cry. "I lost everything. I plunged from the top of the mountain to the bottom of the valley, just like that. I managed to finish the semester, but I couldn't return to teaching. Ohio State granted me a leave of absence. Then Buck offered a place to land here in Friendly. Everything changed in the blink of an eye." Max stopped. What had made him spill his guts? He'd meant to just get some advice about what to do about the troll and Mariah.

"Grief consumes us and takes time. You've been through hell. I'm so sorry, Max. That's really hard. Loneliness, the anger, angst. How are you doing now?"

"Actually, I've been coming around. I've developed a place for myself here. Buck helped a lot." Max reflected. "You know he lost his wife, too?"

"Yes," Pastor Amy said. "You two have a lot in common, don't you?"

"Yeah. I honestly don't know what I would have done without Buck."

"Sometimes, God gives us help when we need it, don't you think?"

Sure, Max appreciated Buck, but a gift from God? "God was the last thing on my mind when I came here," he reported. "You think God sent me Buck?" He chuckled. "I've been touched by an angel?" What would Buck say about that?

"Maybe so," Pastor Amy said. "The Spirit moves in our lives more than we often realize. I know the grief is hard, but God is with you, loving you through the people in your life, helping you to come out on the other side." Pastor Amy gave him a moment to digest that, then asked, "Where are you now? What brings you here today, Max?"

He'd hoped the pastor would help him resolve his dilemma, figure out a way to protect Mariah and the baby. "I don't know where to start," he said.

"Take your time," Pastor Amy said. "There's no hurry."

She let the silence sit between them. Max looked around the room, searching for words, for how to begin. Should he tell her about Isabella, the ghost, showing up each morning? Or about Mariah and the baby? Or should he just tell her about the precipitating event that once again had his world standing on end? He decided to bite the bullet and spill it out.

"The first day I arrived in Friendly, I stopped by the diner for lunch and met Mariah. We connected. From the first moment, I felt something there. Do you believe in love at first sight? I enjoy her, always have. In the dark tunnel of my life, she brought some bright light. Almost blinded me, you know? I didn't plan on another woman. Probably I'm not ready for it. But we sang together, in your church, one night. I couldn't get her out of my mind. I still can't.

"I'm a wind scientist. We study the climate. It may be hard to believe, but the fossil fuel industry hires public relation firms to convince the American people that we don't actually have a climate problem. They spend millions of dollars on this effort. They've been very successful. Not only that, but they bankroll our government, and finance political campaigns.

"It's a sinister operation, really. They focus not only the federal government, but also the state governments. Did you ever wonder why the Ohio Legislature is rolling back the alternative energy incentives established in recent years? Money controls what happens.

"Part of their operation includes roughing up climate scientists, folks like me. Every single climate scientist that's gone public has gotten death threats. They pay trolls to frighten us. We don't back down, but still, it's a scary way to live.

"I don't know if the deaths of Gabrielle and Isabella were accidental. Buck's a climate scientist, too, and he's not sure about the deaths of his family, either. In different times, we'd call in the FBI to investigate. But when the fossil fuel industry's in bed with our government leaders, any investigation would be tainted."

Pastor Amy interrupted. "Wow, Max. That's a heavy burden to carry. That's very scary."

"Yes, and part of me wants to believe it's not true. But there's another part of me that feels haunted and hunted. And just when I thought things were looking up, he's back. It's not the first time. Did you hear about it?"

Pastor Amy stayed quiet. Her eyebrows lifted, but she didn't respond.

"No, I guess you wouldn't know," Max realized. "We kept it quiet, but maybe you heard about the bomb scare, and the guy with the gun who came to Buck's tavern last fall?"

Amy nodded.

"It was him, the troll. They arrested him, booked him to jail. But he got out on a technicality of some sort. Rigged, I'm sure," Max said. "The good thing was he hightailed it out of town and disappeared. But I couldn't take any chances. I left Friendly myself. After things quieted down, Buck encouraged me to come back.

"I returned to Friendly after Christmas, after spending the holidays with my family. I even attended church for the first time since my wife died on Christmas Eve and it felt right. Maybe I'm healing. Once back in town, I couldn't miss Buck's New Year's Eve party at the pub, and there was Mariah again. The attraction is so strong between us. We ended up at my place, all night long. And now Mariah is pregnant, as you probably know."

Pastor Amy didn't deny or admit. Instead, she said, "How are you feeling about being a father again, Max?"

"Surprised, scared, not sure I'm ready. But, you know, Mariah and I are good. I'm beginning to think of our baby as a gift. Maybe it's just what I need right now."

"That sounds positive. Mariah is a gem. She has a heart of gold."

"Yes, I'm learning that. We moved too fast, but the attraction is strong. The feelings are unfolding, more and more each day."

"You sound happy about Mariah. Max, you sound really happy, after all you've been through. Are you finding new light in this relationship and the promise of family?"

"Yes, that part seems almost too good to be true. I lost everything, and now here comes a second chance. But that's not why I came to see you." Max frowned. "Can I share my screen with you? You probably need to give me permission."

Amy smiled. "Okay. I'm still learning Zoom, but that I can do. I'm getting more experienced with our worship services and groups."

"Nice job, by the way," Max said. "Buck raved about your Easter service, then Mariah invited me to watch with her on Easter afternoon. You're doing a good thing. You helped Buck turn over a new leaf. He's a hard nut to crack."

Amy smiled. "Thanks, that means a lot. It's not easy being a pastor right now, holding virtual church. It's a real learning curve, but I'm trying to do my best. We need God and each other now, more than ever. The church is the people in communion, not the building. Church transcends time and place."

"Right," Max agreed. "You got this." Then he shifted back to the topic at hand. "You need to give me permission to share my screen."

Pastor Amy said. "I did that already. You're good."

Max found the picture he'd taken of the note from the troll and it popped up on the screen.

Pastor Amy scanned it silently. "Oh, Max," she said. "I see why you're upset. Tell me more about your feelings and any options you've considered.

Max didn't know what to say. It felt good to share, but he wasn't sure what came next. He felt terrorized, immobilized, and unable to think or even consider what to do. "I just don't know anymore," he replied.

Pastor Amy nodded, and held the silence for Max to continue.

"I'm scared. I think they got me. But if I give in to the terror—and it is terror—they win. That's how terrorists operate. They win by scaring you enough to make you stop doing your work. Buck and I don't want that. Long ago, we agreed we wouldn't let them win."

"You don't want to give in, but you're scared," Amy reiterated.

"Right. If it was just me, I could stay and fight. But now, I have to worry about Mariah and the baby. What do I do?" Max turned it back on the pastor.

Pastor Amy replied, "It's a hard place to be, a hard decision." She tossed the ball back to him. "Have you considered all your options?"

"Well, first off, I can't leave. Our factory's up and running. Buck needs me. I should tell the sheriff. He knows all about the guy from the last incident when he had a gun. I still don't understand how he got away with that. This is a threat to my life, to Mariah and our unborn child. I need law enforcement."

"That sounds reasonable," Pastor Amy agreed.

"I don't want to put Mariah in jeopardy. I couldn't live with myself if she got hurt. I started coughing the other day, right after an evening with Mariah. I figured it was my allergies acting up with all the spring pollen in the air, but with this pandemic, every cough seems like it could be COVID-19, right? I got a test and kept my distance from Mariah. I found out this morning, I'm negative."

"That's a relief," Pastor Amy said.

"I thought, though, maybe I could tell Mariah I have the virus, and we need to keep our distance, so I wouldn't be seen with her, wherever this guy might be. That would keep her safe, don't you think?"

Pastor Amy looked at him.

"You don't like the idea."

"Well, it's up to you, Max. But why don't you just tell her the truth?"

"I don't want to scare her. That's not good for her or the baby."

"Mariah's stronger than you think. She's been through some rough times."

"I know she's strong, but I don't want her to worry."

"I don't recommend lying."

Max wanted to do the right thing and he wanted Mariah with him all the time now. But she'd be safer in town than out in the country, going back and forth to work each day. "Maybe you're right," Max admitted. "I can tell her the truth and ask her to stay in town to be safe."

"Are you going to talk to the sheriff?"

"Yes, I will," Max said. "I don't like this guy getting away with all of this. Social media trolling may be idle chatter, but a written threat is criminal business. I want him stopped. It's not just me, it's others, too, and it's plain wrong."

Pastor Amy nodded again. "Let's pray about it. Okay?"

Prayer again? But this time, Max realized he wanted her to pray, which surprised him.

"Remember, God is always there. We forget sometimes, but we don't have to carry these burdens alone," Pastor Amy said.

"Thank you, Pastor," Max said. "Thanks so much."

"You're welcome," Pastor Amy replied. "We can talk again if you'd like."

"I'll call you again, I'm sure," Max replied. "Now, you can get back to work and I'm off to see the sheriff."

57. HOWARD DECLINING

Howard tossed and turned all night, and just when he got back to sleep, he heard knocking on the door. *What the?* At first, he thought the noise came from a dream, but then, as it increased in intensity, he reconsidered. His cell phone rang. He picked it up.

"Howard? Are you home?" a voice asked. "We're outside. Remember, I said we were coming by to check you at eight thirty?"

"Oh, right," Howard said, trying to shake off the stupor of too much coughing and fever. "I overslept." He started coughing and couldn't talk.

"You need to come out to get checked," the nurse said.

When the coughs subsided, he responded. "Okay, let me get dressed." He slipped on a mask, pulled on some jeans. and went to answer the door.

The nurse and her assistant were dressed in protective gear, not only with masks, but also plastic shields. They wore rubber gloves. It wasn't enough that his body ached all over, but now he felt like a leper. Fortunately, they'd brought a folding chair and instructed him to sit, while they checked his oxygen levels, quizzed him about his symptoms, and checked on his state of mind. They took his temperature and listened to his lungs.

"How are you feeling?" the nurse asked Howard.

"Oh, not so hot," he reported. "Coughing a lot. Can't sleep. Sometimes I feel like something's growing in my lungs. Makes it hard to breathe."

He appreciated that she seemed kind and really cared about him. Too bad he was in no shape to pursue her. After a few minutes of examination, she took her assistant off to the side where Howard couldn't hear as they discussed something in low voices.

"What's the verdict?" he called to them. Meanwhile, he tried to enjoy the fresh morning air, but it just wasn't helping. His lungs felt heavy. Overnight, his breathing had become labored. He felt like something was growing inside his throat. The more he coughed, the more it hurt.

The nurse kept chatting with her assistant. Howard didn't like being talked about. Why weren't they talking with him about his illness? She made a phone call. A little while later, he heard a siren.

What's going on, he wondered. An accident? A speeding violation, maybe? He'd noticed coming in, the speed limit was ten miles an hour in the cabin area, and 25 before that. Not easy to drive a car that slowly.

The siren got louder. The nurse walked back over, close to Howard. "We're going to admit you," she said.

"Admit me?" Howard asked in disbelief.

"To the hospital," she said.

"Do I have a say in this?"

"You're very sick, Howard," the nurse responded. "You can stay here, but I wouldn't advise it. Your oxygen level is eighty, which means you're not getting enough air into your lungs. Your temperature is a hundred and two. Your lungs are congested. COVID-19 already has a strong grip on you. In the hospital, you can get oxygen. If the disease progresses, they will have a ventilator for you."

Howard listened, knowing he was sinking fast. For the first time in his life, he realized that he could die. Soon.

"I'll go," he said as the ambulance pulled to his cottage. "I'll go."

58. MARIAH AND HER MOM

Mariah saw her mom's car pull up in the parking lot and skipped over to the door. During the pandemic, they kept the door locked. They now conducted all business through a new drive-in window the owner had installed at the request of the mayor. Mariah slipped on her mask and opened the door to her mom who flew into her arms.

"Oh, honey. It's so good to see you," her mother said with a warm embrace.

Mariah pulled away. "Uh, Mom, should we be hugging?" she asked. "Where's your mask?"

"Oh, I didn't tell you, Mariah, did I? I've already had COVID-19. Working in the hospital in the early days, we didn't know what precautions to take. Some people come in sick after traveling abroad. By the time we figured out they had the virus, it was too late. But I'm one of the lucky ones. I felt a little sick and spent a couple weeks at home. Then I tested negative and went back to work."

"Did your partner get it?" Mariah asked.

"Yes, he got sicker than me. Probably because his lungs aren't that healthy from the cigarettes he smokes. He still has a lot of fatigue. He's convinced he's one of the long haulers."

"What's that?" Mariah wanted to know.

"Some people who get COVID-19, after the worst of it passes, continue to have headaches, tiredness, aches, and more. We're still learning about this novel virus. Sometimes it may attack the heart and other organs. Those who smoke tend to inhale deeper, bringing the virus throughout their respiratory system, causing more havoc."

"I'm sorry," Mariah said. "Don't they say some people get it twice? Are you sure you're safe?"

"I think so," her mom answered. "Let me look at you. You're getting bigger." She placed her hand on Mariah's tummy.

Mariah touched her mother's hand, moving it over her bump and they felt a ripple of movement.

Her mother smiled. Mariah did, too, but she still felt nervous about her mom not wearing a mask. "Mom," she said suddenly. "Would you mind wearing a mask when you're with me? I just think the jury's still out on this virus. You're exposed all the time. Some people have gotten it twice, at least that's what I hear in the news."

Rebecca looked alarmed. She pulled a mask out of her purse and put it on, covering her nose and mouth, securing it on her ears. "I don't want anything to happen to you or the baby. You're right. There's a lot we don't know about this illness. Better be safe than sorry."

"Do you think it's a girl or a boy?" she asked her mom.

"Ah, I can't predict the future. What do you think?" Her mother copped out, batting the question back to Mariah.

"I think it's a girl. I just can feel her in my bones." Mariah felt her baby bump. "The baby feels like a girl."

"Okay," her mom said. "Have you named her yet?"

"No, not yet. I just started talking with Max again. I'm not quite ready to name her. I'm hoping maybe I'll find a name with Dad's family. Wouldn't that be nice?"

Her mother didn't reply, but a strange look came over her face, one that Mariah couldn't read. Mariah didn't ask, not wanting to dampen her own excitement and anticipation. "Let's go," she said. "I packed us a lunch to eat along the way."

"It's only noon," her mother cautioned. "Didn't you say the appointment is at four? It only takes a couple hours to drive over there."

"I know," Mariah said. "But I want to be early. Maybe we could stop at one of the Columbus metro parks for a hike?"

"Okay," her mother agreed. "Let's go."

As it turned out, a traffic jam, caused by an accident outside of Columbus, turned the highway into a parking lot, and slowed them down an extra hour. They stopped at a rest stop to eat their packed lunches, which took another half hour. When they finally approached Mansfield, they only had minutes to spare.

Mariah squeezed her mother's hand. "I'm excited, but also scared," she said. "How do you feel?" As soon as she asked, Mariah wished she hadn't, not sure she really wanted to know, or to let her mother's feelings overshadow her own.

"Oh, honey," her mother started to explain, "I feel so many things. Mostly sad. I came to this town with your father several times while we were dating. When we came back to announce our engagement, your grandfather treated us horribly. He didn't want his son to marry me. I was not the woman he wanted for his son. We were cast out. He forbade the family to talk with us. That was terrible. Your father lost his whole family."

Mariah nodded. "I can see why you're not excited. But maybe grandfather eventually regretted what he did?"

"Yes, I think when your grandfather got sick and almost died, that changed him. Your dad's brother told your dad, but by then, it was too late. Your dad didn't want any part of him or his money."

"But, Mom, what about forgiveness? Why didn't Dad forgive? Maybe that's why he got sick. When we hold that anger inside, it turns on us. Not forgiving someone hurts you more than the person you refuse to forgive. Didn't Dad know that?"

"Mariah, you were born an old soul," her mother said. "You may be right. Your dad never seemed quite whole after his family cut him out. And he was extremely stubborn later when his father sought reconciliation. If they'd reconciled, maybe he'd still be with us. It's possible. I loved him so much."

Mariah watched her mom's eyes get glossy as tears began to flow. She pulled a couple tissues from the box on the floor and handed them to her. A thought crossed her mind suddenly and she asked, "Mom, have you forgiven him?"

Her mother kept crying. "I haven't thought about this for a very long time. To tell you the truth, I'm not sure. When your dad died, his father tried to communicate with me, but I felt it was too little too late. I also didn't think your dad wanted me to reconnect. We'd survived without his money all of those years. It just didn't seem right to accept his help then.

"I went to church for a while after your dad died, before I met Bill. I did try to forgive him then, but it was all so raw. Forgiveness is hard. You have to wait until you're ready. Then Bill came along and the whole situation faded into the background. So, honestly, Mariah, I can't say one way or another. I just know that driving up here today brings it all back and I feel the pain and the sadness." Her mother wiped her eyes and blew her nose.

"I'm sorry, Mom," Mariah said. As they pulled into the small parking lot by the lawyer's office, Mariah reached over and gave her mom a hug. "I'm sorry. Thanks for coming with me. I didn't think about how hard this would be for you."

Her mother sniffled and nodded. "But for you, Mariah, I want to do this. I know how painful it was for your dad to lose his family. They are a good family. It's not fair for you to be estranged from them. After all these years, that's one thing I regret. Your life would have been much better if I'd returned your grandfather's calls. I see that now. That's why I want to be here now with you. It's hard, yes, but I think it will be good for you."

"Thanks, Mom," Mariah said, appreciating that her mother had opened up. She felt happy deep inside that her mom wanted her to know her family. That meant a lot. For so many years, after her mom left, she'd felt so alone. She'd longed for a family. Now, not only would she soon be making a family of her own, but she might have a brand new extended family, as well. "We better go in. It's time," she said, then put her mask on.

"Yes," her mother said. "That trip took a lot longer than I expected. Let's go."

59. A VISIT WITH LAW ENFORCEMENT

Max wasted no time going to talk to the sheriff. Mariah's and the baby's safety came first. He took the crumpled note with him. Its dangerous absurdity pushed his blood pressure into the stratosphere. That the fossil fuel industry had gotten away with this stuff for so long really bugged him. The climate scientists seemed for the most part to accept it as the price of truth-telling, but he faulted the large companies accruing fortunes while heating up the earth. That they kept sending their minion to rough him up irked him to no end. He wished he could just thumb his nose at them and buckle down with his work, but he'd tried that before and lost Gabrielle and Isabella. He would not quit, but he wanted to make sure the troll got nowhere close to Mariah.

The sheriff welcomed him into the office. "Have a seat and you can take off your mask. Tell me, what brings you here. Something with COVID-19?"

Max left his mask on, bothered that the sheriff didn't follow the Health Department's orders, although the sheriff kept a bandana up over his nose himself. "No, not today. Remember that guy who shot a gun in the pub? I think he may be back."

The sheriff nodded. "Yes, I remember. An odd one, with a strong legal team as well. I didn't feel right letting him go, but the judge gave me no choice. I felt very bad about that when you left town. Glad you're back. We don't need more of that man in Friendly. What you got?"

The sheriff's candid speech surprised Max. At the time, he'd thought the troll had the sheriff wrapped around his finger. Hearing otherwise helped. "This," Max said, sliding the crumpled note onto the desk in front of the sheriff.

"Do we need fingerprints?" the sheriff asked before picking it up.

"Mine are all over this. I'm not sure it would do much good."

"You'd be surprised," the sheriff countered. He photographed the note with his phone and called to an assistant in the backroom. "Could you dust this for prints and get Max's print while you're at it. If other prints show, we need to compare it to our records. Max, do you remember the date of that shooting?"

"November 25," Max said. Some things were too hard to forget.

"Check the files. We booked a man in who shot a gun in the pub. Find his prints on file."

"Righto," the assistant said as he opened a drawer and pulled out a thumbprint kit. He took Max's prints before disappearing back into the other room.

Meanwhile, the sheriff read the note, using the picture on his phone. "Who is he referring to here? Your lady friend?"

Max turned beet red. Did the sheriff know Mariah was pregnant? In a small town, secrets spread like wildfire. "Mariah Landtree," he said. "We've been seeing each other for a few months." And because she was the reason he came, he came clean. "And she's pregnant with my child."

The sheriff's eyes widened, but then shifted into his professional poker face. Max realized the sheriff didn't know the gossip, but it was too late now. He needed to protect Mariah and his child, anyway. "When and how did you get this note?" the sheriff quizzed Max, starting to fill in a form which Max imagined was a police report.

"Last Sunday night. Easter," Max said. "Er, I found it on Monday when I got my mail."

"What time? Why do you say Sunday night? Could the mailman have dropped it off?"

"Well, no envelope? I don't think so. Sunday night, my dog started to bark, woke me up, but he quieted down. I went back to sleep. But I thought I heard someone coughing."

"Got a ghost out there?" The sheriff laughed. "They used to tell stories about that."

"I don't know. Maybe I dreamed it. Maybe I'm losing my mind. But the note is real enough."

"What's this guy got on you?"

"I thought I told you before. I'm a climate scientist, focusing on wind energy. Buck and I just opened a factory to build little windmills that could help provide energy for your house. You just put them on the roof like an old-fashioned antenna."

"I'll be darned," the sheriff drawled. "Think I could have one of those things?"

"It'll cost you." Max laughed.

"But what does that have to do with this?" the sheriff asked.

Max gave the sheriff a look. He remembered telling the sheriff before but answered the question. "The fossil fuel industry hires these trolls to intimidate us. Mostly, they use social media sites, but this guy takes it further, roughing us up in person. I don't know how far he'll go. My wife and three-year-old daughter died. They were run off the road in a storm a little more than a year ago. I have no proof. It was high water. If could have been just an accident, or maybe another car nudged her off the road. There were bumps and scratches on the car. Police said it hit a tree on the way into the river."

"Gosh, I'm sorry," the sheriff said. "I can see why you're spooked. This guy's serious trouble. I apologize for my forgetfulness. My wife tells me I need to have my head examined. I'm not as sharp as I used to

192

be. I'm worried about this guy, too."

"Yes," Max said. "I'm extremely concerned."

"Let me get on it, then," the sheriff said. "Since we booked the guy, we might be able to track him down and figure out where he's at. In the meantime, I would recommend that you keep Mariah away from your house; it's too secluded out there. I can have our patrolman drive by, but we can't watch twenty-four seven. Might not be a bad idea to get a camera up. They don't cost too much these days. If he comes around again, and you catch him on camera, we can pick him up."

Max nodded. "Okay, I'll do that. Any other advice?"

"You and Buck keep your eyes open. If you notice anything amiss, give me a call."

"Thanks, Sheriff. I'd shake your hand, but it's not recommended with this pandemic. Know I appreciate you." He slipped on his jacket, feeling a whole lot better. The pastor and the sheriff both reminded him of the benefits of living in a small town. He'd stepped out of his comfort zone twice today, but whatever it took to keep Mariah and the baby safe, he was on it.

60. MR. MARLEY AND A FATHER'S LEGACY

Mariah pulled open the door, holding it for her mom. Her excitement flipped into apprehension. Now that they'd actually arrived, she realized she had no clue what to expect from Mr. Marley, her grandfather's attorney.

A young receptionist greeted them. "Good afternoon, ladies." She looked squarely at Mariah. "Are you Mariah Landtree?"

Mariah nodded. "And this is my mother, Rebecca. She was once married to the late Joseph Landtree, Junior."

"Oh, yes," the receptionist said. "I don't believe Mr. Marley knew you were coming, Rebecca. It's not a problem, but he might not be prepared for you."

"I just came for my daughter," Rebecca said. "This is all about her."

The receptionist nodded. Mariah could read people well and saw that the young woman didn't agree with her mom. Mariah thought for a moment. Yes, of course. Realization flooded Mariah. Regardless of the fact that she'd refused to come earlier, honoring her late husband's wishes, her mother still was the widow and heir.

"Just a minute," the receptionist said. "Let me tell Mr. Marley you've arrived." She rose and slipped through the door to his office.

"This is so weird," Mariah said once the woman disappeared. "It's like walking into a retro movie set. How old do you think this furniture is, Mom?"

Her mom laughed. "I know. It's like the twilight zone. Da-da-da-da. Da-da-da-da. Remember that funny noise?" Mariah nodded and her mother continued. "Some people don't like change. Mr. Marley must be old school. I guess that's what you want in an attorney. I believe he was quite good friends with your grandfather."

"What was my grandfather like?" she asked.

"Oh, very proper, but a very nice man. Well-respected here in Mansfield. Very generous, too. And a church-going man. But he held very rigid ideas about his children. He wanted your dad to settle down in Mansfield and become his business partner. He groomed him for it, beginning when he was a little boy. But you know how children can be, they have to do their own thing.

"Your granddad cut your father out when we married. Your dad thought he was rejected because of me. I wasn't good enough for his son. But, really, the problem was that I took him away and slammed the door on your grandfather's dream. However, your dad never planned to join his dad's business. He repeatedly told him so. Our marriage put the final nail in the coffin."

Before Mariah could ask another question, the door opened. "You can go in now," the receptionist instructed.

Mariah's mother came up along beside her, squeezing her gently with a side hug. "You've got this, honey."

"I'm glad you're here, Mom."

In the large office, an old, wrinkled man sat behind a desk stacked with folder and papers, his large face mostly hidden by a red Ohio State mask. But Mariah could see his smile in the crinkles of his eyes. The sparsely furnished office matched the reception area, a throwback to the past. 1970s, Mariah thought, her conclusion based on the old movies she watched on Netflix. The moment they walked through the door, Mr. Marley put his hands on the desk and pushed himself to a standing position, although with great effort. "Welcome, ladies," he greeted. "I would shake your hands, but they tell me that's not a good idea with this COVID thing we have spreading around right now. And I apologize for the masks, but that's what we can do to be safe. When you're as ancient as me, you know you're living on borrowed time. I must be very careful." He chuckled, putting Mariah and her mom ease.

"Absolutely," Rebecca said. "I'm a nurse. You don't need to apologize. Those of us in the health profession appreciate people and businesses like yours that aim to maximize safety, which slows the spread."

"Yes, I thought the virus would be gone by now, but guess not. I rely on our public health experts to lead the way," he said. "Thank you for your service, Rebecca, during these dangerous times."

Rebecca said, "Thank you. And again, thanks to you for leading by example."

Mr. Marley nodded appreciatively, then looked at Mariah. "Thank you for coming, Mariah," he said. "And you, too, Rebecca. You know I tried to get you here when your husband passed away. His father was adamant that you should be given full rights as an heir. And it pained him greatly that he never met you, Mariah. He never wanted you to lack for anything. Either of you."

Mariah looked at her mom in surprise. "Joe didn't want his father's money," her mom explained. "Maybe I should have called. God knows we were poor after my husband died. I just didn't think it was right, after all those years."

Mr. Marley cleared his throat. "Rebecca, I respect that. But, Mariah, I take it you feel differently about this? Or you wouldn't be here today."

"Yes, sir. I want to hear this out. My father wrote me a letter before he died, which I just read last week. He wanted me to come here, so here I am. I want to meet my family," she added. "Is anybody still around?"

"Yes, indeed. You have a family, a very large family. They'd love to meet you. But first, you need to listen to this video."

"Video?" Mariah asked.

"You see, your grandfather knew his days were numbered. He tried to make amends with your dad, but your dad refused to listen. So he planned for the future, preparing a video for your dad's heirs. If you ever came around, he wanted to tell you himself."

"Cool," Mariah said. "I get to hear him in a video?"

"Are you ready?" he asked.

"Yes," Mariah exclaimed. How awesome that she would see and hear the grandfather she'd never met. "This is so exciting," she told the attorney.

"I'm sorry your grandfather couldn't be here today. He would've loved to hear you say that," the attorney said.

Mariah thought she detected a tear running down his cheek. "You were good friends?"

"Oh, yes," Marley said. "We go way back. We grew up together here in Mansfield, played ball together as boys, linemen on an award-winning football team at Mansfield High, and then we roomed together at Ohio State. I knew your grandfather very well. He was a very good man, but also very stubborn. And that cost him his son. I don't think he ever got over it. His death certificate said he died of heart disease. I call it a broken heart."

Rebecca bristled. "He kicked Joe out, sir. Joe didn't want anything to do with him and I don't blame him. I mean, who would do that to their own son?"

"We all make mistakes," Mr. Marley said. "Your father-in-law made an error in judgement. Of course, at the time, he thought he was doing the right thing. By the time he realized his mistake, it was too late to turn things around. God knows he tried. He used to come in my office and cry. Perhaps if your husband had seen his dad crying, he might have forgiven him."

Mariah watched the tears streaming down the old man's face and now her mom's as well. Her mom cleared her throat. Mariah handed her a tissue from the desk and handed another to Mr. Marley.

"So much pain in this broken family," her mom said, sobbing.

Silence hung in the room. Mariah waited patiently, trying to fathom all this pain and sadness in her family. She vowed not to let history repeat itself in the life of her child.

"Can we hear the video?" she asked finally, ready to turn the corner now.

Mr. Marley called to the receptionist, "Gretchen? Can you come help us with this new-fangled contraption?"

Gretchen appeared at the door, smiling. "Yes, Mr. Marley," she said as she turned on the DVD player connected to a large screen. "Could I have the DVD?"

"Did they have DVDs back then?" Rebecca asked.

"Good point," Mr. Marley said. "This was recorded on a videotape, but we converted all our videos to DVDs a few years ago when the VCRs started becoming obsolete."

Mr. Marley took a disk case out of the open folder on his desk and handed it to Gretchen. She opened the DVD drive and popped the disk in. "Ready?" she asked.

Mr. Marley nodded. "It's showtime."

Gretchen handed the remote to Mariah. "You can control the volume if you like." Then Gretchen spun around and left just as a very old man appeared on the screen.

Mariah looked carefully at the tall, extremely thin bald man, her grandfather. How she longed to reach out and give him a hug, but, nevertheless, she savored this opportunity to see him alive on the screen. He obviously had taken much care in dressing for the occasion, all spruced up with shiny black dress trousers, a silver belt, a white dress shirt, and red bow tie. Her eyes lingered on the embroidered emblem on the right side of his shirt. A black tree trunk, covered with green leaves and red apples, towering over the silhouette of a dark, long-haired woman sitting beneath. Underneath, cursive letters spelled out Landtree Farms.

Her grandfather sat in a sturdy mahogany chair. To his right, she noted a large rectangular desk, and, behind him, a large bookshelf filled the wall. Beyond the shelves, a picture window looked out onto a green lawn, with a barn in the distance. Hanging on the wall, near the window, hung a portrait of a lady very similar to the one on his shirt. Mariah could see kind eyes, a warm smile, and radiant beauty. Could that be her Native American great-grandmother?

As she looked more closely, at first the beautiful lady and then the wrinkled old man, she caught a resemblance, in their pronounced cheekbones and dark eyes. Suddenly, Mariah also saw her father's eyes and face reflected in them both. Her own eyes began to tear up. The man picked up a framed photo off his desk. There she saw a picture of a younger version of the old man sitting in the very same chair, with hair as dark as the beautiful lady's and a smile similar to hers. On his lap perched a little boy holding an apple.

The man looked at the camera, and then touched the child in the photograph. *That must be my father*, Mariah realized as the man began to speak. "Joseph, I've always loved you. I made a huge mistake in casting you away. First, I want to say I'm sorry. I can't forgive myself for what I did. It's literally killing me. The doctor calls it heart disease. I don't want you to suffer like me. Don't hold it in, Joe-Bo.

"I also want to apologize to you, Rebecca, if you're watching. You became a scapegoat in a situation that had nothing to do with you and everything to do with a stubborn old man who didn't know his ass from a hole in the ground. Pardon my language, but I want you to know I'm sorry. You weren't the problem. It was always all about me.

"I've suffered for my mistake every day of my life since I made that fateful choice to send you away, Joe-Bo. Your mother tried to stop me, but I wouldn't listen. I think it killed her, too, eventually.

"And, Mariah, if you're there, I'm so sorry I never met you. It's all my fault and I want to make it up to you, your dad, and your mother. Maybe you can convince them to accept my love. Maybe it's not too late."

Mariah started crying. "It's too late for Dad."

"I've put together a little adventure of discovery for you." Her grandfather grinned. "I want you find the treasure buried in my heart that I'm opening up to you. Marley holds the directions. Go out, seek, and find. When you've completed your tasks, come back and I'll have a few more words for you."

The video stopped. "You can turn that off," Mr. Marley told Mariah.

Mariah clicked it off and the screen went black. She looked at Mr. Marley expectantly. "An adventure of discovery?"

Mr. Marley nodded, pulling a large envelope out of his folder. "Let me read the instructions." He opened the large manilla envelope which contained three smaller envelopes. He held them up for Mariah and her mother to see that they were labeled with the numbers 1, 2, and 3.

He pulled a sheet of paper out and began to read. "During our estrangement, some good things have happened. The Good Book says that all things work together for the good for all of those who are loved according to His purpose. Some of the things, Joseph, that you urged me to do came to pass. I waited for a while, hoping you'd come back to take charge. When that didn't happen, I went ahead and implemented your suggestions, without you. I'm sorry it took me so long to see the wisdom in your plans."

"What does that mean?" Mariah asked.

Mr. Marley smiled. "You'll see. The adventure of discovery is designed to explain it all to you. Let me finish this letter." He picked up where he left off.

"Joseph, Rebecca, and Mariah, may you all reap the goodness of Joseph, Junior's keen intellect, future vision, and love for this beautiful planet of ours.

"Son, I'm mighty proud of you. Probably the single best thing I ever did in my life was to be your father, and I'm so sorry I got it all wrong. Maybe this will help right my mistakes, or at least teach you to live your life much differently than I have lived mine.

"Love, Dad"

Rebecca looked as surprised as Mariah. "What did Dad want to do? Did he tell you, Mom?"

Rebecca looked off into the distance before answering. "Your dad was a dreamer, Mariah. He had all kinds of ideas. I'm afraid I didn't pay much attention to him. I guess your grandfather didn't either, until it was too late."

Mr. Marley smiled. "Actually, Senior was quite a dreamer, too. Joe-Bo was a chip off the old block. Of course, back when Joseph was building his business, things looked quite different. Later, Joe-Bo's recommendations helped bring him into the 21st century. But he wanted you to discover this for yourself.

"Now, ladies, it's rather late in the day to begin the adventure. I apologize for my forgetfulness when we arranged this late afternoon visit. My old mind doesn't remember the important things these days. I need to alert the places you'll be visiting. Let's schedule a time for you to come back for the adventure. Or, if you prefer, you could stay overnight and start the hunt at the crack of dawn. I'll be glad to put you up in a hotel overnight, courtesy of Marley and Masters."

"I need to get someone to cover for me at the diner where I work," Mariah said. "I think my coworker could do it. She's been learning the ropes for when I have the baby. And I need to call Mrs. Bee."

"I didn't realize you are with child," Mr. Marley said. "Another Landtree heir. It's a good thing you came now."

Mariah touched her baby bump. "I'm not showing a lot yet. I'm due in October," she said.

Rebecca said, "Well, I don't have to be home until Monday. I was planning to stay until Sunday anyway. I could do that."

"Let me call to see if she can cover for me, and touch base with Mrs. Bee." Mariah said.

Rebecca cautioned, "The thing that concerns me about all this is the pandemic. I've already had the virus, but Mariah hasn't. And it's possible to be reinfected. Will we be safe in the hotel and on this so-called adventure of discovery? Will people be wearing masks and what about sanitizing surfaces?"

"Good point, Rebecca," Mr. Marley said. "We've covered those bases. The hotel assured me that they will take precautions and all their staff will be wearing masks in common areas. The hotel requires masks, as well. You can order meals through room service. As far as the adventure of discovery goes, everyone you visit will wear masks, as I'm sure you will also. In fact, we have a pack of masks for you with the Landtree logo on them. I almost forgot about that. Someone dropped them off yesterday." He pulled out a package of green Landtree Farm cloth masks with the same image Mariah had seen on her grandfather's shirt. "Here's the cellphone number of my assistant, Thomas. If you have any concerns at all for Mariah's safety, please call Thomas and he'll help you out. Okay?"

Rebecca nodded. Mariah took the phone number and the package of masks. "These are awesome. Thank you," she said.

"Don't thank me. Thank Jacob Landtree. You'll meet him at your first stop. Enjoy your adventure, ladies."

61. HOWARD RECKONING

Howard's ambulance ride unfolded in rapid motion, terminating at the ER. He remembered paramedics moving like zombies, covered from head to toe in white body suits. They'd handled him as if he were a pariah, communicating over him in mysterious whispers. Only one man had addressed him in a steady one-sided conversation, explaining the procedures as they connected him to their medical machines. He hadn't wanted this ride, but the oxygen made it easier to breathe. They seemed eager and very happy to dump him at the hospital. Only the nice man had stayed for a moment to say good-bye. "They'll take good care of you," he said in closing.

After a quick exam, the ER doctor had him admitted to the COVID wing, where he had the dubious distinction of being their first patient in the newly-established section. Again, the medical personnel all wore white zombie suits, and handled him with kid gloves, as quickly as possible. It became perfectly clear to him within hours that they aimed to minimize time in his room.

The first night, Howard had considered working from the hospital. His oxygen levels had improved with the little plastic thing in his nose providing oxygen. He'd opened his laptop, but couldn't quite get into the mood, so he put it away. They offered him something to help him sleep, which sounded like a better idea.

When he woke up on Saturday morning, he felt like a zombie himself. His whole body ached, the coughing had returned with a vengeance, and his lungs felt heavy. The nurse turned up his oxygen, but, even then, he struggled to breathe. They offered him a ventilator.

At first, Howard refused, but by Saturday evening, he feared each labored breath would be his last. His lungs burned. His heart struggled as well, as evidenced by the monitor interpreted for him by the nurse.

In the twilight of illness, Howard longed to take stock of his life. He felt a nagging sense of error but fighting to breathe consumed all his remaining energy. Something tugged at his heart. As he considered his work, the business of trolling, and his harassment of the climate scientists, all color shifted to gray. But his time to contemplate life evaporated. He needed a miracle. When the nurse came in on her evening rounds, he managed to whisper, "Ventilator."

"Good. You need it, Howard. We'll have to take you to the ICU for that," she said. "Give me a few minutes to make the arrangements. You will be sedated. Just to confirm, you're giving your consent to be put on a ventilator?"

"Yes," Howard whispered, barely pushing out a quiet, raspy assent before lapsing into a coughing fit and gasping for air in between the coughs.

The nurse hurried out of the room. He didn't blame her. Who would put themselves in jeopardy of catching this terrible virus?

Time stood still. He waited. The hands on the clock on the wall moved ever so slowly. Eventually, an orderly came to wheel him up to the ICU. There, they transferred him into a different bed. An anesthesiologist arrived to explain the sedation meds. It sounded like they were going to knock him out for the duration, until he got better or he died, but they didn't tell him that. Frankly, as bad as he felt, he didn't care. He just wanted release, however it came.

The drugs permeated Howard's system and he faded quickly. When he woke after some undetermined length of time, he found himself floating near the ceiling of the room, looking down on his own body. He could watch treatments being administered. They stuck a ventilator down his throat. It looked ever so painful, but he couldn't feel a thing. Instead, he experienced the lightness of weightlessness, floating in the air above himself. It was an extremely cool experience.

A loudspeaker announced, "Gentlemen, start your engines."

Howard glanced around, searching for the speakers. Were they the hospital's public address system? Before he could figure it out, he found himself perched on the roof of the hospital in front of a landing strip. But before all that completely registered, he sat in the cockpit of a little plane that looked just like the Blue Angel and Thunderbird jets that performed in the air shows he loved to watch.

"I can't fly," he yelled. He scanned the roof for assistance, but he was strangely all alone. He wondered exactly who had said, "Gentlemen, start your engines," and where were the other men. He heard noise above and, looking up, saw three identical blue jets circling in formation. Howard started shaking.

Now the voice called him by name. "Howard, start your engine. Just turn the key in the ignition and let's go. Put your foot to the pedal and speed your baby up. When you get to the end of the runway, use the lever to lift off. Turn your steering wheel left and right for direction and use the lever to move up and down." The lever lit up bright red when referenced by the voice. "Once you're in the air, control your speed with the dial to the right of your steering wheel. I'll let you know if you're getting off course."

Of course, sure. He could just fly a plane without any instruction at all. Right. But what did he have to lose? A few minutes ago, he hadn't been able to breathe. Now the voice offered him the invitation of a lifetime: to fly with the Blue Angels. *There must be a God after all*, he thought. He turned on the plane, gunned it to the edge of the runway where he pulled the lever and, sure enough, lifted off into the wild blue yonder.

He noticed the wing of one of the other planes tip toward him, as if to say hello. The voice didn't teach him to wave, so instead, he raised the lever to lift up to their height. Then he steered his plane into their formation, completing their diamond in the sky. After that, he hung on to the steering wheel for dear life and followed the direction of the lead plane, keeping an equidistance between himself and the other two nearby planes. It was a lot simpler than he'd imagined. By God, he could fly!

"Where are we going?" he asked aloud. "Are we in an air show? Out for a joy ride? Are you taking me home? Is this a pathway to heaven?"

"Enjoy your trip," the voice startled him as he finished his string of questions. "But to answer your question, Howard, this is your wake-up call. Observe closely and listen up. You can put your plane on autopilot now."

Autopilot? Right, Howard thought. There might be such a thing, but not with the Blue Angels.

The voice instructed, "Push the blue autopilot button to the left of the steering wheel." A blue button lit up and started blinking.

Howard muttered, "Even I am not stupid enough to believe this plane can fly itself."

"Howard," the voice repeated, "push the button. You can't do this by yourself."

Howard figured what the heck. He pushed the button and waited to crash. Better to go down in glory with the Blue Angels than coughing out on a ventilator in a hospital bed. But instead, the button quit flashing and the plane actually took control. The steering wheel rotated itself and the lift lever moved up and down, adjusting altitude as needed to keep pace with the other planes. No way could he figure this all out, so he didn't even try. Instead, he just sat back and enjoyed the ride.

62. MAX IN THE MORNING

On Saturday, Max crawled out of bed at dawn. The morning came early now, after daylight savings had returned a few weeks ago. He decided to run to clear his head before Gabrielle's visit. Then he'd check on Mariah. He wanted to learn about her trip to Mansfield to meet with her grandfather's attorney. He knew it was big deal for her. He wanted to listen and be there for her as she discovered more about her family — and he needed to tell her about his COVID test and warn her about the troll.

He hit the path running and felt free, moving effortlessly down the lane past Buck's house and out into the country road that led into town. Other than concern for the bad guy, for whom he did keep an eye out, his heart brimmed with happiness, full of life for a change. Possibly now he could begin to dream and enjoy life again. With Mariah at his side, his life was brand new. He felt a growing excitement about the child forming in her body. He offered up a prayer of gratitude for this new life, surprising himself after months of anger at God.

Kicking up his heels, Max pushed himself hard. He ran his heart out, elevating his heart rate. He slipped into the third realm, moving with the flow. He immersed himself in the meditative now, somewhat oblivious to the details of his surroundings, vaguely aware of houses as he neared the town. Before he knew it, he'd circled the main block and started back.

Once home, he took a quick shower to wash off the sweat, after starting a pot of coffee. When he came out, Gabrielle smiled at him from kitchen table. Not wanting to break the spell of his good mood, he just smiled back and said, "Howdy, honey. How are you?" She'd liked his cowboy act back in the day when they were an alive couple.

She responded with her usual, "Hey there, handsome cowboy. Are you ready to ride?'

Max gave her a questioning look, even though he doubted she meant a sexual offer in her words. Angels couldn't, could they? "What do you mean?" he asked stiffly.

"Just a little joke, dear. Just a little joke. How are you?"

"Actually, I feel great," Max said. "Just finished a morning run. Despite the pandemic, things are looking up."

"I'm glad, Max," Gabrielle said. "I know it's rough to be left behind."

Max nodded. "That's an understatement."

"I'm sorry. I didn't want this for you."

"Not your fault, dear. Don't apologize."

"But it was my fault, Max. I shouldn't have been driving in that storm."

"You didn't know. You didn't do that on purpose. Flash floods are like that. They come without warning. There's no way you could have avoided that situation," he comforted her. "I don't blame you. Please don't blame yourself."

Gabrielle smiled, sharing that warm gaze he loved so much. When their eyes locked, her love connected deep with his soul. In the past, that had awakened him in other ways, too, but that was out of the question now. And for the first time, that felt okay. He treasured Gabrielle, but his heart belonged to Mariah now, his woman in the land of the living. Gabrielle was just a visitor from his past life, the ghost of his former wife.

"What's up, Doc?" he asked instead. Although Max had the Ph.D. and Gabrielle had stopped with her Master's degree, he still liked to call her Doc from time to time because of her work as a public health official.

"Now we just stay the course," she told him. "This virus might go away if people across the country practice social distancing with masks. However, it appears that your President minimized the threat and wants businesses to open right back up. This may draw out the pandemic. Your job is to keep Friendly on task. It won't be easy."

"The hospital received their first patient last night," Max told her. "That traveler they put in quarantine at the state park on Easter. I'm so glad they cut him off at the pass. The checkpoint worked well there."

"Yes, and they were ready. Now it's just a matter of implementing all the policies and procedures we've discussed. I think Friendly is in a good place, honestly."

"As long as it doesn't spread. As long as the contact testing works and people take precautions. Big ifs," Max cautioned.

"But they've got you to show them the way, Max."

"Right. All they need is me."

"You underrate yourself. You've got this, Max. Just be persistent. You can do it." And with that, Gabrielle disappeared.

Max lost no time in dialing the sheriff. Enough of ghosts. "Anything new?" he asked.

"Oh, Max," the sheriff said. "Do you read minds? I was just getting ready to call you. Could you come down to the station? I think we just hit pay dirt."

63. CLOSING IN ON HOWARD

Max covered his face with a mask and walked into the sheriff's office with a spring in his step, feeling hopeful. Perhaps truth could win over falsehoods. Maybe he'd find light at the end of the tunnel. *The arc of the moral universe is long, but it bends toward justice.* Max remembered the quote from Martin Luther King, Jr. Today, he wanted to land at the end of the curve.

"Max," the sheriff called. "Come see what I've discovered. Look at this." The sheriff wore a splotchy camouflage bandana around his neck, pulled up over his nose and mouth. It matched his khaki-colored uniform in places. "Come back here, behind my desk, Max, and look at my computer."

"You found him on the computer? Do you know where he is now?"

"You are not going to believe this, Max. Come look. You'd be surprised what you can turn up in computer searches these days. It's getting harder for people to hide every day. Now some may say that's Big Brother watching, but when you're trying to solve a crime, it's our best ally."

Max positioned himself behind the desk, peering over the sheriff's shoulder. He felt a little awkward not maintaining a six-foot distance. He knew Gabrielle wouldn't approve, but he wanted to see for himself.

"Look at this." The sheriff pointed to the screen. "This is the guy we booked into our jail after that incident at the pub. Then we got his driver's license, his Social Security number, his license tags, the whole nine yards. We even got his thumb print. Now, with the Social Security number, we can track his income and with that, comes addresses of employers, addresses of employees. With the Board of Motor Vehicles, we can track license plates and renewals." He showed Max.

"Here he is. When he left Friendly, he went to California. He used his credit card to pay a fine, here. We can track credit card spending, so we can also track his purchases. He stayed near L.A. for most of that time, then headed back east. He purchased gas outside of Friendly on Easter, but that's not all.

"Sometimes you get a hunch about these things. Remember that man who stopped at our pandemic checkpoint Easter with a fever? We quarantined him at the state park? When they checked him in, they took his picture, got a copy of his ID, wrote down his driver's license, and asked for his employer information. I made a little visit to the Health Department to look at his records. And look at this."

"That's him," Max said excitedly. The photo ID from the previous incident matched the photo at the state park. "You found him!"

"And look at this," the sheriff said. He pointed to the man's employer's name. Then he flipped back to the previous screen to reveal the same name: the public relations firm paying the guy to harass climate scientists. "Interesting, the driver's license and plates don't match up, but the picture on the driver's license? Dead ringer. We got our man. Must've changed his name and tags before coming back to Friendly, thinking he could fool us. He underestimated small town cops."

Max smiled. "We got him. Quarantined. But wait, isn't that guy in the hospital now?"

"In the hospital? Really?"

"The health commissioner updates me daily on the pandemic response," Max explained. "They took him by ambulance to the hospital a couple days ago. He's the first patient on the COVID-19 ward. Not in very good shape, either, from what I understand."

"Well, well, well," said the sheriff. "I wouldn't wish that on anybody, but it drops him right in our laps, doesn't it?"

"At least I feel safe for now. But with COVID, we can't pay him a visit, you know?" Max said.

"Right, but we can ask the hospital staff to keep an eye on him. When he gets ready to walk, we'll issue a warrant for his arrest and bring him in for questioning. From the hospital to our door. We've got time on this."

"What makes you so sure?"

"If he's sick enough to be in the hospital, it's going to take time to recover. If he does recover. If he was having difficulty breathing when they picked him up, he could end up on a ventilator."

"Oh, you're right. He might be really bad off. Maybe we should give the hospital a call," Max suggested.

"Good idea. I'll do that right away."

Mariah woke up early and decided to go for a walk. She left a note for her mom, and took her cellphone along, thinking about Max. A residential neighborhood bordered the hotel. She ventured out to enjoy sidewalks and spring gardens.

Stately old two-story houses faced each other across the tree-lined street. Surely once proud homes, now they looked tattered with age. Cracks in the sidewalk, peeling paint, and boarded-up windows lent a sad overall feel to the place. Yet here and there, tulips bloomed in full force. *Nature overcomes ruins of humanity time after time,* she thought.

She speed-dialed Max. "Good morning," she said cheerfully when he answered. "How are you?"

'Good. Things are going well here. How are you feeling? How's our baby?"

"Oh, Max, I'm feeling great. The baby? It flutters a little from time to time. It's so nice to be over morning sickness. Today, I'm going to meet the Landtree family, my father's people. Can you believe I've never met any of them before? We're going on an adventure of discovery to three places. The first is the Landtree Farm."

"Is that safe, Mariah, for you to be going out, meeting people? Are you taking precautions? You know COVID-19 first came to Ohio up there by Cleveland. You're not too far away. You need to be careful," Max warned.

Mariah laughed. "Yes, I know, Max. They gave us Landtree Farms masks. My mom asked the same question when we met with the attorney yesterday. He told her that everyone would be very careful, all wearing masks in our presence. I think we'll be okay, but thanks for asking."

"I just don't want anything to happen to you and the baby. So you're going on an adventure? What does that mean?"

"My granddad wanted us to learn about the family and their businesses, I think. He said he implemented some of my dad's ideas. I didn't know my dad had a lot of ideas, but my mom says he was a dreamer. I guess his dad didn't like my dad's suggestions, but eventually, he came around. He implemented them all. He kept hoping my dad would come home and see for himself, but my dad died without ever knowing. It's so sad, Max. I don't want this kind of pain for our child. You gotta promise to get along with our families, okay?"

"You know my family and I are very close. I don't know how I would have survived without them when I lost Gabrielle and Isabella. I stayed with my mom and dad for long time. They were there for me. They're everything to me."

"That's good, Max. I'm so glad you have them. I want to meet them," Mariah said. "Do they know about the baby?"

"No, I haven't brought it up yet. I want to go tell them in person, but it's hard with COVID. My parents are getting up there in years and have some health problems. I don't want to do anything to jeopardize them. Once we get this pandemic behind us, I'll take you to meet them. I know they'll love you," Max said. "Do you want me to come on this adventure with you? I'm not doing much today. I could drive up."

"Um," Mariah paused. "Um, I don't want to hurt your feelings, but I think this is for me and my mom. That's the way Granddad wanted it: a family affair. And aren't you coughing?"

"Yes, but just allergies. My COVID test was negative."

"Thank God," Mariah exclaimed. "I'm so glad, Max. I was worried about you, about us, and the baby. That's great news."

"Yes, great news," Max agreed. He decided not to spoil it with worrying her about the troll since she was out of town anyway. "Okay, then, you have fun and call me tonight. I want to hear all about it."

Mariah checked the time. "Thank you. That means a lot. I've gotta leave now, but I'll try to call you tonight and tell you what we find. Ooh, I need to get back to the hotel and get something to eat. They're sending a driver for us at eight. I didn't realize I've been walking for so long."

"You're on a walk?"

"Yeah, I needed some exercise and it's so pretty out this morning. I'm just walking in a neighborhood close to the hotel."

"Be safe, Mariah. Be careful. Call me and tell me how things go today, okay?"

"Yes, I will. Good-bye, Max," Mariah said. She clicked off, happy that he seemed so concerned about her well-being. It felt good to have someone watching out for her. Then she picked up her pace to a light jog, getting back to the hotel just in time to shower, dress, and prepare for an adventure.

***

At eight sharp, a knock sounded on their door. Mariah jumped off the bed, where she'd just sat beside her mom who was watching a morning TV show. She opened the door with a greeting. "Good morning."

A tall man with a mask identical to the ones they'd received at the lawyer's office stood at the door. "Hello, Mariah? My name is Charlie Landtree."

"Awesome. I'm Mariah and this is my mother, Rebecca. Pleased to meet you." Mariah offered her hand, then pulled it back remembering she shouldn't be shaking hands because of COVID. She explained, "It's not safe now to shake. Consider yourself welcomed."

The man nodded and then Rebecca asked, "What's your father's name? I think I met him years ago."

"David, ma'am. David Landtree."

"Yes." Rebecca remembered. "He's as tall as you, right? Back in the day, he had black hair and was quite athletic."

"That's my dad. Actually, I'm a little taller, though." Charlie chuckled, then said, "We better get on the road. They're expecting us for breakfast at the farm."

Mariah's head spun with the possibilities of the day. Her cousin picked up their suitcases as if they were paper bags and carried them out to his SUV, which looked like an expensive model. They followed him out. After their luggage was loaded, he held the door open for the front seat.

Rebecca deferred to Mariah. "You sit here, dear. This is your adventure. I'll be right behind you."

"Thanks, Mom," Mariah said, perusing the expensive leather interior of the car. "How far to the farm?"

"Just out of town a bit. We'll be there in no time." Then Charlie turned on some soft rock and silently focused on the road.

Mariah enjoyed the peaceful music and the view out the window. As they left the downtown area, the road dipped up and down with hills filling the surrounding countryside. The fields were still brown but looked recently tilled. "So, this is where my dad grew up," she commented. "It's very beautiful."

"Yes, I think so," Charlie replied. "But I'm a little biased. You know there's a place here for you, if you want it, Mariah."

"What?"

"Oh, I'm getting ahead of the plan," Charlie said. "You'll find out soon enough. Did you bring your envelopes? This would be a good time to read number one, as we approach the farm."

Mariah reached into her big bag of a purse and pulled out the envelopes. She read aloud, "Number One. Landtree Farm. This one?" she asked.

"Right," Charlie said.

"Did you create the treasure hunt?" she asked him.

"No," Charlie said. "Our grandfather created the treasure hunt before he died, but he left my dad detailed instructions. Dad really wanted to do this himself, but he's recovering from knee surgery, so I'm doing the honors. You'll meet him soon enough."

Mariah opened the envelope and took out a typed piece of paper. She began to read.

"Your first stop will be Landtree Farm. The farm has been in the family for four generations. The original settlers came from Germany. They changed their name during the first world war, when anti-German sentiment ran high. Because their farm included many orchards, they called themselves the Landtrees. Simple, truthful, a name directly connected to this piece of earth we call home.

"Joseph, I know you weren't happy with our ways of modern agriculture. You didn't like the newfangled seeds and pesticides and fertilizer we used back then. You wanted us to go a different way. I had David read up on organic farming and heirloom seeds. And we've made some changes on the farm. We transitioned to organic farming. We also continue to plant trees and utilize permaculture techniques for our crops. Thank you for the suggestion.

"I want you to have a tour of the farm and learn a little more about what's new around here. Enjoy your breakfast and tour and I'll catch up with you in a little while.

"Love, Dad "

"Are you crying?" she asked her mother.

Rebecca nodded. "Your dad would have loved this. He talked about this stuff all the time," she said. "Mostly, he complained about his dad's farming style. He used permaculture techniques in our backyard back then. He worried about overuse of fertilizers and how modern farming techniques destroy the good soil. He started a degree in horticulture at Ohio State, Mariah."

Charlie seemed guarded when he said, "Actually, Rebecca, my dad kept in touch with Uncle Joe about all of his new ideas. They traded information. Your dad taught my dad a lot, even though Uncle Joe never came back home."

"Wow," Mariah said. "Did you know that, Mom?"

"I suspected as much," her mom replied.

Charlie said, "You'll be surprised by what you learn today, ladies. Uncle Joe left quite a legacy at Landtree Farm and Industries. Our greatest family regret is that he never came back to find out. He's our hero."

They pulled up to colorful sign announcing Landtree Dairy. Behind the sign, Mariah could see what looked like a restaurant and, to the right, a barn. Were those goats in the yard? The large complex included a miniature golf course and, farther over, she saw a sign: Landtree Fine Dining, announcing a larger building, shaped like a barn, but, a restaurant.

"This doesn't look like a dairy," Mariah observed.

Charlie laughed. "No, this is an experience, our public relations manager tells us. The place started as a dairy store, serving milk and ice cream. Over time, it evolved into a recreational mecca. The lines of people stretch out through the store here all summer long. In the fall, we have a corny maze and hayrides. We offer clubs for children to come and do crafts and get an ice cream cone. Companies hold their annual picnics back in our shelter and conference space. Little ones come to visit the goats and cows. This whole place really took off after my Uncle Barney—your uncle, too, Mariah—took it over after getting a business degree at OSU. I believe he's going to serve you breakfast. We closed the dining room because of COVID, but our drive-through service keeps the kitchen staff pretty busy. A lot of high school and college students work here and it's funded quite a few of their educations. We want to protect you both, so we'll all be wearing masks. We'll talk with Uncle Barney first and then you can eat. After that, my dad will come to show you around the farm."

In the dairy store, ropes defined lines leading up to the ice cream counter. Other ropes led to the left, where Mariah noticed a menu hanging on the wall behind another counter. Charlie led them to a large dining room filled with picnic tables and booths with wooden benches.

"Have a seat," Charlie said. "I'll go get Uncle Barney."

Mariah slid into a booth on the side wall. Her mother slid in after her.

"How are you doing, Mom?" Mariah asked.

"I'm surprised," her mother said. "I had no idea, no idea at all. Dad would have been so happy. I'm very sad that he didn't, that I didn't, ever come up here."

"But, Mom, this is so very cool. We can be proud of Dad. It's not too late for us to enjoy Dad's legacy."

A large man with a fuzzy full white beard, wearing farmer's overalls, entered the room. He had a red-checkered mask sporting a black cow, also branded with the now familiar Landtree Farms logo. Charlie trailed behind him.

"Rebecca?" his large voice boomed out. "If you aren't a sight for poor eyes. Let me give you a hug, pretty lady. You've only gotten better after all of these years." Then he stopped. "I guess we better not do a hug. Have to be careful with COVID, right?"

Rebecca's eyes watered as she replied. "Right."

Instead, he gave her a warm smile and said, "Consider yourself hugged, then."

Charlie slipped into the booth opposite Mariah. Barney joined them, across from Rebecca, commenting, "So here you are. I'm glad you ladies finally came to visit Landtree Farms. There's been an ugly gaping hole a mile wide in our family for years since Joe left. You have no idea how much you being here means to all of us. Rebecca, what are you up to these days? How long has it been since I've seen you? Almost thirty years?"

"I live in Myrtle Beach. I'm a nurse," Rebecca said. "I'm doing okay, although all of us in the unit where I work caught COVID."

"You got it? Were you very sick?"

"Not too bad. I was off work a few weeks. I was lucky to get it over with early."

"And Mariah? You sure are a beautiful young lady. What are you doing with yourself?"

"I lead a simple life in Friendly. I work at the diner. I love the Earth. I think I got that from my daddy. We used to have a garden together. He taught me to love creation. I help at our community greenhouse and I'm going to have a baby. I'm so excited."

Barney raised his eyebrows and looked at Rebecca, who smiled. "Well, okay then," he said. Whatever he was thinking, he didn't probe or judge. "Now, I guess you noticed this is more than a dairy."

"We did," Mariah said, happy to change the subject. "Charlie said it's an experience."

Barney chuckled. He perched on the edge of the booth's bench with his hands resting on his generous belly, stretching his long legs out away from the booth. He was clearly a man comfortable in his own skin. "Well, if he's already told you all about it, let's bring on the food. I asked for a little of everything. You eat whatever strikes your fancy. But I have to warn you, it's all-American fare here. Over in our restaurant, we have a variety of dishes, but here you get sausage, cheese, eggs, coffee, toast, and orange juice. The basics."

Barney picked up his cellphone and texted something. A few moments later, two masked young people appeared at their table with plates of scrambled eggs, hash browns, and sausage. They took drink orders and provided napkins and silverware.

"We'll leave you two to enjoy your breakfast," Charlie said. "I've got to make some calls. I'll eat in the backroom to keep you safe."

Barney said, "It's good to see you both. I'll catch up with you at noon. I believe there's a family dinner planned out at the homestead. You ladies enjoy your meal." He added, "I'm going to show you a little film about the dairy and its story. You can watch while you eat." He walked over to a big screen TV on the wall and used the remote to start it. Then he retired to the kitchen with Charlie close behind.

65. HOWARD'S TRIP

Howard pinched his hand and then his cheek. Could he really be in formation with the Blue Angels, flying through the sky? Was he awake or was he dreaming? Did it matter? He decided to just relax and enjoy. Below, he could see the countryside getting smaller as they gained in attitude. The roads and rivers formed lines through the landscape as they climbed up. He watched the instrument panel and the controls moving without his help. Autopilot seemed to be doing the job.

The loudspeaker began again. "We're heading west. First, the Mississippi River. Do you see a problem there?"

The planes dipped down closer to earth, made a sharp turn south, and followed a path of water, spilling its banks, flooding small towns along its course. "Is that a flood?" Howard asked. "Is the Mississippi overtopping its banks?"

The voice continued, "One result of the changing climate is a disruption of weather patterns here in the United States and around the world. Spring rains become torrential downpours that last for days. Yes, that's a flood you see. Unprecedented rainfall caused this problem. The farmers can't get their crops in when the ground remains wet through the spring."

Howard realized that the announcer did not know what he was talking about. "But you can't blame that on climate change," Howard countered, still on his game.

"Oh, really?" the voice responded. "Do you truly think climate change isn't wreaking havoc on our Earth? Why would the fossil fuel industry need to hire people like you to convince people there's no problem, if everything's hunky-dory?'

Howard shut up. A sinking feeling started in his gut and continued up to his heart. He knew that the climate was changing. His bosses knew, too. It was just that they were trying to make sure nothing stood in the way of the fossil fuel industry's expansion. The American Dream required American industry. And American factories ran on fossil fuels. They could not let tree huggers shut down progress.

"Howard, you are a part of a fragile ecosystem. You depend on this planet for life. The air you breathe, the food you eat, your very life relies on this amazing creation. But if you destroy an aspect of the system, you destroy yourself. Take this pandemic, for example. It's a symptom of a larger problem."

"Now there you're wrong," Howard argued. "There were plagues long before the climate began changing."

"You'll see," the voice said. "What's happening now is much different."

Howard looked back down and followed the swollen Mississippi to its mouth where he knew it spilled out into the Gulf. Again he saw flooding and too much water. "Is that New Orleans?"

"Yes. Hurricanes changed the face of New Orleans. Katrina caused over fifteen billion dollars in damage. And the hurricane season becomes more costly every year, with more storms of greater intensity. As the ocean warms, the tropical storms build more quickly. In recent years, hurricanes have hit the east coast hard, destroying island playlands of the wealthy. You don't hear much about it because the tourist industry doesn't want you to know."

The planes turned abruptly ninety degrees to the right. Howard could see the gulf as they veered west. *Ah*, he thought, *that must be Texas on the horizon.*

"Hurricanes are nothing new," Howard said. "You know, back at the turn of the century, a hurricane put Galveston under water. It's just part of the way our planet works."

"Yes, Howard, you're right. We have had hurricanes here for hundreds of years, but if you study the numbers, they're getting worse, causing billions in damages. This is well documented by our climate scientists. And the sea level is rising. In parts of Florida, the ocean is already mixing with ground water."

"Now, that's just a construction issue," Howard said. "Those cities were built too close to the ocean."

"True. But they were fine until the glaciers started melting. Did you know that at your military base in Virginia Beach, it's regularly flooding, without even a big storm, due to the rising ocean? The ice caps are melting. People are going to have to move inland soon."

Howard remained silent. He didn't want to think about those things. Most of the time, he pushed the negative reports out of his head. He believed in American progress. Environmentalists were always slowing that down, ringing alarms and pushing for more regulation. His job was to smooth over the truth so the dream could continue.

"Howard," the voice said. "We're passing over the desert now."

"Oh, yeah," Howard said. "Been there for centuries. I just drove across it a few days ago."

"Yes, but did you know that our changing climate increases droughts in the west? The desert gets bigger every year. Water supplies are dwindling in Colorado, for example. People flocked there from California. The water table can't support them."

Howard felt concern as they crossed the desert and headed to his home state of California, yet also so very happy to be going to the place he loved. "Ventura Highway" played in his head. Then he started whistling his favorite Beach Boys' tune, "Everybody's gone surfin', surfin' USA."

As they flew over Colorado, they circled over a runway in a small airport below. Six little red, white, and blue jets appeared ready for takeoff. Howard looked closer. Were those the Thunderbird jets of the Air Force? He really did die and go to heaven! Flying with the Blue Angels and the Thunderbirds? "Here we go, into the wild blue yonder" he hummed as the six planes followed each other across the runway, then lifted into the sky, The gold and blue Blue Angel jets enlarged their circle, making room for the Thunderbirds to join. Together, all ten jets came full circle, then one plane broke formation, leading the others out toward the coast. Howard cruised in pure bliss as they crossed over into his very own California.

But then the voice interrupted his joy. "And the west is burning."

Howard peered down to watch flames engulfing trees from the south to the north. They flew low enough that Howard saw not only the fire, but parched land left desolate in the aftermath of the blaze. They sped up north where trees flamed over mountainous ridges, ravaging Oregon and the State of Washington.

"With our changing climate," the voice continued, "we have experienced unprecedented wildfires, destroying thousands of acres of our forests, and burning houses. Just last year, wildfire changed the face of Santa Rosa forever. The Cascade Mountains of Washington lost thousands of acres of forest growth."

"Wildfires are a part of nature," Howard countered, not sure who might be listening. "Nature does that. Lightning strikes clear out old growth, allows for new seedlings to break through." Howard knew what to say about these things. "Poor forest management causes wildfires," he added.

"Yes," the voice agreed. "But because of climate change, we have more droughts. Dry summers cause more wildfires. Did you know that the State of California lost a third of its trees in recent years to the fires? Loss of trees leads to soil erosion and quicker desertification. California will never be the same."

"What do you want me to do about it?" Howard began to argue. "I don't have the power to change this." His voice increased in volume. He heard himself shouting. "Why are you telling me these things? What can I do?"

"Howard, think." A long pause made Howard feel very anxious, but then the voice continued. "You know the error of your ways. You know exactly what you can do about all of this. Just think about it."

The plane started vibrating, then shaking. The controls flashed. The plane tilted, until Howard was suspended sideways in his seat. Then it flipped all the way over. Howard hung upside down. The planes started flying in circles again. He saw one plane above and two below. They spiraled downward as the circles became smaller.

"You are in the eye of a tornado," the voice said. "As a result of climate change. tornadoes are also becoming more deadly and destructive, increasing in frequency every year."

Howard held on for dear life, bracing himself for a collision. They were descending rapidly; he knew they couldn't be more than a hundred feet above the ground. Suddenly, he heard a loud smashing noise, followed by a series of beeps.

He opened his eyes. The tube stuffed down his throat made it impossible to breathe. The beeping came from a nearby monitor. He looked for his plane. What happened to the tornado? Where was he now?

Where had he been?

66. LANDTREE FARM

The morning passed quickly for Mariah and her mom. They enjoyed a delicious breakfast while listening to the story of the Landtree dairy store that had become a destination for people far and wide with fun and activities offered year long.

After breakfast, Charlie treated them to a tour. Before they left the car, he showed them a short documentary on the car's video screen which explained the organic farming techniques, permaculture, and preservation of heirloom seeds. Mariah learned that their strategies of farming helped rejuvenate the soil and also helped draw down carbon.

At the end of the film, a still picture of a young man filled the screen. Rebecca gasped. "Joe!"

"This farm celebrates the vision of Joseph Landtree, Junior, who conceptualized this land producing as it does today. We thank Joe for his vision and his good work. We dedicate our future to the memory of his creative genius."

Then the Landtree logo filled the screen. The dark woman with the long hair morphed into the painting of the woman Mariah remembered from the office of her grandfather in the video. The narrator explained. "We owe who we are today to Joe, and also to our great grandmother, Naomi Cyclone Thunderbird. True to her Native American heritage, she taught us that in our work with the land and vegetation, we must consider how the changes will impact seven generations into the future. If you pollute the land, what will happen to the animals and the people? Will the crops still grow? If you cut down too many trees, will you damage the ecosystem? She believed we are caretakers of the land for our children and their children's children far into the future.

"She's our mentor and our guide. Once hidden from public view, we now display her proudly. She holds the wisdom needed for our common future."

Mariah's mouth hung open in surprise. How could all of this be happening just a few hours away and she'd never known about it? How could this all be possible? The image of her father lingered in her mind, superimposed with that of her great-grandmother Naomi, as they toured the farm and its fields and orchards. Charlie explained the permaculture techniques in great detail. At the end of the tour, he presented Mariah and her mom pouches of seeds labeled Landtree Heirlooms.

Charlie ushered them back to his truck. "Next up, Landtree Homestead for lunch, but first I need to go check on something," he said. "I'll be right back, ladies."

Rebecca's eyes were red, her face still wet from tears, yet Mariah questioned her. "Why? I don't get it. Why did Dad want me to come here, if he refused? And why make me wait until I'm all grown to meet my family?"

"Your dad had some strange ideas, Mariah. He also suffered with mental health issues. One time, they diagnosed him with bipolar disorder, but he was never treated for it. That illness causes you to fluctuate between mania and depression. Your dad would get crazy with fantastic ideas and angry when people challenged him on them. Probably that's what happened with your grandfather. It's hard to communicate with a person when they're upset. They can be very unreasonable."

Bipolar disorder? Mariah couldn't believe it. "Are you sure? Why didn't I know this? Could my baby have that? Could I?"

"You were so young, Mariah, and you loved your father. Like I said, they never treated him for it. Maybe I should have explained when you got older. Yes, it can be genetic. You could have it, but I've never seen evidence of those behaviors with you, honey. I don't think you have it. And hopefully your child won't have it, either, but it can sometimes skip a generation. Maybe your dad didn't even really have it. I'm not sure."

"You've been crying a lot today, Mom. Is there something else you haven't told me?" Mariah asked.

Her mother paused, stared out the window, took a very deep breath, and then started to explain. "Well, yes. I feel guilty for all of this. I wanted to protect Joe from his father. I told him to stay away and never to trust the man. I didn't want that pain, either. He kicked me out, too. I think I made some mistakes back then."

Mariah nodded. "I understand it was hard for you, but forgiveness is important. Look at what you both missed."

"Yes. Just before someone dies, they often have moments of clarity. Your dad pepped up like that. I even thought he might pull through. He started writing letters to his family, to you, and to me. He obviously thought he was dying, leaving orders on when and how they were to be handed out after he passed on. But one night he became very angry. He threw the letters into the fire. Fortunately, I'd already stowed my letters away. The next morning, after his rage had subsided, I found your letter on the floor and showed it to him. At first, I thought he might burn it, too. But then he handed it to me. 'Give it to her when she's grown, Rebecca, when she's ready to have a child of her own.' He died the next week."

67. MAX CALLS HOME

For the first time in weeks, Max could relax. However, he didn't enjoy the fact that the man who terrorized him was fighting for life in the local ICU. He still felt compassion for the guy. Knowing the sheriff was keeping Howard under surveillance brought a sort of peace that Max hadn't experienced for a very long time. He knew they could, and probably would, assign a similar troll to his case, but for now, his nemesis was out of commission.

This was the day Max planned to come clean with his family. They deserved to know about Mariah and the baby. It might be weeks before he could actually go home for a visit. The pandemic now seemed likely to stretch out into the future, much longer than he'd originally imagined. So he invited his folks to a Zoom call. He wanted to see their faces when he shared the news. Part of him wanted to wait until Mariah came home, but he realized it made more sense to give them some time to digest the news before they met her. He was afraid they'd be more than a little upset.

Max knew his parents wanted him to find love again. His mother had relentlessly offered to fix him up with various women after Gabrielle and Isabella died. Eventually, they would welcome Mariah and love her. She might not have academic credentials, but no one who spent time with Mariah could say anything negative about her.

He had no intention of telling his parents that the child was conceived on one of their first dates, a night when they'd both drank too much. He was embarrassed by that, and knew they'd have harsh words about having raised him better than that. And he didn't want Mariah to begin her relationship with them on a sour note. First he'd break the news and get their support. Then he'd introduce her.

Situating himself in the recliner, he rocked back and extended his legs. Might as well get comfortable for this uncomfortable chat. He searched for just the right words to break the news. He wanted to sugarcoat the situation a little bit. After a few moments' thought, he decided he wouldn't discuss the timing at all.

His dog plopped down by his side and he stroked his soft fur. Gus had accepted Mariah at first glance, eating out of her hand and paying almost as much attention to Mariah as the dog did to him. He hoped for the same from his parents.

Max opened his laptop and started the Zoom meeting, waiting for his parents to join. He turned on his video, smiling at himself in the screen, enjoying the nice little beard gracing his face, along with his shaggy long hair. Living in the woods this past year, he'd thoroughly enjoyed the freedom to go a little wild. His parents, he suspected, probably would not appreciate his new look.

He received notification from Zoom that a participant was in the waiting room, so he took a deep breath and admitted them to the meeting. *Show time.*

"Good afternoon," he said. "It's great to see you. You're both looking good."

His father smiled. His mother greeted him warmly. "Hi, Max. It's good to see you, too. We've missed you around here since Christmas. How's everything going?"

"Well, of course, this is a difficult time with the pandemic. Things seem upside down in Friendly. We've got our first cases, but we're doing well, compared to some places. I hear Franklin County is one of the hot spots."

"Yes," his dad said. "Your mother and I are being very careful. We wear plastic gloves when we go to the store, and always masks. Unfortunately, there are quite a few people without masks."

"You could do home delivery or curbside pickup, Dad. You can afford it. That's much safer," Max suggested. "I think the first few deliveries are free."

"Right," his dad said. "Reel them in, get them hooked, then wham, the fees start skyrocketing. No, thank you I'll do my own shopping."

"We do try to go when they open the store for senior citizens early in the morning," his mother added.

"Shouldn't have to," his dad grumbled.

"You're a little grumpy, Dad. Are you okay?"

"Just keeping it real, Max. You know I don't like change. This year's been a bear for old codgers like me."

"For all of us," Max agreed. "How's the family doing?"

"Just fine," his mother said. "You should come up some weekend and we'll have everyone over. Kids grow up fast. You're missing out."

"That's a great idea. I'll look at my schedule and get back to you on a good weekend.

"So, what's new with you, Max?" his mother asked. To change the subject, Max suspected.

"Oh, I'm good. Buck and I started production in our wind machine factory and that seems to be going very well so far. We've made the first shipments with more orders than we can fill anytime soon. Fortunately, the governor's letting the factories keep churning out the goods. Essential workers, they call us. Energy is essential."

"I'm real proud of you, son," his dad said. "I admire you. You might get knocked down, but you dust yourself off, get back up and start running. Another man might've gone into a tailspin after what happened to you. But here you are, doing something new, something very amazing, no less."

Max frowned. The not-so-perfect son had called to drop a bombshell. He wanted to set the record straight, before he lost the nerve, rather than drag out the inevitable. He still hadn't found the right words, but decided it probably didn't matter in the long run.

"I have something I need to tell you," Max said. He paused, took a deep breath and continued. "I met a woman. Her name's Mariah Landtree. We're going to get married. She's pregnant."

"What?" his mother asked. "What did you say?"

"You heard him," his dad said. "He got her pregnant."

"George," his mother protested, "don't talk like that. Max, tell us the story so he'll understand."

Max laughed. He loved his mom for giving him the benefit of the doubt, even though his dad was absolutely right. But he wanted them to like Mariah and trust his decision to get involved, so he decided to embellish their story of romance, knowing the truth might be somewhere between his tale and what really happened. "Do you believe in love at first sight?" he asked.

His mother giggled. His father frowned. "Tell him, George," his mother insisted.

"What?" Max asked. "Have you not told me your whole story?" He thought he knew it all. His mother liked to talk. The romance began in the summer, after his dad's junior year in college. He interned at a law firm and his mother was a paralegal at the time. They worked on some cases together and started to date. The romance carried them through his senior year and the relationship survived three years of law school before they tied the knot. He never doubted the love his parents shared. But they'd never mentioned love at first sight. "Dad, what? Tell me."

His father laughed. "Okay. It was June 2, 1975, at eight a.m. when I first showed up for my internship at Gabrielsen and Mason's Law Firm in downtown Columbus. The secretary showed me in, and they assigned me to your mother to orient me to the firm, get me situated at a desk, and give me a few assignments. I don't need to tell you, son, that your mother is a beautiful woman. Beautiful now, beautiful then. She batted her big brown eyes at me and I was a goner. Haven't wanted any other woman for thirty-eight years. It took a while for her to come around, but for me, I fell off the deep end that very first day and never looked back. First impressions don't lie. Yes, I admit, I fell in love at first sight, but I think it's extremely rare."

"Wow, Dad. Who'da thought?" His conservative father, known for measured decisions and meticulous practices, jumped in from the get-go when it came to love? Max seized the opportunity to launch into his story. "When I moved to Friendly, you know I was lower than low. I fully expected I'd never love again. I didn't want to grow into a bitter old man, but I sure seemed to be headed in that direction. And in a small town, you know there aren't a whole lot of options anyway. But one day, I got tired of my own cooking and checked out the local diner, the Wind Song Café. I'd been out hiking on a very windy October day. I practically blew into this little restaurant, along with some leaves, and there, to my surprise, was a beautiful young woman behind the counter, looking at me with a curious smile. Mariah." He paused and smiled, looked at his little camera squarely so that his parents would feel the intensity of his words. "From the beginning, I felt drawn in like a moth to light.

"One night, she invited me into the church. She lives next door to the Episcopal church, with the late pastor's wife, and had the key. She started singing. You know how much I like to sing. We sang a duet. It was breathtaking, listening to her soprano voice fill that sanctuary, and when I joined her with my tenor? A match made in heaven. It just seemed like we were meant to be, you know? You'll like her. She's the sweetest person—"

His father interrupted. "Did she finish college?"

Leave it to his father to ruin a good story. "She's working on it. Her father died when she was very young, then her mother went into rehab after a run-in with an abusive second husband. Her mother just came back a few months ago after five years."

"Be careful," his dad warned. "Those experiences mess with a person. You may not like what you're getting into here. Why did you go and get her pregnant, son? We taught you better than that."

Max shrugged. "I know, I know. We should have been more careful, but accidents happen. Having another child was the last thing on my mind. As a matter of fact, I told myself I'd never open my heart again. After losing one family, I did not want to put myself in a position to suffer like that again. Yet here I am, starting up all over and you know what? I'm happier than I ever thought possible. Mariah's sweet and strong at the same time and she shares my love of nature and the wind. It feels right. And just like you, it was definitely love at first sight. Like father, like son." Max knew he was stretching the truth a little bit here to get them on his side. The truth was that love was developing, but not yet spoken of.

"I'm so happy for you, Max," his mother said.

His father grunted, but then said, "A chip off the old block, I guess."

"So when's the wedding? Can I help?" his mother asked.

"I haven't even given her a ring yet. Really, we haven't talked about it beyond I've told her I'm there for her. I'm taking it slowly. I'd like to wait until this pandemic is behind us so we can do this properly. I just wanted to tell you and I'd like you to meet her," Max explained to try to slow his parents down, knowing he couldn't backtrack now.

"Yes," her mother said. "When? By Zoom? As soon as possible. I'm dying to meet her. I'm so glad you've found someone."

His father frowned again, but then agreed. "Yes, I'd like to meet this Mariah myself. She must be a very special woman."

"Okay," Max said. "I'll arrange that real soon. And thanks for the support. It means the world to me. I've got to get to work now, but I'll talk to Mariah and find a time we can chat online. Okay?"

"Sounds good," his mother said. "We're not going anywhere. Who knows how long this pandemic will last."

"Right," Max said. "I'll call you. Bye for now. Love you."

"We love you too, dear," his mother said. "Talk with you real soon."

Max ended the meeting and took a moment to reflect. Did he have their support? His mother seemed happy, but his father had cautioned him about Mariah's background. Once they met her, they'd come around. He was sure of it.

Charlie returned before Mariah and her mother could finish their discussion. As much as Mariah tried to understand, she really couldn't. How her father and mother had kept her separated from the rest of her family for all her life didn't make sense. She realized, though, that nothing could change her past, and that, starting today, her life seemed be changing with each new discovery on this adventure.

"Next up, Landtree Homestead," Charlie announced. "Get ready to meet the fam."

Goosebumps formed on Mariah's arms as they cruised down the highway. Soon, Charlie turned onto a tree-lined lane. Straight ahead stood a traditional white farmhouse with several additions. But the lane also branched off into what looked like small neighborhoods, where she could see newer houses in the distance. A large circular drive provided ample parking for the numerous cars already present. Charlie pulled right up to the front door, under a portico with white columns, and ran around to open the doors for Mariah and her mother.

Charlie left the truck parked in front of the door as he ushered them into a large foyer. At first, Mariah didn't see anyone, but then all of a sudden, a multitude jumped up and out from every corner. All sizes and ages of people, all covered with the signature Landtree COVID masks that Mariah and her mother wore as well. "Surprise," they yelled.

After the noise died down, a little girl with brown hair hanging in ringlets down her back, stepped forward. "I'm Molly Landtree," she said and handed them each a bouquet of daffodils. "Welcome home."

Mariah reached down to accept the flowers. Although she couldn't see the girl's face, her eyes looked very familiar. They looked like her own in the photos lining the pages of the one treasured album she kept of the days before her father passed. "Thank you, Molly. Thank you so much," Mariah said.

Behind Mariah, a tall, beautiful woman stepped forward and, again, Mariah instantly saw familiar features. This woman's body reminded Mariah of her dad. Even with her face hidden behind a mask, her big eyes with long lashes felt like a gaze from her father. Her luscious long hair flowed around her face and down her back. Mariah noticed her well-manicured, painted nails as she bid Mariah and her mom welcome.

"I'm your Aunt Julia," she said. "Welcome home. We're glad you both came. Rebecca, great to see you again. Our family has been incomplete for such a long time. You two fill a gaping hole that we've suffered since my father kicked my brother Joe out of the family fold.

Afterwards, he regretted that decision every single day of his life. I wish he could be here to welcome you home, but I think he's watching from up above and I have a feeling he's finally made amends." She handed Mariah a large book. "This is our family story. You can read it when you have time."

Aunt Julia seemed genuinely happy to see her mom, but Mariah noticed her mother struggling to manage composure. She didn't return the smile, but instead seemed to be fighting tears. Mariah got it. They'd kicked her mother out. It must be hard to remember the trauma of the past.

With her arms now laden with these precious gifts of the daffodil bouquet and the large bound book, Mariah murmured, "Thank you, Aunt Julia." Her heart overflowed with love. She looked beyond her aunt to the many people standing around the room, knowing they were her relations as well. "It's good to be home," she told her aunt and realized she really meant it. After feeling orphaned for so many years, she could barely contain her joy.

Uncle Barney appeared and announced, "Lunch is served in the great hall. Please take your seats. Sit with your family units in the plexiglass stations. I apologize for the separation, but we want to keep everybody safe. You can remove your masks once you sit at your tables."

Mariah tried to beam a smile at him with her eyes. She doubted he could see the emotion bubbling up from her heart into her face. She wished she could hug these newfound family members, but she needed to keep herself and her baby safe and not risk infecting anybody else as well, if by some chance she had the virus herself.

Mariah's mother took her hand and they followed the people streaming from the foyer down a long hall into what looked like a banquet hall. Once again, she saw tears on her mother's face. "You sure are crying a lot today, Mom," she observed.

"I know, honey. I'm happy and sad all at once. I just wish your dad could see all this. I feel sorry he never knew about his impact in the family business. He lost out on so much by never forgiving his father. And I feel guilty for encouraging him to stay away. I see now he missed out on just so much good here."

Mariah nodded as they entered the room. "I feel sad for Dad, too," she said. "If only he could have seen the farm and his ideas being implemented. Such a tragedy, for him and for us. But we're here now, and I, for one, am going to treasure this family of mine for the rest of my life. Thank you for giving me Dad's note, Mom. Thank you for keeping it and remembering to honor his wishes. I wish I'd known years ago, but maybe this is perfect timing. Maybe Dad knew exactly what he was doing."

"Maybe," Rebecca said. "But you deserved to know your family, Mariah. Looking back, I'm not sure we did the right thing. But you're right, we're here now, and for that, I'm grateful."

Barney motioned to Mariah and her mom to take seats at the small table in the middle of the room, circled with plexiglass. Their place settings both faced the side of the room where a podium and microphone stood. She noticed the other tables, although round, also had the chairs facing the microphone. "Do you think we're going to have a program, Mom?"

"We'll see soon, I guess."

"I'm glad my appetite's back," Mariah, said. "I'm getting hungry again. But if I wasn't pregnant, I don't think I could eat again after that big breakfast."

"I know," her mom said. "I still feel stuffed."

Charlie poked his head into their plexiglass enclosure. "I forgot to give you this," he said. "Your second note on your 'Adventure of Discovery.'" He placed it on their table and backed away. "Enjoy your meal."

"Another message from Grandfather?" Mariah asked. Charlie nodded before leaving. "This is so very cool, Mom. I don't ever want this day to end. I feel like I'm dreaming and I'm going to wake up and find out it's not true. I mean, really. This is amazing. Doesn't it feel like a dream?"

"I know what you mean," her mother said. "I had no idea. Never in a million years would I have expected anything like this."

She picked up the envelope Charlie placed on the table and, once again, marveled at how her grandfather designed the day for them. The envelope simply read "#2". She pulled the paper out of the envelope and read:

Your second stop will be Landtree Homestead. We welcome you home, Joe. I know the farmhouse will be familiar to you, although you'll be surprised at the many additions since you were here. You may also be interested in knowing that we took your advice. The house is now powered entirely by a mix of solar and geothermal energy. No fossil fuels used in this structure, Joe.

We've also developed a subdivision for your siblings and their families who want to stay around, and so you can see the houses we've built, also fueled with alternative energy. I know you recommended this. We thank you.

Our family keeps growing and we've missed having you and your wife and little girl at our family gatherings. I hope that will change now that you're back home with us. There's always a place for you at the table, and we'll build you a house if you want to move back.

I know you were also offended by our use of the migrant, undocumented workers, son, and you complained to me about their living conditions on the edge of our farm. You were right about that, too. I want you to know that we now work with our government to bring our migrant workers in legally, and that they, too, have modern housing. We provide health insurance and options for them to stay year-round, working in our factory when the farming season comes to a close, if they wish.

I'm so sorry I lost you, Joe. I've regretted my decision every day of my life for many years. And now, as I know my days are few, I wish I could make it up to you somehow. I'm trying, son, but it will never be enough. I apologize and pray someday you might find it in your heart to forgive me.

Love, Dad

Mariah looked at her mom. "This is unreal! Can you believe it? How did Dad not know what was going on? This is like a tragic movie! How could he not know how his dad did a three-sixty, taking all of his advice? Somebody should have gotten in Dad's face and demanded he come home."

"You know, Mariah, I think they did. His brothers and sisters visited, more than once, and tried to convince him to come home. Especially the year your grandfather died, they tried very hard. Your dad wouldn't listen. Not until his last few days. I think he started to come around, but there was no time."

Mariah tried to comprehend the past, but she couldn't. And then, the feast began. Young people from some of the family tables stood up, put their masks back on and began to serve the salads, soup, and sandwiches to all the tables in the room. It was simple, but also elegant. A strawberry avocado salad, a black bean soup loaded with veggies, and a platter with a selection of mini subs, some with veggies and cheeses, others with turkey and cheese, and still others, chicken salad. Mariah knew there was way too much food on the table for just the two of them, but she appreciated that they offered a selection of sandwiches to be sure to meet their dietary preferences.

And after a few minutes, a screen rolled down from the side wall, above a stage which Mariah hadn't noticed earlier. A video began, introducing the Landtree Family who'd received land grants in the early 1800s after Ohio became a state in 1803. Three brothers had come across the Atlantic on a boat and changed their name once they settled and began their orchard. The film summarized the family's story over the past two hundred years with family portraits, highlighting the family business milestones and the development of the Landtree Family Homestead as well. The narrative reviewed the history explained in her letter, explaining that they intentionally built houses around the original farmhouse, gradually building a community for the extended family.

Mariah thought, *How nice that must be, to have cousins and aunts living right down the street and all over the neighborhood. Perhaps I could visit and bring my child to know of this amazing family legacy.*

When the pictures of her father's era began popping up on the screen, she watched her father grow from a baby to a little boy and finally a teenager. There was even a picture of her dad and mom together, a wedding photo. Images of her father with his brothers and sister as they stood together on family occasions through the years were displayed on the screen. These group pictures ended abruptly, probably signaling the time her parents were banished. And yet, somehow, pictures of herself displayed also, as a baby and a small child. In one picture, her father held her under the apple tree in their yard. Then she saw herself in school and even a brief video of her singing in church. She asked her mom, "How did they get all these pictures of me?"

"I remember your dad sent his sister pictures from time to time," her mother told her. "Maybe she found the others on the internet. Doesn't the church website have videos of the services? I'm surprised no one tried to contact you before this."

Mariah had a great number of questions now and so much she didn't understand. Many of the answers undoubtedly had gone to the grave with her dad and grandfather. However, someone in this family had kept tabs on her all along.

"Mom, I need to go to the bathroom," Actually, she just needed to get away for a moment.

"Do you want me to come?"

Mariah laughed. "No, Mom. I can go to the bathroom alone now, remember?"

Her mother laughed back as Mariah rose and walked toward the door where they entered. She could find her way to the restroom if she started where they came in. She walked down the hall to women's powder room, as the door named it. She happily discovered the room empty. Mariah felt the silence envelope her in calm. As much as this day meant to her, she was also completely overwhelmed. After a few minutes, she summoned the strength to return.

All eyes turned on Mariah as she returned to her seat. She nodded to Barney who stood at the lectern. Uncle Barney then said, "Mariah and Rebecca, turn to page one hundred and twenty in the Family Book on the table between you to see the families listed with their names. We will now begin introducing ourselves."

Individual family groups came to the microphone and introduced each member of their nuclear family. She opened the large volume between her mom's plate and her own and kept flipping through the pages to find the family standing at the mic. She wanted to etch their faces and names on her heart and in her memory.

Her extended family suddenly became very real. She opened her heart to her uncles and aunts, her cousins, and all the children standing together like family portraits in the room. She couldn't keep it all straight, but she knew the book would help her learn who was who.

After the introductions, her father's siblings stood up and started to talk about their brother Joe. This time, Mariah cried along with her mother as they learned about his childhood, his vision for the future, and the pain they'd shared when their father cast him out.

When the presentation ended, slices of apple pie and bowls of ice cream were served to all the tables. Then Aunt Julia took the microphone and looked directly at Mariah and Rebecca, saying, "You always have a home with us. If at any point in the future either of you would like to join us here, know that we will build you the house of your dreams. You can live right here on the Landtree Homestead for the rest of your lives. Welcome home."

For a long time after Howard woke up, he kept reliving that dream in his mind. In his younger days, he'd dreamed of flying with the Blue Angels, but his eyesight issues had killed any hope of entering pilot school. Grounded, his life took a different turn. And now, just as he was prepared to bite the dust, he'd soared into the big blue yonder. The spectacle of the experience gave him something to savor in the pits of his current situation.

Fortunately, after a few hours, they removed the ventilator. His throat burned from the damage and his voice sounded raspy. Not that he had much to say, and not that anyone really cared to listen. The nurses seemed friendly enough, but they weren't lingering in his room any longer than absolutely necessary. He felt like he'd been run over by a Mack truck. He couldn't find the energy to reach for the remote to turn on the television. That gave him an idea of just how sick he really was.

The afternoon nurse came in, masked and covered from head to toe with the hospital isolation garb. He felt like a pariah, one of the untouchables, as she reached to adjust his equipment with plastic gloves. He wanted to engage her in small talk, even as lousy as he felt. He needed to break the bone-chilling isolation of his COVID room.

"Well, good afternoon," he half-whispered, half-spoke in his hoarse voice. "Did I die yet?" He could only hope she had a sense of humor.

"No, your vitals are improving. You're not ready to go to the Friday night dance, but if you continue like this, we might get you out of here in a few days. But you did give us a scare the other night."

"What happened?" There was no way she could possibly know about the plane crash. Hell, he could barely remember it himself. Then he self-corrected. No, that was a dream. He needed some answers. "What day is this anyway? How long was I out?"

The nurse looked at his chart. "You've been here five days," she reported.

"Five days? I don't remember that," he said. "Where have I been?"

"We keep you sedated when you're on the ventilator. You were struggling for your life. The other night you coded. We thought we lost you. Your heart stopped. They called in the code team to get it started again. They hook you up to a machine and it shocks your heart to hopefully get it beating again. In your case, it worked. And, fortunately for you, once your heart came back to life, you started to turn the corner. Your fever subsided and we were able to wean you off the ventilator and switch to a CPAP and now just oxygen. You're one of the lucky ones."

Howard grimaced. "Wow. I died and came back to life. I'm a modern-day Jesus! Every bone and muscle in my body aches and I can't even pick up the remote. If this is lucky, I wonder what the alternative might be."

As soon as he said it, he felt bad. He heard himself and the lack of gratitude in his voice. Hadn't she just told him he almost died? Suddenly, his mother came into his mind. She'd been gone for years and, with her had gone most of his childhood memories. It was too painful, reliving what he lost. But now, he remembered his mom. "Your life will make a difference, son," she'd liked to tell him. When he got hit by a car, his mother nursed him back to health. She told him back then that God still wanted him around. "God's got some big job out there for you, Howard," she'd insisted. Now, suddenly, he grasped the truth. He let the Boss in the skies down, big time. Yep, he'd messed up royally.

"Can I get you anything to drink?" the nurse asked, interrupting Howard's inner soliloquy.

"What?" he blurted, somewhat embarrassed he'd forgotten she was in the room with him. "I'm sorry," he recovered. "What did you say? I must've been dozing off."

"Can I get you anything to drink?"

"You serve beer in here?" he asked, thinking he could get her to laugh.

He thought maybe she smiled before she gave him her prim answer. "Of course not, no. You're on a clear liquid diet until the doctor clears you for soft food. Water, tea, coffee. Those are your choices now."

"I'd love some coffee with sugar," he said. The next words out of his mouth surprised even him. "Could I speak to a priest?"

"Sure. I'll get you some coffee and call our chaplain's office about a priest. Anyone in particular?"

"I'm not from around here. Just your run of the mill priest will do. I'm Catholic. A Catholic priest, please."

This nurse seemed to be staying longer than most. Maybe now that his fever was down, perhaps he wasn't contagious?

Did I just ask for a priest? I must be losing my mind. Which seemed as fuzzy as his energy, or lack thereof. He closed his eyes and slipped into a very deep sleep.

Charlie showed up at their table right as the luncheon presentations ended and handed Mariah the third envelope. Mariah's mouth opened wide as she took the envelope, realizing that their journey of adventure continued. "This is a lot," she told him. "It's all good, but I'm completely overwhelmed. I think I'm in a dream, but then I pinch myself and I know I'm really here."

"Give yourself time," Rebecca said. "Maybe you need a break."

Charlie looked at his watch. "We're due at Landtree Solar at three thirty. We have a couple hours. Would you like to go for a short hike? There's a nature trail not too far from here. Would that help?"

"I'd love that," Mariah said, "but I think I need a nap."

"How about I take you to my house? We have a guest suite You can both take a nap and freshen up a bit. Would an hour be enough?"

"That would really help," Mariah said. "My baby takes a lot of my energy. Naps are good. But a walk in the woods would be awesome, too. It always refreshes me."

"Me, too," Charlie replied. "Must be in our genes, you think?"

"It's our DNA," Mariah agreed. "I mean, we are nature, all of us."

"And also, being out in the natural world helps refresh us. A walk in the woods helps slow us down so we appreciate life more and realize the miracles unfolding all around us."

"Wow. That sounds like something I'd say. Let's get the nap over so we can get outside." she told him. "Mom, are you up for a hike in the woods?"

"Sure thing," Rebecca said. "But I like the idea of a nap first, too. I'm not getting younger. Days like this wear me out."

Mariah half-listened to Charlie's monologue as her mind raced with the new realities of her life. She kept thinking about her family, her new family, all of the people gathered there for lunch who had welcomed her and wanted to know her, who'd invited her to come live with them. After a life of being an only child, losing her father and then her mother moving away, it was hard to believe.

After a nice nap, Mariah felt revived, ready to face the rest of the day. She loved Charlie's idea to visit the nature park. As they strolled along the soft path, the smells of the earth and green things growing filled her lungs with oxygen and her heart with joy. Late spring wildflowers decorated their way, and she kept pausing to snap pictures with her cell phone. She loved that Charlie and her mom didn't talk. Together, they walked silently through the woods. It gave Mariah a chance to catch her breath from the happenings of the day. She felt incredibly blessed and began to cry. Pregnancy hormones kept her emotions close to the surface and this was big.

She remembered the third note. She searched for it in her small backpack of a purse and slowed her steps as her mom and Charlie forged ahead. She wanted to read it now. She sat on a bench by the path, opening the seal to read the final note from her grandfather.

The envelope was marked with nothing more than a 3, but the note inside again was addressed to her father.

Joe,

You have so many great ideas and I apologize again for not hearing you out at times. You were always learning, suggesting new possibilities, and I was like an old dog, set in his ways. But I did listen to you and after you left, I started exploring some of the things you were talking about.

Remember the day you came home and wanted us to go solar? You told us we could put solar panels on our roof and it would provide electricity for our house. You said that we could put them on our barn to provide the energy for the milking machines. And you told me about how the Earth is heating up and we need to switch to renewable fuel sources to quit putting so much carbon in the air.

At the time, I didn't think you knew what you were talking about. But after I started reading and learning, I discovered that, instead, I didn't know which end was up. Your brother Tim took an interest in solar panels and decided to get a degree in industrial engineering from Ohio State. Before long, he graduated and we began scheming to start our own solar factory.

How many times I called you, Joe. I wanted you to come back to see what good your ideas have produced. I wanted you to be here with me, son. If you're reading this letter, I guess you finally decided to come home. I'm sorry I can't be here for you, but your brothers can.

You'll be amazed at what Tim has done with Landtree Solar. You are an owner. Even though you didn't even know it existed, you have a share. Go visit your factory, son, and be proud of what you've accomplished.

Know I never stopped loving you and I hope someday you'll find it in your heart to forgive your old man who made a very serious mistake.

Love, Dad.

Mariah sat on the bench, crying. She carefully folded the letter and placed it back in her purse. Her heart ached for her dad and his broken relationship with his father. Once she let the floodgates open, her sobbing expressed all that she missed, growing up so out of touch with her Landtree family. And mingled with the grief, she felt great joy. Today, her whole world had opened into the embrace of her unknown extended family They'd showered her with love and acceptance.

"Mariah?" her mother called. "Mariah!"

Then she heard Charlie. "Are you all right, Mariah?"

She brushed her tears off on her sleeve and ran down the path toward their voices. At a sudden turn, she collided with her mother, who enfolded her in a big hug.

"Mariah," her mom said, holding her tight. "We were worried about you. We were walking along and, all of a sudden, realized you weren't behind us anymore."

Charlie came up behind her mom. "Are you okay?"

Mariah smiled. "I'm sorry. I remembered the third letter you gave me and sat down to read it. I'm okay. This is a lot. I'm happy, but also I'm sad for Dad and his father, and for not knowing all of you before today."

Charlie said, "It is very sad, but also so wonderful that you're here with us today. Let's keep walking so we can make our appointment at Landtree Solar."

They walked briskly along the trail, circling back to the parking area and then drove the short distance to the factory. "Everything seems so close together," Mariah remarked.

"Yes, all part of the original land grant. Well, several brothers came here and so they each had a grant and, over the years, purchased neighboring property. The farm expanded, and eventually provided space for the subdivision, and also the factory," Charlie explained.

The rest of the afternoon passed in a whirlwind as Mariah met her dad's brother, Timothy, as he liked to be called. He told them they now held a patent for a new version of a solar panel that didn't require the rare mineral that earlier panels required. "When we first started, we paid for the common design. Over time, we developed our own panels and patents. Our research division continues to focus on innovation. We turn out traditional solar panels, roof panels, and also little solar panels to power smaller items, such as laptops and outdoor lights. One of our most recent designs involves an antenna-like structure that can be mounted on the roof of a house. When the sun shines, it activates a switch which causes the panels to open, kind of like an umbrella. When it gets too dark for the panels to absorb the light, the panels close, and lower, and retract close to the roof."

Mariah enjoyed her Uncle Timothy's enthusiasm. He reminded her of her father in some ways. She remembered her father's excitement about his dreams. She tried to imagine how he might feel if he could be here right now and hear his brother talking.

At the end of the tour, Timothy gave both Mariah and her mom a Landtree Solar kit that included several solar-powered devices, including a calculator, an outdoor lamp, and a garden fountain.

At four o'clock, Charlie loaded them back into the truck, telling them, "Now I need to take you back to the law office."

"Why do we need to go back?" Mariah wanted to know.

"You'll see," Charlie said. "You'll see."

Rebecca looked at her watch. "We're going to hit rush hour in Columbus if we don't get on the road soon."

"Yes," Charlie agreed. "You will, but I don't think you want to skip this next stop. Why don't you stay for dinner and then drive home after rush hour? Otherwise, you'll just be sitting on the highway anyway. Columbus has the healthiest economy in the state and along with that comes too much traffic."

"Great idea," Mariah chirped. "Not that I need much food."

In a few minutes, they arrived back at the Law Offices of Marley and Masters. The receptionist greeted them as they entered. "Mr. Marley has been waiting for you. Go on in."

They found the old man snoring at his desk. Mariah moved a chair to make some noise, startling Marley who jerked his head back and opened his eyes. "You're back," he announced, perking up quickly. "Have a seat, ladies. How was your day?"

"Amazing," Mariah said. "I feel overwhelmed. It's all good. I can't believe I have all of these relatives I never knew about it. I'm afraid I'll wake up tomorrow and learn this was all a dream."

The old man chuckled. "No, Mariah. This is very real. Now that you've learned about your family and their farm and factory, you also must be aware that their financial holdings are considerable. You are both Landtree heirs, and, as such, part owners of all you've seen. If you wish, you will have a house built to order on the Landtree Homestead. You will always be welcome to work in one of their enterprises. Of course, you also will be issued a monthly check, regardless of whether or not you work here. Should you choose to work with Landtree Enterprises, your shares will grow even more over time. Now, I just need to get you to sign some papers saying you accept your inheritance. Then you can be on your way."

"Wow," Mariah exclaimed. "We learned about most of this today, but now to hear it all together, it's a lot to process. It sounds like I'm rich." Although she'd come to claim her inheritance, finding her family and learning about her father's legacy dwarfed any thoughts of financial gain.

Her mom smiled. "Yes, Mariah, you're a wealthy woman now."

Mariah's tears began flowing again, embarrassing her. She could go for days without crying, but once she entered that emotional spot, her tears were difficult to contain.

Mr. Marley handed Mariah the tissue box, and then, perhaps to give Mariah some privacy, he turned to Rebecca. "This all belongs to you, too, ma'am, if you want to accept."

Her mom looked hesitant. Mariah dried her tears and quickly signed the paper that Mr. Marley had placed on the desk. Her mother picked up the document to read it and said, "I'm not sure I should do this."

"Mom," Mariah said, "come on, this is for you. Granddad wanted to make it up to Dad. He wanted you to have this. It's yours."

Her mom nodded, but didn't sign.

"Mariah's right," Mr. Marley said. "Senior felt so bad about what he did to you, ma'am. He longed to make amends. I would say this inheritance could go a long way to doing just that."

In the end, Mariah's mom signed and then Mr. Marley treated them to a private meal at the country club, where the waiters wore masks and served them lobster and steaks. Mariah wolfed it all down, realizing the baby must be growing a lot. An hour later, they left Mansfield. Mariah felt full of not only the delicious food, but of the bounty of gaining a huge extended family and a new friend in Mr. Marley.

On the way home, Mariah questioned her mother. "I still don't understand why you didn't come here a long time ago. Why did you keep me from my family?"

Her mom didn't answer, maybe only now realizing the gravity of her mistake. They rode home in silence. The sinking sun created a splendid light show with bright oranges fading into pink and blues just above the horizon. As Mariah watched the sunset, she knew she would never forget this incredible day that had opened her life into a brand new world of connection and family.

***

The next morning, Mariah and her mom shared breakfast with Mrs. Bee. They recounted their adventure of discovery in Mansfield. Mariah talked nonstop and showed her the family book. She told her about Aunt Julia, Uncle Barney, and Charlie. "Can you believe it, Mrs. Bee?" she asked. "This incredible family is all mine! They love me. They want to build me a house. I would live next door to cousins and down the street from them all. I can work for Landtree Enterprises. My baby will have an amazing family and home."

Mrs. Bee smiled. "I'm so happy for you, Mariah. You deserve all of this. I'm so glad you discovered your family. But does this mean you'll be leaving me?"

Mariah stopped. She'd never considered the ramifications of moving to Mansfield, hadn't thought about what would happen to Mrs. Bee if she left. She took a deep breath, wondering what she should say.

"Maybe you could move with us," she suggested.

"Oh, my," Mrs. Bee said. "You have such a generous heart. Let's think about this, dear. We don't have to make any decisions today. Let's just see what the future brings."

Mariah nodded. "Everything happened so fast. You're right. Let's think about it. If you could excuse me, I need to call Max."

Max answered on the first ring. "Mariah? You're back?"

"Yes, I am. I want to tell you all about it. Max, it was so amazing. I have a big family! They want to build me a house. They want me to work in their business. I have an inheritance. I'll start receiving monthly checks. I never have to worry about money again. It's all so much. And you'll love the business. The farm is organic and they're doing everything with permaculture and renewable energy. And it's all because of my dad."

"Renewable energy, really?"

"Yes, Landtree Solar. Can you believe it? My dad and you, both visionaries! He knew we needed to stop using fossil fuels, too. And the whole Landtree enterprise works to limit the use of fossil fuels as much as possible."

"Mariah, that's wonderful. I'm so happy for you. I want to meet your family. This is incredible. But does this mean you don't need me?"

"What?" Mariah said. "Max, I love you. Of course I need you. Our baby needs you. This doesn't change a thing. Not now, not ever. You hear me?"

"Okay, okay. I just wondered. You know, some people get rich and they leave their old life and friends behind. You promise you're still my Mariah? That's all I need to know. I'm glad you have such an awesome family."

"Yes, Max. "It's absolutely wonderful. And I need to get to work. For now, I'm still going to work at the café, at least until the baby comes. I'll talk to you later."

She signed off with a happy heart, hurrying downstairs to say good-bye to her mom and Mrs. Bee. She literally skipped all the way to work as the spring sun illuminated her path. She laughed and smiled, enjoying thoughts of her new family and life.

71. MAX PLANNING THE FUTURE

After the conversation with his parents and the call from Mariah, a plan began to form in Max's mind. But first, he needed a ring. He deliberated until Gabrielle solved the problem at her breakfast visit one morning. She picked up on his consternation and gave him permission to do exactly what he wanted.

"Max, do you still have my ring?" she asked. When he nodded, she said, "That's your family heirloom. I loved wearing that ring, knowing it has been passed down from generation to generation on your mother's side of the family. Maybe it's time for a new look. Use the stone, get it reset into something special for Mariah."

Max called in a favor from the jeweler the very next day. Although the store was closed due to the pandemic, his friend met him at the shop and let him pick out a new setting for the diamond. The jeweler promised to have it ready within the week, telling him to bring cash to complete the sale. He said he'd ring it up later when he got permission to reopen.

Now Max needed to craft the rest of his plan. Although it could technically be called a shotgun wedding, Max's reframe labeled it pure joy and an incredible blessing for them both. He refused to allow any negativity or the appearance of coercion taint their relationship. He wanted to start off on the right foot, acknowledging the blossoming love they shared. Absolutely nothing would short Mariah the happiness she deserved. He personally loved the big deal engagement events people posted on Facebook and YouTube. He planned to make his ask for Mariah's hand out of this world. He consulted with Buck, Pastor Amy, and Mrs. Bee. He even decided to give Rebecca a call, and Mariah's Uncle Barney, who she'd raved about ever since she'd returned from Landtree Farms. It would be difficult in the midst of a pandemic, but that also provided a unique opportunity for him.

As Max called in favors and planned for the big day, he realized he was truly happy. Finally, the cloud of grief had lifted completely, as he looked forward to his new life with Mariah and their child. He knew a pandemic wedding wouldn't be ideal, but perhaps they could have a celebration whenever things started to open up again. For now, he just wanted to solidify their bond and begin to build a home together. He hoped Mariah would agree.

Just as Max finalized arrangements with Uncle Barney, who would put the icing on the cake, his cell phone buzzed. A text from the sheriff appeared on his screen: Made deal with Howard. Call me.

When the sheriff answered, he asked, "What's up? You got Howard back in a cell where he belongs?"

"I'm afraid not," the sheriff said. "But I made a deal. He's going to quit that job and he volunteered to do victim-offender mediation with you. I'd like to do that Friday, if you're willing?"

"What in the hell is victim-offender mediation?" Max asked. The last thing he wanted was to negotiate with Howard. He wanted the man gone.

"Before you dismiss this out of hand, hear me out. This is something OSU set up for us a few years back. They provide mediators so people can make amends for their crimes. It's good for first-time offenders, you know. Keeps them from continuing in a life a crime. Howard's the perfect candidate. His record was clean before he came to Friendly. His goals were to make life difficult for you; it was part of his job. He tells me he had no intention of hurting anybody."

"You're barking up the wrong tree. Don't try to tell me or Buck that those trolls for the fossil fuel industry's public relations team are harmless. We both lost our families, and no one will ever convince us that was accidental." After the words left his mouth, Max remembered what Gabrielle had said. For so long, he'd blamed the fossil fuel trolls, but she'd said it was purely accidental and blamed herself. She ought to know, being an angel and all. Maybe he should try this.

"Okay," the sheriff said. "I get it, but Howard is going to resign his job. He'll let me verify it. He wants to help you. He almost died last week. He had an incredible dream about climate change, and even went to confession after that. I think you'll be surprised. I think you should hear him out."

Still, Max didn't trust Howard. He could easily fake quitting his job and come back after Mariah and the baby. Max didn't think this was a good idea. "Why should I trust the man after what he's done? How can you?"

The sheriff didn't answer for a moment. When he did, he spoke very cautiously. "I don't know, Max, how to explain it, but I believe the guy. I don't think he's lying. I believe he genuinely experienced a shift. He's not the same man we met before."

Max took a deep breath, considering his options. He said a little prayer and as soon as he did, he felt thumbs up emerging from somewhere deep in his soul. "Well, okay then, I'll give it a try," he told the sheriff. "But you've got my back, right? He will still leave town as soon as he gets out of the hospital?"

"Yes, he committed to do that, if that's what you want."

"If that's what I want? Come on, sheriff," Max complained.

"We'll see. Let me hang up here and set up a Zoom meeting for us

Friday morning. Watch your email for a link."

Max called Mariah and asked if she could reserve a Saturday night for him in three weeks. "I have a surprise for you," he explained.

"Sure, Max. I'll look forward to it. Let me put it on my calendar. What time will you pick me up?"

"No, I'll come to the café. Do you get off at three?"

"Yes," she replied, "but don't you want me to go home and freshen up a bit?"

"I'll pick you up and take you home, first thing," he said.

"Okay, it's a date. What's the surprise?"

"If I told you, then it wouldn't be a surprise, would it?"

Mariah laughed. "I guess not. And, Max, do you want to come to dinner tonight at six?"

"Yes, I'd love to."

"Great. I'll see you then."

72. THE MEDIATION

Howard started to feel much better after resigning his job. He asked his boss to send a letter verifying the termination to the hospital, which he then forwarded to the sheriff. Not that he didn't harbor some second thoughts, but he'd kept his word and did feel a heck of a lot lighter.

Early on Friday morning, the nurse brought him an iPad for a call. "You sure are popular," she said cheerfully. "For being a stranger here, you're getting a lot of attention."

"Not the kind of attention you want, though," Howard said. "Is that the sheriff again?"

"Yes, how did you know?"

"We planned this. I thought maybe you overheard," he said, knowing the nurse had sat through the entire talk between him and the sheriff earlier.

"Oh, no. I have enough to keep me busy without listening to your calls. They just want me in the room to make sure you don't get medically stressed, especially with law enforcement."

"I'm fine, really," Howard assured her. "I actually haven't felt this good for a very long time. But you can stay if you want."

The nurse waved and walked out the door.

"Howard," the sheriff said, "are you ready?'

And then began what the sheriff called Victim-Offender Mediation. A couple volunteers from Ohio State led the discussion. They spent quite a bit of time outlining the whole process, explaining it was a way to deal with crime that helped provide restoration. The victim got a chance to explain how the crime impacted them personally and to ask for what they needed to move forward. The offender might apologize and make amends. It reminded Howard of when his mother required him to make up after a fight with his best friend back in childhood. He asked how a little town like Friendly could offer such a service. The mediators explained that they provided the service throughout the state, and, during the pandemic, virtual meetings suited well enough, although, they preferred face-to-face meetings.

After all the introductory stuff, the mediator asked Max to explain what had happened and how he felt about it. Howard had to listen to Max explain about his work at Ohio State, working to tame the wind and teach about alternative energy options to slow climate change. Then he began to talk about the fossil fuel industry's trolls who targeted climate scientists. He laid it all out, telling not only what had happened to him personally, but also to his colleagues across the country.

Howard could hear the anger in Max's voice. He began to realize his impact on Max. His old self would laugh, imagining the rise he could produce with his scare tactics. His new self, squarely facing Max front and center on the screen, found nothing funny at all. More than anything, he felt regret. Howard knew that Max was a learned and decent man, well-respected as a wind scientist. Now he had to face the error of his ways.

"Their goal is to intimidate us," Max told the mediators. "They want to shut us down and shut us up. We know that they're employed by public relations firms, but that really doesn't help when you're getting blasted on social media day after day. Not only are they threatening our credibility by using false science, the death threats are the hardest part. And attacking on social media is one thing, but when my wife and child died, going off the road in a rainstorm? It sure seemed like they'd made that threat come true. Man, I've been a Christian all my life, but that was too much for me. I'm pretty convinced now that it was an accident, pure and simple, but it sure didn't seem like it back then."

Howard interrupted, "No, man, we wouldn't do that. No, sir."

The mediator stopped Howard and asked him to let Max finish.

"Just recently, I've been able to step back into a church again and get myself right with God. But try as I might, I can't figure out how the fossil fuel industry, their PR firms, and their trolls can sleep at night. Why are they trying to pretend climate change isn't a problem? Why are they trying to make sure enough carbon is released into the atmosphere to destroy the human race? It just doesn't make sense. It's evil. Pure evil, from my point of view."

For Howard, hearing Max explain it that way really opened his eyes. Max's question was valid, and Howard had no answer, except he could say that the fossil fuel industry hired PR firms that hired men like him because they all wanted the same thing: money. It was a money-making scheme. That was all. Howard hung his head. How had he ever gotten caught up in this mess?

The mediators then asked Max to talk more specifically about Howard and what had happened in Friendly. Max complied, starting with the graffiti telling him to go home. He explained the threatening notes, culminating with the bomb threat and Howard firing a gun in the pub.

"He ran me out of town," Max said. "I would've been crazy to stay in Friendly after that. Do you understand? I was still grieving the loss of my wife and my daughter. I escaped to my parents' house to be safe. He's very effective. He got exactly what he wanted. He's pure evil."

The mediator asked Max to focus on his feelings. Max talked about his anger, his exasperation, and his depression. He explained that dark night of his soul.

"But then you came back to Friendly?" the mediator asked.

"Yes, my friend Buck told me that the sheriff had kicked Howard out of town. He hadn't been seen for over a month. You see, Buck was a target, too, because we work together. Buck convinced me the coast was clear. I came back after Christmas."

"But the coast was not clear?" the mediator asked.

"Well, nothing happened for a while," Max said. "Not until a few weeks ago, when the social media posts started up again. Then last week, a threatening note appeared in my mailbox. Handwritten, no stamp. The note told me to stop my work with our wind factory. He threatened both me and my girlfriend. I freaked out. My girlfriend is pregnant. It felt like déjà vu. I could not let anything happen to her and our child. I could never live with myself."

"So, this has been very scary for you?".

"Damn right," Max replied. "Until I learned this guy was in the ICU with COVID, I could barely sleep at night. I didn't want to upset my girlfriend by telling her, but I wanted her to be safe. I wouldn't wish that virus on anybody, but I must say, it gave me some peace of mind to have him incapacitated by it."

Howard hung his head in shame. "I'm so sorry," he said. He realized Max had been terrified by the ordeal and overcome with worry about his girlfriend's safety.

The mediator continued, asking Max to explain what he would like to have as the outcome of the mediation. "I just want this man out of my town and off my social media. Make the rest of the trolls leave me alone, too."

Howard didn't blame him one bit, and said so when the mediator turned to him. Howard put it all out there for Max. He explained that, for him, it had been a job, a good-paying one that had given him an opportunity to be a bad boy while doing what he thought was the right thing. But a week in the hospital and almost dying from COVID had changed everything.

"I don't know what I was thinking," Howard said. "Honestly, looking back, I don't know how I did all that. It makes no sense to me anymore, none at all." He went on to explain his Blue Angels climate change dream in great detail. Always a great storyteller, Howard gave the mediators and Max a lively recounting of that incredible night. He noticed the mediators' eyes growing very round, even though they remained silent.

"Yes, that was quite a ride," he concluded. "I fulfilled a life-long ambition of being a Blue Angel pilot and got smacked with the reality of climate change at the same time. My dream came alive with our collective nightmare. I can't get those images out of my head, I toss in bed at night, tormented with the reality of the damage caused by increasing carbon in our atmosphere. I remember raging forest fires, rampant flooding, and destructive hurricanes, all changing the face of America. I thought I was helping my country in my work. I am so sorry, Max. I am so very, very sorry."

Then the mediators asked what both of them thought they could do at this point, telling them that, although the past couldn't be undone, sometimes apologies, forgiveness, and making amends could go a long way to make the future better for both of them.

Howard started out by apologizing, repeatedly and sincerely. He asked for forgiveness. Max accepted the apology but said he didn't feel ready to forgive him. Howard said he understood. He watched Max's face relax, but it was still very guarded. He hoped that Max would feel better in time.

As the mediators let them both sit with silence for a while, an idea started forming in Howard's mind. Could he do more than just apologize? Could he go to work for the other side? Could he counter the trolls and speak the truth? He knew enough about their work to be effective. He presented his newly formed idea to Max, who, surprisingly, was receptive to it.

"Yes," Max said. "I love it. You're exactly what I need. I tear my hair out trying to understand how they get away with their lies. I can't understand how they can create so much doubt in the American psyche that people can think we don't have a problem with our climate. You could take them on because you know exactly how they operate. I love, love, love it."

The mediators were smiling as they started to craft an agreement. Howard and Max would start a new public relations venture to challenge fossil fuel trolls. And, in the end, Max even extended forgiveness and said he'd be willing to let Howard stay in Friendly after all so they could work on their plan.

Howard called the priest in once more that night to pray a prayer of thanksgiving and to ask if he could share the priest's copy of *Laudate Si* with his new friend, Max. He knew he didn't deserve all of this, but, for once, he felt like he was walking in the clouds and didn't even need the Blue Angels to take him higher.

The past month had exceeded all of Mariah's expectations. Ever since visiting her grandfather's attorney, her life had opened into so many possibilities. Now that she'd accepted her place in the Landtree family, not only did she enjoy a large extended family, but her inheritance also provided her with all the tools she needed to live her dreams. At the same time, her relationship with Max seemed to be lifting higher and higher. Ever since he'd committed to her and the baby on Easter, they couldn't spend enough time together. She felt incredibly blessed to have him in her life.

Yet whenever she talked about the Landtree Homestead, he clammed up. More than anything, she wanted their child to grow up as a part of a large family, something she'd never had. Max listened to her yearnings but didn't share his own thoughts. Even when she came right out and asked, he shrugged the question off and changed the subject.

Max did, however, want to talk about Landtree Solar. He prodded Mariah for details again and again. Finally, Mariah arranged a socially-distanced tour of the factory for him. Max was impressed and told her so. In fact, Max talked with the CEO, her uncle, Timothy, for quite some time after the tour. Mariah used the ladies' room, made some phone calls to pass the time, and finally asked Max if they could leave. On the way home, Max explained that working in alternative energy created a brotherhood of sorts.

Finally came the day of Max's surprise. For three weeks, Mariah had tried to figure out what Max had in store. Today, all through her shift, she pondered what kind of surprise Max possibly planned.

She finished her clean-up in record time, then went into the restroom to freshen up for Max. She smoothed her belly and gave a prayer of thanks that, so far, her pregnancy was progressing without problem. Now in her twentieth week, she found it hard to believe that her pregnancy was already halfway completed. The baby was still on schedule to come out kicking and screaming in October. She loved having forty weeks to prepare. They needed to start getting a place for the baby ready, physically. She still didn't know if she should plan to have the baby live with her at Mrs. Bee's, move in with Max, or ask for a home at the Landtree Homestead. He still hadn't told her which he preferred. Maybe today she could pin him down for a talk after the surprise.

While Mariah waited in a booth near the door to keep an eye out for Max, she finished tallying the receipts for the week to make a report to the owner. The café seemed to be weathering the storm of the pandemic quite well. She guessed people liked to get diner food, even though they had to stay home to eat it.

Before long, she noticed Max's red truck pulling into the lot. He covered the few steps from the truck to Mariah in a matter of seconds and embraced her warmly. It felt good to hug someone during this time of social distancing. Sometimes she thought perhaps they should keep a distance, too, but Max didn't think so. He pulled away for a moment, far enough to give her a kiss, and she felt the warmth of it all the way down to her toes.

"So, what's my surprise?"

"Just wait," he told her, smiling. "I thought you wanted to wash up first. Let's get you home. We've got time. Be patient, dear."

As Max drove the short distance to Mrs. Bee's, Mariah felt relaxed and happy. Max seemed different today. She couldn't quite put her finger on it. He seemed happy, too, but it was something more. His smug smile told her he was excited about whatever the surprise might be.

When they arrived at her house, Max suggested, "Why don't you go freshen up? I'll wait for you."

"Oh, okay. Come in and talk with Mrs. Bee while I'm getting ready," Mariah suggested. They found Mrs. Bee sitting at the computer. "What are you doing?" Mariah asked. It had been a very long time since Mrs. Bee had come anywhere close to that computer.

"Oh, I just decided I need to enter the 21st century. I need to get a life," she said with a wink.

Mariah laughed. "Oh, my gosh! I can't believe it. You go, girl!" Mrs. Bee never ceased to amaze her. "I'm going up to get ready. Max can help you if you have any questions."

She hurried upstairs to change. When she came back down, she found Mrs. Bee and Max working at the computer.

Mrs. Bee said, "Thanks, Max, for your help. Have a good time, you two." Happy that Mrs. Bee seemed to be in good spirits, Mariah threw her a kiss on the way to the front door.

"Wait a minute," Max instructed. "We're going out back first." He opened the back door and motioned for Mariah to come.

As they walked onto the back patio, a nicely dressed older couple, sitting on the loveseat swing, greeted them. Mariah looked at Max. "Mariah, I'd like you to meet my parents, Gloria and George Wahlberg."

His parents stood. Gloria spoke first. "It's good to meet you, Mariah. I would give you a hug, but with COVID, I better not."

"Same here," George said.

"Wow," Mariah said. "Thank you for coming, It's wonderful to meet you, too." She felt a little nervous then. What should she say? This must be her surprise.

After an awkward pause, Max's mother started the conversation. "Max has been telling us about your Landtree family. They are well known in the Columbus area. I imagine you're very happy about that."

"Oh, my gosh," Mariah said happily. "It is just so big. Did he tell you about my father? My dad was estranged from his family and passed away when I was young. His father actually kicked him and my mother out when they got married, so I didn't really know any of them. And then, right before Easter, my mom told me that my dad had written me a letter. It was buried near his grave and he left instructions to give it to me when I was grown. In the letter, my dad encouraged me to reach out to my family. And all of a sudden, I have an aunt and uncles and cousins that I didn't even know about. This has been an amazing spring for me."

Gloria smiled and George said, "And I hear you have a baby on the way."

"George," Gloria reprimanded.

"It's okay," Mariah said. "Yes, Max and I are going to have a baby and I'm thrilled. I want you to know that I love your son very much. I know you suffered a great loss when Gabrielle and Isabella died. I know they can never be replaced, but I hope that our child will bring you new joy.

Mariah watched Max's parents for their response. She didn't think George looked very pleased. He frowned, but his wife smiled at Mariah, her warm eyes tearing up. "We're so happy for you, Mariah and Max. When is the baby due?"

"October tenth," Mariah said. "That's coming very soon,"

"Yes, it is. I can help you get ready," Gloria offered.

"Mom, Dad," Max interrupted. "Can we continue this discussion later? I need to take Mariah somewhere in a few minutes. Maybe we can have dinner together, if you can stay?"

"Of course," his mother said. "You go and let us know where to meet you when you're done. And maybe over dinner, George can share our love story and you'll see there are some parallels with yours."

"Okay," Max said. "We need to get out of here now. We'll see you soon, Mom and Dad."

So maybe his parents aren't the surprise, Mariah thought. They walked around the house to the front lawn and back to Max's pickup. Max, pulled open the large door, helping Mariah climb up and in. "Where are you taking me?"

"Not very far," Max replied. "Not very far at all."

He pulled out onto the street and took the first left into the church parking lot.

"We're going to church? It's not open, you know."

"That didn't stop us before."

"Do you need me to unlock the door?"

"Let's see," Max said. "I think it might already be open."

Sure enough, when they walked up to the church door, it pulled right open. A masked Pastor Amy waited on the other side.

"Did you know she was here?" Mariah asked Max, confused.

"Perhaps," Max replied, smiling at Pastor Amy.

Mariah pulled a couple of Landtree masks out of her pocket and offered one to Max. Together, they stepped back, donned their masks, then stepped into the church and greeted the pastor.

"Welcome," Pastor Amy said. "Everything is all set up for you. I'll just be up in the back balcony if you need me. Need to maintain social distance, you know." She winked at Max.

"What's going on here?" Mariah asked.

"Shh! It's a surprise. You'll find out soon enough," Max said as he took her hand, holding it firmly as they walked down the center aisle of the dimly lit church. When they reached the front, he said, "You sit right here in the front pew."

She did as she was told while Max walked on up to the chancel area and pulled out a guitar from behind the pulpit. Suddenly, the large screens on the walls on either side of the chancel lit up. So that was what Pastor Amy was really doing in the balcony. Now, spotlighted on both screens, Mariah saw herself. She smiled and waved, not sure what else to do.

Max chuckled and pulled out a chair, situating himself in the open space in front of the altar. The screen display split into two parts with an image of Max, with his guitar, and still Mariah on the other side. "I wrote a song for you," he said.

"Ohhh," Mariah crooned. "Is that the surprise?"

"Part of it," he said cryptically. He began to sing a song all about her. Mariah's mouth dropped open. He sang about the wind and her love of nature, about the first time they met and about the way they sang together in this same place. His resonant voice filled the sanctuary, and his beautiful body filled the screen before her. She could watch him and her own response at the same time. They looked bigger than life on the screen which amplified the moment. Her eyes shone with love for this incredible man, the father of her unborn child, who'd welcomed her into his life and composed this beautiful love song just for her.

When he finished, she clapped. Her applause sounded a little strange in the large, empty sanctuary, so she told him, "That's incredible, Max. I love it. You wrote that for me?"

"I've been working on it for a while. I wanted to get it just right. I love you, Mariah." Just as he professed his love, the screen shifted a few times and other faces began to appear. First her mom, then Buck.

"Mom? Buck? What are you doing here?"

"Max invited us," her mom said. "We wouldn't miss this for the world."

Miss what? Mariah wondered. And then more faces appeared. "Uncle Barney! Mrs. Bee! You knew about this, didn't you, Mrs. Bee? That's why you were sitting at the computer."

Mrs. Bee's eyes twinkled. "Yes, I needed to get online to join in the fun."

Mariah turned around to look up at Pastor Amy who sat behind a computer, controlling the screen. "So that's what you're doing up there! Maintaining social distance, right?" She started to laugh. "Now that we've got you all here, now what? Did you hear Max's song?"

"Of course," Buck said.

"Your boy's got some pipes," Uncle Barney announced.

"Nice job, Max," her mom said. "A beautiful song about my beautiful daughter."

Mariah continued to laugh. "I can't believe you're all here." Even though Zoom meetings had started to become a part of everyone's lives in the past few months of pandemic, it still felt incredible to be sitting in the large, familiar, but vacant. church with her loved ones talking to her from the big screens on the wall.

The door opened at the back of the church and in walked Gloria and George Wahlberg with masks on. "Your parents! Is that why they were here? Did they know about this, too?"

Max winked. "Mom and Dad, you can come up to the front if you want." Max waited for his parents to walk up to the front row, where they took seats on the left side, not too far from Mariah. "Mariah, there's more. Could you come up here for a moment?"

Max placed his guitar on the chair and stood as she approached. When she arrived by his side, he knelt down on one knee. Mariah looked up at the screen in the back of the church and saw that now the spotlight was on the two of them. Familiar faces lined the bottom of the screen, all with wide smiles, looking on. She looked back at Max, now having an idea of what was coming.

"Mariah Melody Landtree," Max said, "one day last October, I stopped by the Wind Song Café. I walked in and a beautiful woman greeted me. You didn't seem too eager to serve me at first. I think I'd come right as you were getting ready to close up for the day. But you served me anyway and engaged in some small talk with my grieving self. You were a breath of fresh air, stirring up my life that day. You have the voice of an angel and the spirit of the wind. You lighten up my days and share my love of nature. You love the wind and want to help me save our planet from the fossil fuels. And now you're carrying my baby. The more I get to know you, the more I love you."

Max pulled a box out of his jacket and opened it to display a beautiful gold rose ring with a large diamond sparkling in the center. Mariah's hand covered her mouth in surprise. She started to cry tears of joy.

"Mariah Melody Landtree, would you marry me?"

"Yes," Mariah said. "Yes. Yes. Yes."

"Before I put this ring on your finger, I want you to know this diamond has been passed down for several generations in my family. My first wife wore it until she died. For that reason, I hesitated to give it to you, but I decided to get a new setting to make it new for you. And now, it will be all yours, but it's also all mine, a symbol of the continuity of life as we look back and look ahead together. Is that okay with you?"

Mariah nodded through her tears. "It's beautiful. Yes, I love that this is from your family. And I love the setting."

"I thought you'd like that flower, "Max said and placed the ring on her finger. "You are my rose." He stood and embraced her to the sound of people cheering from the screen at the back of the sanctuary.

"Kiss her," Buck yelled and started a cheer.

Mariah laughed as their audience chanted, "Kiss her," in disjointed bedlam, which happens when people try to talk at the same time on a virtual call. Max wasted no time in turning his embrace into a long kiss that tingled Mariah from the top of her head to the tips of her toes.

When Max came up for air, he pulled away, but kept his arm wrapped around Mariah's shoulder as he announced, "And now Uncle Barney wants to have his say."

Mariah looked up at the screen. "Can we sit down in the pew?" she asked. "I can see better down there." Max followed her down to the front row where they could both look at the big screens, rather than looking all the way to the screen in the back of the sanctuary.

"Congratulations, Mariah and Max," Uncle Barney's big voice boomed into the sanctuary. "First, I want to welcome Max into our family. And second, I want you to know that Max has asked that we start building your love nest on the Landtree Homestead, if that's okay with you?"

Mariah looked at Max. "Max! You never answered me when I talked about it. Is that why? Did you have this up your sleeve all along?"

"Maybe," Max said. "I just want you to be happy, Mariah. I know you want to be with your family. We can design Mrs. Bee her own suite, if she wants to join us."

Mrs. Bee looked surprised. "Well, I'll be," she said.

Then the screen shifted. Uncle Timothy appeared on the screen with the others. "Uncle Tim?" Mariah said. "You're late! You missed it!" She held up her ring for him to see.

"Beautiful ring, Mariah. Congratulations, Max. I'm sorry I'm late. I couldn't get away in time, but I'm here now. Is it time, Max?" he asked. "Should I make the announcement?"

Max nodded. "You're on, sir!" Uncle Timothy pulled out a sign from behind him that read *Landtree Wind and Solar*.

"What's this?" Mariah asked. "I thought it was Landtree Solar?"

Uncle Timothy said, "It was, until today. That fiancé of yours has been busy, Mariah. Max and Buck are now partners in our firm, which is expanding to include their wind machines. We'll continue making them right there in Friendly so your town won't lose any jobs, but our team will oversee the operation. And we're going to hire Max's man Howard to help us do some good public relations to counter the fossil fuel giants he used to serve.

Mariah hugged Max. "Oh, my gosh!"

"This is a wonderful opportunity for us," Buck said. "Neither Max nor I are really trained as manufacturers. Now we can get back to what we're good at: teaching and doing research at Ohio State. But we'll still oversee some of our products. We'll also lead the Landtree Research Division."

"Wow," Mariah said. "Wow. That is so cool." She took a tissue out of her purse to catch the tears of joy that continued to stream down her face.

Pastor Amy appeared on the screen. "Mariah, are you ready to set a date? I've done a couple virtual weddings already and I'm ready to roll whenever you are."

Mariah looked at Max. "Well, I know we don't want to wait until October, but I'd like to see if the pandemic clears up. Do you think by the end of the summer, things might be back to normal? I'd really like a regular wedding to have all of my friends and my family to be with me. Let's say Labor Day weekend?"

Max replied, "Sounds like a good plan to me."

Mariah clapped and laughed. "Thank you, Max. Thank you, Uncle Barney and Uncle Timothy! Thank you all for being here. What an amazing day. I am so happy."

Her mother said, "I'm glad I could be here with you for this moment, dear. Now we're going to leave you love birds alone." One by one, the people on the screen offered their congratulations as they signed off, until the screen showed only Max and Mariah, until Pastor Amy turned the video off as well. Max's parents wished them well and said they needed to get back home, but would like to have Max and Mariah over for dinner soon.

Max and Mariah sat quietly for a long time, holding each other, celebrating their love and the beginning of their new life together. Eventually, Max drove her over to the closed pub, which Buck opened up just for them and catered in an engagement dinner with candlelight. They sat and talked long into the evening, planning their future life together.

EPILOGUE

A year and a half later, on a windy October day, Mariah decorated a large sheet cake with blue icing. She drew a large yellow leaf in the center with a happy face and wrote Happy Birthday, Baby Joe along the bottom. She placed a single candle squarely on the nose of the happy face and laughed. As if on cue, the doorbell rang. "Max," she yelled, "can you get that?"

While Max greeted their guests, Mariah scooted back to Mrs. Bee's first floor suite to wake the older woman from her nap. "It's party time!" Then she climbed the stairs to the second-floor nursery where she woke Baby Joe with a kiss. When his eyes fluttered open, she gently whispered, "Happy Birthday, Baby Joe," before scooping him up to change him for the party. She tickled his belly to make him laugh, then dressed him up for his big day in new Landtree bib overalls with a bright onesie covered with orange, red and yellow-colored leaves.

By the time she made it back downstairs, several families were gathered in their living room. Most hadn't had to do more than walk down the block, as Mariah now lived in her extended family's neighborhood.

Everyone brought something to eat, along with a present for Baby Joe's first birthday. She handed the baby off to one of her cousin's daughters and returned to the kitchen to organize the food.

"Here's your ice cream for the party," recently arrived Uncle Barney announced. His wife Sylvia handed her two half gallons of Landtree Vanilla Bean. "That's to go with the cake," he explained, "but I also brought some Pumpkin and Cookie Dough, because I know that's your favorite." He gave her a kiss on the cheek. "Is there room for this in the freezer?" he asked, pulling open the door at the top of the refrigerator. "Guess not."

"Could you put it out in the freezer in the garage?" Mariah asked, as the doorbell rang again.

Mariah answered this time, finding Howard with a gift in his hands. Their former nemesis had become a trusted ally. Now that he worked for Landtree Solar and Wind, he spent his days debunking lingering myths about climate change while promoting the transition to a fossil fuel-free future.

A steady stream of arrivals kept Mariah busy. She loved the Landtree approach to family gatherings. Everyone pitched in, providing infinite variety and making it super simple for the hosts. All you had to say was "potluck party" and everyone brought their favorites. Uncle Timothy and his wife brought apples and apple pie from the farm. Charlie brought hamburgers and helped Max begin grilling out back. The younger children enjoyed the play equipment now filling the back yard. The swimming pool was fenced off and covered for the winter, but the balls, swings, slides, and climbing structures kept them engaged.

So much had transpired in the past year. As Mariah looked out the kitchen window at the happy scene, she offered a prayer of gratitude. The pandemic had stretched out much longer than any of them could have imagined, which had required a virtual wedding. Pastor Amy had conducted the wedding in the church, but her mother and Buck, along with Max's parents and the others, participated virtually.

A month later to the day, she'd gone into labor and, after twelve long hours, Baby Joe made his entry into the world, kicking and screaming. Fortunately, he'd settled down to become a relatively calm and happy baby. The pandemic had given Max and Mariah much at-home time to bond with their amazing little boy. Mrs. Bee had welcomed the new family into her home until work on their house was complete in April. Then all four of them moved into their new home, in the Landtree Homestead subdivision, surrounded by Mariah's extended family. Mrs. Bee settled into her own suite of rooms on their first floor and sold her house in Friendly. She enjoyed helping with Baby Joe. Mariah loved having Mrs. Bee close and keeping an eye on her as well.

Now, on Joey's first birthday, the pandemic continued with the Delta variant. All members of the Landtree family who were twelve and older were fully vaccinated. They took precautions in public around the unvaccinated, wearing masks, so they did feel comfortable having family gatherings again.

The doorbell rang yet again, announcing Buck with Mariah's mom. Mariah rushed to give them both a hug. The two seemed happy together. Rebecca had decided to move back to Ohio the previous summer and now worked at the OSU hospital. In fact, wedding bells were in the air and construction was underway down the road for the new house where the couple planned to live after their wedding at Thanksgiving.

When the burgers were all gone and everyone seemed happily content with full bellies, Max came back inside and pulled the highchair into the living room. He grabbed Baby Joe from one of the cousins and situated him in the chair, putting on his plastic bib. "Get the cake," he told Mariah. "Time for the family tradition."

The doorbell rang again and in walked his parents. Max said, "Mom and Dad, you're just in time for Joey's first cake."

Mariah placed the cake in front of Baby Joe, who wasted no time in grabbing a fist full of the blue icing and digging down into the white cake, putting some of it in his mouth while smearing it all over his face. Cell phones captured the moment amid much laughter.

"Wait! Wait!" Mariah's mom said. "We need to light the candle and sing!"

"I don't think that's happening today," Max said. "We're not lighting that candle at this point."

"Okay." Mariah's mom laughed. "But we can sing." She started out and the others joined in.

Mariah looked at them all, feeling very, very fortunate. She regretted that her father would never meet his namesake grandson. But Baby Joe would grow up feeling the love of his great uncles and great aunt, right here in the midst of the Landtree family, while Max worked to push development of wind energy to save the planet. Mariah hoped to join him in wind work one day. For now, she continued remote learning, making her way through classes at Ohio State. That way, she could be home with Baby Joe, and the child they hoped to have on the way soon.

Mariah cleaned the baby off and pulled him out of the highchair, standing by Max and Buck who'd opened some bottles of Landtree wine, from the winery recently opened by Uncle Tim's daughter. They passed out wine glasses to all the adults in the room. Max started banging a spoon on a glass, which quieted the chatty crowd.

"And now I'd like to make a toast. Hear! Hear! Let us toast to the power of love! To this remarkable woman, Mariah Landtree, my wife, who is the mother of this child we celebrate today. Cheers!"

The people knocked their glasses together and took their sips.

Max continued. "And to Joseph Landtree Wahlberg. Happy first birthday, son. May you feel the same joy you bring to all of us."

Mariah gave Baby Joe a kiss and looked at the happy crowd as she downed her own glass, telling Max quietly, "I love you so much." As Max enfolded her and Baby Joe in his arms, she knew there was no other place in the world she'd rather be. She asked Alexa to play her favorite song, "At Last" with Etta James, and pulled Max out into the center of the room. She hugged him close with Baby Joe as they began slow dancing to the music. Surrounded by family and friends, in their new home, Mariah danced on top of the world.

About the Author

Nancy Flinchbaugh is an award-winning author who writes as spiritual practice. She wrote this book during the pandemic, in celebration of God's creation, as she grappled with climate change.

Her other books include the MAMs Book Club series: *Revelation in the Cave* (2012), *Revelation at the Labyrinth* (eLectio Publishing, 2017), and *Revelation in the Roots: Emerald Isle* (All Things That Matter Press, 2022). She has also written a memoir, *Letters from the Earth* (Higher Ground Books and Media, 2018), and *Awakening: A Contemplative Primer on Learning to Sit* (Higher Ground Books and Media, 2020).

She enjoys nature, gardening, bicycling, traveling, leading contemplative experiences, community building, and writing books with purpose. Nancy is a member of First Baptist church and mother of two wonderful sons, Luke and Jacob. She lives in Springfield, Ohio, empty nesting with her husband, Steve, and cat, Emily Rose.

Learn more about her work at spiritualseedlings.com and nancyflinchbaugh.com. Connect with her on Facebook at Nancy Flinchbaugh, Author.

Made in the USA
Middletown, DE
13 April 2023

28638745R00149